KENTUCKY BLOOD

BOOK I OF THE
KENTUCKY BLOOD SERIES

BY: ASHLEY THOMAS SHEIKH

Dedicated to My Youngest Brother, Ali (2001-2023)

He didn't like me writing about bad things,

but told me to keep writing anyway.

I am truly blessed by God to have such amazing alpha and beta readers. Thank you.

ALPHA READERS

Curtis Brown
Megan S.
Forrest
Trey Woody
Jessica B.
Coralie Bengoechea

Damien B.
Josh V.

BETA READERS

Curtis Brown
Megan S.
Shawn Miller
Trey Woody
Jessica B.
Coralie Bengoechea
Aaron M. Carpenter

Caitlin M.
Josh V.
JBO

AUTHOR'S NOTE

This is not a standalone story, and this book is not a complete arc. It's the first chapter of a single, continuous saga: one long descent that will span many books and many years.

You'll find no neat resolutions here. The questions raised in these pages—about truth, motive, and the darkness we carry—aren't meant to be answered quickly. This book sets the stage, sharpens the knives, and draws the map. The journey won't be clean, and the people you meet may lie to themselves more than they lie to you.

Some doors will open. Some won't. Not yet.

But everything you notice matters. Every hint, every clue, every lie, every truth. I haven't written a puzzle with missing pieces—I've written a slow descent. You're not meant to solve it.

You're meant to feel it coming.

- ATS

Let's read Kentucky Blood!

* indicates a flashback

*** indicates a scene change

PART I

GIRLS EAT IT BETTER

CHAPTER I

TIME TO RODEO

Sometime in the 1990s

Raven County, Kentucky

"Daddy, can we take him to Strawberry Fields now?

I'm gettin' tired of feedin' him..."

WHEN YOU KIDNAP people, tie'em up, and torture'em in your garage, it changes your view on life.

The way you look at garages is changed.

The way you look at everything is changed.

Probably forever.

Rhonda stared at the garage.

Every time she drove past somebody's house, she'd wonder if they hid people in their garage, too.

Her right hand trembled as she lit her cigarette. She let the smoke hang in her mouth, taking comfort in its taste: slightly sour, rich and earthy—with a hint of truck-stop coffee. Nearby birds chirped their afternoon melodies, but she barely heard them. Before her stood the most important garage in the whole wide world.

("we're gonna find it, daddy...")

("the temple...")

The garage stood alone, near but separate from Daddy's house. Little white ghosts, grinning jack-o'-lanterns, vampire bats, and buck-toothed witches decorated its sides, some hanging from the roof. Felt like overkill now, a mask to hide what they inflicted upon the asshole within. No hidin' the violent necessities of their Quest for The Temple, though—a pig, no matter the lipstick, still squeals *"Oink!"*

("no, please stop, I don't know any—")

These days, the garage door, off-white and ominous, stood out the most. Damn thing pulled at her like a magnet, like it had something to say.

But what?

Didn't know—but it felt beyond her. Beyond her family. And far beyond the pieces of shit they dragged inside.

She took a hit of her cigarette.

The garage door. When had they last even opened it?

Tilting her head to the afternoon sky, she blew smoke toward the clouds.

Maybe when they brought the fucker in. Tied his ass up.

Got him ready for the Family Welcome.

They always screamed a lot then—

—during the Welcome.

4

("please don't do this!")
("y'all don't have to do any of this!")
("i don't know nothin' about no temple!")

The garage absorbed their screams, like the mop she used to soak up their blood. Sometimes, when she looked at the garage—any garage—she couldn't help but hear those screams, like she couldn't stop the blood oozing from the mop.

("not my fingers not my fingers not my f—")

The tremor in her right hand worsened.

What about *his* perspective?

The perspective of the dipshit inside?

Do you feel different about garages now, too?

Her gaze drifted down the gravel driveway, settling on blades of grass poking between the rocks. She scratched the back of her neck and sifted her fingers through her wildly cropped blonde hair.

Not like it matters...

You ain't ever gettin' out...

'Til we take you to Strawberry Fields.

Taking a final drag of her cigarette, she blew out smoke in rings, a trick an older boy had taught her around ten years ago, when she was eleven or twelve. The last ring drifted toward the garage door, then dissipated. She raised her hand to flick the cigarette away—

No.

Not on Daddy's driveway.

After sliding it in her pocket, she pulled out a new one. Marlboros. Medium. The red-and-white label kind. The kind Daddy smoked. Tiny golden sparks flickered as she struck her lighter.

Fuckin' thing won't light...

The tremor in her hand made it hard to steady the lighter, the flame dancing just out of reach.

"C'mon, motherf—"

The cigarette ignited, but the lighter slipped from her grasp, falling to the gravel driveway.

"Shit!"

As she bent to retrieve it, something *pulsed* from the garage door—like a heartbeat. A new possibility, both fascinating and unsettling, dawned upon her:

What if the piece of shit *sensed* her standin' near the door?

What if bein' tied up, blindfolded, and gagged for so long had increased his other senses tenfold, like how blind people just knew somebody nearby watched'em?

She took a hit of her cigarette, letting the smoke drift from her mouth.

Can you sense me lookin' at you, you piece of shit?

Narrowing her eyes at the door, she tried to read his thoughts.

Bet you're thinkin' of how to escape, ain't ya?

I would, if I was you...

Her eyes widened.

But good thing I ain't you.

A strange hum arose—like the buzzing of a thousand bees—before piercing the air with a needle-sharp whine. She glanced about, only to realize it came from her mi—

That sound!

It whined sharper, louder.

That fucking sound again!

Her right hand trembled so hard she dropped her cigarette.

That sound that sound that soun—

She only saw the garage door now, only *the white*—that terrible off-white of the door and she didn't see herself, she didn't see anything except the door, the white, the off-white and the whining got louder and louder and it hurt her brain it hurt her mind it hurt her insides and she felt—

sick.

(what are you doing, rhonda?)

(what are you and your family doing?)

Ripping her gaze from the door, she turned and fell to her knees, coughing and spitting. The whine faded, but the driveway gravel melted into puddles of gray and white. For one terrifying moment, she lost herself in those puddles *(what are you doing, rhonda?)*, but soon enough the rocks solidified, providing clarity and stillness to focus on.

Still on her knees, she grabbed her cigarette and brought her twitching hand to her mouth, mustering just enough lung power to take another drag.

Gotta remember what the doctor said...

(breathe)

(breathe)

(focus)
Focus on somethin' peaceful...
(breathe)
(breathe)
(focus)
She looked at the trees.
(breathe)
(breathe)
(nature)
A calm fell.
(focus)
(focus)
(calm)
The sick feeling faded.
(breathe)
(breathe)

(peace)
The tremor in her hand eased.
(focus)
(focus)

(strength)
Branches rustled nearby. Two sparrows fluttered and chirped at each other, fighting or mating; she couldn't tell. Either way, the smaller sparrow kept trying to escape the bigger one. Why didn't it just fly away? Maybe it couldn't—maybe something bound it to this spot, like she and her family remained bound to the garage and the assholes inside. Or maybe it just hoped the other sparrow would give up.

Maybe the piece of shit we got tied up is thinkin' like that...
The garage beckoned her gaze once more.
Maybe he thinks we'll just give up, and let him go...
Rising, she kicked a piece of gravel.
Bet they all thought that...

She turned toward the garage.

But especially him.

She felt okay now.

Everything felt okay now.

She could look at it now.

We've never kept one alive as long as him...

Of course, he may have just accepted his fuckin' fate. Slowly, she exhaled smoke through her nose, wondering which was the case.

The smoke drifted before her eyes, obscuring the garage.

***

They called this one "AB," short for "Alabama Boy." Didn't remember his real name—not that it mattered anymore, not that it *ever* fuckin' mattered—but they kidnapped him in Alabama and "AB" proved short and easy to say.

Did that with most of 'em now.

Gave 'em little nicknames.

How long had they kept him in there?

Two months?

Three?

It was warmer back then—

—the night of his Family Welcome.

*

"No..."

"P-Please..."

"W-What are y'all doin'?"

AB begged and screamed as Daddy dragged him across the gravel driveway with a rope.

"We got a big one this time, didn't we, Daddy?" asked Rhonda.

Daddy grunted.

AB twisted and squealed like a pig, leaving a speckled trail of blood across the gravel. Rhonda hurried into the garage and hit the button to raise the door.

The hammer and the strawberries were ready.

She smiled.

*

What month was that?

June, July, August...

Couldn't remember.

Time flies when you're havin' fun...

Don't it, motherfucker?

She drew in smoke from her cigarette—deeper this time.

This one seemed different, though.

Hadn't cried yet.

Oh, he was scared shitless, alright. Beyond a doubt. So why no tears from him?

She shook her head.

Still didn't make no sense.

Oh well.

We'll see if you end up cryin' or not, AB...

She kicked a piece of gravel—it made a *"ding!"* against the garage door.

Little pussy-ass bitch.

She stretched her arms to the sky, smoke from her cigarette curling across the face of the afternoon sun. The October air felt just right. Chilly, but not too chilly. Just cold enough to remind you that Halloween lurked around the corner. Rays of orange sunlight illuminated the forest leaves behind the garage, casting a warm glow over the open field beside it.

They took good care of AB, all things considered.

Fed him.

Gave him water.

Cleaned his bucket.

Even gave him leftover pain pills when he complained about hurtin' too much. One time he got a real high fever, so they just kept on givin' him more and more until it went away. *"Don't need no doctors,"* Daddy had said. *"Just Advil and Tylenol and shit. Cures most things. Most of the time."* He was right—and even though AB didn't deserve nothin' nice they did for him (like the free medical care they provided), they took good care of him, anyway. They were *good people,* after all. Daddy even washed him with the hose every couple weeks or so.

Never kept one over Christmas, though. Never needed to. Probably get too cold in the garage come wintertime. Now, if they got him a little space heater, it might keep him warm enough, but that'd run Daddy's electric bill real high.

Maybe just dress him real warm?

Throw a Christmas sweater on him or somethin'?

Or shit, maybe he's *already* cold at night?

Could buy him a Halloween sweater at Walmart, one of them black ones with a big orange pumpkin on it.

But nah, it ain't that cold yet.

He'll live.

Probably.

She made a mental note to discuss this later with Daddy. Wasn't worth AB dyin' yet—they still kinda-sorta needed him alive a bit longer, even though everyone was tired of feedin' him. Daddy still felt AB had another Clue in him—another Clue to the Temple. At least, that's what his dreams told him.

And they didn't argue with Daddy's dreams.

"Maybe we should be real nice to him," her little brother Zachary had said, *"and trick him into tellin' us what he's hidin'!"*

"Nice idea, numb nuts," she'd said. *"Who'd believe us suddenly bein' nice to'em after we kidnapped'em, tied'em up, and tortured the fuck out of'em?"*

"I sure wouldn't," she'd said. *"Not me."*

But that tactic might've worked on a few others, like FB—the weirdo one they'd had before AB and GB, but after MB. (MB was the one who'd escaped—*that fucker.*) FB ranked among the most gullible of the assholes, the easiest for her and her little sister Taleiah to kidnap. Like a deer walkin' up to ya and lickin' your gun...

*

FB's mouth hung open while he stared at Taleiah.

Looked like he might drool.

"You s-so cute...and s-s-smaaaall..."

He licked his lips and fumbled with his belt.

"...s-so...so..."

He swallowed.

"...in-innocennnnt lookinnn'..."

Rhonda peered through the slats of the hotel closet door, waiting for the right moment to strike. They'd learned the hard way that timing was everything—you fuck up the timing, shit hits the fan real quick.

"I'm g-gonna take r-real good c-care of you, l-little girl..."

Within his bulgin', googly-ass eyes, burned that same desire she'd seen in all the others—

"...p-pretty, pretty l-little girl..."

—the desire to both worship and consume her younger sister.

"...so pr-etty, pre-tty..."

He unbuckled his belt.

Taleiah's voice held just above a whisper:

"...lemme take care of you first, get you real hard..."

She sauntered toward him, tracing her finger across his chest.

"...is that okay, mister?"

Rhonda had taught Taleiah to ask her questions real innocent-like, the way all the pieces of shit preferred—like she ain't never fucked before.

"Ohhh," he said. "I'm-I'm already real haaard..."

He inhaled his words as he spoke. This one might be an easier takedown than the rest.

Taleiah guided him to the bedside. "Well...lemme get you harder..."

Rhonda gripped her cattle prod.

Time to rodeo.

CHAPTER II

PRISMS

"Why ya eyeballin' me, girl?"

RHONDA HELD SMOKE from her cigarette longer than she should have, letting it burn her lungs.

Not all the dipshits proved as easy as FB.

The moment a lot of 'em walked into the hotel room, they'd try to take charge and grab Taleiah or start touchin' her—some of the real assholes even hit her.

Once the door closed, the monster came out.

FB was different. Even after kidnappin' him, he didn't squirm or scream much (well, not *that* much), as if he didn't believe it was real. Even when he finally cried after Daddy smashed his elbow with the hammer, she swore she caught a twinkle in his eyes—like he was just playin' along. The supposed theater of it all.

Even at the end, when they took him to Strawberry Fields, he still had that *just playin' along* twinkle in his eyes, like it was all a practical joke for his birthday—which, coincidentally, was the same day they fielded him. ("*Happy fuckin' birthday, bitch,*" she'd told him.) As if he truly believed the garage door would rise and they'd all be standin' there with balloons, party hats, and birthday cake, yellin' together in one gigantic roar:

"*SUR-PRIIIIIIISE!*"

"*HA-PPY BIRRRRRTH-DAAAAAAY!*"

Rhonda smiled and nodded.

FB was such a fuckin' weirdo...

Each piece of shit was unique, though, makin' 'em all special to the whole family every time they fielded one.

Of the recent assholes, GB had been the best lookin' of the bunch. By far. Like a member of the Backstreet Boys or one of them other shitty boy bands, but with a *"I like to hunt and fish"* vibe.

She'd had fun with him.

Real good fun.

OB was the guy before him, the dude who liked Skittles and shit. Demanded Taleiah eat Skittles with him before, during, and after he had his way with her—of course he never got that far. They intended to bury him with a bag of Skittles (seemed like the right thing to do) but Zach got into 'em, then Taleiah and her ate some and before you knew it they didn't have no more Skittles.

Daddy got real pissed.

"*I bought those at fuckin' Walmart,*" he said, "*and I ain't goin' back again!*"

They still buried him with the bag, though.

Better than nothin'.

And now, they had AB—the human puddle of water who, for some reason, hadn't shed a tear.

(why doesn't a human puddle cry, rhonda?)

(still doesn't make sense, does it?)

She shrugged and took a hard hit from her cigarette. Despite the slight chill of a typical October day, she'd chosen not to wear a jacket over her black tank top, admiring the colorful tattoos running up her arms. *Yep, glad I got'em*, she assured herself for the thousandth time. They made her stand out from other girls in Raven—the square bitches, at least. And they looked especially badass when she wore tank tops.

Not like her legs.

She always wore jeans to cover her legs.

After what *he'd* done to her.

The blue-eyed boy.

Her breath quickened while an inner voice cried, *"You're too self-conscious,"* and *"No one would notice most of the time."*

She told that voice what she always did:

"Fuck you."

and

"I'll keep wearin' my jeans."

Taking a nervous puff of her cigarette, she tried to push all thoughts of her legs and the blue-eyed boy and his piercing eyes from her mind.

But she heard his voice.

("you gon' be my b—")

No.

No.

Just gonna enjoy this fuckin' day.

After one last hit from her cigarette, she headed down the driveway to the red-and-white Marlboro ashtray on the table in front of Daddy's house. One of Daddy's rules: always put your cigarettes out in the ashtrays and never toss'em on the ground. *"We got fuckin' standards,"* he'd say—usually while puttin' his out right there at the table where he smoked and drank all day, like most days.

Crushing her cigarette, she let her eyes drift to the white cordless phone.

Daddy always forgets to put that back on the charger...

She glanced around.

No sign of Taleiah—had last seen her walkin' toward Strawberry Fields with one of them trashy romance novels. Probably thought it might help with her "little problem."

Rhonda smirked.

No sign of Zach, either—he'd been standin' in the driveway, lookin' all zoned out, but then ran off to play with his Game Boy or whatever weird shit he liked to do these days.

And her Daddy, Bill, was likely decidin' with care which pizzas to order tonight.

But would he go with Domino's, or Pizza Hut?

God, I hope it's Domino's.

Not that Pizza-Hut-bull-shit.

"Yesss..." she whispered.

She snatched the phone, pulled out the long metal antenna, and strode away.

***

A chorus of chirping birds greeted Rhonda in the forest, as if awaiting her arrival. The phone felt solid and heavy in her hand—big-ass battery, long-ass range. *A good fuckin' phone.* She knew just who she'd call: Darla. Some of her friends she'd made since moving to Raven were okay—close, even—but none as close as Darla. They had history.

Crisp autumn leaves crunched underfoot, releasing a familiar, musty scent into the air.

"I'm-usin'-Daddy's-long-diiis-tance..." she sang.

She punched Darla's number into the phone, swaying her hips with each digit. Still had Darla's number memorized, along with all the numbers of her old friends back in the Crow, Zion, and Hazard counties of the Tri County area.

"I'm-usin'-Daddy's-long-diiis-tance..."

Rays of sunlight pierced the canopy, strobing across her tattooed arms. She savored victories like this—saving money through secrecy. Hell, with long-distance rates as high as they were now, she'd probably save twenty dollars today. *"Savin' money is earnin' money,"* Daddy always said. *"If you saved twenty dollars, you fuckin' earned twenty dollars. That's true financial shit."*

The phone kept ringing. She stepped over a log, careful not to disturb any Halloween decorations along the winding path. Passing AB's car under a camo tarp, she grinned at the little white ghosts scattered across it—a subtle touch from Taleiah. Still hadn't fenced his car yet—might need to park it far from Kentucky if news ever broke that cops were lookin' for him.

So far, though—they weren't.

At least, as far as they knew.

But just in case...

"Rhonda? Rhonda Jean?" a voice asked from the phone.

"Darla!"

Rhonda's eyes lit up.

"Wait," she said, "how'd you know it was me?"

"Just guessed!" said Darla. "I *sensed* ya."

"Oh, come on!"

"I tell ya, I'm turnin' psychic..."

"Darla, you ain't no psychic. I bet you got that Caller ID thing."

Darla laughed. "You got me!"

"Ain't that expensive?"

Darla laughed again. "About twenty dollars a month, but we like it. Anyway, how you been doin', girl?"

"Twenty dollars a month?"

"Yeah, well...anyway, how ya doin'?"

Daddy's new phone number was supposed to stay *top secret* from anybody and everybody back in the Tri County—he'd made that clear as crystal.

"Don't tell nobody our phone number or address," he'd said. *"Especially people back in the Tri. Startin' a new life now. Don't want none of that bullshit."*

Rhonda bit her lip.

But it's just Darla...

Who cares?

Besides, she already knows now...

Can't put the toothpaste back in the tube.

"Girl," said Rhonda, "I am *so happy* I reached you!"

The sunlight shone through the trees even brighter.

"I can only talk real quick," said Rhonda. "I'm usin' Daddy's long-distance. He don't know, though..."

Darla chuckled. "You're just a little ninja, ain't ya?"

"I am, Darla. *I'm-just-a-little-ninjaaa, walkin'-through-these-woooods,*" she sang. *"Hopin'-I-don't-get-cauuught, usin'-Daddy's-long-distaaance..."*

"He ain't gonna notice when he gets the bill?" asked Darla.

"Pssh, he won't notice shit. To him, all the bills are already too high, and he don't even try to figure'em out."

"Oh, I'm about the same way," said Darla. "Everything's so expensive these days, especially long-distance. It's like twenty cents a minute now, and we're in the same-damn-state!"

"Mmm-hmm," said Rhonda in a slow, Southern kind of way.

"You ready for Halloween?" asked Darla.

"You bet your ass I am," said Rhonda. "We have gone all-the-fuck-out with decorations this year!"

They still had leftover money from fencin' GB's car, so Daddy called for a Family Meeting to decide how to spend it (she respected how democratic Daddy was about everything: *The American Way*). After hours of debate, they agreed to splurge on Halloween decorations. About the only thing they reached real consensus on—nobody jumped for joy, but nobody stood dead set against it, either.

"That's what you call a fuckin' compromise," Daddy had said.

"I'm tellin' ya," said Rhonda, "we could make these woods out here a literal spookfest, open it up like a verified haunted attraction, like them Haunted Woods of Hazard County we used to go to back in elementary school. You remember that?"

"Uh-huh," said Darla. "Y'all'd make a shit-ton of money with that."

"Ohhh, we'd make a killin'..." said Rhonda.

But we won't need any fuckin' money—

—not after we find The Temple.

A pleasant chill ran up Rhonda's spine.

(the temple.)

The mere thought of it evoked a sensation of floating—

(the temple.)

—as if Heaven itself pulled her skyward.

(all for the temple.)

She closed her eyes,

(temple above all.)
reveling in the pull.
We're gonna find it, Daddy...
Everything they did,
We won't stop...
everything they'd do—
Not 'til we find it...
—all to find The Temple.
Not 'til we make The Run...
They would make *The Run on The Temple,* just like Daddy's dreams prophesized, and receive the untold riches, the glory that God would bestow upon them.
The Run on The Temple!
Oh, how glorious it would be!
She squeezed her eyes tighter, Darla's voice fading.
Oh, the Glory!
If only she could tell Darla!
About the glory they'd receive!
All about Daddy's dreams, and how they came true!
If only she could *teach* Darla about The Temple, about their Quest—to explain it in a way that made it sound *not-crazy,* in a way she'd understand.
She would understand—
wouldn't she?
(what if she didn't?)
(what would you do?)
Rhonda's eyes widened.
What *would* she do?
(you know...)
(there's only one th—)
No.
She clenched her hand into a fist.
Best to tell Darla *after* The Run—then she'd believe her.
But by then, it wouldn't matter.

The Run on the Temple would change everything.

***

"How's life outside the Tri?" asked Darla. "Still ain't shit to do out there?"

Rhonda kicked a fallen tree limb out of her way. "I mean, there's bars and house parties and shit. Ain't like we're out in Appalachia or nothin'."

"So you still tearin' shit up?"

"Girl," said Rhonda. "You know me. 'Course I'm still tearin' shit up."

"You better be!" said Darla. "You better be teachin' them Raven bitches how us Crows get down!"

"Oh, I have to teach'em how to *get down* over here! They don't even get fucked up!"

A scraggly branch from a hollowed-out elm brushed against Rhonda's arm. She'd caught Zach standing inside there before, staring off into space. Kids did weird shit.

"But it ain't like Crow," said Rhonda. "Ain't like the Tri..."

Her gaze drifted to a lone wicked witch figurine poking from the ground.

"And I ain't as wild as I used to be..."

She bent over, pulling the witch from the ground. Dirt smeared its face.

"Well," said Darla, "after I got knocked up and hitched, I couldn't keep track of you, girl! You went off the rails, you was so wild. How many times you get arrested back then? Two, three times, right?"

"Yeah, I got a little wild..."

Rhonda rubbed her thumb across the witch's face, trying to wipe off the dirt.

"Once or twice for possession..." said Darla.

The more she rubbed, the more it smeared.

"Only one of those times was it *my* fuckin' drugs," said Rhonda. "Second time was *theirs*. Not mine. That was some bullshit."

She stuck the figurine back in the ground, the witch's face even dirtier now.

"*Aaaand,*" said Darla, "you were fuckin' guys for their cocaine back then, too..."

Rhonda gazed at the dirt on her thumb, rubbing it between her fingers.

"It was usually a two-for-one..." said Rhonda. "...got a free fuck and free drugs on top o'that, too..."

Darla laughed. Rhonda wiped her hand on her jeans and continued strolling through the woods.

"What about that one time?" asked Darla. "When you beat that girl's ass? At that bar?"

"Which time?"

"You know, the time you got in *real* big trouble..."

"Oh, *that? That* girl? She was talkin' shit!"

"You beat her so bad she was in the hospital!"

"*'That's what happens when you run your mouth!'* I told her!"

"You ripped out her eye, Rhonda..."

Rhonda paused, her gaze drifting into the forest. The red and orange of the leaves, the yellow shafts of sunlight pouring through the canopy, the birds flying amongst the stillness of the trees; it all reflected in her eyes, and they glimmered like prisms.

She'd never forget how that girl screamed.

("my eye!")
("you fucking bitch!")
("you ripped out my eye!")

A strange mix of satisfaction and awe fell upon her face.

"Hey, Darla?"

"Yeah?"

"If you ever see a one-eyed bitch, tell her I said hi."

CHAPTER III

AIN'T NOTHIN' WRONG WITH ME

"Does your family have a history of mental illness?"

"Don't think so."

"Have you had any trauma recently? Or in your

past that you have trouble dealing with?"

"Not really."

"Have you done anything to anyone, even a long

time ago, that you feel guilty about?"

"Nope."

RHONDA'S SQUEALS OF laughter rang through the forest.

"I'm cryin'!" said Darla, between laughter.

Rhonda wiped her eyes, too, laughing harder when Darla pointed out the one-eyed bitch could now only cry with *one fuckin' eye.*

"Now remember," said Rhonda, "back then you were right there with me! For *all* that shit!"

She resumed walking. Had almost forgotten how much she craved her easy, relaxed banter with Darla.

"No...I...wasn't!" said Darla through gasps of laughter. "Not when you ripped out that girl's fuckin' eyeball, I wasn't!"

Rhonda's laughter faded. "Yeah, guess you weren't there for that one."

"Wasn't there all them other times you got arrested, either! That was all after I got hitched!"

"I guess so," said Rhonda. "But we used to do all kinds of crazy shit. Remember when we'd take road trips out to Texas and ride them cowboys?"

"Oh, that was only once..."

"You was right there with me! Right there in the backseat, ridin' them cowboys!"

"That was forever ago!"

Rhonda fell silent, lost in memory.

*

Country music wafted from the car windows, drifting into the Texas night. Rhonda and Darla's naked bodies bounced up and down atop their cowboys in the backseat.

Up and down, up and down—

"...God, you fuck so good..."

—finding a rhythm that transcended the music.

"...look at me..."

Rhonda bit her lip. A faint yellow glow from the parking lot revealed her cowboy's face.

She wanted to see his eyes while she fucked him.

"...show me those eyes, boy..."

She tried to look into his eyes—into him—but they stayed closed as he drifted off.

"...look at me, now..."
(show me those fucking eyes, boy)
Maybe she should peel his eyelids back—
(you son-of-a-bitch I wanna look into you)
—fuckin' hurt him so he opened his fuckin' eyes.
(lookatme)
Maybe drag her nails across his face—
(showmethosefuckingeyes)
—make him bleed make him bleed make him bl—
(no!)
(stop thinkin' like that!)
Her pace slowed.
Her grind weakened.
This wasn't workin' for her.
Couldn't cum like this.
Not if she couldn't see his eyes.
She turned to watch Darla ride her cowboy, her little body bouncin' up and down, up and down in a hypnotic, sensual rhythm.
Darla took the hat off her cowboy and put it on.
She giggled.
Rhonda grinded harder.
(look at me, darla)
She took the hat off her cowboy and put it on, too.
(look at me)
Darla turned toward her and smiled.
Rhonda smiled back.
Darla tipped her cowboy hat, giggling again.
Rhonda did the same, giggling back.
Their eyes locked.
(oh god, darla...)
(don't stop lookin' at me...)
That look on Darla's face.
(intoeachother)
That look in her eyes.
(intoeachother)
Those big, brown eyes...
(intoeachother)

Oh God, her eyes...
(don't stop lookin' *into* me!)
(into me!)
(into me!)

(LOOK)
(INTO)

(ME)

*

"Rhonda? You there?"

Rhonda started walking again, the image of Darla's little body atop the cowboy burned into her vision.

"Rhonda? Can you hear me?"

"Yeah..."

Darla's little body.

Up and down, up and down...

Ridin' and ridin' that cowboy while lookin' into *her* eyes.

Not the cowboy's.

Hers.

And only hers.

"I said I only did that once!" said Darla. "You went a couple of times with other people, too! And I'm sure you rode a hell of a lot more of 'em than I did!"

"Well, somebody had to..."

Darla laughed. "I guess that's true. Those cowboys can't ride themselves, can they?"

"Nope, sure can't..."

(look into my eyes, darla)

(look into my fucking ey—)

A rapid knocking startled her. She glanced up and spotted a woodpecker hammering at a nearby tree.

But that's all ancient history...

No need to linger.

"But I'm tellin' ya," said Rhonda, "I've calmed down a bit over here in Raven. Not quite the bad girl I used to be."

"Well, at first when you moved out there and called me," said Darla, "I remember you were still bein' the bad girl, datin' a guy with *real* blue eyes, said he was a *real* thug..."

Rhonda froze.

"You know," said Darla, "the one you was afraid to introduce to your daddy he was so bad?"

The blue-eyed boy.

"You-gon'-be-my-bitch?"

Rhonda's right hand spasmed.

No.

She released the phone.

No.

It hit the forest floor with barely a sound.

No.

"Rhonda?"

She leaned against a tree for support.

No, no, no, no.

"Rhonda? You there?"

No-fucking-no.

A frigid hand clasped the back of her neck and *squeezed*. Darla's hypnotic gaze sank into a dark sea.

(darla...)

(don't leave me...)

For a moment, Darla's face bobbed to the water's surface *(look into me...)*, but then it distorted into *his* face, his fucking face and the sea turned into that dark room with *his* face staring down at her with those fucking blue eyes and—

"Aah!"

She gripped her head.

That sound again!

She fell to her knees,

I don't wanna remember!

gripping her head tighter,

I don't wanna fucking remember!

pressing her fingers into her skull,

Please....
tighter,
tighter,
Please...

tighter.

*

"You-gon'-be-my-bitch?"
The words poured out in a deep, melodic drawl,
"You-gon'-be-my-bitch?"
like molasses flowing from a jar.
"You-gon'-be-my-bitch?"
His hand clasped the back of her neck and squeezed.
"You-gon'-be-my-bitch?"
She couldn't move, she couldn't breathe.
"You-gon'-be-my-bitch?"
He spoke with such a slow, terrible melody.
"You-gon'-be-my-bitch?"
A terrible, enchanting melody.
"You-gon'-be-my-bitch?"
Even then, she still felt enchanted—
"You-gon'-be-my-bitch?"
—by that fucking melody.
(daddyhelpmedarlahelpme)

(pleasegodhelpme.)

*

"Rhonda, can you hear me?"
Birds, trees, and sunlight spun around Rhonda.
pleasegodpleasegodhelpme.
(birds)

(trees)
Please, God.

(nature)

(sunlight)
(remember what the doctor said)
(birds)

(trees)
("breathe when it happens, breathe")
(breathe)

(breathe)

(focus)
("make sure to breathe")
(breathe)

(breathe)
("and focus")
(focus)
("focus on something around you")
(breathe)
(breathe)
(focus)
("something calm and peaceful")
(breathe)
(breathe)
(focus)
("like nature")
(trees)
(sunlight)
(nature)
("it's all in your head, rhonda")
(sunlight)
(trees)
Help me.
(breathe)
(breathe)

(focus)
(*"it's all in your head"*)
(calm)
The whining faded.
(calm)
The tremor in her right hand lessened.
(strength)
She pushed herself off the tree.

Strength.

She picked up the phone.
"Sorry, Darla..."
I'm strong again.
"Lost reception there for a second..."
I'm fucking strong again.
"Oh, can ya hear me now?" asked Darla.
"Yeah..."
Just like the doctor said...
(blue eyes blue eyes blue eyes)
Focus on something calm and peaceful...
(blue eyes blue eyes BLUE FUCKING EY—)
and it'll go away.
"Can hear ya real good, now..." said Rhonda.
Away...
She resumed walking down the forest path.

Don't need no medicine...

Ain't nothin' wrong with me.

CHAPTER IV

A CARDINAL SIN

"Daddy's gonna like his new present so much..."

"OH, OKAY," SAID Darla. "I was askin' about the blue-eyed b–"

"Oh, he was an asshole," said Rhonda. "Don't need to talk about him. He's long gone."

The phone crackled. Started to lose reception this far out.

"Well, tell me what happened," said Darla. "I'm your friend, and I wanna know."

Rhonda slowed her walking pace. She needed to change topics, and fast. Lies came naturally to her—hell, it was a family talent—but there'd be no fibbin' to Darla. Knew her too damn well.

"Oh, I don't wanna get into it," said Rhonda. "He ain't worth talkin' about. Besides, ain't got much time before Daddy calls us to the house for supper."

"Oh," said Darla. "Okay..."

A moment of silence passed.

Halloween decorations hanging from branches fluttered in the wind.

"I'm focusin' on myself right now," said Rhonda. "On my job, and helpin' Daddy out with Taleiah and Zach."

"Oh, that's good..." said Darla. "You still workin' at the Dairy Queen over there?"

Good, she's moved on...

Could probably tell I'm hidin' somethin', though...

"Yep," said Rhonda. "And I got promoted to manager last month."

"Oh damn, you're alr—" The line crackled, hissing briefly before Darla's voice cleared. "—ready manager now?"

"Yep, and I'm a badass bitch," she said. "They call me Boss Rhonda, and I keep their shit in check."

Rhonda pushed the antenna in and out, then waved the phone like a lasso. Somehow, that always improved the reception. Turning a corner, she headed toward a semi-hidden path, deeper in the woods—drawn by something she'd caught in the corner of her eye.

A huge...*pumpkin?*

Way out in the underbrush?

Didn't used to be there. They'd gone all-out decoratin' the forest this year, but there wasn't much sense in puttin' a jack-o'-lantern way out *there*.

Especially not one so huge.

"Congratulations, girl!" said Darla. "Boss Rhonda! *A badass bitch.*"

Rhonda beamed. *A badass bitch*—it suited her well. Maybe better than anything she'd ever been called before.

She stepped onto the narrower trail toward the distant pumpkin. The phone crackled as its antenna grazed against gnarled limbs above. The canopy and underbrush thickened here, casting shadows that felt darker, colder. Submerged in twilight. Fallen branches clawed at her jeans as she marched forward.

She sniffed the air.

What's that smell?

Darla said, "I remem—" A crackle cut her off before her voice returned, warped and distant. "—you was tryin' to become manager at the DQ over here, 'fore you moved."

"Yeah, they didn't wanna promote me anymore after I ripped that bitch's eye out…"

She sniffed again.

Somethin' stinks…

"Well, no wonder!" said Darla. "They was probably afraid you'd blind a customer one day!"

Rhonda laughed.

"I'm serious!" said Darla. "Everybody in the whole dang Tri County couldn't stop talkin' about it! I bet they was all afraid to go to the Crow Dairy Queen after they knew *you* worked there! They just went out to the one in Zion!"

"Oh, come on…" said Rhonda. "Wasn't *that* big of a deal."

It was, though—

—a gigantic-fuckin'-deal.

In the paper, on the news, everywhere. The incident and its aftermath had propelled her to stardom across the whole of Tri.

"It was *huge!*" said Darla. "And if I wasn't your friend, I'd have been afraid to go to the Dairy Queen *you* worked at, I'll tell ya that right now."

"Oh, now you're exaggeratin'…"

"I can just imagine if I went up to you and complained about somethin'," said Darla. "I'd be like, *'Excuse me, miss, but I asked for extra pickles on this burger,'* and then you'd be like, *'Oh, I'm sorry, you want extra pickles, you stupid bitch? I got your extra pickles—right the fuck here!'* And then you'd yell, *'Hee-ya!'* and yank my goddamn eye out! Like a motherfuckin' ninja!"

Rhonda laughed. "Well, I don't know no karate," she said, "nor am I some, fuckin' ninja, but I do know how to beat a bitch's ass. I'll tell ya that right now."

Pushing aside branches, she sniffed again. The odor sharpened—pungent, sour.

"And yeah," said Rhonda, "maybe rip a bitch's eyeball out or two..."

The stench worsened as she neared the pumpkin, now visible as a carved jack-o'-lantern.

"But I'd *never* do that to a customer," said Rhonda. "At least, not over extra pickles and shit."

Inside the jack-o'-lantern, something *flickered*—

—or were her eyes playin' tricks?

They didn't light candles out here in the woods.

Wasn't no point.

"You makin' more money now?" asked Darla. "Now that you're manager over there?"

"Not a lot more, you know I ain't no millionaire or nothin', but—"

She stopped in her tracks and gasped.

A perfect circle of six rotting birds surrounded the jack-o'-lantern. Their necks and wings twisted into grotesque angles, while their pried-open beaks left them trapped in a frozen, perpetual agony, as if caught in an endless scream. Gaping, incision-like holes marred their backs and breasts, revealing the insides as hollow—like their organs had been scraped clean out.

The sour stench hit her face like a truck.

"*Gaack!*"

She retched.

"Rhonda? You th—re?"

The phone crackled, sharp and sudden, mirroring the nausea curling in her stomach. She returned her gaze to the jack-o'-lantern. Within its hollow interior lay a mound of bird entrails, carefully arranged around a flickering white candle.

What the fuck...

Bones and organs and whatever else was inside the birds, all scooped out and piled up.

A pile of bird guts.

Inside that fuckin' jack-o'-lantern.

With a lit white candle pokin' out of 'em.

"*Gack!*"

The acrid taste of bile hit the back of her tongue. Bending over, she tried to spit, but retched once more. This time a little vomit came out.

"Rhonda? You okay? I was just askin' how much you make now that you're m—"

"S-six dollars...and f-fifteen c-cents...*gaack!*...a f-fuckin' hour now..."

Strings of saliva and vomit dangled from her mouth, just shy of touching the ground.

"That's *gooooood*," said Darla. "You rich now, girl! You can call me long-distance from your place, then!"

Rhonda spat out the remaining vomit and drool. Goosebumps freckled her tattoos as she wiped her mouth with the back of her hand. She lifted her gaze to the barely lit canopy (*why is it so dark here?*), then lowered it again.

"Rhonda? You alright?"

Darla's voice barely registered.

"Gimme a second, Darla..."

Rhonda stepped back from the stench of the dead birds and their innards, attempting to grasp just what the fuck she'd discovered.

All the birds sported bright orange breasts—*robins*. Tiny red ants crawled over their carcasses and the innards nestled inside the pumpkin. Only a few had eyes left (likely the softest parts for the ants to chew on), and as the eyeless birds stared back at Rhonda, she couldn't shake a sense of *familiarity;* as if they saw her more clearly than anything else in her life.

She counted six of 'em, but what was that...*bright red thing?* At the top of the circle?

Tentatively, she took a step forward.

The fuck is that?

Pinching her nose, she bent over, peering closer.

That...red thing?

"Rhonda? You there?"

"*Oh-my-God...*" The *red thing* came into focus.

"What is it?" asked Darla.

Rhonda stepped away from the pumpkin, away from the bird innards and the ants feasting on the bird innards.

Away from the *red thing.*

"Darla, you are not gonna believe this..." she said through her pinched nose, sounding like she'd sucked on a helium balloon.

"Why's your voice so funny?" asked Darla. "Are you...pinchin' your nose?"

"I sure fuckin' am," said Rhonda. "And you sure as fuck would be, too, if you were right here with me."

"What do ya mean?"

Rhonda sighed, backed away from the stench, and unpinched her nose.

"It's Zachary..."

The eyeholes of the birds stared at her—*into her.*

"...he's killed birds again."

"Again?"

"But that's not all..."

"What do you mean?"

"...he...he scraped all their damn guts out..."

"What? *He scraped all their guts out?*"

"Yep...and stacked'em up real high in the middle of this jack-o'-lantern out here..."

"You are fucking kidding me!"

"Nope, I ain't kiddin'...all their intestines and everything...scraped'em clean out, then—"

"What the fuck?"

"—put a birthday candle in the middle of'em."

"A birthday c—dle?"

The line crackled, as though the phone itself wanted to avoid hearing more.

"Or some kinda candle..." said Rhonda. "But looks like a birthday candle to me..."

"Why in God's name would he do that?"

"I have no fuckin' clue..."

They fell silent.

A fly buzzed near Rhonda. She shooed it away.

"Well..." said Darla. "...is it one of y'all's birthdays?"

"Nope..."

The hair on the back of her neck stood up.

"...not any of *ours,* at least..."

"That is so fucked up, Rhonda."

"It is."

"That is just insane."

"I know."

She didn't even wanna say the next part—the part about the *red thing*.

"...and...that ain't all, Darla..."

"What do you mean?"

"...you won't fuckin' believe this, but..."

Her voice shook.

"...he killed a *cardinal*."

"What?"

Rhonda stared at the remains of the bright red cardinal, twisted and contorted with its mouth pried open, its carcass hollow and scraped *clean out* like the others. It had chewholes for eyes, too, but the cardinal's chewholes stared back at her in a way that felt more haunting than the robins'.

"You're fuckin' kiddin' me!" said Darla. *"He killed a fucking cardinal?"*

"Yep...and it's a big fucker, too...biggest cardinal I ever seen..."

Well, it was *a big fucker...*

Before Zach scraped all its guts out.

"Rhonda, you are fucking joking!"

"Nope, I ain't..." said Rhonda. "He laid all the dead birds around this jack-o'-lantern, down this kinda secret path out here in the woods. Like he was doin' some fucked-up, dead-bird ritual or some shit."

"That is so messed up, Rhonda..."

"I know..."

"...and one of 'em's a *cardinal*?"

"Yep...six of 'em are robins, but the one at the top..."

Rhonda gulped.

"...that's a cardinal."

"That's-our-state-bird!"

"I know..."

"I think that shit's illegal," said Darla. "At least in the state of Kentucky. You can go to jail for that kinda shit."

"Yeah...probably is illegal..."

Rhonda clenched her hand into a fist.

"And even if it ain't, it should be."

"Well..." said Darla. "Maybe he did it as...part of the Halloween decorations?"

Rhonda fixed her gaze on the rotting pile of innards in the center of the jack-o'-lantern.

"No...don't think so..."

A chill wind caressed her bare arms. The candle's flame jutting from the innards flickered in response.

"At least, he better not have," said Rhonda. "'Cause that'd be pretty *fucked up* if he did..."

She considered blowing out the candle, but that required getting closer to the innards than she preferred. Maybe just let it burn out. Wouldn't cause no forest fire or nothin'—not stuck in the middle of them bird guts.

Shuddering, she turned and marched out of the cold darkness of the dead birds and that God-awful smell and the tiny red ants feasting on their innards and that poor, dead cardinal—back toward the warmth of the October sunlight.

She un-pinched her nose and sighed.

"I swear," said Rhonda, "I don't know what I'm gonna do with him. I got a little monster for a little brother..."

"My cousins shoot robins and sparrows with their BB guns all the time, ain't nothin' wrong with that," said Darla. "But a *cardinal?*"

Rhonda grimaced.

And he did a hell of a lot more than shoot'em with a BB gun, too...

She stepped back onto the main path, letting the sunshine bathe her bare tattooed arms and warm her up again.

Little Zachary had crossed a line this time.

That little psychopath!

Did they not teach in schools now that the cardinal was *Kentucky's state bird?*

Did he not fuckin' *know* that?

"...so he's still killin' birds and animals and shit?" asked Darla.

"Guess so...thought that had stopped for a while now..."

Rhonda closed her eyes and shook her head.

Poor little cardinal...

She'd confront young Zachary about this later, and she knew just what to say and how to fuckin' say it: *"It-is-a-sin to kill a cardinal!"* She'd look at him real intense-like, puttin' special emphasis on the word *sin* so he'd know how fuckin' bad it was. And if he acted like he didn't give a shit, if he just kept on playin' with his fuckin' Game Boy, like a weirdo, then...

Might have to tell Daddy.

She didn't want to, though; Daddy had *flipped the fuck out* last time he'd pulled shit like this. That time, she sensed Zach might've done something even *more* fucked up, but Taleiah wasn't there that weekend, and neither Zach nor Daddy would say what happened. All she knew was that when she got to the house, Daddy was shakin' and cryin', starin' into a big-ass bonfire while little Zachary looked like *he was afraid for his fucking life.*

And then there was the jar of peanut butter.

What in God's name was *that* about?

Daddy had screamed at her, *"Get that fuckin' peanut butter offa my property! Take it to your house and throw it away! Don't even let me see it!"* like he was afraid of a damn jar or something.

But what did *peanut butter* have to do with anything?

After that incident, Daddy put Zach on new medication and it did seem to chill him out a lot.

But maybe he wasn't takin' it right?

Why else would he kill a cardinal?

"How's little Taleiah doin' by the way?" asked Darla, seeming eager to move on from the subject of little Zachary and the birds he mutilated and especially, above all else, the dead fucking cardinal.

Rhonda turned her gaze to the canopy, looking past it to the open sky.

Shake it off, Rhonda...

Just shake it off...

Strings of saliva and vomit glistened on her chin. She wiped it with the back of her hand, then smeared it on her jeans.

Time to move on.

As she walked away, the phone hissed with static one last time, a lingering hum in her ear.

CHAPTER V

HANDICAP

"Ain't no love in Kentucky.

Just fuckin'."

RHONDA QUICKENED HER pace down the forest path, eager to distance herself from Zach's gruesome mess. The static on the phone had finally lessened, making Darla's voice clearer.

"Taleiah's startin' to date them young bucks out here," said Rhonda. "Told ya that last time, right?"

"Yeah, good for her!" said Darla. "I remember she was real cute, but always so quiet..."

"Lil' cute-and-quiet Taleiah's got issues now," said Rhonda. "'Bout to put her ass on *Jerry Springer!*"

"Oh, I love that show!" said Darla. "You still watchin' it?"

"Hell yes, I am," said Rhonda. "We all do. Except Taleiah. She watches that *Oprah* bullshit."

"The fuck? *Oprah?*"

"I know," said Rhonda. "It's like we ain't even kin. When my Daddy catches her he gets pissed and says, *'Turn that bullshit off! Right the fuck now!'*"

"Well, he should!" said Darla.

"Right?" asked Rhonda. "I mean, Oprah herself is alright. She's a strong-ass black woman. I respect that. Could definitely beat some ass."

"Hell yes, she could," said Darla. "I wouldn't fuck with her."

"Oh, I wouldn't, either," said Rhonda. "She'd kill a bitch."

"She'd probably rip *both* a bitch's eyes out!" said Darla.

Static crackled on the phone as they laughed.

"She would indeed, Darla," said Rhonda, grinning ear-to-ear. "She would indeed..."

Rhonda arrived at a fork in the path. The left led to the pond where Zach liked to hang out, playin' his Game Boy like a weirdo; the right led to the huge oak tree in the field behind Daddy's house. She wasn't ready to talk to Zachary yet *(that little psychopath!)* and didn't wanna risk him squealin' on her usin' Daddy's long distance, so she chose the path to the oak tree.

"I got a lot of respect for Oprah as a person," said Rhonda, "ya know, especially since she's a lady of color..."

"Uh-huh..." said Darla.

"But her show, no," said Rhonda. "Just no."

"Don't need none of that self-righteous bullshit," said Darla. "Gimme *Jerry Springer* any day!"

"With *Jerry Springer*," said Rhonda, "people are *real.* Real people, like you and me, dealin' with real-life, everyday issues that normal, everyday people go through."

Darla laughed. "But sometimes they got crazy stuff on there. You see that one episode? 'Bout the dude who married a horse?"

"A horse?"

"Yep."

"And was he..." said Rhonda. "...fuckin' it, too?"

"Well, they was married, so yeah. I assume so."

Rhonda shook her head.

Maybe Zach wasn't so bad after all.

At least he wasn't no horse-fucker.

"Lil' T ain't bangin' no animals," said Rhonda, "at least, I don't think she is. But she's got somethin' *fucked up* with her, that's for sure."

Static buzzed faintly in the background, and Darla's next words broke through:

"...like what?"

"Somethin' *sexual...*"

"Hmm, somethin' *sexual?*" asked Darla. *"Now* you got me interested."

They laughed.

"Guess!" said Rhonda.

"Gimme a hint!"

"It's somethin' she *can't do...*"

While waiting for Darla's guess, Rhonda admired the sights and smells around her. Forest air always smelled so damn good. She breathed in its fragrances: damp moss, wet tree trunks, musty fall leaves, and pine needles.

Mmm...

Love those fuckin' pine needles...

She breathed in deeper, almost tasting them.

"...can't swallow?" asked Darla.

Rhonda's grinned.

"Can't swallow *what,* Darla?"

"You know..."

"No, what you talkin' about?"

"Her boyfriend's..." said Darla.

Rhonda gripped the phone tighter.

"...jism."

Static hissed briefly, almost emphasizing the word, and Rhonda leaned back, cackling.

"No, that ain't it!" she said. "And you got a nasty mind, by the way!"

"You makin' it nasty by makin' me guess!"

"Guess again!"

Rhonda stepped onto a nearby log, her left hand gripping the phone, her right extended for balance.

"...*butt stuff*?" asked Darla. "Somethin' to do with a guy's butt, or hers?"

Rhonda cackled again, almost losing her balance (*fuck!*) on the log. Darla's guesses made it clear where her mind went whenever the topic of fuckin' came up.

"Darla Rhodes, you have the nastiest mind, I swear! Imaginin' my little sister doin' all that nasty stuff!"

Darla laughed. "What else was I supposed to guess?"

Rhonda stepped off the end of the log. Darla had a point—not much else *to* guess, once she really thought about it.

"Oh lord, I give up," said Darla. "Just tell me."

Rhonda lowered her voice.

"Alright...*I'll tell you.*"

She took a breath.

Two squirrels scampered up a nearby tree.

"My sister Taleiah..."

Rhonda bent over, pressing the phone against her lips.

"Can't..."

She grinned so hard her face hurt.

"...cum!"

"What?"

"She can't orgasm, Darla! The bitch can't cum!"

"Ohhh!" said Darla. *"Well-oh-my-Gawd!"*

Rhonda shot up, delight smeared across her face. She spotted another log and made her way across it.

"She can't cum, Darla. My sister cannot cum."

She teetered left, then right as she made her way across the log.

"Poor little Taleiah!" said Darla. "But, you know, that's not a huge problem. A lot of girls can't orgasm."

"I know. And I feel sorry for every one of them bitches. Must be like livin' through hell, every single day!"

"Oh, it ain't that bad!" said Darla. "They still feel good down there!"

"They might be feelin' good, but it'd be like eatin' and never gettin' *full*, ya know what I'm sayin'? I'm afraid it's givin' her mental problems. Ya know, psychologically and shit."

She focused on balancing atop the log, tilting left and right as her thoughts drifted to Taleiah.

Was Lil' T okay?

Like, *mentally* okay?

Little Zachary had problems—*that's for damn fuckin' sure*—but he was takin', or *should* be takin' his new medication. But Taleiah...always so quiet, reserved. Kept to herself. Probably a good thing for family balance—if Taleiah was like her, they'd be fightin' all the time or gettin' into trouble together (or both) and turn Daddy's blood pressure real high. But Taleiah was always *too* quiet—like the fuckin', anomaly of the family. Never really knew what she was thinkin' or up to.

'Til she asked her for advice.

About not bein' able to cum.

Of all the things Lil' T could ask for advice on...and the way she'd asked about it...with such *intensity*...

Was it healthy to be so focused on one single thing?

When there's so much else goin' on?

When they were gettin' so close to The Temple?

To The Run?

To The Glory?

But even findin' The Temple...

Even that...

Probably couldn't help her cum.

She returned to her balancing act on the log. "I can't even imagine what it'd be like to not be able to cum. Can you?"

"Tough for me too, I guess," said Darla. "I mean, I orgasm all the fuckin' time."

"So do I, Darla...so do I..."

Something—a squirrel?—rustled in the nearby bushes. Branches cracked, and a tree limb swayed overhead. Yellow, orange, and red leaves spiraled down, twirling like helicopter blades.

"Ya know," said Rhonda, "out of all the handicaps a person can have, that has gotta be the saddest of'em all..."

Stepping off the log, she ventured along the path toward the spot she'd glimpsed deer crossing before.

"Oh, come on!" said Darla. "It ain't like your sister's handicapped..."

"Nah, it is! I mean, think about it. Even a blind, deaf and dumb bitch can cum," said Rhonda. "I assume. Most of'em."

"But that's different, those are *real* handicaps, it ain't like—"

"And this is worse! If you was blind or couldn't walk, other people would know, right? *'Oh, this chick's blind, so don't bump into her.'*"

"Mmm-hmm..." said Darla.

"'Oh, this bitch can't walk, make way 'cause she's in one of them, goddamn wheelchairs.'"

"Yeah..."

"'Oh, this ho's deaf, don't talk to her 'cause she can't, ya know, hear ya and shit.'"

"Mmm-hmm..."

"All *those* kinds of handicaps," said Rhonda, "can be fuckin' dealt with."

She stepped onto a narrower log that shifted with her weight. The long metal antenna of the phone sliced through the air as she lurched forward, then back, barely catching her balance.

"All problems solved," said Rhonda. "Easily!"

She almost fell from the log *(shit!)*, but managed to catch herself.

"But if ya can't cum..." she said. "...ain't nobody know. 'Til ya mess around and shit. And yeah, most guys won't give a fuck. But it will fuck you up, mentally."

She stepped off the log.

"I guess you're right..." said Darla. "I guess it could..."

"It's like this dark secret..." said Rhonda. "That ya gotta keep with ya... for the rest of your life..."

She stepped over one of the trap holes Daddy had dug in the woods after MB *(that fucker!)* had escaped. Most of'em were out closer to the road, though.

"Now I'm startin' to feel sorry for her..." said Darla. "I guess she *is* kinda handicapped..."

"Right?" asked Rhonda. "And I bet in the future, we'll be givin' handicapped people robot arms and legs, ya know? So legless dudes can walk. And armless bitches can grab shit."

"Uh-huh," said Darla. "And they won't be handicapped no more."

"That's right," said Rhonda. "But if you can't cum, if you lack that fuckin' *ability*—can't imagine inventin' somethin' to fix that."

"A robot clitoris," said Darla, "just ain't gonna happen. Not even in *Star Trek.*"

"Not even in *Star Wars,*" said Rhonda.

"You can tell her what makes *me* cum the easiest," said Darla. "I always cum when someone..."

Rhonda slowed to a stop.

"...licks me down there."

("did it feel goo—")

"You know," said Darla, "maybe lil' Taleiah just needs somebody who's up—"

Static buzzed.

"—to snuff... in the—"

Another crackle.

"—pussy-eatin' game."

Rhonda stood still. Two nearby sparrows had started to mate again.

Or were they fightin'?

Maybe both.

How could you tell?

("did it feel good this time?")

Memories trickled inward—

("it felt good this time, didn't it?")

—like water seeping into a basement.

("i made you cum this time, didn't i?")

How old were they back then?

("didn't i?")

The trickles gathered into streams, and the streams into a flood.

She reached down—

("didn't i?")

("DIDN'T I?")

—and found warmth.

"Did it feel good this time?"

Rhonda lifted the blanket from her head and wiped her mouth.

Darla leaned back against the bed's headrest, eyes closed, thighs quivering. Beads of sweat rolled down her forehead.

"It felt good this time, didn't it?" asked Rhonda.

She needed her to say it.

(say it)

She knew the answer, but she needed her to say it.

It had to have felt good this time.

(fucking say it)

Her pussy was warm this time.

Darla's eyelids parted, revealing a vacant, glazed stare.

"...y-yeah..."

Finally.

Fucking.

Finally.

Rhonda bit her lip.

"I made you cum this time, didn't I?"

(say it)

(i need you to say it)

"Didn't I?"

"...I th-think so..." said Darla.

(yes)

(yes)

(now, you do me)

"Now that I did you," said Rhonda, "you do me."

(you're gonna make me cum this time, girl)

Darla looked away.

"...I dunno if I wanna keep doin' this..."

(oh, yes you do)

(and you're gonna make me cum, too)

"Nah, I did you, so you do me. Come on, now."

Rhonda ripped the covers from Darla's hands.

"Switch places with me."

*

"Maybe he ain't eat—"

Static crackled, breaking up Darla's words.

"...what?"

"I said, maybe he ain't eatin' it right?"

Rhonda gazed at the two sparrows circling each other, chirping and fluttering their wings.

("i dunno if I wanna keep doin' this...")

"Her pussy," said Darla. "Maybe her boyfriend or whatever ain't eatin' it right?"

"Oh..." said Rhonda. "...yeah..."

("stop actin' up, darla!")

("i did you")

She resumed strolling toward the treeline.

("so you do me!")

"You know," said Rhonda, "that just might be the problem..."

"Maybe simple as that," said Darla.

("switch places with me")

Emerging from the woods, Rhonda's stroll turned into a trudge uphill toward the oak tree standing sentinel over Daddy's house.

("do what I say, darla!")

("i said switch places with me!")

"Why you breathin' so hard?" asked Darla.

("always do what I say!")

"Goin' up a hill now," said Rhonda, fighting to catch her breath, "and it's a big one..."

("good, that's right...")

"Lemme guess—still smokin' a pack a day?"

("lick harder...")

"Nope, down to half a pack now," she said, panting. "Thank you very much..."

("faster...")

"Oh, well that's an improvement."

("use that tongue")

"Told you," said Rhonda, straining to push up the hill. "Not as wild as I used to be..."

("use that tongue, darla")
Upon reaching the summit, she grasped her chest,

("use that fucking tongue!")

struggling to breathe.

CHAPTER VI

NO MORE PRACTICING

"Best stop actin' up, now..."

THE GNARLED BRANCHES of the oak tree sprawled across the field like tarantula legs, clawing at the sky. Rhonda leaned against the trunk and caught her breath. Despite efforts to focus elsewhere, her eyes kept darting to the garage in the distance, drawn toward it like her true north.

"I tell ya what," said Rhonda, still panting. "Taleiah needs to get *a girl* to eat her out. At least once. I bet that'd make her cum."

"That might do the trick..." said Darla.

"Girls eat it better," said Rhonda. "They just know what to do. Ya know what I'm sayin'?"

"Yep, I'll admit it," said Darla. "Can't believe I'm sayin' it, but I'll admit it. They really fuckin' do."

Rhonda paused, caressing the rough bark of the oak tree.

Maybe she should change topics.

She wanted to ask *more,* though.

(into her)

But maybe she shouldn't...

(into her)

No—maybe she *should*...

(into her)

They hadn't talked about it in such a long time...

(into her)

She glanced at her arms—so badass with all the tattoos.

The sun still felt *good* on her arms.

She could talk about it.

She remembered.

("I did you, so you do me")

She remembered the first time she'd made Darla cum, and the first time Darla had made her cum.

(you're gonna make me cum this time, girl)

"So," said Rhonda, "how's it goin' with that dude you married..."

Should she really bring this up?

"Is he...ya know..."

She caressed the bark faster.

"...satisfyin' you?"

"Oh, he gets the job done," said Darla. "Ain't nothin' perfect, but satisfies me alright."

Rhonda's hand froze mid-stroke against the bark.

That was some *bullshit.*

Ain't no way that what's-his-fuckin'-face satisfied Darla the way *she* did.

On numerous occasions.

("did it feel good this time?")

("did it?")

Something pitter-pattered inside Rhonda like crawling insects.

She wanted to keep going, ask more questions.

But should she?

The garage loomed in the distance.

(ask it, rhonda)

(ask it)

She caressed the bark even faster now; no longer stroking but rubbing with force.

(ask it, rhonda)

(ask it)

"...do you remember..."

The line crackled, distorting her voice.

She swallowed hard.

(ask it, rhonda)

(ask it)

"...when you ate..."

(ask it, rhonda)

(ask it)

God, she hated sounding weak.

(fucking ask it)

"...*my* pussy, Darla?"

Everything darkened.

The thumping in her ears grew louder. Faster.

Vulnerable.

Vulnerable.

God, she hated being—

—*vulnerable.*

Something sucked all sound from the air and she plunged deep underwater, under that sea, that dark fucking sea and she couldn't breathe she couldn't breathe she couldn't hear she couldn't move she couldn't breathe oh God she couldn't breathe.

(why did i ask that?)

(why did i fucking ask that?)
She waited for Darla's reply, her gaze locked on the distant garage.
And waited.
Stared.
Waited.
Stared.
(i can't breathe)
Waited.
Stared.
Waited.
Stared.
(oh god i can't fucking br—)
"Yeah..." said Darla.
Static buzzed, warping her voice.
"...I—I th—ink—I do..."
Rhonda exhaled.
She filled her lungs with air—
(i can breathe)
(i can breathe)
She could breathe.
—and exhaled again.
Thank God, she could breathe.
But what should she say next?
She didn't know what to say.
Hadn't planned that far ahead.
(wait)
Was that...*guilt* she detected in Darla's answer?
Why'd she say it *that* way?
There wasn't nothin' to feel guilty about.
Nothin' at all.
The garage loomed closer, sharpening into focus.
(darla...help me...)
(don't let the garage inside me...)
"But that was a long time ago..." said Darla. "...we were just kids experimentin'...that's all..."
("that's all.")
The words held a heaviness, an unnecessary finality that didn't sit right.

And what Darla had said before that:

"*...just experimentin.*"

The phrase burned through her.

Just...experimenting?

That's what she called it?

Like they'd been in science class, mixing fucking chemicals together just to see what would fucking happen?

Just,

fucking,

experimenting?

She clutched her head.

No!

A buzzing, like a million bees had been unleashed—

Fucking no!

—morphed into a high-pitched whining.

(remember what the doc—)

That same fucking sound.

(the doctor sa—)

The field,

(neuro—)

the tree,

(—logically trigg—)

the garage,

the sky,

(—ered tinnitus)

all spun around her.

Please!

She grasped at the tree but her right hand trembled too hard,

(breathe)

(breathe)

(foc—)

but she knew she should,

(brea—)

(br—)

(f—)

because she felt herself *falling.*

Falling.

Falling.
Everything spun.
(*"stop actin' up!"*)
Falling.
Falling.
(*"no more!"*)
Everything melted.
(*"i don't wanna do this no more!"*)
Falling.
Falling.
Everything merged.
(*"do what I say, darla!"*)
Falling.
Falling.
(*"always do what I fucking say!"*)

She remembered when it ended.

*

*The crickets chirped through the night air, a backdrop to the stillness.
Rolling fields of wheat and corn surrounded Rhonda and Darla, stretching as
far as the eye could see. One of their usual spots—nobody for miles.*

*Darla sat before Rhonda, facing away, clutching her legs to her chest. She
hadn't said a word all night—wouldn't even look at her—but Rhonda tried
to ignore it. Lying behind Darla, arms outstretched, hands behind her head,
she chewed on a strand of wheat. Whenever Darla acted up like this, staying
relaxed had proven key to get her acting right again.*

Darla wiped her eyes. "I want us to stop, Rhonda."

"Stop what?"

"You know..."

Rhonda sat up. "No, I don't."

"...I want us to be..." said Darla.

She tilted her head to the night sky.

"...just 'normal' friends again..."

Rhonda squinted, trying to peer into *her—to pierce the back of her skull
and reach into her fucking mind.*

To control her.

(let me control you darla you always let me)

"Just 'normal' friends…" said Darla.

Rhonda clenched her jaw.

She's actin' up worse this time…

"What does that even mean?" asked Rhonda. "Just 'normal' friends?'"

"You know."

Rhonda gazed at the twinkling blackness above. The stars seemed to watch them more closely tonight, as if this time might play differently from all the other times Darla acted up.

It wouldn't, though.

Tonight, a script replayed, one of tired and predictable behavior that tended to come in cycles. As long as Rhonda played her part, the cycle could continue and Darla would start actin' right again.

So they could play *together again.*

"Darla, we are just 'normal' friends."

She pulled the wheat strand from her mouth, laying it on the ground.

"It's fine," said Rhonda. "We're fine. And normal. And you're gettin' worked up over nothin.'"

(stop actin' up, darla…)

(do what i say)

Darla glanced back with red puffy eyes, then looked away.

"No, we're not," she said. "Just normal friends don't do that with each other."

"So?"

"So, Jake said he loves me and I only wanna do that stuff with him."

"Oh, fuck Jake."

She scooted closer to Darla, trying to work her magic again, her secret power she used whenever Darla acted up like this.

"Listen, Darla…"

This part had to be said so, so softly—she'd learned the hard way that delivery was everything. If she fucked up the delivery, Darla might react badly again, and she didn't wanna take another fucking "break."

(i need you now)

(i need you tonight)

(i need you every fucking night)

"Jake can be your boyfriend," said Rhonda, "and…"

She laid her hand on Darla's shoulder, massaging it.
"...we can still do that kinda stuff together, as friends..."
(best stop actin' up now...)
Darla always liked it when she massaged her shoulders.
Helped get her actin' right again.
"Ain't nothin' wrong with it..." said Rhonda. "...just practicin', that's all..."
She pressed her thumb deeper into Darla's favorite spot, right between her shoulder blade and spine.
(you like it when i touch you here...)
(don't you?)
"...just practicin'..." She caressed Darla's bare arm. "...for when boys do it to us...ain't nothin' wrong with it...and you can sti—"
Darla flung Rhonda's hand to the ground and bolted up.

"No."

"No more fucking practicing."

*

In all the years Rhonda had known Darla, she'd never seen that same look on her before or since.
Why had Darla felt so...*guilty* about it?
Why'd she get that *look*—that awful, nasty look in her eyes?
She loved Darla and Darla loved her—right?
Right?
("i did you...")
And why'd she cry the whole time?
("so you do me...")
She just had to fuckin' cry, didn't she?
(you're gonna make me cum this time, girl)
In that fuckin' field.
Fuckin' crybaby.
("i dunno if i wanna keep doin' this, rhonda...")
Wasn't nothin' to cry about.
(oh yes you do and you're gonna make me cum, too)
Just practicin' for when boys did it to'em, that's all.

It felt good, didn't it?

(*"switch places with me"*)

Didn't it?

(*"i said switch places with me!"*)

She glanced around. Felt cold now.

The sun sank into the horizon.

The nearby forest, once cheerful, now loomed darker.

Ominous.

Her hand slipped from the bark. She marched toward the garage, drawn by an invisible force.

Finally, Darla spoke.

"I love you, though, Rhonda...you know that, right?"

(*no you don't*)

(*you don't love me*)

Rhonda's lips barely moved when she answered:

"...love you, too...Darla..."

(*you ended it*)

Silence fell, broken only by the phone's faint static. Rhonda fixated on the garage.

(*everything was fine and you fucking ended it*)

A crow cawed.

The sky darkened to a cold Kentucky gray.

(*you don't love me*)

(*you never loved me*)

"So..." said Darla. "...you got anyone over there? In Raven?"

"Got a couple guys..." said Rhonda. "Nothin' too serious...just lettin'em get the job done..."

(*i have no one*)

"That's good..." said Darla. "...you can show them Raven boys how a Crow girl gets down..."

(*you say that every time we talk*)

(*it ain't funny no more*)

"Yeah...I guess..."

(*and you ain't came to see me even once yet*)

Vulnerable.

Vulnerable.

God, she hated feeling vulnerable.

"Ain't got no girls here, though..." whispered Rhonda, not meaning to say it but only think it.

"Better be careful..." said Darla. "You remember what happened to Abby—"

Static crackled, distorting her words.

"—by My—ers—don't ya?"

Rhonda winced.

Not her again...

Why's she keep poppin' up lately...

"Yeah, I know..." said Rhonda.

Her eyes fell to the ground.

"I remember..."

("ohhh, abby myerrrrs...")

She remembered Abby Myers—the girl in high school who had *"FUCKING DYKE"* scrawled on her locker for weeks.

("where ya hidin', abby?")

She remembered Abby Myers—how girls snickered and covered their mouths as Abby walked by in the halls.

("we ain't gonna hurt ya...")

She remembered Abby Myers—clutching her books and staring at the floor as guys fake-coughed and yelled, *"Dyke alert!"*

("we just wanna play with ya...")

And she remembered how it made *her* look down, clutching her own books, too.

("come play with us, abby...")

Abby Myers killed herself the day before graduation.

Her parents found her swinging from a tree. A piece of paper clung to her shirt, the words *"I AM NOT A DYKE"* scrawled across it.

That's all it said.

"You'll find someone, though..." said Darla.

Rhonda lifted her gaze toward the garage.

("ohhh, abby myerrrrs...")

The pull grew stronger.

***

Rhonda marched downhill toward the garage, eyes unblinking, phone loose in her hand. Darla seemed eager to change the subject *(why?)* and started blabbin' about her *(stupid)* family. She and her husband were doin' *fiiiiiine*, but still havin' money problems *(that's what you get for spreadin' them legs)*. Havin' a baby cost a lot *(no shit)*, and they didn't wanna have another until her dumbass husband got a higher-payin' job *(good fuckin' luck)*. Money was tight, you see, *(yeah, i see—that you're a stupid whore)* especially once you had a *(dumb, useless)* baby. The expenses kept addin' up.

Rhonda shook her head.

Dumb bitch...

Shouldn't have let him nut inside you, then...

The garage drew closer.

The sky darkened.

The air turned frigid.

Her face descended into a vacant stare.

And on top o'that, you're payin' twenty dollars a month for Caller ID...

Darla went on about her baby, *he was doin' fiiiine*, eatin' a lot now *(fat, fuckin' parasite)*, and spoke his first word *("Momma," or the usual bullshit)*. Then she babbled about her husband *(whatshisfuckin'face)* maybe gettin' a new job in Zion County *(he won't, he's a retard with a record)* and some nonsense about takin' their baby to Lake Gilead where he did the cutest thing...

(hope he drowns next time, bitch)

She truly didn't give a fuck about Darla's useless baby or her rock-for-brains husband or what cute bullshit happened at the fuckin' lake.

But that kinda shit mattered, didn't it?

It was *so damn important* to talk about babies and listen to your *"normal"* friends when they prattled about their dumb kids and shitty husbands, and she *did* want Darla to be happy—after all, who wouldn't want their best friend to be so fucking happy?

"Oh wow," said Rhonda. "His first word was 'Momma?' That's great..."

Just so fuckin' great...

She approached the garage.

I bet whatshisfuckin'face don't eat your pussy like I used to...

Or like you ate mine...

Turning the knob on the side door, she sighed.

Hadn't had a girl eat her in a long time now.

She *yearned* for that again.

"Uh-huh...ya don't say..."

She stepped into the darkness of the garage, slamming the door so hard the markerboard almost fell off.

"FED @ 4 PM - ZACH"

CHAPTER VII

THE BLOOD, THE MUSIC

"I love you, Darla..."

RHONDA GAZED UPON the piece of shit tied to the pillar in the garage. A Kentucky state flag bandanna covered his eyes while another bound his mouth.

"Hel-...hel-me..." said the piece of shit. Cold, gray light from the windows illuminated the bloodstains and splattered SpaghettiOs on his white t-shirt. The ropes had chafed his arms raw and his thinning hair had matted into an oily mess.

"...pl-se..."

"Shh..." Rhonda clasped her hand over the phone receiver—Darla was goin' on about what her baby liked to eat, or something.

"...pl-se...hel-hel-me..." said the piece of shit.

You still sayin' that, AB?

Even after all this time?

She placed her finger on his lips.

Ain't no one gonna help you...

Get it through your thick fuckin' skull.

Leaning close to his ear, she whispered:

"How ya doin', AB?"

He did his best to mutter through the bandanna. "Mm...nee's...Bah... bby...m-my...mmname—"

"Shut the fuck up!"

Rhonda clasped her free hand around his face and *squeezed*.

"Your name isn't Bobby, it's AB!"

She pushed her nails into his cheeks.

"Why don't you fucking get that?"

The piece of shit whined and moaned.

"...I...I-'m...s...s-orr-y..."

Good...

Best stop actin' up...

"Now," she said, *"what's your fucking name?"*

"...A...B...."

"Gooood..."

She released her grip.

Bobby, Jim, James, Michael—never gave a shit about their *old names*, and most of the fuckers usually had bigger things to worry about than their new monicker, ya know, bein' fuckin' kidnapped and all. This one was different, though—still hadn't given'em a *real* Clue yet and still hadn't fuckin' cried.

But, whatever.

He'd cry.

Eventually.

Maybe when they took him to Strawberry Fields.

"Aaaay-Beeeeee..."

Drifting through the darkness around him, she tugged on his ropes, making sure they held tight.

"Urnnf!"

With each pull, the piece of shit moaned.

"Urnnnff!"

"Shh..." she whispered.

The ropes had grown worn, but held firm. She traced her finger across the asshole's face, sensing a slight electricity between them. Smooth as a baby's behind—Daddy must've shaved him today.

"You ready to tell us The Clue yet?" she asked. "Hmm? The Clue to The Temple?"

"...d-n't-know...a-out...Te-ple..."

"Mmm-hmm..."

They all said that.

They all fuckin' knew.

She slid her tongue up his left cheek, nice and slow, stopping shy of his blindfold.

AB squirmed like a worm on a hook.

She frowned, then dragged her tongue up his right cheek, wiggling it under the blindfold, licking his eyelid.

"Pl-s...stop!"

His ropes creaked as he struggled.

She withdrew, her frown deepening into a scowl.

Just don't make sense...

You're one of the biggest sissies we ever fuckin' kidnapped...

Stutterin' all the time like a little pussy-ass bitch...

So why ain't you cried yet, boy?

"Where's your fuckin' tears? Why don't you cr—"

Huh?

She sniffed.

What's that smell?

Her face twisted with disgust.

Oh no.

She sniffed again.

Oh, hell no.

She tightened her grip around the phone receiver.

"Did you shit your pants?"

AB stopped squirming.

"*You little...*" she said.

She unclasped the phone receiver.

"Darla?"

"Rhonda?" asked Darla. "Thought I lost ya for a second, I—"

"Listen, I'm real sorry but I'm gonna have to let ya go," said Rhonda. "Pizza's comin' soon and we're havin' a big family dinner tonight."

"Oh, okay," said Darla. "Well, it was so good talkin' to you! You call me anytime, now!"

Rhonda reached for the metal-pronged whip on the countertop. Daddy had told her not to use it yet, but she didn't give a fuck. Not today.

"Uh-huh..." she said. "...you too..."

She flipped the light switch by the door. Pale blue light washed over the garage, casting everything in a ghostly teal. It had been Taleiah's idea to paint the light bulb blue.

Darla's voice crackled through the line. "And don't worry too much about little Zachary, now. Boys will be b—"

A burst of static interrupted.

"—boys..."

Rhonda's hand relaxed, then tightened around the whip in a pulsating rhythm.

"Besides," said Darla. "Ain't like he k—k—"

The line hissed, breaking her words.

"—k—killed no—"

"—one."

Rhonda grit her teeth.

"That's right, Darla..."

Her muscles tensed.

"Ain't like he killed no one..."

"L—ve you, girl!" said Darla. "Have a good—night, n—ow!"

"Love you, too…"

Rhonda's voice shook like Darla's that night when she said she wanted it to stop—that she wanted to be *just 'normal' friends.*

(normal friends)

(just NORMAL friends)

(normalnormalnormalnorm—)

"Have a good night…" said Rhonda.

After sliding the antenna in, she laid the phone on the countertop and turned back to the piece of shit.

"Now, you and me…"

She pulled on the whip to hear it tighten.

"We're gonna have a little talk…"

AB made a muffled protest.

"You can't even control your bowel movements?"

She pulled on the whip again.

Loved that sound.

The tightening.

"Do you know how fuckin' *disgusting* that is?"

"…a-m…s-ry…"

"Sorry? *Sorry that you shit your pants?*"

With all her strength, she reared the whip back and unleashed it forward, cracking it to his left.

CRACK!

The sound ripped through the air.

AB yelped like a dog.

His whole body shook.

"*'Sorry'* don't fuckin' cut it, AB…"

She cracked the whip to his right.

CRACK!

AB yelped again.

Like a little fucking dog.

CRACK!

Again.

CRACK!

Again.

CRACK!

Her heart beat faster.

God, she loved that.

That sound had *power.*

Her right hand trembled.

"I bet you can't look at me with those blue eyes now, can ya, boy?"

"I-don-ave-bur-eyes!" he said.

Lies!

Lies!

(LIES)

She saw *his* eyes now, shinin' and shinin' from behind that blindfold.

They shined *blue.*

Blue blue blue like the blue-eyed boy's.

She remembered the blue-eyed boy, and what he done to her.

("you goin' by my b—")

Pulling the whip back,

She remembered the blue-eyed boy,

and cracked it on his face.

and what he done to her.

He screamed.

"Boy," she said, "you got anything to say for yourself?"

Spittle gathered in her mouth.

She remembered the blue-eyed boy,

and what he done to her.

"...blue-eyed boy?"

She bit her lower lip.

It bled.

"I can see your blue eyes shinin' and shinin' from behind that blindfold..."

"Ah-don't-a-ve-bl-eyes!"

(LIES!)

(they all have'em!)

(they all LIE!)

Her right hand trembled harder.

She gripped the whip tighter in response.

CRACK!

He screamed and screamed.

"You-gon'-be-my-bitch?"

Her right hand spasmed.

No!

She dropped the whip.

No!

A high-pitched whine pierced her ears.

That sound!

She bent over, grabbing her head.

That fucking sound!

The off-white garage door appeared before her—only that fucking door spinning and melting and merging with his fucking bl—

"*You-gon'-be-my-bitch?*"

She gripped her head tighter,

No!

pressing her nails into her skull.

"Your eyes..."

She ripped her gaze away.

"I can't stand those eyes!"

"*You-gon'-be-my-bitch?*"

"I don't wanna remember!"

"*You-gon'-be-my-bitch?*"

"Your eyes hurt!"

She tried to push the memories away.

"*You-gon'-be-my-bitch?*"

"Your eyes fucking hurt!"

She bit her lip harder.

I don't let no one see my legs!

Blood trickled down her chin.

Not after what he did to me!

She grabbed the whip off the floor.

"*You-gon'-be-my-bitch?*"

"Stop askin' me that!"

"*You-gon'-be-my-b—*"

"I said stop askin' me that!"

CRACK!

The whip hit his arm.

It bled.

He squealed and squealed.

She flicked her eyes to the blood.

(yes)
The blood on his face,
the blood on his arm.
(yes)
The tremor in her hand eased.
She pulled the whip back again—
CRACK!
hitting his stomach.
(yes)
He screamed like a dying cat.
(yes)
When he screamed—
she felt better.
When he bled—
she felt better.
(yes yes yes)
Slowly, the high-pitched whine morphed into something else—
I love this!
a distorted symphony,
God, I fucking love this!
a dark orchestra,
I love hearing the music!
harmonized with heavy metal,
When I see the blood!
and a choir of angels.
And hear the music!
An orchestra unlike anything she'd ever heard,
Every time I hear different music!
nor could replicate outside her mind.
The music makes it good again!
And rising above it all:
Makes it all good again!
a violin.
She smiled.
"I-know-what-I-can-doooo..."
With her left hand, she yanked at her jeans button,
"I'm-gonna-get-re-veeeenge-on-yooouuu..."

gazing at AB with a vacant, unplugged look,

"Bluuue-eyed boooyyy..."

her mouth agape and drooling.

(pussy in the left)

(whip in the right)

She whipped him again with her right hand,

CRACK!

her left still grasping at her jeans.

CRACK!

He screamed.

(pleasure in the left)

(pain in the right)

She unclasped the button *(finally! fucking finally!)* and ripped the zipper down.

God, she fucking *loved* this.

It felt so dirty.

So wrong.

Just like when Darla licked me down there...

A narrow string of saliva dripped from her mouth.

CRACK!

The whip crashed over the blindfold.

She said she'd only do it a little...

He screamed and screamed his dyin' cat screams.

That she didn't like doin' it with girls...

But she'd do it for me...

For me.

Was his eye bleedin' now?

Had never hit one in the eye before.

CRACK!

Blood dribbled from behind his blindfold.

Yep!

Got his eye that time!

"...do you remember..."

She licked her left middle finger and stuffed it down her underwear, feeling for her clit.

"...when you ate..."

There it was.

There it was.

Already wet for her.

"...my pussy, Darla?"

The violin halted.

(no)

The orchestra fell silent.

(no)

She was so stupid for asking that.

Why the fuck had she asked that?

She pulled her finger away.

The whip hung to her side.

Shame.

Shame.

(what the hell am i doing?)

She looked around.

Shame.

Shame.

(i don't wanna hurt anyb—)

Darla's face.

Oh God, those eyes...

Darla's big, beautiful eyes.

I could drown myself in'em...

The violin's cry returned.

The orchestra thundered anew.

Those eyes!

She shoved her finger back down, moving it in a familiar, circular motion.

(look at me darla!)

(look at me!)

Leaning her head back,

(pussy in the left)

she moved her finger faster and faster,

(whip in the right)

cracking that fucking whip harder and harder.

(pleasure in the left)

God, this felt so good.

(pain in the right)

Hadn't done this in such a long time.
(pussy in the left)
The whip kept crashing down.
(whip in the right)
Didn't even know where she hit him.
(pleasure in the left)
Just heard his screams.
(pain in the right)
His beautiful screams.
"I did you..."
"So you do me..."
She remembered.
"Switch places with me."
She bucked her hips.
"I said switch places with me!"
The violin cried louder.
No one ate it like Darla did!
The orchestra swelled.
No boys!
Her finger moved faster and faster.
No other girls, either!
She whipped him harder and harder.
Not even the bitch who killed herself!
Not even Abby Myers!
The violin shrieked with emotion.
("ohhhhhh abby myerrrrrs...")
The orchestra surged to a crescendo.
Darla ate it so much better than that fucking bitch, Abby!
Her eyes rolled back.
Darla's little tongue!
She whipped him harder, faster.
Darla's little tongue wigglin'!
AB howled and howled.
God, I fucking loved that!
I miss that, Darla!
She arched her back,
I miss you!

turning the whites of her eyes toward God.

I miss you and I fucking need you!

Her left finger moved faster and faster,

(yes)

her right hand whipped him harder and harder.

(give it to me)

She was gettin' close now,

(fucking give it to me)

real close—

(GIVE IT TO ME)

Oh, Darla...

*

—it felt so dirty, so wrong, and that's what made it so hot, when Darla licked her down there she said she'd only do it a little bit, that she wanted to be just-normal-friends *but she held Darla's head there, just held it* (keep goin', darla) *and gripped her head tighter* (please) *and then Darla relaxed, became resigned to it, yep, fuckin' resigned to it then she started gettin' into it,* (keep goin') *yep, gettin' real into it* (don't stop), *and then once Darla got good* (use that tongue) *she started grindin' her hips, grindin' her pussy into Darla's little face, grindin', grindin', feelin' that little tongue wigglin' everywhere, oh God it was* everywhere, *up her pussy up her ass lickin' her thighs lickin' her knees* (get back here, now!), *that little tongue wigglin', wigglin' and lickin' everywhere all at once* (get back where you're supposed to be, darla) *and she gripped Darla's head* (please) *and pulled her back to where she was* supposed *to be, where she should always fuckin' be, and then she started gettin' close,* oh God she was close, *"Use that tongue, Darla!"* she said, *"Use that fucking tongue!" and she gripped Darla's head harder and harder* (do what i say, now) *and pushed her fingers deeper and deeper into her fucking skull and that made her lick harder and harder* (always do what i fuckin' say) *and the fact that Darla didn't even wanna do it but she pressured her, she pressured her to—no! she'd* convinced *her, she'd convinced her just like she'd convinced Abby, and that made it hotter, oh yes, that* always *made it hotter,* (keep fuckin' goin'!) *and now Darla was gettin' good, yes, so good so-so-so fucking good* (almost there) *she was close,*

yep, gettin' close yes yes yes *keep fuckin' lickin',* (don't fucking stop) *keep on goin', bitch* (i said don't stop!) *you're my bitch now, lick that fucking pussy, Darla! Lick it! Eat it good, now! Eat it right! Eat it* the right *fucking way! Use that tongue, now!*

Use that fucking t—

*

"Oh God, I'm gonna—"

CHAPTER VIII

A PURPLE WAVE OF LIGHT

"Do you see the colors?

Do you hear the music?

When you—"

UPON REACHING ORGASM, Rhonda often soared on a brilliant wave of light. Sometimes red, sometimes yellow, one time orange. This time, *purple*—a purple wave of light, freeing her from this realm and allowing travel elsewhere.

Elsewhere...

She didn't know where the purple light took her, nor did she care. Sometimes other planets, other galaxies, occasionally the sun. Trusting the wave like one trusts solid ground, she let it propel her into a kaleidoscope of rays and beams of every color of the rainbow, then relaxed something inside herself to melt and merge with those colors, still riding her pleasure like a purple wave, an interstellar fucking purple wave crossing the galaxy at the speed of a solar flare, onward toward—

The sun...

This time, the wave delivered her to the sun.

She slammed past the inferno of the sun's surface. Here, as always, a single, clear image appeared in her mind's eye: a moment of perfect clarity that escaped her muddled daily existence. Often, she witnessed scenes of nature—a pine forest viewed from the sky, a creek running through an open field, or a rust-colored mountain bathed in hues of twilight.

This time, an image of Darla—perfectly still and eye-searingly vivid.

Darla, with her little cowboy hat.

Darla, naked atop the cowboy.

Darla, frozen in time as she gazed back, looking *into* her, *into* her *into* her *into* her—

(*darla!*)

(*oh, darla!*)

Rhonda's whole body quaked.

(*pussy in the left*)

(*whip in the right*)

Every muscle, every fiber of her being quaked.

(*pleasure in the left*)

(*pain in the right*)

Blood trickled down her chin as she fell to her knees, her rolled-back eyes turned toward Heaven and God. The violin and orchestra overwhelmed her now; so loud and terrible in their beauty.

(*the blood*)

(*the music*)

74

(clarity)
(it gives me clarity)
(FUCKING CLARITY)

She smiled, her whip snapping limply through the air, like a dying insect kicking its leg out.

(...clar...ity...)

Sobs wracked her body as truths, fundamental truths echoed in her mind:

When Darla did it
It was the best
The fucking best!
The contrast
Oh, the contrast!
Pain in the right
Pleasure in the left
Oh God, the contrast!

She fell over sideways, her whole body quivering just like Darla's little legs quivered the first time she'd made her cum, and she was with Darla and the contrast and the memories of them—

—together.

Darla...

Rhonda's eyes rolled forward, her irises visible once again.

CHAPTER IX

GIRLS EAT IT BETTER

"Always do what I say, Abby…"

THE VIOLIN AND orchestra finally quieted; now a gentle hum. Water *drip-dropped* from Daddy's hose, echoing through the garage.

Darla...

Before her, Rhonda saw only Darla, their presence together undisturbed, like it had never ended, *like that bitch Darla had never fucking ended it,* and they held each other in a warm embrace.

My God...

Her left leg spasmed.

She squeezed Darla's little body real tight.

Girls really do eat it better...

...don't they, Darla?

She squeezed her tighter, tighter,

—tighter.

"Yep, I'll admit it..." whispered Darla. "...*can't believe I'm sayin' it, but I'll admit it...*"

"They really fuckin' do."

Her little body felt so warm.

CHAPTER X

RHONDA'S MISTAKE

"Sometimes you fuck up so bad there ain't no fixin' it."

RHONDA LAY DROOLING on the cold concrete floor, eyes locked in a vapid stare, seeing everything and nothing at the same fucking time.

"I love you, Darla..."

"I love you, too, Rhonda..."

Saliva and blood pooled at her mouth.

She could've lain there for hours.

Days, even.

That concrete floor felt so damn good.

But she heard a sound.

What's that?

She heard it again.

No...

No way...

Her left thigh twitched as she lifted herself, unsteady as her jeans slid down her legs.

There it was again.

A sniffle.

A moan.

No way...

Clutching her halfway-down jeans, she hobbled toward AB.

No fuckin' way...

"Are you..."

Another sniffle.

"...fuckin'..."

She leaned in closer.

"...cryin'?"

A slow, mournful weep poured from AB, echoing through the garage like a whale's cry beneath the sea.

Unbelievable.

Un-fuckin'-believable.

She stared in amazement, mouth agape and eyes sparkling, like a child witnessing their first shooting star.

"You finally cried."

Tears streamed down AB's face, now riddled with lash marks and blood.

Guess they all cry, eventually...

Just takes time, that's all.

Realizing she still held the whip, she tossed it behind her.

"Rhon-daaa!"

Daddy!

Daddy callin' her from outside!

"Pizza's here! It's Dominoooo's!"

Shit, he ordered Domino's this time?

Didn't wanna be late for that.

She glanced at her left hand and tried to wipe it on AB's pants, but he flinched, screaming *"Nooo! Stop!"* or some bullshit like that.

"Oh, calm the fuck down, you little bitch..."

After wiping her hand on his still-flinching legs, she pulled her jeans up and turned to leave. He wailed louder, but she no longer heard it—the violin played behind her now, as did the orchestra.

As she flung the door open, a final drop of blood rolled from her chin, landing with a muted *plop*.

She slammed the door shut.

AB cried and cried.

The drop of blood congealed on the concrete floor.

She'd forgotten all about the dead cardinal.

She never noticed all her whipping had frayed AB's ropes.

PART II

THE SHAPE OF THINGS TO COME

FIVE MONTHS EARLIER

1990s

CHAPTER I

FAMILY MISSION

"Don't none of y'all use that whip yet unless
I say y'all can," said Daddy.

"Got a bad feelin' about it..."

THE CUNNINGHAM'S BUSTED-UP Toyota Corolla came to a stoplight.

Bill slammed his fist against the steering wheel.

"Ten percent off everything you buy, for the rest of your fuckin' life!"

The sky radiated blue, and the heat, though present, remained at Bill's preferred level—not *too* hot. Perfect for driving with the windows down. Saved gas that way.

He glanced in the rearview at his son, young Zachary.

"You understand that, Zach?"

"Yep!" said Zach.

He flicked his eyes to his daughter, Taleiah.

"Taleiah, you listenin' back there?"

"Yes, Daddy," said Taleiah.

The stoplight turned green.

"How much discount does it give us?" asked Bill.

"Ten percent!" said Zach and Taleiah.

"And what do they sell at Super Walmart?" asked Bill.

"Everything!"

"That's right, kids..." said Bill. "Every-fuckin'-thing..."

He slowed to make a left.

"And what're we gonna save *the most* money on?"

"Guns!"

"And what do we need them guns for?"

"Killin'!"

"Killin' who?"

"The Guardians of the Temple!"

"And when we gonna *killllll* them Guardians?"

"On The Run!"

"The Run on where?"

"The Temple!"

Sunlight glinted off Bill's aviator sunglasses.

"That's goddamn right..."

They slowed at a red light that quickly turned green. Bill floored the gas—no need, but no cars ahead and he liked the engine revvin'. *It sounded badass.* Wind pressed his sleeveless WWF white T-shirt against his body, while his long hair streamed behind his *"GETTIN' LUCKY IN KENTUCKY"* cap.

"If we can get a Super Walmart Employee Discount Card," said Bill, "that means we can get ten percent off everything we buy! For the rest of our life!"

He hit the steering wheel *hard*—the thud audible over the White Zombie tape blasting from the speakers.

"And y'all know *why,* don't ya?"

"Yes, Daddy."

"Because they sell *everything* at Super Walmart..." said Bill. *"...every-fuckin'-thing..."*

One way or another, he *had* to get that Discount Card.

For his family.

For The Quest.

Temple above all.

He glanced in the rearview mirror.

"Y'all hearin' me back there?"

His eyes darted between Zachary playing his Game Boy and Taleiah staring out the window. All the car windows, except Taleiah's, remained rolled down, with hers only cracked.

"Taleiah," said Bill. "You hear me back there?"

"I hear ya, Daddy," She rolled her window down further. Her dark hair billowed in the wind.

"Zach," said Bill, "you hear me back there, or you just playin' with your Game Boy?"

"I'm listenin', Daddy!" He switched off his Game Boy.

"Good," said Bill, "because, *I swear to God,* this is quite possibly the best, and most simple fuckin' financial education I'm ever gonna give y'all..."

Both Taleiah and Zach had heard this *"best and most simple fuckin' financial education"* a million times before, but they knew to keep silent when Daddy got pumped like this.

Bill looked in the rearview mirror at Taleiah.

"Real simple math, Taleiah."

Taleiah nodded.

"Zach, you listenin'?"

"Yes, Da—"

"Savin' money, is earnin' money," said Bill.

He paused to let it sink in, to let them reflect on that simple-fuckin'-truth.

"When you *save* a dollar on somethin'," said Bill, "you've *earned* a dollar on somethin'."

He paused again, really wanting it to sink the fuck in.

Deep.

"And how much does the Super Walmart Employee Discount Card save us?" asked Bill.

"Ten percent!"

"That's-damn-fuckin'-right!"

Bill slammed his fist against the steering wheel with each word.

"That's why y'all gotta keep applyin' to Super Walmart every week! Every chance we get!"

"But Daddy," said Zach, "I still ain't old enough to work yet."

"We been over this before, Zach..." said Bill.

At least, he *thought* they had.

Could've sworn they'd talked about this—multiple fuckin' times. But maybe he only imagined it, or dreamt it, and took those dream conversations as real memories.

That happened sometimes.

Probably came with age.

(you know why it happens, bill...)

"Anyway," said Bill, "that's why you lie, and write that you're sixteen, and if they call us about hirin' you, we say *sorry,* you already got a job at, *uhhh,* somewhere-fuckin'-else, but my daughter Taleiah is, ya know, fuckin' available, and then we get *her* hired! So we can get that motherfuckin' Discount Card!"

Taleiah narrowed her eyes. They'd tried this plenty of times now, and still hadn't gotten any phone call yet.

"Y'all already filled out your forms, right?" asked Bill. "Zach, did you write that you're sixteen?"

"Yes, Daddy."

"Good."

They came to a four-way intersection. Bill made a full stop, taking his time to look both ways. Cops loved to get ya for shit like that, and he didn't want *any* interaction with the Raven County deputies—especially not during The Quest.

Nothing could interfere with The Quest.

Fuckin' nothing!

He took another look around, then drove forward.

"Oh," said Bill. "Don't lemme forget to get Tylenol or Advil and shit for GB...Rhonda done fucked him up this mornin'..."

Taleiah narrowed her eyes. "Did you tell her to do that, Daddy?"

"Hell no, I didn't!" said Bill. "And I tell ya what, I'm gonna have a *serious talk* with her about doin' shit like that..."

"When?" asked Taleiah.

"Soon," said Bill.

"She won't listen, Daddy," said Taleiah.

"Yes, she will," said Bill. "She's endangerin' our Quest. Gotta be strategic about torturin' them fuckers. Can't be all random-ass about it. And if one of 'em died and shit before they told us a Clue, we'd be in *real* fuckin' trouble, I'll tell ya that right now."

Zach spat out the window. "Then why's she do stuff like that? Without your permission?"

"Why does Rhonda do *anything,* son?" asked Bill. "Why'd she rip that poor girl's eye out? Huh?"

The White Zombie tape clicked to a stop.

Bill pressed rewind.

"What was that girl's name? Jessica? Brittany?"

Taleiah and Zach shrugged.

"Bethany?" he asked.

Silence.

He slowed the car as it rounded a curve.

"Well, she's *Ol' One Eye* now...that's for damn sure..."

Bill shook his head. The girl's real name didn't matter no more; she was likely just *"that one-eyed chick"* or *"ol' cyclops"* to everyone she fuckin' knew. Probably even to her own family.

Sad, but true.

"Ya know," said Bill, "for the rest of her life, that poor one-eyed girl is gonna have to wear an eyepatch or somethin'. Can you imagine that? Like a pirate. Which is kinda cool, I guess..."

He cleared his throat.

"...but she probably don't think so."

***

The Cunninghams rode in silence for a while, nodding along to White Zombie as wind streamed in through the open windows.

"Daddy," said Taleiah from the backseat. "I didn't have my oatmeal this mornin'. 'Cause Rhonda ate it all."

"Now Taleiah," said Bill, "Rhonda didn't eat *all* the oatmeal, did she?"

"She did," said Taleiah. "She ate it *all.*"

Zach leaned forward. "She ate all the oatmeal *and* all the eggs, Daddy!"

"I ate oatmeal yesterday," said Bill, "and there were like, six packets left. And about half a carton of eggs."

"She ate *all* six packets, Daddy," said Taleiah.

"And all the eggs!" said Zach.

"Shit..." said Bill.

"Why'd she eat breakfast at *our* house today?" asked Zach. "She can eat her own food. At her own house."

"She eats *all* our food, Daddy," said Taleiah.

"Yep," said Zach. "She eats all our food and complains about Mrs. Dash!"

"What is her problem with Mrs. Dash?" asked Taleiah. "It's *so* good..."

"It's good on about everything," said Zach. "Except SpaghettiO's."

"Yeah," said Bill. "I wouldn't ever put Mrs. Dash on my SpaghettiO's or nothin'. Not really made for pasta and stuff. But it *is* good on about everything else. And it's salt-free, ya know, so good for your health and shit..."

He slowed to make a left.

"And you know," said Bill, "I have no idea why she's always talkin' shit about Mrs. Dash..."

Zach asked, "And why's she eat so much?"

"She does eat a lot," said Bill. "Like a horse."

Zach said, "She eats more than you sometimes, Daddy!"

"She does, son," said Bill. "She really fuckin' does."

"I don't see how she don't get fat!" said Taleiah.

"Me neither..." said Bill.

He patted his belly, relieved his loose shirt helped hide it.

"Some people just got a real high metabolism..." said Bill. "And Rhonda's got a motor in her..."

"I think she's got, like," said Zach, "a *nukyular* engine inside her, or—"

"It's *'nuclear,'* Zach," said Taleiah.

"No, it ain't," said Zach.

"Yes, it is," said Taleiah.

"No, it ain't!"

"Yes, it is!"

"Daddy," said Zach, "is it *'nukyular'* or *'nuclear'?"*

"I do believe it's *'nuclear,'* Zach," said Bill. "I believe your sister's got ya on that one."

Taleiah stuck her tongue out at Zach.

"Okay, Mrs. Smarty-pants," said Zach. "Whatever. *Nuclear."*

"Well, anyway," said Bill. "Let's just hope Rhonda don't have a fuckin', nuclear meltdown anytime soon..."

"Disaster Blaster" by White Zombie blared from the car speakers. Bill cranked up the volume.

("this shit goes hard, don't it?")

("hell yeah, it does...")

He fell silent, grasping at the edges of memory.

"This shit goes hard, don't it, kids?" asked Bill.

They said *"Yeah,"* nodding to the chorus.

"Me and Charlie Young," said Bill, "we used to listen to heavy metal and rock and roll and shit, all the fuckin' time..."

Zach and Taleiah exchanged a look—the one they often shared whenever Bill mentioned Charlie or other guys from his old days. A look he detected but never understood.

"We'd go cruisin' around town..." said Bill. "...lookin' for shit to get into..."

A small laugh escaped him. He shook his head.

"...lookin' for trouble is what we were doin'..."

("you ever tried coke before?")

"...never had to look long, though..."

("i know a guy who's got a shit-ton...")

"...trouble always found us..."

("and he won't notice if we take some...")

"...real quick..."

("even if he does, what's he gonna do? call the cops?")

"...wherever we went..."

("easy breezy, man...")

("money in our pockets, candy up our noses...")

"I ran with a wild-ass crew back then..."

He glanced at the rearview mirror.

"I told y'all about my *Posse* back then, right?"

Zach and Taleiah nodded, silence etched on their faces.

"There was Nice Guy Paul..." said Bill. "Now, he was kinda like, the hippy-guy of our group. Back then, every group of friends had to have, like, one fuckin' hippy in'em. At least one. That's just how shit was. Y'all know what I'm sayin'?"

He glanced at the rearview mirror. Taleiah kind of nodded.

"But I tell ya what," said Bill, "ol' Nice Guy Paul, he wasn't so nice when he had to get that business done!" He laughed. "He'd forget about peace and love and all that bullshit real quick..."

Zach's face darkened.

"And Skinny Kenny..." said Bill. "That boy was crazy! Didn't even do no drugs or nothin'...but wild as shit..."

Taleiah turned her gaze to the window, caressing her arrowhead pendant.

"And, of course," said Bill, "can't forget Charlie Young. AKA Young Charlie. We was *mejores amigos*. Now, Charlie was the smartest of us, to be real honest with ya. Clever as a fox. Saw stuff comin' even before I did sometimes..."

("no matter what happens, bill...")

("we'll always be mejores amigos...")

"...spoke that Spanish stuff real good, too...even though he wasn't Mexican..."

Bill took off his *Gettin' Lucky in Kentucky* cap and scratched his head.

"And, uhh...who was that other guy? I swear there's a few more..."

"Graham," said Zach. He switched his Game Boy back on.

"Yeah, Graham-cracker!" said Bill. "Good ol' Graham-cracker, he was as big as a fuckin' house! Biggest ol' boy I ever seen, I'll tell ya that right now. He'd just *look* at guys and they'd 'bout shit their pants..."

He nodded, stroking his beard. "Yep, yep..."

"Now, ol' Graham-cracker, he started thinkin' people were talkin' shit about him, even when they fuckin' weren't. Or maybe they were, I dunno.

And that caused us lotsa trouble back then. But he fuckin' *saved* our asses, too. More times than I can count!"

Bill checked the rearview mirror. Zach and Taleiah had those weird looks on their faces again. Still didn't know what that was about. But whatever. Kids these days.

"But, ya know," he said, "deep down inside, Graham was a big ol' softy... even though he acted all tough..."

He slowed the car to make a right.

"Oh, and the...the..."

Staring out the window, Taleiah mouthed, *"The Bedford Twins."*

"The Bedford Twins!" said Bill. "I remember now! The fuckin' Bedford Twins..."

Taleiah shook her head, gripping her arrowhead pendant tighter.

"Them Bedford Twins," said Bill, "they knew how to *tear shit up.* I ain't ever met boys like them before. Knew how to fuck shit up *real* good. And if you had a problem with one of 'em, then you had a problem with both of 'em. Ain't *nobody* fucked with the Bedford Twins. Not even Graham-cracker. I mean, if push came to fuckin' shove, he could've whooped'em, probably. Just chose not to..."

A cop car appeared in the distance.

Shit...

Bill slowed down.

Is that the one Rhonda saw this mornin'?

Never saw cops out here before...

"...and you could always depend on'em, too, them Bedford Twins..." said Bill. "...real reliable...plus, it was cool they were twins and shit..."

The cop passed, driving until out of view.

Bill let out a *"Phewww..."*

Thank God...

"Hey," said Bill, "did I ever tell y'all how the Bedford Twins used to wear the same outfit when we went to bars and shit to pick up girls?"

"You told us, Daddy..." said Taleiah. She held her arrowhead pendant closer to the window, admiring how it sparkled in the sunlight.

"Pretty much always fuckin' worked..." said Bill. "...made me wish I had a twin back then..."

Bill rapped his knuckles against the steering wheel.

"...just had Wayne, though..."

Wayne.

He took off his cap and ran his fingers through his long hair.

("bill, will you pleeease play this dungeons and dragons game with me?")

("it's gonna be awesome!")

Bill grimaced and placed his cap back on.

"...anyway, ol' Graham-cracker was built like a brick fuckin' house... ain't ever seen a boy as big as him...not since we moved out here, at least... have y'all?"

Zach and Taleiah shot each other another look.

"Wonder what..." said Bill. "...whatever happened to those guys..."

Fragments of memories danced through his mind, slipping his every grasp.

("we follow your dreams, bill...")

("tell us what to do...")

("just tell us what to fuckin' d—")

"Daddy!" said Taleiah. *"The stoplight!"*

"Shit!" said Bill.

He slammed on the brakes. The car lurched forward with a deafening screech, halting inches from the truck ahead.

"Fuck!" said Bill.

His heart raced. He'd come so *close* to slamming into that truck.

("because you made bad decisions, bill...")

("you still do.")

Bill shook his head.

Whose voice was that?

Wayne's?

"Daddy," said Taleiah. "You okay to drive?"

Bill inhaled, then exhaled. "I'm fine..." He glanced at the rearview mirror. "Y'all okay back there? Got your seatbelts on?"

Zach and Taleiah gripped their respective door handles, eyes wide.

"Yeah, Daddy..." said Zach. "...but are *you* okay?"

"I'm alright..." said Bill. "...stoplight came outta nowhere..."

He looked back at his children.

"Good thing Taleiah was keepin' an eye out. If it'd just been me and you, *Zach,* you'd just kept playin' your Game Boy! And we'd be fuckin' dead right now!"

Zach flipped his Game Boy off.

"Now," said Bill, "what was I talkin' about?"

"Family Mission, Daddy," said Taleiah.

"Oh, yeah," said Bill. "We're gonna get that Discount Card! To save money on *everything,* includin' the most expensive shit we gotta buy!"

He glanced in the rearview mirror.

"And y'all know what that is, don't ya?"

"Guns and ammo!"

"And what do we need that for?"

"The Run on the Temple!"

"That's goddamn right..."

A cloud drifted above, and for a moment, everything around the Cunninghams darkened.

Taleiah whispered to her arrowhead.

1970s

CHAPTER II

MEJORES AMIGOS

Crow County, Kentucky

"Ain't nothin' worse than what we did, Charlie.

And ain't nobody worse than us."

"THIS SHIT GOES hard, don't it?" asked Charlie Young.

"Hell yeah, it does," said Bill. "They're fuckin' *metal*, dude."

Black Sabbath rocked from Charlie's boombox, vibrating the warm afternoon air as they sat on the back porch of Charlie's dad's place. Just a little two-bedroom house, but plenty big enough to serve as their summer HQ before senior year.

"You like'em more than Zepp, *ese?*" asked Charlie.

Bill grinned. Charlie said *ese* like *ess-aaay,* and although Bill didn't speak no Spanish, he felt pretty sure Charlie stretched it out with a redneck twang.

Sounded cool, though.

"Dunno about that, man," said Bill. "I'll have to listen to'em more."

"Fair enough, *amigo,*" said Charlie. "Fair enough."

Charlie leaned back in his chair, took a long drag from his cigarette, and exhaled perfect smoke rings that drifted and hung in the air before dissipating.

"Which you like better," asked Charlie, "Marlboros, or Camels?"

"Marlboros." The last smoke ring faded—a trick Bill had tried to master but couldn't quite nail yet. Chicks might dig it, if he ever got it right.

"Me too," said Charlie. "I mean, I'll smoke a Camel if you got one, but somethin' about havin' a cartoon camel on those packs...*estúpido...*"

"Yep," said Bill.

They sat there for a while, allowing a comfortable silence to pass as they smoked and enjoyed the music.

Enjoyed chillin'.

It felt good, sittin' there with Charlie, smokin' cigarettes and listenin' to metal. Away from his dad and little brother Wayne always naggin' him to play those nerdy-ass games. He'd grown to more or less enjoy Dungeons & Dragons, but not all day, every day. He'd rather hang with Charlie— drinkin', smokin', chasin' girls.

Rinse and repeat.

That's what *he* liked doin' everyday.

Not spendin' forever rollin' dice, pretendin' he was a half-elf archer on some bullshit *"quest"* to find a *"temple."*

"Your hat looks good on ya, man," said Charlie. "It suits you."

Bill ran his fingers across the brim of his cowboy hat. He felt cool wearin' it—different from everybody else.

"Really?" asked Bill. "You *really* think so?"

Charlie smiled and winked.

"I sure fuckin' do. You should keep wearin' it."

"My dad says I shouldn't wear it inside," said Bill. "Says it ain't good manners and shit."

"Nah, fuck it," said Charlie. "Wear it inside, man."

"Really?"

"If ya want to, why not?" asked Charlie. "I mean, if you're gonna hang with old people, maybe take it off. But you see any old folks around here, *ese?*"

Bill took a long drag of his cigarette, nodding to the metal.

He sure as fuck didn't, and told Charlie so.

"*Eso es cierto,* my man," said Charlie. "People our age won't give a shit, and even if they do—" He blew smoke upward. "—who gives a fuck?"

He paused, letting his question hang.

"You don't get cool by bein' like everybody else," he said. "You get cool by bein' *different.*"

Bill felt the weight of Charlie's words shift to him.

"You're probably right..."

No, not probably—

—he was *absolutely right.*

A hundred-fuckin'-percent.

"Is that why you grew your circle beard?" asked Bill.

"Kinda." Charlie leaned back and stroked his beard. "I just like havin' a beard, though. Think I look better with one."

Charlie ranked among the few guys Bill's age who could grow a short beard and mustache that actually looked *legit*, not half-peach-fuzz, half-scraggly bullshit. Bill intended to grow a beard, too, and not that "circle beard" or whatever Charlie called his, but a huge, *badass* beard, like one of them heavy metal rockstars.

"Thought about growin' my hair long, too," said Charlie. "But nah. Doesn't fit me like it does you."

Bill nodded. His asshole dad threw a fit about it, but he didn't give a fuck. Having long hair set him apart from other high schoolers—gave him presence, style.

"Is that why you go by 'Young Charlie'?" asked Bill. "To be different?"

"Kinda," said Charlie. "And to be honest, man, I actually preferred

'Charlie the Younger' or 'Charlie the Young,' but those never stuck. Too long or somethin'. So Young Charlie it is." He grinned. "And also, I get to say—"

"Yeah, your thing," said Bill. "*'Don't call me Ol' Charlie, call me Young, 'cause I'm Charlie Young.'*"

Charlie beamed, his smile bright enough to blind.

"*Sí*, fuckin' *sí*. Never gets old."

Bill couldn't help but smile back. It *did* get old—after about the fourth time. But with Charlie's ear-to-ear grin and that twinkle in his eye, it always *worked* on a certain level.

"You should start goin' as Wild Bill," said Charlie. "Just like I told ya, like that cowboy in that movie we saw. Especially now, with the hat."

"Been thinkin' about it." Bill ran his fingers across the brim of his cowboy hat. He liked doing that. It felt cool.

"But" said Charlie, "you gotta do somethin' *wild* to earn a name like that, man. If you want it to stick."

"Somethin' wild, huh..."

Bill allowed his thoughts to wander, fragments of dreams floating through his mind like shards from a mirror adrift in space. He'd glimpsed these shards before—

("bitch, i am wild bill and this is young-fuckin'-charlie!")

—and he *knew* that Charlie's nickname for him would catch on.

("and we got sixteen of our cowboys surroundin' this place!")

Eventually.

("now y'all come the fuck out with your hands up!")

Just wasn't sure when.

Or how.

("or y'all know what the fuck's gonna happen!")

Charlie's smile flipped into a frown.

"What's wrong, man?" asked Bill.

With a strange, nervous intensity, Charlie wiped ashes from Bill's cigarette off the table.

"Oh," said Bill. "My bad, dude..."

"It's okay, man, it's okay..." Charlie wiped the table over and over, attempting to remove every fleck of ash.

"I'll be more careful, man..." said Bill.

After a few more tense wipes, Charlie finally relaxed, sighing as he returned his cigarette to his lips.

"My bad, man…" said Bill. He then decided to stop apologizing and let Charlie chill. Proof again of the *one thing* he had to be careful of, the only big thing they were *not* on the same fuckin' wavelength about—

—cleanliness.

Charlie liked his shit *clean*.

Bill wasn't no slob—merely average in keepin' shit neat and tidy—but Charlie resided on a different level.

"It just bothers me," Charlie had said, *"when shit's out of place, or gets messy or dirty. You know what I'm sayin', ese?"*

"Yeah, I see where you're comin' from, man," Bill had said. *"Kinda bothers me, too. Now that I think about it."*

It really didn't, though.

Who gives a fuck about a bit of ash on a table?

But it was Charlie's home, not his—and, so far, messiness stood as the *one* thing Charlie didn't tolerate.

Bill could handle that, though.

Not a big deal in the grand scheme of things.

"Dude," said Charlie. "I got somethin' for ya." He crushed his cigarette in the Marlboro ashtray, went inside, and returned handing Bill a book titled *Blackbeard: The Man Who Scourged the Seas.*

"Now, this guy's fuckin' badass," said Charlie. "Metal as shit."

The cover featured a pirate with an enormous, badass beard—he certainly looked metal as shit, with just the beard Bill wanted to grow.

"I mean, Wild Bill was cool and all," said Charlie. "He was a cowboy and everything. But in terms of who'd really be best to fuckin', *emulate*, Blackbeard would be the better choice. I'll tell ya that right now."

"You think so?" Bill liked it when Charlie used words like *emulate*. Made their conversations feel more sophisticated and shit.

"I sure fuckin' do," said Charlie. "Dude, this Blackbeard guy, he had zero tolerance for bullshit. I mean *zero-fuckin'-tolerance*. You know what I'm sayin', *ese?* Makes Wild Bill look like a straight-up pussy, man."

Bill flipped through the pages. He hadn't read much about Wild Bill in school, but in the movie he'd been only *mildly* badass. Wildest thing about him was his name—didn't even kill that many people.

"So this Blackbeard guy," asked Bill, "was that badass, huh?"

"*Absolutamente,*" said Charlie. "*Abso*-fuckin'-*lutamente.* Now, Blackbeard wasn't no fuckin', leader of no empire or nothin'. Definitely no Genghis-fuckin'-Kahn. Didn't invade no countries and shit. But man, I tell ya what, he was one of the most brutal, badass motherfuckers that ever lived. *Esa es la* fuckin' *verdad,* man."

Bill read the book's back. "I remember learnin' about him in school..."

"They didn't teach us half of it, man," said Charlie. "This Blackbeard dude, he didn't even *have* to fuck shit up when he approached other ships. Once they knew who he was, they just gave up."

"Gave up?"

Charlie nodded. "They just put their hands up and said, *'Hey, we know you're Blackbeard and shit. We heard what you done to them other motherfuckers. Just don't fuck with us and we'll give ya our shit.'*"

"Hmm..." said Bill. "So he ruled the seas through his reputation alone..."

"Damn fuckin' straight he did," said Charlie. "He did just enough badass, brutal shit in the beginnin' to spread the word, so later he didn't have to do nothin'. Most of the time."

"And he's got a badass beard, too..." said Bill.

"He sure fuckin' does," said Charlie. "Didn't you say you wanted a beard like that, too?"

"Uh-huh..." Bill pictured himself with the same beard—truly badass and metal, like Blackbeard, ruling by reputation alone. He traced his finger across the cover.

"I sure fuckin' did..."

("you tell your boys!")

("you tell'em what we did here today!")

"But man, listen up," said Charlie. He lit another cigarette. "It's about more than Blackbeard himself. It's about havin' zero-fuckin'-tolerance for disrespect, and livin' like *he* fuckin' did, and how bein' brutal—I mean exercisin' full-fuckin' brutality—can actually be a good thing. It *saves* fuckin' lives, man."

"*Saves* lives?" asked Bill.

"*Sí,* fuckin', *sí,*" said Charlie. "In the longrun, bein' brutal saves lives and saves ya a whole lotta trouble, *ese.* This Roberta Stevenson chick, the chick who wrote this book, she did her fuckin' *research,* man. She understands how the world works. *She fuckin' gets it.* And she uses examples in history and shit that'll blow your mind."

He blew smoke upward, then brought his gaze back to Bill.

"You gotta read it. And once ya do, you won't be able to deny the truth in what she's writin', even if you don't like it at first."

Charlie's face turned serious and cold.

"Sometimes the hardest fuckin' truths," he said, "are the things ya don't wanna hear."

Bill had never seen that look on Charlie before. The hair on his neck bristled and he *sensed* something—something wrong and—

("open his mouth, bill!")

("open his fucking mouth!")

With a shiver, he set the book on the table.

"Sounds pretty badass."

"I'll let ya borrow it," said Charlie.

"You sure?"

"Lo-fuckin'-*estoy."*

"Thanks, man," said Bill. "I mean, uh...*muchas gracias, amigo.*"

Charlie smiled and winked. "There ya go, *ese...*"

Bill smiled back. Another reason they clicked so effortlessly: not only was Charlie *a good dude* and generous to a fault, but he held a wide range of interests—real smart about all kinds of shit without showin' off. And even though he didn't have no Mexican in him, he spoke that Spanish shit real good, too—no problem orderin' food *en español* at Mexican restaurants. *("Tacos, dos. Por favor.")*

Charlie also loved history, like he did, and they'd share anecdotes about badass dudes like Julius Caesar, Genghis Kahn and fuckin' Atilla the Hun—dudes who knew how to tear shit up, and didn't take shit from nobody.

"Hey, you taught me to shoot," said Charlie. "Still owe ya for that."

"Your dad's got a good gun," said Bill.

"Said he's never even fired it, though. Just carries it around. For protection."

Bill crushed his cigarette and lit a new one. Charlie's dad likely carried a reputation that removed the *need* to fire his gun.

Always good to have protection, though.

Just in case.

"Always good to carry protection on ya..." Bill took a puff from his freshly-lit cigarette and tried to exhale the smoke in rings, but it billowed out in plumes instead.

"Be honest with me, *ese,*" said Charlie. "Did your dad *really* start teachin' ya to shoot from the second grade? Or was that bullshit?"

Bill gazed at his right hand as it opened and closed, seemingly on its own, squeezing air.

Even now, it *ached.*

Ached with that *gunlust.*

"Nah, he really did," said Bill. "More like military drilled the shit outta me."

"*Muy impresionante.* No wonder you shoot like them cowboys on TV."

Bill shook his head. "Still not as good as my dad..."

"That *hombre's* got about twenty or thirty years on ya. By the way, been meanin' to ask ya somethin'."

He leaned across the table, lowering his voice.

"*You ever tried coke before?*"

Bill's eyes widened. Even with no one around, he lowered his voice, too. "You mean like...*cocaine?*"

Charlie grinned. "Nah, I mean fuckin' Coca-Cola, *ese...*"

Bill shook his head. "Heard that shit's expensive..."

"I got some," said Charlie. "If ya wanna try it..."

"You got *cocaine?*"

Charlie nodded, excitement flashing in his eyes. "I sure fuckin' do. I mean, technically my dad does, stashed in his closet. But we could do a little and he probably won't notice."

"You for real, man?" Suddenly, Bill didn't give a shit about his cigarette or the music or the ache of gunlust in his hand. *He was gonna try cocaine.*

"Have you tried it before?" he asked.

"Nope, not yet..." said Charlie. "All I've done is weed..."

Bill had smoked weed, too—including with Charlie. Wasn't a fan. Just made him dizzy, light-headed, and lazy as shit, infecting him with brain fog that lingered for days, blurring his dreams.

He had to see his dreams *clearly.*

As clear as The Ethereal would allow.

He also found heavy weed smokers obnoxious. Looked and acted like dumbfucks.

"*Hey maaan, wanna smoke some weeeeed, maaan?*"

No—no thanks, dude.

Don't wanna be as stupid as you.

Not to mention his clothes and long hair absorbed the pungent weed stench, informing the world and his dad he'd toked up. The allure of weed lay only in its illegality, in doing something risky, wrong, and sinful. Beyond that, weed was pretty much bullshit, and he'd do just fine without it.

"How's it different from Mary Jane?" asked Bill. "You know I ain't 'bout that weed bullsh—"

"Oh man," said Charlie, "it's *real* fuckin' different. I'm pretty sure it gets ya real pumped and shit."

"Real pumped, huh…"

"*Sí,*" said Charlie. "And if I do try it, I wanna try it with my best bro. Know what I'm sayin'?"

He drew deeply from his cigarette, seeming to appraise Bill.

"Bros I can trust."

Bill nodded.

Bros he could trust.

Although him and Charlie had been hangin' for a while now, it felt good to vocalize their friendship level. Make it concrete and official.

Bros he could trust meant fuckin' *best bros.*

Best bros who liked to smoke, chill and listen to heavy metal—best bros who were gonna try *cocaine* for the first time.

Hell yeah.

This was the life he wanted to live.

These were the experiences his dreams had shown him.

This was only the beginning.

"*Mejores amigos,*" said Charlie.

"What's that mean?" asked Bill.

"'Best bros, my bro…" said Charlie. He winked.

Bill chuckled. "You speak that Spanish shit real good, man."

"*Gracias,*" said Charlie. "*Listo para probar,* fuckin' *cocaina?*"

He leaned forward.

"That means, '*You ready to try some fuckin' cocaine with me?*' "

Bill laughed again.

Charlie's such a hoot…

"Hell yes, I'll try it with ya," said Bill. "And I'm honored to be your *mejores amigo.*"

He extended his hand and Charlie clasped it, looking him in the eyes.

"Best bros," said Bill. "*Mejores amigos.*"

"There ya go, *ese,*" said Charlie. "That's what I'm talkin' about."

Bill looked out into the distance. "You're my only friend who knows, man. Ya know, that I got a…"

He still couldn't say it.

Charlie nodded and blew smoke from the side of his mouth, his eyes reflecting quiet acceptance, free of judgement.

"When ya see her next?" he asked.

Bill grimaced. "Maybe in a few weeks or somethin'…"

"Bring me with ya, dude," said Charlie. "Introduce Uncle Charlie to Lil' Rhonda."

Bill crushed his cigarette in Charlie's Marlboro ashtray.

"Thanks, *amigo,* but…dunno if even *I* wanna see her, man. I know it's shitty as hell to say that…"

He took off his cowboy hat and ran a hand through his long hair.

Not after…

Not after what happened.

"*Está bien, está bien,*" said Charlie. "Your secret's safe with me, *ese.* No worries."

Bill considered revealing other things to Charlie—things about his dad, his mom, his brother and the dreams he and his brother witnessed through their connection with The Ethereal—but for now, this was enough. He trusted Charlie almost completely, but drip-feeding information still seemed the safer play.

"Anyway," said Charlie, standing up. "Let's try some fuckin' *cocaina* together."

As they headed into the house, Charlie glanced back at Bill.

"But we can only do a little…"

Time to read that fuckin' book Charlie gave me...

Blackbeard: The Man Who Scourged the Seas

By: Roberta Stevenson

PROLOGUE

(pg.03) Lightning streaks across the sky as waves crash upon the ship's wooden bow. Inside his dimly lit quarters, Captain Joseph Stannis nervously twirls his mustache while the ship's timbers *creak* and *groan*. He's experienced ocean storms before, both in the North and South Atlantic, but this one feels...different.

Different due to the particular Atlantic waters they traversed.

Waters particularly known for something—

—someone—

far worse than storms.

Stannis drums his fingers across his desk. The nearby oil lamp casts a dancing shadow of his hand against the wall.

Who created such monstrous storms?

Such monstrous people?

God?

He'd always presumed that God, in His infinite wisdom, crafted all creation, but why would God create such...*things?*

Things that destroyed, like storms.

And things that did worse, like pirates.

Perhaps the Devil, then?

He pats his powdered wig. The ship's rocking not only makes him nauseous, but often shifts his wig out of place. The wigmaker in Bristol, skilled as he is, has nevertheless sewn it a bit too large. Either that, or his head has shrunk, a possibility even more troubling than the dangers that threatened his ship.

"Captain!"

First Mate Leonard barges in, breathless and pale.

Stannis grabs the corner of his desk and *squeezes*. In times of anger, upset, or worry, he finds solace in touching, stroking, and *squeezing* his desk, a tangible reminder of his blessings in life. Indeed, possessing a desk crafted from African blackwood—the most prized and resilient timber in the known world—remains a privilege few can boast.

"Now, Mr. Leonard..." He prepares to remind his subordinate of the requirement to *knock* before entering a captain's quarters.

What if he'd been caught without his wig?

A situation to be avoided at all costs, especially for a man of his reputation.

He switches to his authoritative voice. "Need I remind you that—"

"Another ship, sir!" says Leonard. "Another ship has approached us!"

Stannis reels back, *squeezing* the corner of his desk.

"In this weather?" he asks. "What in the devil could they—"

"They're readying their cannons, sir!"

Lightning flashes, illuminating his quarters.

No.

It can't be.

Surely even *he* wouldn't dare attack in the middle of a storm?

***

Not far away, Captain Edward Teach, a very different breed of captain, stands perched on his ship's deck, stroking his massive black beard. Despite the storm's fury, he remains resolute, the lightning and thunder serving as a fitting backdrop to the epic grandeur of his mission.

He tilts his face to the swirling clouds of the night sky.

Please, God...

Grant me victory...

One more...

Ocean spray stings his face, mingling with the cold raindrops. He's never considered himself a religious man, nor does he now, but his belief and faith in God have strengthened as of late.

After all, if it wasn't God who helped propel him to such success...

...then who?

Removing his black tri-corner hat, he shakes the collected rainwater from its crown. He doesn't worry about his powdered wig as he hasn't worn one since childhood. He wasn't the wig-wearing type then, nor is he now.

"Approachin' firin' range, Captain!" yells First Mate Israel Hands, his voice barely audible over the storm.

Teach nods. Unless things truly go south, the cannons are only for show.

He grips his scabbard.

But if things *do* go south, he won't hesitate.

Death comes first to those who hesitate...

His ship, *The Queen Anne's Revenge,* lurches as a colossal wave strikes, throwing him and his men off balance. He quickly steadies himself, refusing to let his gaze drift from the approaching prize.

"Steady, men, steady!" he shouts. "We've been through far worse than this, boys!"

A lie. They'd been through worse storms, but none *far* worse. Were it any other night, such a storm would worry him. Indeed, countless ships and crews, no matter their worth, have succumbed to the unforgiving might of the sea, bested not by enemy cannons but by the awesome fury of Mother Nature.

Another huge wave strikes, sending him and his men reeling. He steadies himself, barking orders.

Not tonight, Mother Nature...

Tonight, you aren't what I care about.

Tonight, Teach cares about one thing only—capturing the *HMS Zion*, a British treasure ship laden with vast fortunes of gold, diamonds, and riches beyond imagination.

His heart beats faster.

So...

Much...

Plunder.

Capturing a prize of such magnificence would etch his name into legend, chronicled in history books for generations to come.

A smile creeps across his face.

And surely send all those powdered-wig aristocrats in Parliament into *quite* the tizzy.

"Bring me my fuses!" he barks.

"Aye-aye!"

Four men spread a canvas overhead to block the rain while two others light slow-burning fuses, placing them in his beard.

There it is.

There it is.

Already smelling good for him.

He loved that smell.

The smell of conquest, victory, freedom—

—and *destiny*.

A deckhand shouts, "They're readying their arms on deck, sir!"

"Let them!" says Teach.

He marches to the edge of the deck, his men holding the canvas overhead.

"Little men, little men..."

Through ribbons of smoke, he surveys the British sailors scramble for their swords and their powdered wigs and their courage, none of which can help them now.

"Do you know who I am?" he yells.

They likely can't hear him over the storm, but it doesn't matter.

Once they see his beard, they'll know.

They always know.

His voice booms across the ocean:

"Do you know who I am?"

***

How could *The Queen Anne's Revenge,* armed with a mere twenty cannons and crewed by a modest hundred, possibly contend with a ship boasting seventy cannons and manned by more than three hundred?

The *HMS Zion* commanded admiration as the most heavily armed treasure vessel of the British Empire. To attack such a ship, even during the best of circumstances, bordered on recklessness beyond imagination.

And to attack during a storm?

Insanity.

Any other pirate driven to attempt such an act would be called a fool, a madman, a daredevil.

But Edward Teach was no normal pirate—

—he was *Blackbeard.*

The most legendary pirate of all.

Turn the page to learn more about Blackbeard!

1990s

CHAPTER III

FAMILY MISSION, PART II

*"Daddy," said Rhonda, "I bought that whip
on QVC at sixty-three percent off.*

And it's a damn shame if we don't use it."

SUPER WALMART EMERGED in the distance, massive and breathtaking, like Camelot on a hill.

"God, there's a lot of people today!" said Bill.

Their car stopped a light packed with traffic. Bill glanced at a fine-lookin' momma in a nearby van with her kids—no husband in sight. He nodded along to White Zombie blasting from his windows, trying to look as cool as possible. The momma smiled, then, perhaps reluctantly, looked away.

Bill grinned.

Chicks still can't resist me.

"This is gonna be a good fuckin' day!"

He glanced in the rearview mirror at his kids.

"And y'all remember Plan B, right?"

Silence.

"Taleiah?"

He turned to look at her as his seatbelt stretched with a tightening sound.

"Gimme Plan B."

"Plan B," said Taleiah, "is that you get a girl at Super Walmart to be your girlfriend so you can use her Discount Card to—"

"*We*," said Bill, "so that *we*, as a family, can use it."

Taleiah nodded.

"To get how much of a discount?" asked Bill.

"Ten percent," said Zach.

"Damn it!" said Bill. "I want *both* of y'all to fuckin' answer!"

"*Ten percent!*"

"*That's damn-fuckin'-straight!*" Bill slammed his fist against the steering wheel, driving past the now-green stoplight.

Zach turned to Taleiah, her face hidden beneath a cascade of dark hair as she stared out the window, caressing her arrowhead pendant.

"Can I borrow your arrowhead?" asked Zach.

"No," said Taleiah.

"Daddy," said Zach. "Taleiah won't lemme borrow her arrowhead!"

"Well, now," said Bill, "it is *her* arrowhead necklace, son..."

"But she should share!" said Zach. "I'll share my Game Boy with her!"

"I don't wanna play your Game Boy!" said Taleiah. "Game Boys are for weirdos and dweebs, like you!"

"Now Taleiah," said Bill, "don't be callin' your brother no weirdo or—"

"You're so selfish!" said Zach. "You never share!"

Zach's shifted his glare from Taleiah to the red SpaghettiO stains splattered on his jeans.

She didn't even feed their prisoners, either.

It wasn't fair!

"Now, Zach," said Bill, "Taleiah *is* the one who found that arrowhead, fair and square. I'd like to *hope* she'd share it with ya, but I can't make her."

"But she—"

"Nope!" said Bill. "Don't wanna hear no more fightin' about that arrowhead now, ya hear? Don't want *no* bullshit today. None of that!"

Taleiah flashed Zach the briefest of smiles, then turned back to her window and resumed rubbing her arrowhead—this time, it seemed, with even greater enthusiasm.

"I'm real tired of y'all fightin' all the time," said Bill. "Tired of makin' new rules, too. We're probably the only family in Kentucky with a no-ridin'-in-the-front-seat-rule, because y'all can't even agree on basic shit like that. And I'll tell ya what, me and your Uncle Wayne, we fought, too, but we took *fuckin' turns* when it came to shit. Y'all can't even even agree to that!"

Zach stomped his feet. "That's 'cause—"

"Nope!" said Bill. "No bullshit, now! Not today!"

Zach fell silent, seething.

"Now, Zach," said Bill, "maybe you can discover your own arrowhead out there, too, when you're on your little adventures. Where there's one, there's bound to be another..."

Zach glared at the back of Taleiah's head, wishing he could shoot lasers from his eyes like Cyclops in *X-Men* and splatter her brains inside the car. He'd searched all across their property but still hadn't found a single arrowhead.

Just animals and birds and stuff.

Stuff that needed killin'.

"What ya need to be focused on, Zach," said Bill, "is our Family Mission."

"We get it, Daddy," said Zach. "We know it's important."

"It's *more* than important, boy," said Bill. "It's worth its weight in gold..."

The car rolled to the final stoplight before the parking lot. Bill gazed in awe at the retail behemoth in the distance.

We're gonna get that Discount Card today...

I can feel it.

The grandeur of Super Walmart grew as they drew near.

"We're gonna get that fuckin' Discount Card, y'all!" said Bill. "It's worth its weight in gold!"

He bounced in his seat, throwing up the heavy metal horns and headbanging to White Zombie. The seatbelt strained against his body as the car shook with his weight.

Zach burst out laughing. "Daddy, you're shakin' the car!"

"It's worth its weight in gold, son!" said Bill. "Diamonds and fuckin' gold! Get pumped!"

Even Taleiah couldn't hold back a giggle as Bill rocked back and forth, channeling Rob Zombie.

"Diamonds and gold, y'all!"

"Get pumped!"

***

As the Cunninghams pulled into Super Walmart, Bill stopped rocking out and lowered the volume to focus on finding a parking spot—but also out of respect for the majesty of the place.

("it's worth its weight in diamonds and gold, son...")

Once parked, his kids got out, but he stayed glued to his seat, staring at the giant *S-U-P-E-R W-A-L-M-A-R-T* letters on the front of the store.

Will today be the day?

When we can finally start savin' ten percent?

On every *fuckin' thing we buy?*

Zach squinted in the sunlight. "Daddy, can I check out the video games?"

Bill hung his aviator sunglasses on the rearview mirror, took a deep breath, then opened his door.

"Yeah, that's fine..."

He stepped out of the car, grunting as pain jolted up his right leg and forked at his hip like lightning.

"God..."

Gritting his teeth, he focused on the clear azure sky.

(it still hurts, doesn't it?)

(it'll never stop hurting...)

Heat radiated from the parking lot pavement. Beads of sweat ran down his face as he waited for the pain to subside.

"...after we turn in our applications, ya can..." he said through clenched teeth. "...and if your sister goes with ya..."

Bill hobbled behind his kids as they ambled toward the entrance, moving slowly enough to let him catch up without being too obvious about it. The pain shooting up his leg mercifully dulled, easing his hobble into a limp.

"Y'all know where I'll be while y'all check out them video games..." he said.

They nodded.

They knew.

The Guns & Ammunition Department.

This Blackbeard dude sounds badass...
Wish I could be like him...
(you can be, bill...)

(obey your dreams.)

Blackbeard: The Man Who Scourged the Seas
By: Roberta Stevenson
CHAPTER 1
Which Pirates Do You Know?

(pg.09) When you think of pirates, who comes to mind?

Long John Silver?

Guess what—he never existed!

Though his name may be linked to a delicious fast-food chain, he's a fictional character in *Treasure Island,* the classic pirate novel.

Maybe Captain Hook?

He's not real, either!

Just the fictional villain in the magical universe of Peter Pan.

What about Cap'n Crunch?

Surely, he must be real, right?

Nope!

Just a mascot for a popular cereal!

Chances are, the only *real* pirate you've ever heard of is Blackbeard.

But why?

After all, Blackbeard wasn't even the most successful pirate. It's recorded that he captured sixty ships, an impressive number, but nothing compared to Peter Easton, the Scottish pirate who captured over one hundred, or the most successful pirate of them all, Bartholomew Roberts, who captured *over four hundred ships*—a staggering number by any measure.

Then there's Henry Every, William Kidd, Sir Francis Drake...the list goes on. Even French pirates like Francois l'Ollonais achieved greater success than Blackbeard. Not to mention Chinese pirates, like the pirate queen Zheng Yi Sao.

→ ***Did You Know?*** *Every country in the world bordering an ocean once had pirates. Even China and Japan!*

But you're not reading a book about Francois l'Ollonais or Zheng Yi Sao, are you? In fact, you'll likely forget their names within minutes of reading this.

History may be filled with pirates who achieved more success than Blackbeard, but historians across the world agree: none are as famous, legendary, and celebrated as Blackbeard.

But *why?*

Why does Blackbeard's legacy eclipse all others, despite capturing fewer ships?

To answer that question, first let's explore his early life, tracing his journey from obscurity—

—to destiny.

Turn the page and get ready to learn about Blackbeard!

Home Discussion Exercises—Talk With Your Parents!

1) Ask your parents if they can name the most famous pirates in history.

2a) Did they say Blackbeard? If they did, ask them, _"What made Blackbeard so famous?"_

2b) If they didn't, ask them, _"Why didn't you mention Blackbeard?"_ Chances are they knew about him, and it just slipped their mind!

1990s

CHAPTER IV

LITTLE STACEY AND THE VOID

Maplefield, Alabama

"How ya doin', AB?"

"Mm...nee's...Bah...bby...m-my...mmname—"

"Shut the fuck up! Your name isn't Bobby, it's AB!"

WEDNESDAYS USED TO be Bobby's favorite day.

That was the day he fed Little Stacey her breakfast.

(little stacey)

(little stacey)

He stood alone in the middle of KB Toystore, gazing at the Barbie dolls.

This is what it'd came down to—

—a full-grown man reduced to buyin' a dang ol' Barbie doll.

Music jingled from a nearby speaker. Pleasant, upbeat, joyful. Feelings of excitement and wonder from childhood began to stir.

"Can I get a G.I. Joe, Momma?"

"No, Bobby, you haven't been a good boy..."

Couldn't help but tap his foot to that jingle.

"I'll be a good boy, Momma..."

"I promise..."

But he was never a good enough boy, was he?

Never good enough for Momma.

Never.

She'd always find *one* thing wrong, so he bought most of his toys himself, earning money from chores he begged for around the neighborhood. *Toys earned from begging.*

It did make him good with money, though.

When you only got a little, you learned the hard way to make it dang ol' count.

A child laughed nearby, startling him.

He glanced around. Didn't want nobody catchin' him in the Barbie doll aisle. Even as a child, he'd never lingered there before—only passed through, not ever takin' anything in. Just a blur of pink and shiny plastic. Until today, the Barbie doll aisle hadn't really existed to him.

Today it did.

It existed.

It existed more than anything in his life these days.

The fluorescent lights hummed, audible even over the music. He squinted.

Were the lights always this dang bright?

And loud?

He squeezed his eyes shut, releasing his breath in a long, slow stream.

It's okay, Bobby...
You can do this.

It took courage to come here today, and plenty of thinkin' outside the dang ol' box to even come up with the idea of buyin' a Barbie doll for himself. He cast a quick glance left and right, making sure nobody looked at him funny. Wasn't right for a grown man to be buyin' a Barbie doll. He knew that.

But he had no choice.

Dang ol' Mr. Stannis...

He clenched his fists.

That dang ol' rich son of a gun with his fancy degree and his shiny sports car spendin' his days golfin' and "touchin' base" with the clients. Thought he was *real* special, didn't he?

Bobby's eyes tightened.

And now, thanks to Mr. Stannis, he couldn't take Wednesday mornin' off this week 'cause of that dang ol' mandatory Morning Meeting. Everybody reported on what they were doin', what was goin' well and what wasn't. Couldn't think of a worse way to waste time if he tried.

He shook his head.

The lights brightened.

And during those useless bullcrap Morning Meetings, he had to listen to people's words.

Words.

He didn't like words. He liked numbers. That's why he worked there. Not to deal with words, but numbers. Words in contracts and tax documents—they felt okay. Had a concreteness to'em. As concrete as words could be.

But those dang ol' Morning Meetings?

He clenched his jaw.

Listenin' to all their words, their useless empty words and then he had to say useless empty words himself and none of their words *mattered*. None of 'em. Just had to *act* like they did.

They didn't, though—most words didn't matter.

Only the simple ones did. Simple words were okay. Concrete. Like numbers. They mattered.

Like Little Stacey.

She mattered.

Little Stacey...

And now that dang ol' Mr. Stannis had put him in a pickle by not givin' him Wednesday mornin' off again.

"Let me think on it some more, Bobby..."

What was there to think on?

"For now, keep on attendin', just like everybody else. You know how important company unity is, don't ya, Bobby?"

Nope, sure didn't. And thanks to that bullcrap company unity, it'd been three long weeks since he'd fed Little Stacey.

Three.

Long.

Weeks.

Poor Little Stacey...

She must be so dang hungry...

His heart beat faster.

(little stacey)

(little stacey little stacey little stacey)

His breathing turned rapid and shallow.

Every Wednesday, I got to feed her breakfast!

The fluorescent lights dimmed.

Every dang Wednesday!

Saliva pooled under his tongue.

Because she was a good girl!

And always ate it all!

A drop of cold sweat rolled from his armpit.

Like a good girl...

He wet his lips.

"Are you gonna be a good girl, Little Stacey?"

She'd always nod and say *"Yesss"* and smile at him with that happy smile. Oh so happy. Always happy.

Little Stacey was always happy and she always ate all her breakfast like a happy, good girl.

(littlestaceylittlestaceylittlestacey)

He darted his eyes from one Barbie doll to the next, catching glimpses of his reflection in the glossy packaging. For a moment, it looked like his spirit—*the real Bobby*—was trapped inside the doll cases, staring back at an empty vessel of a man.

(what are you doing, bobby?)
(what in god's name are you doing?)
His body jerked.
No, no.
Just his reflection.
Wasn't his dang ol spirit or nothin'.
Didn't mean nothin'.
He closed his eyes and focused on controlling his breathing.
Breathe, Bobby...
Breathe...
Gotta focus on the task at hand.
Come on, now...
Let's get this show on the road...
He opened his eyes.
It has to look like her.
He swept his gaze over the different Barbies, the cases blurring into a sea of shiny pink plastic.
Where is she where is she where is she...
At first, he'd considered getting a bigger doll, like those soft cotton ones—Cabbage Patch Kids or whatever they're called. They were bigger than Barbie dolls, softer, with larger faces you could cuddle. But concealin' a Barbie doll proved easier.

And Barbie dolls had little boobies.

Little Stacey didn't have much in the way of boobies—maybe used to, but likely never real big. Big enough to know they were there, but not anymore. Whatever bosom she had was long gone. That's okay—the doll's tiny nubs turned him on, even if they didn't match Little Stacey's current proportions.

The doll's hair and face remained the most important—and the Barbie doll's face held far more sex appeal than those baby-lookin' faces of the Cabbage Patch Kids ones.

Little Stacey's face...
If only the Barbies had bigger eyes.
Her eyes...
Like the real Little Stacey's.
Starin' into me...
Oh, how he loved to see her eyes starin' back up at him!

(into me)

Little Stacey could see *into* him, his soul, into everything he was and could have been, before things got bad, before his Ruining, and she accepted it, she accepted him as he was: *Ruined.* Every fault and weakness, every insecurity, every barely remaining strength and success clinging on despite his Ruining—she accepted it all into *her eyes,* and he saw himself inside them, free.

(free...)

He saw her now,

(free...)

on her knees like a good girl,

(i'm free when I'm with you...)

starin' up at him with those purty eyes of hers...

(little stacey...)

His penis tingled and stiffened.

(little stacey little stacey little sta—)

A child's laughter startled him.

He sucked in air, his lungs expanding like balloons.

Fully hard now.

But couldn't stand around forever.

Quickly, he scanned the Barbies—only one blonde left.

Only one.

Blondes must be the most popular.

Purty blonde hair...

The Barbie's hair reminded him of Little Stacey's and how it felt when he ran his fingers through it.

Purty, purty blonde hair...

Almost the same color, too.

You so purty, Stacey...

Her hair felt so good when he squeezed her little head...

Gosh dang you so purty...

Suddenly, it was only him and the blonde Barbie—alone in their sacred space, separate from everything else, as he felt himself drawn into a wonderful void.

Little Stacey...

The fluorescent lights vanished.

The jingling music faded.

Darkness enveloped him.

The Void...

The Void was pleasant and numb and soundless and perfect. It shielded him from the stressors of the whole wide world. Nothing existed in The Void but him and the Barbie—nothing but him and Little Stacey.

(little stacey little stacey)

Little Stacey was perfect—perfect like The Void.

She was the Barbie doll, and the Barbie doll was her.

Inside The Void, they became one.

They Joined.

He reached out to touch her—

Little Stacey...

to touch The Void—

(littlestaceylittlestaceylittlestacey)

to touch The Vo—

Everything crashed crashed crashed back into terrible focus: blindingly white lights reflecting off pink plastic cases and that stupid jingling music and his stupid face reflected on the cases.

No...

The Void...

I was inside The Vo—

He glanced down. A small girl clasped her mother's hand.

An intruder.

An intruder upon The Void.

She intruded intruded intruded upon *his* aisle, *his* sacred space.

Little brat!

His penis deflated.

The girl marveled at all the Barbie dolls before her.

Little brat might want the same one I do...

(grab the doll, bobby)

(hurry up and grab it!)

No—didn't wanna grab the doll in front of 'em—that'd be embarrassin'.

(grab it or else!)

(the last blonde barbie!)

(grab it!)

He flicked his eyes between the last blonde Barbie and the encroaching child.

Better not want that one...

The child's gaze locked onto the *same doll*—that *same doll* that he wanted, needed.

You better not...

She reached her grubby little hand out.

"Mommy, I want th—"

(NO!)

(YOU CAN'T HAVE THAT ONE!)

He snatched the Barbie doll box, shooting the child a defiant glare.

"It's mine, you little brat!" he said. *"It's mine and you can't have it!"*

The mother's mouth dropped.

Shock and heartbreak erupted across the child's face.

Clutching the Barbie doll to his chest, Bobby scampered toward the register.

1990s

CHAPTER V

LIGHTS SO LOUD, SO BRIGHT

"Bobby, are you a good boy?

If you cry like a bad boy, then I'll have to—"

"IT'S-IT'S FOR MY daughter..." said Bobby.

His face turned hot.

"A-ain't for me..."

The register girl looked pretty. Not as pretty as Little Stacey, and definitely not as little, but didn't matter. She wouldn't eat her breakfast like Little Stacey. Not like a good girl.

The register girl smiled and laughed. "That's what I assumed..."

Why did I say that?

That it ain't for me?

Just makes it more suspicious...

Better add somethin' else.

"I-it's for her birthday..." he said.

"Oh, okay..." said the girl.

Bobby glanced around. The little brat still cried over in the Barbie doll aisle, pointin' her grubby little finger at him.

Too bad, so sad!

You can't have it!

It's mine!

Had to make his exit fast. Didn't want no confrontation with the momma. Probably crazy and aggressive, like most mommas these days. Always lookin' for somethin' to start a commotion about.

Bobby hated confrontation.

And commotion, too.

"That'll be $12.95," said the register girl.

Good lord that's expensive for a dang ol' Barbie doll...

He sighed and reached for his billfold.

"Hope she has a good one," she said.

"Huh?"

"Your daughter," she said. "I hope she has a good birthday party."

"Oh!" he said. "Yep, yep..."

He cleared his throat.

"My-my daughter..."

He handed her a twenty.

"It's g-gonna be a real, real good one..."

No, that sounded too confident...

Sounded like a lie!

Now she knows I'm hidin' somethin'...

"I mean, I-I *hope* so..." He nodded more vigorously than required.

She nodded in return, pursing her lips.

Oh boy...

I bet she knows...

Bobby gulped.

She knows I don't got no daughter...

His body moistened with sweat.

She knows I'm a full-grown man buyin' a Barbie doll for himself!

A child's cry whined from the Barbie aisle like a police siren.

That little brat!

Still bawlin' her eyes out while her mean ol' momma glared at him as if he'd committed a crime against nature.

Who are they to judge me?

They never walked a mile in my shoes...

They don't understand...

The register girl said something he couldn't catch, so he nodded and said, "*Yep, yep,*" and chuckled. Probably no need to chuckle. But he did, anyway.

Gosh dang, I hate these awkward interactions...

He checked his surroundings, scanning his environment like a commando deep inside an enemy jungle.

Better not be anybody from work or church nearby.

Come on, register girl, what's takin' so dang long...

She bent down, pulling out drawers, searching for something.

Best hurry up, now.

Didn't like standin' at the register too long.

Felt exposed.

She said she'd be back and stepped through the *Employees Only* door.

Bobby's pulse raced.

What's the dang ol' problem?

The walls of the toy store closed in on him now, everything and everyone so dang close to him now.

Why'd they make this store so small?

His stomach tightened as he gripped the counter with cold, clammy hands and *squeezed*.

This is takin' longer than necessary...

Somethin' ain't right...

Wasn't no crime for a grown man to buy a Barbie.

Unusual, sure.

But not a crime.

Did this girl know him?

Or maybe somebody else?

Somebody behind the Employees Only door?

(remember your cover story)

Did he know anyone that worked there?

Did anyone kn—

(calm down, bobby...)

(remember your cover story...)

Cover story: It's for a cousin in another state.

Easy as pie.

But he'd already said it was for his daughter.

Shoot!

Never been good at lyin'...

He scratched his forehead.

Lyin' required skillful use of words.

Words.

He hated'em.

And whenever he lied, people saw through his words and through *him,* they saw his—

The register girl returned carrying a tube of gift wrap.

"W-What's that for?" he asked.

"You said you'd like it wrapped?"

"O-oh..."

"Do you *not* want it wrapped?"

"Uh...n-no thank you..."

(no, ask for it wrapped)

(ask for it wrapped!)

"I mean!"

Cold sweat ran down his forehead.

"Y-yeah..."

Always started sweatin' when interactions got awkward.

"Y-yep...yep-yep-yep..."

Perspiration was the sign of a healthy body. He'd learned that in school and told it to himself ever since.

Why's she takin' so long...

He wiped his forehead with the back of his hand and wiped his hand on his pants.

So dang bright in here now...

Had they turned up the brightness?

Is that what she did behind the *Employees Only* door?

The register girl put her hand on her hip.

"So, you *would* like it wrapped?"

Bobby looked at her like she'd spoken Chinese. She laughed. Maybe to ease the tension, a small act of mercy. But there was something *else* in her eyes—something he could detect, but not understand.

Why's she lookin' at me like that?

It was always like this when he interacted with people—when he had to use dang ol' words.

"Well, I-I mean..."

He never got used to it.

"Uh..."

It never got better.

"...d-does it cost extra?"

The lights brightened to a near-blinding level.

Gosh dang lights...

Why they gotta be so bright...

He chuckled.

There was no reason to chuckle.

"It costs $2.95," she said.

That's highway robbery for wrappin' a dang ol' Barbie doll...

"W-Well, then..."

He looked around.

Was *everyone* starin' at him now?

Why?

"J-just g-give to me wrapped..."

He forced a smile.

"P-Please wrap it for me."

The girl mouthed *"O-kayyy"* and began wrapping it. Didn't seem used to it, though. Just figuring it out as she went.

Big mistake...

Should've never asked her to wrap it...

Big mistake!

Sweat dripped down his thighs, face, back, chest, groin and (especially) his butt cheeks. He reminded himself he must be really healthy to sweat so much. *Sweatin' was the sign of a healthy body.* He'd learned that in elementary school and told everyone when they called him "Sweaty Bobby." Life's most important lessons were learned in elementary school.

"*Let's tie Sweaty Bobby to a tree!*"

"*No!*"

"*Just leave me alone!*"

Those kids.

Their laughter.

All around him.

"*You gonna barf again, Bobby?*"

"*Huh? Barfin' Bobby?*"

He hadn't puked in a long time—not since his *Ruining.* Unlike the sweating, he'd gotten that under control.

Nothin' wrong with sweatin', anyway.

Just the sign of a healthy body.

("*swea-ty bo-bby!*")

("*bar-fin' bo-bby!*")

("*stop pokin' me!*")

And he never cried he never cried he never CRIED.

Momma told him big boys don't cry and he never did. Not once.

Still won't. Can't.

Couldn't even cry even if he wanted to (*sometimes I want to*).

("*just leave me alone!*")

("*what you gonna do about it, huh?*")

("*sweat some more?*")

"Sir?"

("*or barf again?*")

("*swea-ty bo-bby!*")

("*bar-fin' bo-bby!*")

Oh, he *did* something about it, alright.

"Excuse me? Sir?"

And it was the most amazing, glorious moment of his childhood.

"I'll do somethin' about it..." he said.

"Excuse me? Sir?"

The register girl held out his change.

"S-Sorry," he said. "D-drifted off..."

As he reached for his change, something *sparked* when their fingers touched *(littlestaceylittlestacey)*. He glanced at her eyes *(did you feel it, too?)* but she yanked her hand back, keeping her focus fixed on the wrapped box.

"Have a nice day, sir..."

She knocked the box to the floor behind the register.

"Oops..."

Bobby's shrill voice pierced the air:

"BE CAREFUL WITH HER!"

The register girl's mouth dropped.

Everyone in the store froze.

Oh, shoot...

Bobby couldn't move.

Oh, shoot shoot shoot shoot shoot...

(get out of there, bobby)

(get out of there, now)

He hadn't meant to say it loud—hadn't meant to say it at all, only *think* it—but it escaped with such intensity that everyone in the store now stared at him.

(STOP LOOKING AT ME)

He tried to laugh, but it sounded like choking.

(STOP STARING)

The lights brightened—so bright so bright *so bright* now.

"Aah!"

He covered his eyes.

The hum of the lights intensified.

(THE LIGHTS)

(WHY ARE THE LIGHTS SO LOUD, SO BRIGHT?)

He felt the register girl's stare—just starin'-starin'-starin' like there was somethin' wrong with him but there wasn't nothin' wrong with him, no sir, not at all.

She didn't know him.

They didn't know him.

Nobody knew him.

Except Little Stacey.

(GIVE HER TO ME)

(GIVE ME LITTLE STACEY)

All their stares their stares THEIR STARES burned his skin like the sun had when they left him tied to that tree.

"What you gonna do about it, Sweaty Bobby?"

Stop starin' at me!

"Swea-ty Bo-bby!"

"Swea-ty Bo-bby!"

Y'all don't understand!

"Bar-fin' Bo-bby!"

"Bar-fin' Bo-bby!"

Y'all don't know me!

He covered his face, shielding it from their nasty stares—especially that crazy momma and her brat, glaring at him like he was a freak.

(STOP STARING)

(THEY ALL STARE)

(I HATE YOUR STARES)

He tried to force a smile at the register girl so she'd *understand* him— not his words, his dang ol' useless words but his smile and it hurt to smile it hurt to smile and why did it hurt to smile?

"P-please...just-just..."

He tried to grasp the counter and *squeeze,* but his hands, slick with sweat, made it slippery.

"J-just give her to me..."

(PLEASE)

(I NEED HER)

"Just gimme Little Stacey."

***

Bobby sat in his car with the A/C turned full blast. The frigid air felt good on his skin, drying his sweat.

He peered out at the scorching parking lot, sunlight glaring off the asphalt.

Sure was hot today. Even for Alabama.

Thank God for air conditionin'...

He leaned back in his seat, grateful to be safe and cool inside his car.

Asking for it wrapped had been smart—just in case someone in the mall saw him with it, someone who knew he didn't have no daughter. Could use the cousin-in-another-state story, but there was always the risk they'd see through it, like they always did.

Even when Bobby wasn't lying—when he was tellin' the dang ol' truth—he needed time to plan what he said and how he said it. Words in general weren't his strong point. He liked numbers. And ideas and concepts represented by numbers. Like data. Graphs. Financial statements. They had numbers. Lots of numbers. Numbers were concrete. Irrefutable. Words were abstract. Depending on how you said a word, the context, and who you said it to all affected the meaning. He was never sure of people's words and he had to concentrate hard, *so hard* to decipher what people really meant with their dang ol' words. Sometimes he couldn't decipher his own.

He exhaled slowly, releasing stress from his body like air from a balloon.

Felt good to be alone in the car.

Away from people, from words.

He stared at the wrapped box in his hands.

Maybe this could work.

The doll might satiate him.

For a while, at least.

He squeezed the box.

It felt good in his hands.

Solid.

Concrete.

Like numbers.

He liked numbers.

Not words.

Numbers were good.

And he liked Little Stacey.

Even more than numbers.

1970s

CHAPTER VI

CHRISTMAS LIGHTS

Bobby understood that Bill must've led

a wild life, full of hard livin'.

Lots of drinkin'.

Lots of drugs.

Lord knows what else.

FOR THE FIRST time since Bill had started wearing his cowboy hat, he actually felt like one.

A real cowboy.

The sun's early rays peeked from the window behind him. He sat on Charlie's living room couch in a daze, feeling both tired and alert. Nancy, one of the two naked chicks asleep in Charlie's bedroom, mumbled and shifted to her side, giving Bill a full view of her bare ass.

Damn...

He took it in for a second, appreciative of the good things in life, then turned off the heavy metal still humming from Charlie's boombox. After all that craziness, now was the time for silence.

Clear, pristine, church-like silence.

While he stared at a chick's bare ass.

And appreciated life.

He leaned back on the couch, in awe of how cool it felt to have a house to party at all summer. Charlie's dad was back in jail, maybe for a long while this time. Technically, Charlie's mom was supposed to be back to livin' with him, but she was rarely around—and even when she was, she wasn't really *there,* just lost in a haze. She'd ask, *"How's school goin'?"* and *"Do ya have enough food?"* and take'em to the grocery and ask, *"How y'all doin' at school?"* and then disappear again. They'd given up reminding her of summer break.

Besides, her absence meant they had the whole fuckin' house to themselves—and that felt *awesome.*

They both had driver's licenses and their own rides now—Charlie with his dad's black Camaro, Bill with a busted up blue Ford F-150—so they could do whatever the fuck they wanted whenever they damn well pleased. In fact, Bill had already experienced something he thought possible only in his wildest fantasies:

bangin' two different chicks—

("god, you fuck so good...")

—in the same fuckin' night.

Older chicks that Charlie's dad knew—college-age, but not college-attending—which had intimidated Bill at first. Charlie played it cool, though, so Bill followed his lead, and once they cranked up the metal and brought out the coke and liquor, the awkwardness melted away.

Then, at just the right moment, Charlie switched off the lamps and said, *"Hey, check this out!"* as he flicked on the Christmas lights strung along the walls. The vibe shifted instantly. That's when Nancy unzipped Bill's jeans—and he felt like he'd stepped into the pages of a *Penthouse* magazine.

("...whatcha hidin' in there, boy?")

Liquor made girls wild, and if you were lucky, slutty, too—Bill already knew that.

("...ya got somethin' ya wanna show me?")

But how fuckin' *horny* girls got on coke?

("...lemme see it...")

That came as a revelation.

("...damn...you're big for a young guy...")

Like rabbits in heat.

("do ya like this?")

("does it feel good?")

The coke came from Charlie's dad's no longer secret stash that they'd cut with a shit-ton of caffeine pill powder—a trick Charlie had learned from spyin' on his dad. But even ten percent cocaine—or maybe the mere thrill of *thinkin'* they snorted cocaine—mixed with liquor, heavy metal, and Charlie's christmas lights, turned the girls real slutty, real fast.

The other girl, Tina, had asked, *"What are you, some kinda cowboy or somethin'?"*

"A cocaine cowboy..." Charlie had said, pouring a line across the mirror on the table.

Tina—*oh, Tina.*

Petite, dark-complected, and hot as fuck.

Flat as a board, but still hot as fuck.

Her small stature helped him feel less nervous, but she still commanded the elegance and confidence of a hot chick in her twenties. A chick on a different level from high school girls.

Then there was her friend Nancy *(oh, Nancy)*, blonde and kinda thick. Not fat, but tall (for a girl) and big-boned, with amazing tits. Bigger and nicer than most in *Playboy* magazines. At first, Nancy didn't even look at him, making him think she didn't like him, but when the room darkened and the Christmas lights came on, she unzipped his jeans—so, go figure.

("you wanna put it inside me?")

What one girl lacked, the other made up for—probably why they hung out. The best friendships thrived not just on similarities but on differences, too.

Likely the same reason him and Charlie clicked so well.

And why he'd seen Charlie so often in his dreams lately.

("y'all bitches listen up!")

("this is wild bill and i'm young-fuckin'-charlie!")

("and we fuckin' rule kentucky!")

Bill hadn't revealed his dreams to Charlie yet. He'd never revealed them to anyone except his dad and his brother Wayne—and telling his dad when he was younger proved a severe mistake.

("you think you can see the future?")

("like your crazy momma?")

("i'm gonna do to you what i should've done to her...")

But Charlie was his best friend, and witholding something big like that didn't seem right—especially when he'd seen fragments of their future: the good, the bad, and maybe how to prevent the worst.

("bill, do your dreams always turn out like you seen'em?")

("mine turn out different sometimes...")

He shrugged off his little brother's voice, reminding himself how the next steps should play out: the girls they'd fucked tonight would talk to other girls, *spread word of their badassness,* drawing in more girls (primarily for free drugs and liquor, but fuckin' usually came with the package, too). Their newfound prestige would rip through a Crow County gripped in a summer daze. Soon, other guys would wanna roll with'em—the kind who tore shit up, the only kind him and Charlie could kick it with.

Before long, they'd have a hand-picked *posse.*

("you tell your boys about wild bill and his posse!")

("you tell'em what we did here today!")

He gazed at his reflection in the coke-streaked mirror on the table.

My own posse...

And I can be their leader...

Like Blackbeard...

The cocaine residue blurred his face, but he saw past it—

—into his future.

("boys, do we fuckin' rule kentucky or not?")

A future fueled by drugs and alcohol and the possibilities they provided.

("fuck yeah, we do!")

A future fueled by *his dreams.*

("we rule kentucky, man!")

Charlie's house would serve as a base, a launching pad for that future.

("ain't nobody gonna fuck with us!")

He would submit to his dreams now.

Obey them.

Obey them and never question th—

Nancy mumbled in her sleep. She laid her hand on Tina's ass and nuzzled closer, their lips touching briefly.

Bill raised an eyebrow.

Were they—

WHOOSH!

The toilet flushed, and Charlie marched out of the bathroom in that ridiculous bathrobe of his *("It's my dad's, what do ya think?")*. He plopped down on a chair and crossed his legs like the Hugh Hefner of Kentucky.

"Qué tal las putaaaas?"

He smiled and winked.

"...what'd you think of them bitches?"

***

Bill made Charlie close the bedroom door so the girls couldn't hear *("dude, they're asleep")* *("just in case, man!")* as they compared notes from the night before, at first in hushed tones.

"When y'all were fuckin," said Charlie, "did Tina's eyes roll back? 'Cause they rolled *way* back when she rode on top of me."

"Dude," said Bill. "I thought she was possessed. Freaked me out."

"That's when you know bitches are really feelin' good," said Charlie. "When you're fuckin'em and lickin' their pussy and shit. When their eyes do fucked up shit like that."

He fixed Bill with a serious gaze.

"She probably felt better than all of us put together, man. Probably went up to Heaven."

Bill paused, contemplating how fuckin' might feel different for different people, and how everybody might experience sex on different levels. He'd felt good, *real* fuckin' good, but the way Tina had looked, as if in a trance, like she traveled to another planet...

Bill said, "Nancy kept on sayin' shit the whole time we banged. I guess she wasn't as, like, fuckin' *lost* in pleasure and shit like Tina was. But man, the stuff she said..."

"Dude," said Charlie. "That's what sticks with me, man. Not only the fuckin' or the suckin', but what they *say* while they're doin' it. You feel me?"

Bill nodded.

He sure fuckin' did.

"And what they say afterwards, too..." said Bill.

(*"daaamn, you came so much..."*)

(*"you can cum inside me next time..."*)

(*"okay, baby?"*)

(*"i'll let you fuck me on my period"*)

Charlie stared into space. *"Sí..."*

Sharing such raw sexual anecdotes with someone who'd just fucked the same girls felt awkward and intense—even with Charlie. Part of Bill yearned to share, while another part resisted. In the end, though, he couldn't help himself.

"I can't believe we both banged the same two girls in the same night, man..." said Bill. "It's like a dream..."

"*Sí*, fuckin' *sí*," said Charlie. "I didn't even know it'd go down like that, *ese*. I mean, I was pretty sure they'd do *somethin'*, like make out with us and shit, maybe give us handjobs, or if we were really lucky suck our dicks or somethin', but damn..."

"Ya know," said Bill, "when you switched off the lamps and turned on the Christmas lights, that's when shit got real. When everything *changed.*"

"That's what I was hopin' for," said Charlie. "My dad taught me there's just somethin' about Christmas lights. Makes people feel more relaxed and shit, improves the *ahm-bi-ahnce* of things." (Charlie said *"ambiance"* in some kinda grandiose, pseudo-French pronunciation—likely a side-effect of his bathrobe.)

"Whose pussy did you like eatin' better?" asked Charlie. "Nancy's? Or Tiny Tina's?"

"Neither," said Bill.

"What do you mean, 'neither'?" asked Charlie. "You *did* eat their pussies, right?"

"Nope," said Bill. "Don't do that shit."

"What do you mean, you *'don't do that shit'*?"

"Nah," said Bill. "That's gross."

"*Qué?* Dude, you *got* to eat the pussy. You just got to. It's somethin' required of you. As a man."

"Think I'm man enough without doin' that shit," said Bill. He tipped his cowboy hat. "Thanks for the advice, though..."

"Boy, you gonna be hungry later," said Charlie. "If you didn't eat no pussy last night, you gonna be hungry later!"

He cackled.

"Have to call this motherfucker—

—*a Domino's fuckin' pizza!*"

Charlie smacked the kitchen counter, and Bill laughed because Charlie laughed. They collapsed to the floor, cackling until their sides hurt.

***

"I'll tell ya what, though," said Charlie, wiping tears of laughter. "If we'd been doin' the pure shit, we couldn't've even banged *one* of 'em."

Bill's laughter faded. "What do ya mean, dude?"

Charlie's expression turned grave. "Coke can make it hard to get a boner, dude."

"*What?*" asked Bill. "Why? How?"

"I don't know why or how, *ese*," said Charlie, "I ain't no fuckin', scientist and shit. But *sí*, I'm fuckin' serious."

"How ya know?"

"Heard my dad complain about it with his buddies," said Charlie. "Called it 'coke-dick.'"

"*Coke-dick?*" asked Bill. "I don't want that shit!"

Bill couldn't imagine how the night would've gone if he couldn't have gotten hard. Couldn't even fathom such a condition, as he'd only experienced the opposite problem.

"We ain't gonna get *that*, are we?" asked Bill. He felt as if he'd been told he might have cancer. "We ain't gonna get no *coke-dick,* right?"

Charlie stroked his beard and gazed out the window, as if calculating the probabilities of various coke-dick scenarios.

"...we *should* be alright as long as we keep cuttin' it with a shit-ton of caffeine powder," said Charlie. "Even if it does keep us up all night and day."

"Makes me pee a lot, too," said Bill.

"*Yo también, amigo.* Best drink fuckin' *agua* to stay hydrated. And start takin' multivitamins, for our immunity and shit."

Charlie retrieved a bottle of Flintstones chewables and brought Bill a purple dinosaur vitamin with a glass of water.

"Vitamins are like magic pills," said Charlie, "that give ya a hundred percent of whatever your body fuckin' needs. Except for fiber, and protein, and some other shit."

"*Gracias,* Charlie..." He popped the purple dinosaur in his mouth and chewed—gritty, chalky. Like sweet sediment.

"I'm so tired," said Bill, "but I don't think I can sleep, man. Like them other times."

Charlie munched on his multivitamin. "Just gotta stay up all day again and go to bed early."

Bill nodded toward the bedroom. "Caffeine didn't stop them from sleepin' none."

"'Cause they drank enough to kill a horse!" said Charlie.

The girls *had* drunk a shit-ton—downing tequila between sex acts like boxers drinkin' water between rounds. They'd even wanted to drink and snort coke *while* they were fuckin' and suckin', which made Bill wonder, amidst the fever-dream of lust, if there was something wrong with'em.

"And 'cause they probably built up a tolerance," said Charlie. "They been doin' caffeine-infused coke for years, man. I remember my dad sellin' to'em back when *they* were in high school."

Bill removed his cowboy hat and ran a hand through his long hair. He considered asking if Charlie's dad might've banged Nancy and Tina, too, but no. Something felt wrong with asking that.

"And you know what?" asked Charlie.

He looked at Bill carefully.

"Don't think they paid my dad in *money,* either..."

Bill nodded.

Question answered, then.

"Now I see why you invited those two," said Bill.

"There's more where that came from," said Charlie. "But those are two of the hottest. Been wantin' to bang them since middle school."

Bill turned his tired-but-alert gaze to the window, admiring the green of the bushes and the yellow of the morning sunlight. A squirrel hopped around, searching for breakfast.

"You ain't gonna shoot today, are ya?" asked Charlie.

"I will," said Bill. "Once the girls leave. Don't wanna wake'em up."

"Can't believe you shoot every day, man. Even when you're hungover and coked out."

"And tired from fuckin', too..." Bill winced as pain and a mild tingle ran down his left leg.

What the...

Am I gonna have to stretch before fuckin' now?

"You *really* like shootin', don't ya?" asked Charlie.

Bill stood and stretched. "Just somethin' I gotta do. Once ya start doin' somethin' every day, it becomes a habit, and if ya do it long enough, it becomes a part of ya."

Charlie nodded, then froze.

A look of horror fell upon his face.

"Fuck!" he said. *"Did they spill on the carpet?"*

In a flash, he bolted to the kitchen, grabbed cleaning spray and a rag, then scrambled to a spot that looked like it *might* have a tiny dot of orange juice.

"I told those bitches not to spill shit..." he said, spraying and scrubbing.

Bill wanted to feel useful so he paced the living room, searching for more spots.

"I don't think there's any more , dude. They drank a ton, but they didn't like, spill shit or nothin'—"

"Well, they fuckin' spilled on here, didn't they!" said Charlie.

Bill nodded, careful to keep his mouth shut while Charlie sprayed and scrubbed. After several long minutes, he released a long sigh and collapsed into his chair, rolling his head in circles.

"I'm sorry that happened, man," said Bill. "I was doin' my best to watch'em, ya know, so they didn't sp—"

Charlie held out his hand. "It's alright, man, it's alright..." He said it in a way that meant it really wasn't alright, though.

Not at all.

"Well, hey *amigo*," said Bill, "I'm fuckin' glad we had a night like we did. And I wanna thank ya for it, too. From the bottom of my heart."

He looked at Charlie, hoping his eyes conveyed how truly thankful he felt. The night had turned out wilder and better than even his dreams had shown.

("bill, if our dreams are wrong sometimes...")

("...should we really be tryin' to follow'em?")

One thing his brother Wayne hadn't realized yet: their dreams could be wrong in a good way, too.

"If you need me to chip in any more," said Bill, "for the liquor or the coke, I'm doin' a ton of chores for old people in my neighborhood next week, I'll be able to pay—"

"Nah..." said Charlie, still staring at the now undetectable spot on the carpet. Undetectable to all but Charlie.

"We're *bueno*..."

Bill leaned back on the couch, grateful for such a generous friend. He'd throw Charlie some cash next week, anyway—he deserved it.

"So," said Bill, "there's other girls you know from your dad, too? That'd be down to party?"

And fuck?

"*Sí*, fuckin' *sí*. I know a lot more, man. My dad had a shit-ton of customers..."

Charlie's face fell, as if recalling something he'd rather forget.

"...but ain't all of 'em hot, *ese*...

"...some ain't the kinda people you wanna be around."

***

Charlie fixed a pot of coffee (decaf, thank God) since they weren't ready to sleep yet and neither water nor orange juice seemed appealing. The remaining milk, they decided, should be saved for cereal.

"I almost didn't wanna fuck Nancy after she threw up," said Charlie. "Figured I'd just get head or somethin'. But she kept on jerkin' me and talkin' dirty, tellin' me to put it inside her and shit, and I knew I had to fuck her, *ese*. I just had to. So I hit it from the back so I didn't have to smell her barf-breath."

Bill sipped his coffee. Clear and bitter—a nice contrast to all the sweet shit they'd mixed with liquor all night.

"At least she got it all in the toilet," said Bill.

Charlie scowled. "If that bitch would've puked on the carpet, I would've kicked her ass out. I'll tell you *that* right the fuck now."

Bill reminded himself to be extra-fucking-careful not to spill any coffee.

"Dude," said Bill. "Why *did* Nancy start cryin' and shit? That was weird, man."

"Girls get emotional sometimes," said Charlie. "Ain't no explainin' that. They might be doin' drugs other than coke. Got their minds all fucked up, *muy loco* and shit."

"That Tiny Tina chick," said Bill, "she's almost *too* fuckin' skinny. Could 'bout count her ribs."

"Coke probably keeps her thin," said Charlie. "Nancy used to be bigger, too, but she's thinned down and now she's just big-boned. And her tits stayed the same size, thank God."

Bill considered revealing something, thought better of it, then figured, *"What the fuck?"* and revealed it:

"Nancy was still cryin'," said Bill. "While we was fuckin'."

"The fuck?" asked Charlie. "I thought she stopped after she did another line? You talkin' about before, or after she barfed?"

"Before," said Bill. "She cried before she barfed, too. While we fucked. And I'll be honest with ya, it was *weird,* man."

"Sí, fuckin' *sí,"* said Charlie. "But I bet some guys get off on that shit. Maybe that's why she—"

"Maybe *they* do," said Bill. "But not me. I 'bout stopped fuckin' her."

"You almost pulled out? While y'all was—"

"I 'bout stopped fuckin' her! But she told me to keep goin', like, actually *held* me inside her, and then she finally stopped cryin', so...I fuckin' kept goin'..."

Charlie nodded. "If she holds ya inside her, ya gotta finish. You just got to. You gotta nut."

"And then, towards the end," said Bill, "she told me to blast on her face. Couldn't believe that shit, man..."

("cum on my face, baby")

"...it was like..." said Bill.

("...give it to me...")

"...the hottest thing I could imagine a girl sayin'..."

("...give it to me on my face...")

He took a swig of coffee, lost in memory.

"That is pretty hot, ain't it?" asked Charlie. "And at least you got to fuck her without barf-breath."

Briefly, Bill wondered *why* Nancy had barfed, especially since she was so much bigger than Tina and should've held her liquor better—in theory, at least.

"What about Tiny Tina?" said Charlie. "You bust on her face, too?"

"Nah," said Bill. "She—"

"You didn't jizz inside her, did ya?" Charlie's eyes twinkled. "You didn't make that fuckin' mistake ag—"

"*Ha-ha,* Charlie," said Bill. "No, I did *not* jizz inside her. Already got one fuckin' kid. Don't want another."

Got my pull-out game real good now...

Thank God.

Bill shuddered at the thought of another child in addition to Rhonda—

—a true nightmare.

"She said she wanted it on her tits," said Bill. "So that's where I blasted."

"Tiny Tina ain't got no tits, though," said Charlie.

Bill grinned. "It was still pretty hot..."

Charlie shook his head.

"*No, no, hombre...*" said Charlie. "Lemme fuckin' tell ya somethin'. If ya ever meet a girl who says, '*Cum on my tits,*' that's *code,* man."

"Code for what?"

"Some bullshit."

"What do ya mean?"

"B-U-L-L-S-H—"

"You don't gotta *spell* it for me, man," said Bill. "But what do ya mean?"

"I mean *bullshit,* man—the kind when girls say one thing, but mean another. When she says, '*Cum on my tits,*' that's code for '*Don't cum on my face, nor in my mouth.*' Some straight-up bullshit, that's what that fuckin' is!"

Bill sipped his coffee, absorbing Charlie's words.

Bullshit or not, though—

—still felt hot as fuck.

***

Sipping their decaf, Bill and Charlie continued comparing notes on the girls' sexual skills and quirks, but Bill knew what was coming:

Charlie had a plan.

A plan to rob Roy Jameson: a car mechanic and one of his dad's best customers.

Bill knew because his dreams had told him—and warned of its fatal flaw.

"...easy as that, man," said Charlie. "And then we sell half, snort the rest."

He leaned back in his chair, looking satisfied.

"Money in our pockets," he said, "and candy up our noses."

They smiled at each other.

Money in our pockets.

Candy up our noses.

Bill asked, "And what about when he notices his coke is missin'?"

Charlie's smile widened.

"So? What's he gonna do? Call the *policia?*"

"Hmm..." Bill stroked his beard. He'd resolved to grow it as epic as possible before school started, when he'd have to trim it. For now, he aimed to grow it *way* bigger than Charlie's "circle beard" or whatever—big and badass, like Blackbeard's.

("you tell your boys!")

("you tell 'em what we did here today!")

("you tell everybody about wild bill and his posse!")

"Guess that's a good point..." said Bill. "What *could* he do if he couldn't call the cops?"

"And ain't like he got video surveillance or shit like that," said Charlie. "Don't even gotta wear gloves, man. What's he gonna do, dust for fingerprints?"

In the end, though, Bill decided to wear gloves.

Because it felt cool.

1990s

CHAPTER VII

GLASS COFFIN

"I told you not to cry, Bobby!"

"Momma...no...I—"

"BIG BOYS DON'T CRY!"

A DAY AFTER visiting KB Toystore, Bobby pulled into an empty gravel lot by the highway that cut through Maplefield, Alabama. The woods beside it reminded him of the ones behind his momma's house, where he used to play as a child. *"The Good Woods,"* he called'em. His own little refuge. Never got tied up in those woods.

He parked facing the highway, keeping an eye out for anyone. No way he'd let anyone discover him with Little Stacey. Needed absolute privacy with her.

Of course, it wasn't *really* Little Stacey.

Just a Barbie doll.

He knew that.

He wasn't crazy.

His heart raced as he opened the trunk and pulled out Little Stacey, still shielded from the world in her KB Toy Store gift wrap. The store logo adorned the wrapping along with birthday cakes, party hats, and words like *"Fun!" "Toys!"* and *"Happy Birthday!"*

Definitely not worth no extra $2.95—but the wrapping itself wasn't bad.

Kinda made him even more excited.

(little stacey little stacey)

She'd been locked in the trunk for a full twenty-four hours now, and driving her across town felt like smuggling diamonds—equal parts thrilling and nerve-wracking. Part of him didn't wanna take her out yet, didn't even wanna unwrap her. Something about withholding the moment, like a present still under the tree.

But today, he would.

Oh yes.

He had to.

Little Stacey needed her feedin' today.

Must be so dang hungry...

He closed the trunk and returned to the car. Technically, a meal this late wasn't "breakfast." He knew that. He wasn't crazy. More like an early dinner. But semantics didn't matter—if he believed it was breakfast, then it was breakfast. It'd always been breakfast with the real Little Stacey, so it'd be breakfast with the Barbie doll, too.

The highway traffic cast rolling shadows across the parking lot as the sun's final rays slipped out from behind the clouds. Drivers might notice him sitting alone in the small, empty lot, but with the car facing the highway, they wouldn't—or shouldn't—see the feeding.

Not clearly, anyway.

He tore the wrapping and gazed at the Barbie inside the case.

You so purty...

Her plastic eyes stared back at him.

Like a lil' Snow White...

Sleepin' in her glass coffin....

Almost a shame to take her out. So dang pretty and perfect inside her little glass coffin. He marveled at her, caressing the plastic case as the sun dipped below the horizon.

Peace...

Just looking at the Barbie doll, thinking of Little Stacey, brought him peace.

He exhaled gradually, savoring the moment.

Peace...

Here, in the car, maybe he could even re-form The Void. Almost witnessed it back at the toy store—before that brat and her crazy momma interrupted him.

The Void...

As he squeezed the plastic case, the sun's last golden ray faded.

Darkness fell.

His pulse raced.

His breath quickened.

Time for your breakfast...

Time to feed Little Stacey.

The plastic packaging proved dang near impossible to open with his bare hands but luckily *(thank God)* he had scissors in the glove compartment. Couldn't imagine why they made these things so dang hard to open. Probably why global warmin' was gettin' so bad—too much dang plastic everywhere.

After cutting Little Stacey out of her packaging, he ripped off her pink dress, tossing it into the passenger seat.

Better without clothes.

Better naked.

You so purty...

He'd never seen Little Stacey naked, but she never wore anything like the doll's pink outfit. Usually just a stained white tank top. Besides, the doll looked good naked.

Real good.

So good so good *so good* with her peach-colored skin and her little nubs for boobies and her pretty blonde hair and those sparklin' eyes starin' back at him.

Those eyes...

Purty, purty eyes...

He rubbed his thumb across her face, feeling himself sink into her eyes.

"L-Little Stacey...g-gonna eat her...b-breakfast?"

He answered in her voice, *"Yesss, ahhh sure aaam, Bawww-byyy..."*

"G-gonna..."

He smacked his lips.

"...eat it like a g-good girl?"

His penis stiffened.

"Yesss, Bawww-byyy...awww-ways wike a...guddd gurlll..."

Her little nubs for boobs felt real good against his thumb. He'd never touched Little Stacey's boobies (she didn't really have any, maybe she used to, but not anymore) but now he wished he had. Even if she was as flat as a dang ol' board he might've gotten somethin' out of it. Some kind of sensation. And she might've too—mutual sensation.

"...c-can you f-feel me t-touchin' your...your little b-boobies, Little Stacey?"

He exhaled slowly, releasing his breath as his penis grew harder.

"Ah shuuuure can, Bawww-byyy..."

She could.

She could.

She could *feel him* touchin' her little boobies.

"Feels weeeeeel gooood, Bawww-byyy..."

"Ohhh..."

Little Stacey with her little boobies!

He pressed'em harder.

She didn't mind if he pressed'em hard.

She probably *liked* it.

Liked'em pressed *real* hard.

"D-do you like it..."

He gulped.

"W-when I p-press'em *haaard*, Little Stacey?"

"Yesss ah doooo, Bawww-byyy..."

Spittle formed at the corners of his mouth.

"Feels weeeel guddddd wen you pwess'em haaaaaahd, Bawww-byyy..."

"Oh boy..."

Bobby's penis stood fully erect now.

Hard like a dang ol' rock.

"Oh boy, oh boy, oh boy..."

About ready to go.

He touched her hair.

Dang.

Hair felt good, too.

(littlestaceylittlestaceylittlestacey)

Almost like the real thing.

A little harder, firmer than her real hair.

But good.

(hard)

(firm)

(good)

Oh, how he longed to run his hands through Little Stacey's hair again!

And tell her she was a good girl!

The doll's eyes stared back at him just like hers did—like the real Little Stacey's, when he fed her breakfast.

"...l-love the way you s-stare at me..."

He swallowed.

"...L-Little Stacey..."

The doll didn't blink, either, just like the real Little Stacey never blinked, never broke eye contact, not once during all her feedings.

Saliva dangled from his mouth; he sucked it back in and swallowed.

(little stacey little stacey)

He pressed his thumbs against her little boobies *harder*—so hard it hurt.

(hard)

(firm)

(good)

Little Stacey let him grab her real tight, too. She never complained, she just took it, accepted it, accepted him, for all he was and ever would be, despite his Ruining.

Just like the doll—

—it accepted him, *she* accepted him, because the doll was Little Stacey. One and the same now.

They had Joined.

(little stacey little stacey)

"T-time f-for your br-breakfast, Little S-Stacey..."

The doll's plastic eyes watched in silence as he unbuckled his belt.

1970s

CHAPTER VIII

ROBBIN' ROY JAMESON

"Snort half, sell the rest..."

"IT'S IN ONE of his books," said Bill. "Probably his encyclopedias or somethin'."

"His *encyclopedias?*" Charlie eyed Bill carefully. "Like Encyclopedia Britannica and shit?"

"I don't know what fuckin' brand, dude," said Bill. "They just look like fuckin', encyclopedias. He cut out the pages in the middle of one and hid the coke inside."

"Which one?" asked Charlie. "Which encyclopedia?"

"That part's fuzzy..." said Bill. "Maybe 'C' for cocaine or somethin', or 'D' for drugs..."

Bill and Charlie sat on the porch behind Charlie's dad's house, smoking and listening to heavy metal like always, but this time they weren't relaxing, nor chilling. They'd run out of coke, and an odd tension simmered between them after Charlie revealed his scheme to rob Roy Jameson for more, followed by Bill revealing the power of his dreams—dreams that foretold the plan's failure.

"*Mmm-hmm...*" said Charlie. "So these 'dreams' of yours, *ese,* they're like, fuzzy and shit sometimes, too?"

"Charlie, put my dreams aside for a minute," said Bill, "and just consider what you're plannin'."

Charlie glanced away, past the shooting range they'd set up at the edge of the woods. Either he didn't believe him, or he *did*—and that scared him.

Guess I'd be kinda weirded out, too...

I mean, who claims their dreams can tell the future?

Other than crazy people...

"Let's say we do it the way you planned," said Bill. "You ask him to help with your dad's car, and while y'all are outside, I sneak in and grab the coke."

Charlie stared at Bill as if he were part alien.

Bill continued. "Now, after I snatch his coke, what's he gonna think? That night, or the next day, when he realizes it's missin'?"

"He won't think it's me," said Charlie, "because I'd have been outside the whole time. And he won't even *know* about you, *amigo.*"

Bill nodded. Charlie was sharp alright, and his scheme *seemed* clever, on the surface. But Bill's dreams had warned him: this plan would end with Charlie gettin' his skull cracked.

("charlie, did you take somethin' from me?")

("i don't like bein' stolen from...")

"He's smarter than you think," said Bill. "And he's gonna suspect that, somehow, you were fuckin' involved. *'Hmm, my cocaine has magically disappeared. I wonder if that Charlie Young guy, who just happened to stop by recently, had anything to fuckin' do with it'?'* I mean, unless other people happen to visit him that same day, of course he's gonna suspect you, dude. He knows your dad's a drug dealer, and the apple don't fall far from the fuckin' tree."

Charlie turned his gaze to the sky, muttering in Spanish.

"What's your plan, then? What do these magical, fuzzy dreams tell ya we should do?"

Bill looked at Charlie as seriously as he could and laid out his plan.

He prayed his dreams were right.

1990s

CHAPTER IX

FLOWIN' BETTER

"DON'T YOU EVER FUCKING CRY, BOBBY!"

BOBBY STOOD IN the woods beside the parking lot, swallowed by darkness, surveying his night-time surroundings.

He'd witnessed The Void again.

Inside his car.

He'd witnessed The Void and entered it and *touched it* again.

The Void...

The Void was beautiful and still and perfect.

But this time, inside The Void, he'd witnessed something else:

The Joining.

Little Stacey, the *real* Little Stacey, melded with the doll. They had *Joined*. Only for a moment, but a *glorious* moment. Like a miracle sent from God and Heaven. He had to see if he could conjure it again—The Void, The Joining in The Void. He *had* to.

Not as good as the real thing, but close enough.

For now.

Besides, Little Stacey was probably so dang hungry she needed more.

More feedin'.

Heavy panting filled his mind—as if his brain breathed.

Had to feed her again.

Touch The Void.

Witness The Joining.

The Void.

The Joining.

The Void.

Little Stacey.

I'm gonna feed you again, Little Stacey!

But first, he had to make sure this place was safe.

Just enough light glowed from the highway to see, provided he stayed on the edge of the woods, deep enough so passing drivers wouldn't spot him. Didn't want to go too far in, though; might be critters out. Summertime in Alabama brought some nasty ones, too.

Could've fed her in the car again, but it got *all over* the steering wheel, his legs, even dripped onto the seat. Pain in the dang ol' butt cleanin' all that up.

Fed her a lot, though.

And he felt proud of that.

Real proud.

A man's always proud when he feeds the people he loves.

He glanced around, scanning for critters. Risky feedin' her away from the security of his car, but required less cleanup. Besides, feedin' her standin' up felt better—that's how he'd fed the *real* Little Stacey. Her breakfast just flowed better standin' up.

A mosquito buzzed near his ear. He smacked it against the side of his head, pale moonlight revealing black and red smeared across his palm. If he did start feedin' her in the woods, it'd need to be earlier next time. Maybe pick up bug spray at Walmart, too. Couldn't have skeeters interruptin' Little Stacey's breakfast.

He turned his back to the highway, unbuckled his belt and dropped his pants—this time keeping his tighty-whities on and pulling his penis through the fly. A precaution in case someone pulled up. This way, he'd look like he was just takin' a dang ol' leak, and nobody would see his naked buttcheeks.

He took another careful look around—*just in case.*

Lotsa trees.

Grass and weeds pokin' out the dirt.

Scraggly bushes here and there.

Didn't *seem* like there was no critters around, and definitely no peo—

What?

What was that?

Somethin' on the side of that tree...

Squinting, he caught movement in the faint glow of moonlight and passing traffic. He hobbled toward it, his pants around his ankles restricting his steps.

Just a centipede.

A big sucker, too.

That's alright—lil' ol' centipede wouldn't hurt nothin'.

He touched the back of the centipede, letting its smooth, armor-like scales run across his fingertips as it crawled up the tree.

Critters didn't bother him none. Just had to be careful of 'em, give 'em space. Most critters feared you more than you feared them.

Show 'em some dang ol' respect, and they showed ya some, too.

Critters were simple to understand, with simple needs, unlike people with their words and feelings and things they said and didn't say, and sometimes what they *didn't* say was more important than what they said and you never knew what people really meant when they used their words, their dang ol', dang ol' useless words.

He glanced behind him at the highway.

Those people out there can't see me...

...can they?

It'd look mighty strange to see a full-grown man standin' around in his tighty-whities.

Maybe best to move in a little deeper.

Just in case.

His belt buckle jangled against the ground as he hobbled forward. The underbrush grew thicker and the forest darker with every step. Low-growing briars snagged his pants.

"Dangit!"

Bad idea.

Too much underbrush this deep in the woods, and too dark to see, anyway. He had to *see* Little Stacey when feedin' her.

His pants ripped as he pulled them from the briars.

"Dang ol' briars..."

He hobbled back to the edge of the woods and peered out. Cars sped by on the highway—no way they'd see him. Likely nobody would come into this little parking lot at night, either. Wasn't even sure why the lot was here; restaurants and gas stations were on the other side of the highway, and nothing nearby.

Nobody to bother him out here.

Not his mean ol' boss, Mr. Stannis.

Not his co-workers.

Not nobody.

He turned toward the darkness of the forest, his gaze falling on the Barbie doll faintly illuminated by the highway's glow. Still had some breakfast crusted on her face.

You so purty...

Could still see her eyes, though—

—peerin' through her breakfast.

Purty and sweet...

His hand trembled as he brought the doll's crusty face to his mouth.

And special...

He kissed it, just like he'd kissed Little Stacey's forehead before she ate her breakfast, before she ate it all, every time, like a good girl.

I love you, Little Stacey...

He sank deep into her plastic eyes.

Those eyes...

Slowly, he began stroking himself.

I love you so dang much...

Faster.

Harder.

(littlestaceylittlestaceylittlestacey)

A mosquito landed on his hand.

(i'm gonna feed you)

He'd let it live.

(eat it all)

He'd feed it.

(like a good girl!)

Just like he fed Little Stacey.

1970s

CHAPTER X

EASY-PEASY

"Money for our pockets, candy for our noses…"

ROY JAMESON'S COKE had been hidden inside the "F" encyclopedia, which Bill and Charlie could only surmise was for *"fucked up"*—as in when Roy wanted to get *fucked up* on drugs and shit, he reached for that good ol' "F" volume.

Ol' Roy wasn't in the greatest of moods when Charlie arrived, but Charlie, as promised, still managed to get him to look at his car and shoot the shit for a full thirty minutes or so. He was also careful to never enter Roy's house—not even when Roy finally got in a good talkin' mood and invited him inside. Two weeks later, when Bill's dreams had shown him Roy would head to the bars, they snuck in through the bathroom window Bill had unlocked from the inside during Charlie's earlier visit.

Roy's bag of coke turned out to be almost as large as the entire fuckin' encyclopedia, and nearly full to the brim, so likely recently purchased, too. Poor ol' Roy probably threw a fit when he realized it was gone, but he hadn't come after Charlie, so must've suspected someone else.

That suited Bill and Charlie just fine.

So what if he accused some other dude and fucked him up over some bullshit?

Not their problem.

Didn't give a fuck.

But they also knew it wouldn't be safe robbin' ol' Roy again.

At least, not for a while.

***

The next few weeks went by like Charlie had said: money for their pockets, candy for their noses.

Snorted half, sold the rest.

("we are so fuckin' badass, man!")

Felt like badass outlaws.

("we gotta do it again!")

Felt like cowboys.

("find more motherfuckers to rob!")

Deep down inside, though—

("money in our pockets!")

("candy up our noses!")

—something told Bill it wouldn't stay easy.

1970s

CHAPTER XI

A GLIMMER OF DESTINY

Tommy was eight when his older brother killed himself.

He'd taken their dad's pistol, put it in his mouth,

and pulled the trigger. There was no note.

"Mikey..."

"DO YOU SEE it, Tommy?"
    (mikey?)
    (is that you?)
"Do you see *it?"*
    (i see it, mikey)
    (it's beautiful)
    (god, it's so beautiful)
    (but wha—)
"You've gotta find *it..."*
    (first tell me why)
    (tell me why you did it, mikey)
"Find it, Tommy..."
    (it was the pills, wasn't it?)
    (the pills, *the pills* the doctors fucking gave you they fucked you up
and—)

"FIND IT, TOMMY."

"THE TEMPLE."

1970s

CHAPTER XII

THE SMOKETOWN BOYS

Slowly, Tommy began to act like Mikey, think

like Mikey, and then, by degrees—

he became Mikey.

The leader of the new Smoketown Boys.

TOMMY GLICK STOOD in the front yard of the Smokehouse. He tilted his head back and gazed at the moon. A cool breeze caressed his cheek.

Why do my thoughts drift like that?

To a fucking "temple?"

And to Mikey, Mikey's voice telling me to fi—

A cold shiver ran up his spine.

No.

Fuck it.

Gotta focus on my Boys.

And our mission, our destin—

"Hey, Tommy!"

Larry Knowles stepped out of the Smokehouse and strode down the incline of the front lawn toward him.

"You alright, man?" asked Larry. "You been standin' out here forever."

Tommy craned his neck to meet Larry's eyes. One of the tallest dudes in school, and like many who stood freakishly tall, had a long face to match, hence the nickname "Larry Longface." Tommy never called him that, though, and always reassured him it wasn't *that* long.

That's what bros were for.

"Just thinkin' about shit..." said Tommy. He patted his pockets. "Got any Monkey on ya? Smoke with me before we go inside."

"Alright," said Larry. "Everybody's waitin' at the table, though. Jack's gettin' pissed."

"Good," said Tommy. "Let him."

Typical of Jack to get all pissy about bein' late and shit. But that was okay—the Boys needed a guy like Jack. Good for squad balance.

Larry opened a tin of rolled cigarettes packed with Monkey weed. Crickets chirped as they lit their cigs in silence. Tommy brought his to his mouth and inhaled, savoring the taste: pleasantly pungent, slightly skunky, followed by the smokey undertones of tobacco. Like inhaling the essence of a forest—

—a *dank* forest.

"Did I ever tell ya," asked Tommy, "that it was Mikey's idea to cut weed with tobacco?"

Larry exhaled smoke. "Nah, always thought it was your idea."

"He was probably bullshittin' me," said Tommy, "but he said he named it after some dude up in Hazard." He blew smoke upward. "That had a pet monkey."

Larry's eyes widened. *"A pet monkey?"*

"Yep," said Tommy. "Called him Monkey Man."

"Is that even legal?" asked Larry. "Can you even buy monkeys in Kentucky?"

"Probably not," said Tommy. "Probably illegal as shit. But he said the Monkey Man-dude lived like a hermit, out in the middle of nowhere. Had a shit-ton of money, and a shit-ton of drugs, and one of his big secrets was that he lived with a monkey."

"Lived with a monkey?" asked Larry. "Inside his house, in secret and shit? Like his roommate?"

"Guess so..." said Tommy. "His secret bro."

Larry drew from his cig, letting the smoke curl upward. "How'd Mikey even know a dude like that? Especially up in the middle of nowhere in fuckin' Hazard?"

"Dunno how they first met," said Tommy. "But Mikey said he taught him a lot. About drugs and shit. Who knows, maybe he's the one who taught Mikey to cut weed with tobacco. And that's why Mikey called it Monkey."

"Dude," said Larry, "I gotta meet this Monkey Man now. I've *always* wanted to play with a monkey. How cool would it be to smoke with one? And just chill with him?"

"It would be cool, wouldn't it?" asked Tommy. "To smoke Monkey, with a fuckin' m—"

A cold, vivid image flashed through Tommy's mind: a chimp in a party hat.

What the...

The chimp bared its teeth, mimicking a smile, but those bloodshot eyes weren't smiling. They seemed—

"You okay, dude?" asked Larry.

Tommy pushed the creepy chimp image away.

"Anyway, pretty sure Mikey was fuckin' with me. There's no way some dude up in Hazard has a pet monkey."

"Wasn't fuckin' with ya about the Horse People, though," said Larry. "They turned out just like he'd said."

Goosebumps prickled across Tommy's arms.

The Horse People were just like Mikey claimed.

Maybe even—

Jack Kindley's voice rang out across the lawn.

"Hey, y'all!"

He poked his red-haired, freckled face out the Smokehouse door.

"You're late! We're waitin' at the table, like we're supposed to!"

"Gotta wait for Mouse!" said Tommy. "He's always late! So we'll be right on time!"

Mitchell Mouse's voice echoed from inside.

"Fuck you, Tommy! I been waitin', too!"

Tommy smiled. "We'll be there in a second!"

Jack didn't budge. "How long's a second?"

"Just give us a few minutes!" said Tommy.

"How long's a few minutes?" asked Jack.

"Dude!" said Tommy.

Jack sighed and slammed the Smokehouse door.

Larry's long face broke into a grin. "That's the captain of the chess club, for ya."

"At least he cares about bein' on time and shit," said Tommy. "Unlike Mouse."

"Mouse was actually on time tonight," said Larry.

"Oh," said Tommy. "Guess I'm the only asshole who's late, then."

Not good for the leader of the Smoketown Boys to be the only one late to a Table Meeting, but fuck it—once couldn't hurt.

Larry flicked ash onto the ground. "What's up, man? You need to talk about some shit?"

Tommy blew smoke out the side of his mouth.

Larry could tell.

Larry could always tell when he had shit on his mind.

He considered revealing his dreams about that fucking *"temple"* or whatever, but—no.

All just bullshit.

Maybe from smokin' too much.

Had to focus on his Boys, their mission.

He removed his cap and stared at it. An outline of a crow adorned the front.

Mikey...

Guide me, Mikey...

"...you think we can do it, Larry?" asked Tommy.

Help me make the right decisions...

"...be even bigger than them..."

Tell me what to do...

"...and dominate the *whole* fuckin' Tri?"

Larry's eyes sparkled in the moonlight. "Is that what we're goin' for now? Not just Crow, but the whole of Tri?"

"Might as well," said Tommy. He put his cap back on and took a hit of his cig. "Who's gonna stop us?"

Tommy looked up the slope of the lawn toward the Smokehouse at the summit. Lava lamps glowed in the windows. Used to be Grandpa's place, then passed to Mikey after Grandpa died, then to Tommy after Mikey died.

A house earned through death.

Didn't have two stories or a basement, but more than big enough for a squad to call headquarters. Even had two garages. Bigger than any other squad's house, except maybe rich kids in Zion. But even they didn't have a whole place to themselves; just used their daddies' houses while they were on vacation.

We got the house, the parties, and the drugs...

Just like Mikey and his Boys...

"Mikey and the old Smoketown Boys," said Tommy. "They came close. They were *almost* Kings of the fuckin' Tri, they almost..."

His voice cracked.

"...if Mikey hadn't..."

He shook his head and took a hit of his cig.

I can be bigger than him.

Better than him.

And so can my Boys.

He locked eyes with Larry.

"Not just Crow."

"The whole fuckin' Tri."

***

Jack and Mouse already sat at the Smokehouse Table. Jack looked up from his notebook and frowned while Mouse flexed his right bicep, admiring it.

"Look who saw fit to join us," said Mouse.

"Sorry guys," Tommy crossed the the living room. "Larry's outside pissin'. Arms lookin' good, Muscle Man."

Mouse nodded, gazing at his bicep.

Mitchell "Muscle Man" Mouse ranked as the shortest dude in the Boys—shorter than even the Possibles—but by far the most ripped. Anytime he got pissed, complimentin' his physique usually calmed his ass down.

Mouse asked, "Why we gotta have meetin's like this again?"

"'Cause I wanna do stuff more business-like," said Tommy, sitting at the head of the table. "If we're gonna increase our members and fuckin' dominate, we gotta start runnin' shit legit."

He considered adding, *"And because Mikey ran meetings like this, too,"* but decided against it.

"So why you late, then?" asked Mouse. "How's that for bein' 'legit'?"

"That's my bad," said Tommy.

("the temple")

"I was high as fuck,"

("find it, tommy")

and starin' at the stars and shit."

("temple above all.")

He squeezed his eyes shut, then opened them.

Maybe I'm smokin' too much...

Mouse said he liked to smoke and stare at the stars, too, and returned to flexing his biceps.

Jack folded his arms. "Tommy, as leader of the Smoketown Boys, I'd like to think you'd—"

"Said I'm sorry," said Tommy, both annoyed and appreciative of Jack's commitment to follow the rules. "It won't happen again."

After Larry returned and everyone sat in their respective seats at the table, Tommy rapped his knuckles on its hard oak surface *(knock-knock!)*.

"I hereby start the meeting of the Smoketown Boys."

Mouse snickered. "What are you, a judge or somethin'?"

Tommy shrugged. "Just thought I'd start shit more formally."

"A gavel would be nice," said Jack.

"You kiddin' me?" asked Mouse. *"A gavel?"*

"A gavel would be pretty cool," said Larry. "Make it feel more official and shit."

"What're we turnin' into now?" asked Mouse. "The fuckin' chess club? Or the debate team?"

"What's wrong with that?" asked Jack, the captain of both.

Jack and Mouse started bitchin' at each other while Larry poked fun at both. Tommy let it proceed for a while, as it entertained him, then rapped his knuckles on the table again—harder this time *(knock-knock!)*.

"Alright, alright," said Tommy. "I honestly think a gavel would be cool, too." Mouse groaned. "But we got real shit to talk about today. First order of business."

Tommy paused—he didn't know if it was appropriate to say *"first order of business"* in this context or not, but it sounded good.

"Jack," he said, "you said you had an idea to run these meetin's better?"

Jack's freckled face grew serious. He clasped his hands together.

"Robert's Rules of Order."

The table fell silent.

"The fuck's that?" asked Mouse.

"It's how all meetin's are ran," said Jack. "Not only in clubs, but in companies, too. *It's how you get shit done."*

Jack held his notebook high, displaying the cover labeled *"SMOKETOWN BOYS – OFFICIAL MEETING MINUTES"* for all to see.

"You're fuckin' kidding me," said Mouse. "I thought you were writin' in your diary or somethin.'"

"Meeting minutes," said Jack. "Not a diary. This'll help us keep track of what we voted on and discussed. Our history."

"What if someone finds that shit?" asked Mouse.

"They won't," said Jack, his face making it clear: *I hide shit real good.*

"I'm fine if Jack wants to take notes," said Tommy. "In the future, shit might get more complicated. Might help us keep track of everything."

Jack nodded, looking satisfied.

"Anyway," said Tommy, "tell us how these 'Rules of Order' say we should run this."

"Well..." said Jack, writing in his notebook. "...since we only got four official members, and we don't got formal officers yet..." He glanced up. "We can skip straight to votin'."

"What do we gotta vote on?" asked Mouse. "We already voted on the next Smokehouse Party, and—"

Larry raised his hand. "I wanna vote on somethin'."

"Larry, go ahead," said Tommy. They didn't have a hand-raising policy in place, but he liked that—Larry raising his hand. Kept shit disciplined and efficient.

"We should make the next party BYOB," said Larry. "It costs a lotta Smokehouse funds to buy booze, and there's people who come to our parties and drink all our shit, but don't even buy no Monkey."

"We could start chargin' people," said Tommy. "Get the Possibles to collect the money, and—"

"I'm against that," said Mouse. "If we don't have a fuck-ton of alcohol for chicks to drink, for free, then our parties'll suck dick."

Everyone agreed that parties without free alcohol for girls would suck major dick.

"Okay," said Larry. "How about a compromise? We only charge *dudes* who come to our parties."

Jack and Mouse nodded and said they were down with that.

Tommy asked, "How we gonna keep track of who paid, though?"

Larry's long face drooped. "Uhh..."

Silence fell across the table.

"I got it," said Jack, raising his index finger. "We get the Possibles to collect the money, but we get'em to like, tie ribbons or somethin' on dudes' arms who paid."

"Ribbons?" asked Mouse. "That's kinda gay."

Jack threw his hands up. "What should we use then, Mouse?"

"Anything but ribbons," said Mouse. "That's about as—"

Tommy rapped his knuckles *(knock-knock!)*. He liked doing that. It felt cool and powerful.

"Ribbons *are* kinda gay," said Tommy. "Maybe we can think of somethin' else. I dunno, maybe have the Possibles make paper bracelets or somethin'."

Everyone agreed that paper bracelets seemed cooler and less gay than ribbons, except Mouse, who felt they ranked about the same.

"Alright," said Tommy. "Let's go with paper bracelets. All in favor of Larry's motion?"

Tommy, Larry and Jack raised their hands. Mouse shrugged and semi-raised his, too.

"Passed!" said Tommy. He rapped his knuckles once *(knock!)*, then leaned back in his seat.

Was this how Mikey ran his meetings?

Wonder what they talked about...

"I'd like to bring another motion to the floor," said Jack.

"What 'floor'?" asked Mouse. "The fuck you talkin' about?"

"Robert's Rules of Order!" said Jack.

"You keep sayin' that," said Mouse, "but do these things even exist?"

"First time I heard of 'em," said Larry.

The meeting erupted into commotion as Mouse and Larry accused Jack of makin' shit up, but after Tommy rapped his knuckles *(knock-knock-knock!)* everyone quieted the fuck down.

"Jack," said Tommy. "You were sayin'?"

"Like I was sayin'," said Jack, "before I was *interrupted.*" He glared at Mouse, who flipped him the bird. "I make a motion to change our Monkey formula. Increase the amount of tobacco we cut it with to straight-up *maximize* our profits."

"By how much?" asked Larry.

"As much as the market can tolerate," said Jack.

"Fuck's that mean?" asked Mouse.

Jack shook his head. "I dunno how to say it simpler than that, Mouse. Maybe you should read a book sometime, try learnin' new vocab—"

"What he means," said Larry, "is continually fuckin' increase the amount of tobacco we cut our weed with, up until the point people start bitchin'."

"Okay," said Mouse. "And then what do we do? If people start bitchin'?"

"Then we reverse course a little," said Jack. "Until we get the ratio *just right,* so we can have the highest tobacco ratio possible without affectin' our prices or how much we sell."

Mouse stroked his chin, deep in thought—like he actually got it.

Tommy got it, too—in fact, Jack had pitched his idea to him earlier, behind the scenes, and he'd already given his blessing. But he had to *act* like he hadn't heard it yet and avoid seeming too pro-Jack—something that would piss Mouse off *("You always do what Jack says!")* and possibly even make Larry jealous.

Tommy asked Jack, "How much you think we could increase it by? To see how much the market can 'tolerate'?"

Jack's eyes lit up, revealing a flurry of calculations.

A smile crept across Tommy's face.

Every squad needed a guy like Jack. The accountant. The CFO. The math whiz who calculated how much they could sell and how high to price it. Even drew line graphs once. Now *that* was fucking impressive. That was when Tommy knew they needed Jack.

"Fifty-fifty," said Jack.

Larry whistled. "That's a big change. People'll notice for sure."

Mouse furrowed his brow. "But it'd more than *double* our profit..."

"It would," said Tommy.

Mouse glanced up. "Okay, I'm actually for tryin' this. That's actually a good idea, Jack."

"Thanks, Mouse," said Jack. "Glad you learned simple math."

Everyone snickered except Mouse, whose face darkened.

"Alright," said Tommy. "But let's do it in gradual stages. Slowly ramp the amount of tobacco we cut it with over the next month or so, so hopefully people won't notice as much. All in favor?"

Everyone raised their hands.

"Passed!" said Tommy. He rapped his knuckles *(knock!)*.

Feels good—gettin' shit passed.

Makin' things happen...

"Okay, King of Dorks," said Mouse. "That was actually a good idea. What's your pussy-ass 'guidelines' say we do next?"

"The Rules!" said Jack. *"Robert's Rules of Order!"*

Mouse flipped Jack the bird.

Jack scowled. "Maybe if you traded some muscle in, for brains, then you'd—"

"Just tell us what's next, Jack," said Tommy.

"The Rules state," said Jack, "that if there's no more new business, then we share announcements and news and stuff. Then we're done."

"Any announcements?" asked Tommy.

The Boys looked at each other.

Mouse raised his hand.

"Mouse," said Tommy.

"Me and Lacey are fuckin' now," said Mouse.

His face grew somber.

"Like, *a lot.*"

Tommy nodded. "I think we all know that, Mouse. Any *real* annou—"

"I mean," said Mouse, "we're *seriously* fuckin'. She's gonna let me do anal."

Jack groaned.

Larry raised an eyebrow. "Really?"

Tommy's interest, too, had piqued.

"Yep," said Mouse. "Already stuck two fingers up in there, and—"

"Come on, man!" said Jack. His freckled face blazed red, matching his hair. "Tommy, can we move on?"

Poor Jack. Everyone had taken their turns with Lacey, but Jack remained the only one who seemed pissed she'd started fuckin' Mouse on the regular, exclusively and shit. Not like her and Mouse were a *real* thing—they were just fuckin'—but the sudden lack of easy pussy must've rubbed him wrong. Either that, or Jack actually *liked* Lacey, and—

Nah.

Smart chicks, like those in the chess club, probably suited him better.

Just mad he lost a place to nut...

"So even though," said Mouse, "we're like, seriously fuckin' a lot, we ain't like...super serious and shit."

Jack's face flushed a deeper red. Maybe Mouse talked like this to get under his skin—or, he was just bein' Mouse, and didn't give a fuck.

"Gotcha, Mouse," said Tommy. "She's still technically public property, then. Any other—"

"I mean," said Mouse, "I don't think *she's* gonna fuck anybody else. She wouldn't do that. That's *my* pussy, now."

He glanced at Jack.

"But," he said, "if y'all know any girls who might be interested in me, don't be sayin' that Lacey is like, my 'girlfriend' and shit."

"Understood," said Tommy. "Any other annou—"

"You let those ladies know," said Mouse, rising and pounding his chest, "that Mitchell Mouse is single, available, and ready to bone!"

Tommy and Larry chuckled.

Jack didn't.

"Or date and shit," said Mouse, sitting back down.

"Gotcha, Mouse," said Tommy. "Any other announcements? Or news? That don't involve fuckin'?"

The Boys fell quiet. Mouse resumed flexing his biceps, occasionally glancing at Jack, who pensively jotted down meeting minutes.

Larry raised his hand. "I got news. About one of Tommy's favorite people."

"Who?" asked Tommy.

"Bill Cunningham."

Jack stopped writing.

Mouse looked up from his arms.

Tommy's skin turned hot.

("we just went as friends, tommy!")

("we didn't do anything!")

("stop asking me ab—")

His whole body stiffened, like a slab of iron.

"What *about* Bill-fucking-Cunningham?"

1970s

CHAPTER XIII

THE SMOKETOWN BOYS, PART II

"I love you, Samantha..."

"...and I want you to tell me the truth."

("I SWEAR TO god, samantha!")
 ("if you did somethin' with him...")
 ("i said we didn't, tommy!")
 ("please stop asking me ab—")
Blood pounded in Tommy's ears.

"Bill Cunningham," he said, "is sellin' coke?"

"Yep," said Larry. "Him and Young Charlie. Out of Young's house."

"Out of Young's fuckin' *house?*" asked Tommy.

"Yep," said Larry. "Makin' it their little headquarters, callin' it somethin' in Spanish. Forgot what."

Tommy took a deep breath.

("swear to me, samantha")
("fuckin' swear that you didn't—")
He shook his head.

No, no...

That shit's in the past now...

Gotta focus on business.

Mouse asked, "How's he sellin' shit outta his house like that? What about his parents?"

Jack stroked his chin. "Might be workin' with Young's dad. Heard he's a dealer."

"Yep," said Larry. "I thought the same. But his dad's in jail for cocaine or somethin', so now him and Bill got the whole place to themselves and throw little coke parties and shit."

Tommy drummed his fingers on the table. He'd met Young's dad a few times, back when him and Young used to smoke together. Pretty much like an older version of Charlie, sans the *español.*

"His dad's been in jail before," said Tommy. "And if he's back in again, he probably ain't gettin' out for a while."

"What about his mom?" asked Mouse.

Tommy shrugged. "They're divorced and shit. She don't live with him."

Jack jotted in his notebook, then glanced up. "They ain't sellin' weed, are they?"

"Nope," said Larry. "Not as far as I know. Just coke."

"Good," said Tommy. "Better not be tryin' to compete with us..."

He gazed out the window, straining to discern the distant treeline through the dark.

Bill.

Fucking.

Cunningham.

Even though him and Samantha had patched things up, he still wanted to beat that dude's ass. *Teach him a fucking lesson.* If he dared intrude on Boys' business, that'd be just the reason he needed.

Jack twirled his pencil. "Where you think they get their coke? Think they make more profit than we do with Monkey?"

Two very Jack-like questions: one, who's their supplier, and two, what's their profit margin. Two very excellent Jack-like questions.

"Profit margin's probably higher with coke," said Tommy. "Especially if they're cuttin' it with shit. But it's also way tougher to get."

"Sheriff's son, sellin' coke," said Mouse. "Outta his best friend's house, whose daddy happens to be in jail for possessin' coke. Whaddaya know."

"For all we know," said Larry, "Bill's dad's fuckin' in on it. Gettin' some of the profit."

"He could be their supplier," said Jack. "When he busts people for coke, he gives it to Bill and Young to sell, and they all split the profits."

Tommy considered Jack's theory. He'd seen Sheriff Cunningham a few times, and heard shit about him. Seemed like a hard-ass dude. Not the type to sell drugs through his son.

But, you never know.

"I've never even tried coke," said Mouse. "Been wantin' to, though."

"Man, I wanna try some," said Jack, "but I don't think my heart could handle it. Doctor said I can't even have caffeine."

"You ain't missin' much," said Larry. "Me and Tommy tried it a couple of times, and it ain't nothin' to write home about. Expensive as shit, even for a tiny bit. Don't even last that long. Not like weed. At least you get your money's worth with weed."

Tommy agreed. Never felt super-impressed with coke. The high didn't feel that high and only pumped him up for thirty minutes or so, usually just leaving him wanting more coke.

Fuck that.

That's the shit that makes you an addict, fuckin' with hard drugs like that. The buzz and the body high *(oh, the body high…)* from good weed could last a whole day, easy—sometimes even longer. He'd stick with weed over coke any day.

"If they're not gettin' their product from Bill's dad," said Jack, "then the question is, where they gettin' it from?"

Mouse tilted his head. "And how they got that much scratch? To buy enough coke to start sellin' it like that?"

"Might've been fronted to'em," said Larry.

The Boys started comparing the relative cost of coke against weed and how much they could sell coke for and what they could cut it with ("I heard baby laxative works real fuckin' good").

"Hey Tommy," said Mouse. "Didn't you used to be friends with Young?"

"We used to smoke together," said Tommy. "Way back in the day."

"What happened?" asked Mouse.

"Nothin' really 'happened,'" said Tommy. "Not like we had a big fallin' out or somethin'. He just started hangin' with that Bill Cunningham bitch and I started hangin' with Larry."

"I honestly never cared for either of those guys," said Larry. "Especially Young. Always speakin' Spanish and shit, like he's a fuckin' spic."

"I thought he was part Mexican," said Mouse.

"Nope," said Jack. "I thought that, too, but he's just a normal white dude."

"Annoyin' is what he is," said Larry. "Goddamn full of himself."

"He is kinda full of himself," said Jack. "Always speakin' Spanish to girls in the halls, actin' like he's somethin' else."

"I dunno," said Mouse. "If he ain't part Mexican, it *is* kinda cool he speaks Spanish that fuckin' good. Way cooler than playin' chess, or bein' on the debate team and shit."

Jack took issue with that comment and an argument erupted. Tommy reclined in his chair, considering things.

Honestly, he didn't give a fuck about Young either way anymore.

Yeah, they used to be friends.

Yeah, they used to smoke and chill together.

But that felt like forever ago, before he'd even started The Boys. If Young wanted to sell coke from his dad's house, fine by him. As long as he didn't sell weed.

But sellin' with his best pal, Bill-fuckin'-Cunningham?

Throwin' little coke parties, tryin' to increase their rep across the Tri?

Like a two-person squad now?

That irked Tommy.

Everything irked Tommy about Bill-fucking-Cunningham. Never liked that motherfucker, even before he—

(*"we just as went friends, tommy!"*)

(*"nothing happened!"*)

"...well, maybe he *is* part Mexican, then," said Mouse. "Let's ask Tommy. Tommy, you sure Young ain't part—"

"He ain't," said Tommy. "Just into Spanish and foreign languages, all that shit."

"Told ya," said Jack.

"Whatever," said Mouse. "The fact that he ain't got no Mexican in him but still speaks Spanish that good makes him cooler *and* smarter than you, Jack."

"Go fuck yourself, *Mitchey Mouse,*" said Jack.

Mouse resumed flexing his biceps, unperturbed. "Hey, Tommy, since you used to hang with Young and stuff, and if y'all don't got no beef, maybe call him up? Find out where him and Cunningham are gettin' their coke?"

Tommy's tone sharpened. "And why the fuck would I do that, Mouse?"

Mouse, Larry and Jack's eyes widened.

An uneasy silence fell.

"Chill," said Mouse. "No need to get pissy 'cause we brought up Cunningham."

"I'm not 'pissy' 'cause y'all brought up Cunningham," said Tommy. "I just don't see why I need to—"

Jack held out his hand. "We been talkin', Tommy."

Tommy narrowed his eyes.

Oh, great...

This 'we been talkin' shit again...

"Oh, yeah?" asked Tommy. "And what about this time?"

"Diversification," said Jack.

Larry's long face tensed up with worry.

Jack continued. "We been improvin' shit a lot. Possibles are sellin' Monkey to underclassmen, even makin' progress with the middle-schoolers. And we're finally startin' to run our business, like a business."

He clasped his hands together.

"But businesses need to *diversify,* Tommy."

"Burger King don't sell just burgers," said Mouse.

"That's right, Mouse," said Jack. "And Dairy Queen don't sell just chicken strip baskets."

"Or just ice cream," said Mouse.

"Or just ice cream," said Jack. "They sell both."

"They sell a lotta shit," said Mouse.

"They sell a lotta shit," said Jack, looking annoyed. "Anyway, we gotta do the same. We gotta offer a *variety* of products to our customers."

"I told y'all," said Tommy, "we can get new shit from the Horse People. As long as we keep sellin' their shit and buildin' up trust. Might even give us a new strain of weed next time, it's gonna be a different color and shit, like—"

"That's the thing," said Jack. "We need to diversify our *suppliers,* too. Not only rely on the..."

He grimaced, as if a sour taste filled his mouth.

"...Horse People..."

Jack had always been wary of the Horse People, likely creeped-the-fuck-out by the stories Tommy and Larry had shared. Probably another reason he felt so keen on "diversifying" their suppliers.

Mouse nodded. "I actually agree with Jack. It'd be good to start sellin' other products, and get new suppliers, too."

Tommy clenched his jaw. Mouse rarely agreed with Jack on anything, which meant they'd definitely been talkin'—and likely for a while.

"Larry," asked Tommy, "what do you think?"

Larry paused, carefully choosing his words.

"...might be an idea worth explorin'."

Tommy closed his eyes and rubbed his temples.

So they've been talkin' with Larry, too...

Behind my back...

Just waitin' to spring this shit on me...

Politickin' behind the scenes was bound to happen, though—likely even more as The Boys grew in number.

"Larry," said Tommy, "you just said you don't even *like* coke that much. And Mouse, you ain't even tried it, and Jack, you *can't* try it or you'll have a fuckin' heart attack. So why y'all so intent on sellin' that shit now?"

Larry's long face grew apprehensive. "I mean, I do think diversifyin' might be a good idea..."

Jack nodded. "A whole new revenue stream."

"And coke is expensive as fuck," said Mouse. "That's why I ain't tried it yet. And who knows, maybe I won't like it. But either way, I'd love to sell that shit. Especially to rich kids."

Tommy reclined in his chair and stared at the ceiling.

They had a point.

Coke *could* be sold for a higher margin than Monkey.

But it felt...wrong.

Mikey never touched that shit, and none of his Boys did, either. Not hard drugs, not shit that'd make you an addict, not—

Larry cleared his throat. "I know you wanna do things the way Mikey did."

Jack and Mouse's faces softened.

Tommy looked away.

("find it, tommy...")

("the temple...")

"And I know," said Larry, "Mikey was against coke and drugs that weren't all-natural and shit."

Tommy nodded.

Mikey didn't even like Tylenol.

"But," said Larry, "if you really want us to dominate the Tri, not just Crow but the whole fuckin' Tri—"

"—then we have to challenge ourselves," said Jack. "To do shit even *he* didn't do."

Tommy sighed.

They're right...

They're fuckin' right...

After a long silence, he finally spoke.

"Okay," he said. "Here's what I'll do."

He turned to his Boys.

"I'll bring it up with the Horse People again," he said. "And even *if* they give us new product, like coke and shit, we can still scout for new suppliers, check out big cities like y'all been askin'. Sound good?"

His Boys said it did, and they immediately began discussing options.

"Let's check out Lexington or Louisville..."

"I wanna go to Nashville..."

"We could go to Alabama again..."

"Nah, Alabama's too far, and we only bought..."

Tommy focused on the darkness outside the window.

Working with new suppliers carried risks.

As fucked-up as the Horse People were, at least they proved reliable—high-quality weed with no hassles over quantity, either. Even fronted shit sometimes, when Smokehouse funds ran low. Any new supplier had to have quality, quantity, *and* be trustworthy. Since Mikey had trusted the Horse People, so did he.

Mikey...

He removed his cap and stared at it.

Did you ever try buyin' from random-ass dudes?

In cities like Nashville?

He tried to see Mikey, hear his voice, but couldn't. Didn't matter—he already knew the answer:

Doubtful.

Fuckin' doubtful Mikey ever tried shit like that.

High chance of gettin' ripped off, or worse.

Tommy put his cap back on and drummed his fingers on the table. Seemed like his Boys had decided they'd check out either Louisville or Nashville next—neither of which excited him.

Lots of risks, lots of risks...

But better than the alternative.

No way would he buy from *anybody* squaddin' up with Bill-fucking-Cunningham.

("did you fuck him, samantha?")

("did you suck his dick?")

("tommy, please, we didn't do—")

No fucking way.

1990s

CHAPTER XIV

AWAKE

"I get my country fuckin', if that's what ya mean..."

RHONDA AWOKE INSTANTLY, craving the feeling of a gun in her hand. The first few rays of sunlight peeked from the curtain sides. Unless truly exhausted or hungover or fucked-up from drugs, she almost always woke at sunrise, gripping her gun.

My gun...

Where is it?

She opened and closed her hand, squeezing the nothingness in her palm like the bulb of a blood pressure gauge, yearning for the cold heaviness the gun provided.

She always slept with her gun in hand.

Always.

Ever since the blue-eyed boy.

She wanted to shoot something. *God, she wanted to shoot something.* Even before she slept with a gun, even before *him,* she always woke wanting to shoot something. Likely due to the habit Daddy had instilled in her, now ingrained as a core part of her being. Pretty much all habits eventually become part of you, part of your core if you stuck to'em long en—

The voices.

Another thing absent this morning.

The voices she usually heard upon waking.

Sometimes Daddy's.

Sometimes Darla's.

Sometimes *his.*

Sometimes voices from her past—some pleasant, some haunting, some beautiful, some terrifying, some she wanted to remember and some she wished to forget.

And, occasionally, the voices of people she'd never even met.

(you sure about that, rhonda?)

(you sure never met them?)

Those voices remained silent this morning.

But she felt good this morning. Relaxed.

Why?

Why no yearning for Darla and the good ol'days of tearin' up the Tri? Nor any visions of those awful blue eyes starin' down at her?

Something beside her.

Movement.

Movement beside her.

A barrage of images flashed in her mind like projections on a screen, and it dawned on her why she'd woken up so at ease, gunless.

The dude with the beard.

Sleepin' beside her.

He'd ate it good last night.

Real good.

His beard had tickled.

The bearded dude *(what's his name? Jason? Jim?)* flopped his arm on her shoulder, attempting to caress her neck. She recoiled and his arm to fall to the bed with a lifeless thud. He'd fulfilled his purpose well, and she'd helped him, too—no need for that cuddlin' bullshit.

Rising from bed, she stretched, grabbed her Pantera T-shirt from the floor, and tossed it on. A mirror marked with white residue lay on her dresser.

Whoops...

Almost forgot about his party-powder last night...

After the blue-eyed boy incident, Rhonda had sworn to Daddy she'd refrain from all drugs—sworn to God, in fact—but that Columbia marchin' powder always found its way up her nose somehow. She wasn't like, fuckin', *addicted* and shit, though. Maybe back in her wild days she might've been, a little bit, but now she had it under control. Just had to make sure to ask God for forgiveness later on. God always forgave, and as long as she didn't snort too much of that shit, Daddy would, too.

With a relaxed yawn, she strolled to the window and ripped the curtains open. Sunlight flooded the bedroom and the bearded dude pulled the covers over his head, moaning like a zombie.

"Mmmrrrmmf..."

"Rise and shine, bronco," she said.

Time to wake the fuck up.

***

Rhonda sat on her front porch enjoying her morning Marlboro and Walmart-brand coffee. The Walmart brand, she'd discovered, tasted just as good, if not better, than Folgers and them expensive brands, but cost a full dollar less. She let the coffee sit in her mouth before swallowing, savoring the taste—clear and bitter, with a touch of campfire smokiness. Perfect drink for the mornin'. Only drank it the way God intended, of course—strong and black, free of bullshit.

A cool morning breeze blew, tickling her inner thighs. No houses nearby, so she didn't bother putting on any shorts, just sat outside in her T-shirt, underwear and black stockings.

Wait a minute...

She glanced down.

No underwear, either.

That was fine, though. Breeze felt good down there.

Real good.

Open green fields dotted with patches of woods surrounded her house. Wasn't sure what the fields were actually used for, maybe farmland and shit. Lots of empty fields all over Kentucky. Didn't give a fuck.

A long gravel driveway extended to a seldom-traveled paved road, frequented by only a few cars per day. Even by rural Kentucky standards, she lived out in the sticks. A solid forty-minute drive just to get to town, but only a twenty-minute drive to Daddy's; the short distance of the latter more important in the grand scheme of things.

Leaning back in her rocking chair, she took a puff of her cigarette followed by a sip of coffee. Not much goin' on out here, but that was fine—allowed her to enjoy this mornin' peace, this calm she felt. The calm allowed her to push down the voices, the yearnings. *The blue eyes.* All that shitty stuff she felt and saw and heard when first wakin' up—push it all down and let it the fuck go.

Just let it

("always do what i say, darla!")

the fuck

("you gon' be my bitch?")

go.

Wasn't *all* bad shit every morning. Sometimes good shit, too. Warm memories of Darla, not yearnings (she hated those) but memories of warmth, like comin' in from the cold to a cozy fireplace. Memories of kickin' ass back in the Tri, of runnin' around with the old posse, *her* posse that she was leader of, tearin' shit up wherever they went.

Sometimes she awoke with thoughts of Daddy—both pre- and

post-Accident versions of him. Almost like two different people. Loved'em both, though.

And sometimes, on really good mornings, she awoke with thoughts of their Quest. And The Temple.

The Temple.

A fly buzzed nearby. She blew smoke at it, forcing a rapid retreat.

GB still hadn't given'em a Clue yet.

Past time, now.

Might have to *accelerate* things. Pay him a nice little visit this mornin', say hi and give him s—

SSKSHH!

The sound of her bedroom curtains yanked shut—guess the bearded guy wanted to sleep more.

No surprise there.

Pretty much everyone she'd ever messed around with, guy or girl, required more snooze-time than her afterward. She only needed six hours, max—most nights four or five. How shitty would her life be if she slept eight or nine hours a day?

So much time wasted.

So much of life, wasted.

After crushing her cigarette into the ashtray (a rule inherited from Daddy: never smoked in the house, as she had fuckin' standards), she entered the kitchen and flipped on her mini-TV atop the counter. The news came on—OJ Simpson again. Poor guy. Cops only went after him 'cause he was black; everybody knew that. He absolutely didn't fuckin' do it, and even if he did, bitch probably deserved it.

She turned on cartoons, more for the lively noise filling the house than to actually watch. After tossing back her remaining coffee and pouring a cup for the bearded guy, she returned to the bedroom and ripped the curtains open again.

"I said, 'rise and shine,' bronco!'"

The bearded guy threw the covers over his head, mumbling what sounded like *"Oh, God..."* crossed with a dinosaur yell. She tried to yank the covers from his hands, but he held'em in a death grip.

"Let go of the covers, now!" she said. "Give'em to me!"

With one final yank she pulled the covers off the bed, half-expectin' him to burst into flames like a vampire exposed to sunlight.

"I put coffee on," she said. "You want some?"

The bearded pussy-eater remained silent; his face buried in his pillow.

"Hey," she said, snapping her fingers. *"Hey, boy!"*

Shit...

What's the fucker's name again?

Jim, Jason, Jaimey...

"Oh, God..." he said.

Another cry to God, mixed with a dinosaur yell. Louder this time.

"...what time is it?" he asked.

Time for ya to go.

That's what fuckin' time it is.

"It's mornin' time," she said. "Ya know—wake the fuck up time."

He glanced at the clock on the nightstand.

"Five fifty-two a.m.?"

"Yep, time to go." She whistled at him the way one whistles at their dog. "Come on, boy! Time to get up!"

She wanted him out, but didn't wanna be *rude* about it. After all, he'd eaten it good *(real* good) and she'd need that again.

He pulled the covers back over his head.

"....gimme another hour..."

"Nope," said Rhonda. "Time to wake up!"

You did your job good, boy...

Now leave.

"Hey, boy!" She whistled and snapped. "Boy!"

The bearded pussy-eater remained still as a corpse. Almost like the assholes in the garage after her and Daddy fielded'em.

"I gotta go soon!" she said. "Workin' the breakfast shift this mornin'!"

A lie—her shift started early afternoon, but she didn't wanna tell him she was goin' to shoot. Girls who not only enjoyed shootin' but straight-up fuckin' *excelled* at it captivated most guys, like a flyin' dog might. Didn't need him likin' her *too much* and gettin' all clingy—might even try to tag along, a big no-no. Especially if she planned to pay GB a visit today. Besides, sharin' too many details about herself with her pussy-eaters invited lots of questions—

—and questions invited trouble.

"Why'd you say that stuff before you shoot?"

"How the fuck you so damn good at shootin'?"

"You shoot every mornin', but you don't hunt? Why?"

"Why'd you say you moved here again?"

And her favorite, the one every motherfucker in Raven County had asked her at least one fuckin' time: *"'Crow County?' You mean there's a 'Crow' County? In Kentucky?"*

A benign question that didn't lead to no trouble, but after the hundred-and-seventeenth-time, it got old.

"I put coffee out there on the table for ya," she said, marching off to the shower. "You can drink it before ya go."

Ain't no breakfast in bed, boy...

Best go to the Holiday Inn for that shit.

***

Rhonda avoided looking at her legs as she showered. The tattoos running up her arms helped—a colorful distraction. Probably the best gift Daddy had ever given her. He'd promised'em as a high school graduation present (likely to ensure she actually graduated) way back when he had a lot more money. More than he knew what to do with, it seemed. These days she was lucky if he even got her somethin' small from Walmart. That's okay, though—it's the thought that counted, and the tattoos alone could count for her next fifty birthdays.

Steam rose from the hot water splashing against her body. She squeezed shampoo into her hand, working it through her hair.

Fifty birthdays...

Would she even live to see fifty more?

Not if she kept on puffin' them cancer sticks. At least she'd cut down recently—from a pack a day to about half. Wasn't easy. Hard as fuck, in fact. Put her in a *real* bad mood for a while. But she had to be in tip-top shape for The Run.

Temple above all.

Daddy had cut his smokin' down, too—likely out of solidarity, since he couldn't even run after The Accident. Maybe couldn't even walk fast if he had to.

Lathering soap across her body, she stared straight ahead upon reaching her legs.

("you gon' be my b—")

Her preferred soap, Dove—the kind with moisturizer—proved essential for a woman's skin. Daddy used that Lever 2000 shit, less like soap and more like a green brick of chemicals made in a factory. Maybe burly guys like him needed that shit, but a woman (especially a woman as *elegant, fine* and *sophisticated* as her) required soap with a softer t—

James.

That's the bearded pussy-eater's name.

Fuckin' James...

James Smith or Swift or shit like that. Started with an S and was short. He never asked why she kept her black stockings on even when naked—one of the reasons she continued callin' on him. No pryin' questions, just got the job done. She'd helped him out, too, of course. Wasn't selfish. Dude even got it fairly hard despite bein' so drunk. Not rock hard, but hard enough to return the favor.

While lathering her chest, she ran her hands over her nipples, savoring the tingle. He'd licked those pretty good too last night.

She switched to a separate bar of soap for her face—Neutrogena. Daddy used that Lever 2000 bullshit for his whole damn body. Whatever. Seemed to work for him, as he rarely had acne or dry skin. Most women battled one or both. And their menstrual cycles. And had to put on makeup and shave their armpits *and* their legs *(mylegsmylegsmylegs—no! don't need to shave'em as long as people can't see'em)*, and overall put more time and effort into their appearance than dudes did.

Dudes.

Sometimes she wished she'd been born a dude.

But as a woman, she enjoyed certain advantages. For one, she didn't have to worry about whiskey dick. Could still fuck no matter how drunk she got. The bearded guy who'd ate her pussy—*Jim? no, James*—seemed semi-immune to it, damn near miraculous considerin' most men lacked even partial-fuckin' immunity. The older they were, the worse it seemed to get. Or, maybe whiskey-dicked dudes just gravitated to her, skewing her perception of that sad, sad affliction.

Chicken or egg-type problem.

Whiskey didn't affect their tongues, though—

("keep lickin'!")

—that's for damn sure.

("don't you fuckin' stop now!")

The bearded boy's tongue had done its job good last night. Yessir. Thank God there wasn't no such thing as "whiskey tongue."

She leaned her face into the shower stream, rinsing the soap away.

("keep lickin'!)

("use that fucking tongue!")

* * *

After finishing her makeup, Rhonda ran her styling wax through her shortish blonde hair, pulling at it in random directions to make it look all wild. Kinda made her resemble a chick in a punk rock band or maybe one of them glam metal bands—either way, fine with her. She blow-dried her hair afterward, locking the wild style in place.

Next—her electric guitar earrings.

Hell yes, she'd wear them today.

Today's gonna be a good fuckin' day.

Got her pussy ate real good, slept real good, gettin' back in the groove of things. Movin' on after *him*.

Movin' the fuck on.

She admired her guitar earrings in the mirror—last year's birthday present from Daddy. Probably bought'em from Walmart. Didn't ask, and it didn't matter.

She loved them, just like she loved all of Daddy's gifts.

* * *

Rhonda exited the bathroom to discover the bearded pussy-eater (John? No, *James*—his name was James.) sitting at the kitchen table nursing his coffee. Looked hungover as fuck. After shutting the door to her bedroom, she sat on her bed, staring out the window while putting on her black stockings *(mylegsmylegsmylegsmylegsmylegs "you gon' be my bi—")*, sighing once she could look down again and slip her jeans on.

The hardest part of the morning had passed.

***

Donning her Dairy Queen uniform, Rhonda strolled past the bearded guy (*James? Yeah—James.*) to pour herself one more cup of coffee. A risky move, since the pussy-eater might decide to speak, but she really wanted that extra coffee before Temple Trainin'. Hopefully, he'd stay quiet and they'd enjoy the morning together in pristine-fuckin'-silence.

The bearded pussy-eater gazed down at his coffee, head in hands, still lookin' hungover as fuck. Rhonda's head pounded slightly—not a true hangover, but a residual one. Didn't even remember how much they drank or what they talked about. Probably same ol', same ol'—the meaningless but necessary bullshit that led to him eatin' her pussy.

"You got any food?" asked the pussy-eater. His voice sounded hoarse, like he was dyin' or somethin'—kinda similar to the assholes in Daddy's garage.

(*"...please..."*)

(*"...take me to a hospital..."*)

(*...i won't tell anyone that y'all—*)

Rhonda had plenty of food, usually eating oatmeal and eggs for breakfast to ensure adequate intake of protein and carbs, plus fiber—always gotta have that fiber. *"Bein' regular is real important,"* Daddy liked to say. But having a slow, awkward breakfast with *Mr. Ate-My-Pussy-Good-But-Now-I-Want-You-Out-Jimmie-Jim-James-Jaimey* wasn't on the fuckin' calendar today. The haze of alcohol and lust had lifted, revealing an uncomfortable clarity—well, *for her* it was clarity, of the crystal-fuckin'-clear kind, but he probably still needed to "confirm things."

The *confirmin'* type.

She downed a sizeable gulp of coffee. At least she'd gotten to pour it in silence.

Most likely, none of her answers would satisfy the bearded pussy-eater— instead lead to more questions, more awkwardness. Didn't want none of that bullshit. No sir. Had to nip it in the bud so she didn't break his little heart (she wasn't cruel), but still make his questions *linger*, ensuring he'd remain in her pussy-eater pipeline, ready to call up whenever she needed eatin' again.

"I mean," he said, "if you had any, like, cereal, or oatmeal or eggs or somethin'...that'd be great..."

Rhonda brought the coffee mug to her lips.

Best to eat breakfast at Daddy's today.

"Nope, ain't got much and gotta run," she said, looking away from him.

"Oh, okay..." he said.

A hush fell over the kitchen. Only *Tiny Toons* murmured in the background.

Good...

Maybe he'll be nice and quiet now, and won't—

"Well, you, *uhh*..." he said. "...wanna get dinner sometime?"

Nope, sure fuckin' don't.

"I'd love to..." she said. "But I'm just *so* busy the next couple of weeks... lots of evenin' shifts, too..." She pressed the coffee mug to her lips. "Maybe when shit calms down..."

"Oh..." he said. "Cool."

He sipped his coffee.

Maybe this one, the bearded one, got it. Maybe he wouldn't press on with more—

"I mean," he said, "when things calm down, you wanna like, do somethin' sometime?"

"Like what?" she asked.

"Like...talk and shit?"

No, I don't wanna "talk and shit," you dumbass.

You ate my pussy.

And I helped you out, too.

Now shut the fuck up and leave.

"Maybe we can, like," he said, "watch TV together or somethin'? After you get off work? Rent somethin' from Blockbuster?"

She gulped her coffee faster, nearly burning her throat.

"Just got so much goin' on..." she said. *"James."*

That's the fucker's name!

James!

"Jaimey," he said.

Oh.

"That's what I said," she said. *"Jaimey."*

"Sounded like James."

"Well, you best clean your ears out, boy!"

The kitchen fell quiet again, aside from a commercial for Frosted Flakes. *"They're Grrreat!"*

"Hey," he said. "I'm just askin' if you wanna, ya know, hang out sometime. That's all. I wanna get to know you."

Oh, God.

One of those types...

She cleared her throat.

"Why, I'd love to..." she said. "But, uhh..."

She had to modulate her voice *just* right and say things in the nice, pretty way boys liked but with a touch of underlying coldness to make him shut the fuck up. Didn't need no drama out here at the bars and house parties—had to let him know, no; let him *figure out* she was cool to hook up but neither wanted nor needed anything else.

Couldn't actually say that to the bearded pussy-eater, though.

Then she'd sound like a slut.

"Trust me, I'd really love to..." she said. "...but I'm so damn busy these days...I'm a manager at Dairy Queen now, ya know, got a lot on my plate..."

Even without lookin' at the pussy-eater she *felt* his stare, his confusion, like a puppy dog not fuckin' graspin' why his master didn't wanna play no more.

"...maybe in a couple of weeks..." she said, pressing the mug to her lips, hoping he wouldn't mark it on his calendar.

"So, you just wanted to fuck?" he asked. "That's why you called me?"

Rhonda almost spit her coffee. She spun around.

"Did we *fuck* last night?"

"Well, yeah!" he said. "I mean, kinda..."

Rhonda narrowed her eyes.

"What do you mean, *'kinda'*?"

"Uhh..." he said. "...couldn't finish..." He gulped his coffee, then stared at the table like it was suddenly *real* fuckin' interestin' to him.

She nodded, almost asking, *"Front door, or back?"* but if it'd been the back door, she'd know. That door hadn't been used in a while now, and she'd still feel it if he'd been up *there,* even for a little bit. Probably couldn't have gotten it hard enough for that, anyway. Couldn't quite slide in the back like the front.

After chugging her coffee, she grabbed her purse off the counter and pulled her out her keys so they jangled real loud-like—hopefully sending the message: *"I have to go now, and you do, too."*

The bearded pussy-eater stood up all dramatic at first, like he was about to say some epic, romance movie shit, but then hesitated, carefully pushing his chair under the table instead.

"So, that's it?" he asked.

A cool morning breeze flowed through as Rhonda held the front door open.

Yep, that's it.

Until I call upon you again.

For more pussy-eatin'.

She zeroed in on her car in the driveway, noting how his truck blocked her way out.

The pussy-eater sauntered to the door and stood there, awkward as fuck. She glanced at him, then her car, flicking her eyes between the two, hoping it would speed things up.

Take the hint, boy...

James or Jaimey or Jim Bob or whatever the hell your name is...

Take the fuckin' hint.

He cleared his throat. "But you said...you loved me."

Rhonda sighed.

Yeah, sometimes I say that shit...

Makes the pussy-eatin' better.

She mumbled something about needing time to figure things out.

"I understand," he said. "But I really like you, Rhonda...and I hope we can hang out again."

He opened his arms for a hug, a man crucified.

Rhonda gave him *the look.*

The look she gave all pussy-eaters when they acted up like this.

The look that conveyed everything pussy-eaters needed to know without requirin' her to speak.

The look that said:

You fulfilled your purpose.

Done what God built ya for.

Now get outta my house.

And please-oh-please...

Stop actin' like a pussy-ass bitch.

I can't dominate the Tri alone...
I need Charlie with me, and other guys, too...
Guys who are loyal, and know how to tear shit up...

Guys like Blackbeard recruited.

Blackbeard: The Man Who Scourged the Seas

By: Roberta Stevenson

CHAPTER 4

First Mate, Israel Hands

(pg. 75) Now that you've learned about Blackbeard's early life and his ascent to piracy, let's take a look at who he enlisted to aid him on his journey toward fame and fortune. After all, to dominate the high seas, he needed a loyal and able crew—even a pirate as famous as Blackbeard couldn't run a ship by himself!

Israel Hands – Blackbeard's First Mate

→ *Vocabulary Question: Do you know what a "First Mate" is? A "First Mate" is a ship captain's right-hand man.*

Even before joining Blackbeard, Israel Hands had already forged a reputation as a skilled sailor and savage fighter, commanding respect within the pirate community. While those were considered admirable and important traits, Blackbeard prized other qualities, as well. He sought crew members who shared a sense of camaraderie, a hunger for adventure, and a fiery ambition to achieve feats never before accomplished by pirates.

Above all, he sought *loyalty*.

The Loyalty of Israel Hands

In an epic 1718 battle with the Royal Navy off the North Carolina coast, Hands showcased not only bravery and fighting skill, but also intense *loyalty* to Blackbeard. Amidst the chaos, he sustained severe injuries—even gunshot wounds.

→ *Medical Question: Do you know anyone who's been shot? Probably not, because they usually die.*

Despite his condition, Hands remained undaunted, fighting alongside Blackbeard and saving him from a British commander who nearly cut his head off. Luckily for Blackbeard, the commander hadn't noticed Hands approaching from behind, and by the time he did, it was too late—he glanced down to see his entrails spilling across the deck.

Boy, that must've hurt!

→ *Vocabulary Question:* *Do you know what "entrails" are?*
Entrails are like your guts, except more slippery, slimy, and gross.

Blackbeard demanded absolute loyalty from his crew, but rewarded it as well. After Hands saved his life, he delivered a heartfelt speech, ensuring everyone understood and respected Hands' bravery. He then gifted Hands a finely crafted cutlass, adorned with jewels and intricate engravings.

Can you imagine how honored Hands must have felt?

How his loyalty to Blackbeard must have deepened?

Turn the page to learn more about Blackbeard's awesome crew!

Discussion Exercises—Talk With Your Friends!

1. Although you may not have a pirate crew, your friends are similar. Why is it important to have friends who are loyal and have your back, no matter what?

2. If you wanted fame and power like Blackbeard, what qualities in addition to loyalty would you look for in new friends?

3. Would you die to protect your friends?

4. Would they die to protect you?

1970s

CHAPTER XV

RECRUITMENT

"You sure we really need those guys? Do your dreams really tell ya th—"

"They do."

"REALLY APPRECIATE Y'ALL lettin' me in on your plan," said Kenny Moser. He brushed aside his wavy brown hair and clasped his hands, nodding to a rhythm only he could hear.

"This is gonna kick ass," he said. "I can feel it."

Bill and Charlie leaned back on the couch, stroking their respective beards while sunlight poured through the window behind them. Bill always appreciated the way daylight flooded Charlie's house—a nice contrast to the Christmas-light soaked decadence of the nights.

"Also," said Kenny, "I just gotta say again, it's awesome you got this place to yourself, Charlie. Your own *Hacienda*."

Charlie nodded, accepting Kenny's testament to the awesomeness of *La Hacienda*.

"*Gracias,* Kenny," said Charlie. "Straight-up *gracias*. Real glad you can hang with us."

Bill and Charlie had gone back and forth on what to call their headquarters. At first, they'd leaned toward *La Hacienda,* but Bill said that sounded like a Mexican restaurant, so they changed it to Clubhouse, which both agreed had a nice ring to it.

"*Whatcha doin' tonight, girls?*"

"*Come on over to the cluuuubhouse...*"

But later, Charlie changed his mind. "*Clubhouse sounds like bullshit, too, man. What are we, motherfuckin' Boy Scouts?*" When Bill pushed back, Charlie got pissy. "*It's my fuckin' house, and we're gonna call it* La Hacienda*!*" So Bill relented, and they changed it back to *La Hacienda*. Only Charlie said the *"La"* part, though, which Bill assumed meant "the" or shit like that, but didn't care enough to ask.

"And I really like what you did with the Christmas lights," said Kenny. "I gotta say it again—they look *real* cool at night. Add a lot of atmosphere to the place."

Bill and Charlie smiled at each other. Recruiting Kenny Moser into their Posse had been the right play. Also known as Skinny Kenny, he exuded positive vibes and radiated a wild, *crazy* kinda energy—just the type they wanted to roll with. Neither Bill nor Charlie wanted any negative Nancys in their Posse; they preferred pro-active dudes, ready to tear shit up. Kenny fit the fuckin' bill.

A semi-demented, super-positive grin spread across Kenny's face as he sipped his drink of choice—RC spiked with tequila. Thanks to him, Bill and Charlie quickly became fans of the combo. Cheap, tasty and hit hard. The combination of sugar, caffeine, and tang of cheap tequila fucked'em up good, *real good,* but didn't make'em drowsy or sloppy-drunk like beer and shit did.

Kenny did have one flaw, though—nearly fatal: He abstained from both cigarettes *and* drugs.

This had deeply troubled Charlie.

"How can we run with a guy," he'd asked, *"or even* trust *a fuckin' dude, that don't snort coke, nor even smoke fuckin' Marlboros?"*

Bill had almost agreed, but when they witnessed how *wild* Kenny got on liquor alone, they surmised him a horse of a different color.

The type that didn't need drugs.

The type that shouldn't *ever* do drugs.

"I like the Christmas lights, too," said Graham Riley.

"BRAAAAAP!"

He belched.

The recliner squeaked and groaned under Graham's massive weight as he leaned back, hands behind his head, as if relaxing on a beach. His deep, lumbering voice and slow speech reminded Bill of the giant in *Jack and the Beanstalk*—*"Fi, fi, fo, fum."*

"Also gotta say," said Graham, popping a potato chip in his mouth, "it's been fun rollin' with y'all..."

Chip crumbs fell from his mouth onto his shirt, which he brushed onto the chair and carpet. Charlie's face twisted with revulsion.

"Y'all really bang two girlies here?" asked Graham. "In one night?"

"We sure fuckin' did..." said Charlie, eyes seething with disapproval.

"Huh huh huh..." chuckled Graham. His notorious laugh—deep, drawn-out, and dumb-sounding—had earned him infamy at school.

"I want some of that..." he said. "Girlies..."

He crammed chips into his mouth, brushing more crumbs to the carpet.

Charlie shot him a look that could curdle milk, then took a hard swig of his RC tequila.

"That's why we need more candy...bitches love candy..."

("my name's young charlie...")

("and i'm-i'm the f-fuckin' candy man...")

Bill shook his head. Sometimes he witnessed *echoes* of dream fragments—and lately, whenever Charlie referenced cocaine as "candy," cold chills ran through him.

("you girls like c-c-candy, don't ya?")

"So," said Kenny, "after we steal this guy's coke, we sell half, split the profits, and use the rest to pull bitches?"

"Sí," said Charlie.

"Sounds like a plan," said Kenny. "I'm in."

"Some of us are gonna snort that coke, too, K-Boy..." said Graham.

Kenny cast a sideways glance at Graham, and Bill knew what he wanted to say: *"I really don't like you callin' me 'K-Boy.'"*

"Hey Graham," said Bill, "more for us and the girls if Kenny don't partake. So it's actually a good thing. No need to keep givin' him shit about it, now."

Bill made sure to counter Graham's assholish tendencies fast and hard in this early stage of their newfound Posse. Teaching Graham mirrored teaching a dog—you had to say *"No, bad dog!"* clearly and early on to establish good behaviors.

Graham popped another chip into his mouth, crumbs falling onto his shirt, either not hearing Bill or not caring enough to react. He wiped his greasy, crumb-covered hands on the arm of the chair.

Charlie clicked his tongue.

"Graham, your chips..." said Bill.

"What?" asked Graham.

"Your chips, man..." said Bill, looking nervously at Charlie.

"Oh, yeah," said Graham. "These are good. I like the barbecue flavored ones better, but these sour cream and onion ones are tasty, too."

Graham stuffed a handful of chips into his mouth all at once, moaning as he did.

"Gonna be easy-peasy," he said, bits of potato chips flying from his mouth. "Money in our pockets—"

"—and candy up our noses..." said Charlie, shaking his head like an old woman witnessing something just awful on the news. Graham had repeated the *"money in our pockets, candy up our noses"* line about six fuckin' times since Charlie said it, and after the fourth time Charlie started givin' him that *"I'm not impressed with you, Graham"* kinda stare, lookin' less impressed each time.

"Snort half," said Graham, stuffing more chips in his mouth, "and sell the rest!"

Charlie shot Bill a look that screamed, *"Are you sure about this,* ese?"

From the start, Charlie hadn't been too keen on includin' Graham-cracker in their Posse, and even Kenny wasn't too pumped about it, either. Neither of 'em had any bad history with Graham, but Graham-fuckin'-Riley wasn't the type of guy you included in *anything* without careful forethought of the consequences.

Big ol' boy had a reputation.

Graham-fuckin'-Riley, the guy who extracted lunch money from underclassmen with a mere glance.

Graham-fuckin'-Riley, the guy who beat the shit out of the biggest senior in school in front of everyone, then snatched his lunch money—all on his first day as a freshman.

Graham-fuckin'-Riley, the guy who possessed the physique of a bank safe, takin' up half the hallway as he passed through. When you bumped into Graham, *you* fell down.

Bill stood taller than most—but stopped short of *towering* over everyone like Graham—and nobody in the whole of Tri came close to Graham's sheer size, his pure strength.

No one fit the role of their Posse's strongman better than Graham-fuckin-Riley.

*

"Every posse needs a strongman." Bill lit his cigarette. "And Graham can be ours."

"But he's kind of a dumbass..." said Charlie. "And if he gets outta hand, he'd be tough to control. Dude's as big as a brick house. I'm talkin' muy-fuckin'-grande, *man."*

"We got your smarts to outweigh any lack of his," said Bill. "Your smarts—and my dreams."

Charlie looked away from Bill, taking a nervous puff of his cigarette. Since they'd easy-peasey robbed Roy Jameson, Charlie had seemed more comfortable with the idea of following Bill's dreams, but mentioning them out loud still unsettled him for some reason, as if speaking of their power exposed the absurdity of it all to the light.

No—Charlie wasn't quite there *yet.*

"You sure you saw this dream right, man?" asked Charlie. He eyed Bill with suspicion—*something he never used to do.*

"You said before," said Charlie, "sometimes you misinterpret—"

"I didn't misinterpret shit," said Bill. *Yes, he'd admitted to Charlie his dreams appeared foggy sometimes, even contradictory, and yes, he had misinterpreted them before. Not nearly as often as his little brother Wayne, though. Besides, there was no room for mistake when it came to Graham—on this, his dreams had been clear.*

Clear as crystal.

"And Graham-cracker's a softie," said Bill. "Deep down inside. I've talked with him before, bonded with him and shit. He'll listen to me. And once he understands you're tight with me, he'll listen to you, too."

"...I dunno, amigo..." said Charlie. He muttered "No sé, no sé..." under his breath.

"Hey," said Bill, "I called it with Roy Jameson, didn't I? We got off with that scott-free. Money in our pockets—"

"—and candy up our noses..." said Charlie.

Bill narrowed his eyes. That was the first time Charlie had repeated their maxim with a distinct lack of fuckin' enthusiasm. Although recruiting Graham remained absolutely necessary, he still had to sell Charlie on the idea—make him realize Graham's value to the Posse, not just passively go along with it.

"Charlie, you gotta think of the big picture, man," said Bill. "If we start sellin' more and more coke, we might be paintin' a target on ourselves."

"You really think Johnny Law's gonna come for us?" asked Charlie. "Like your dad might arrest us and shit? I mean, even my dad wasn't arrested for drugs—not technically."

Technically, Charlie's dad had been arrested for his third DUI, not drugs. Pulled over for swervin' while some chick gave him head. The cop's unfortunate discovery of all the coke in his car, though, added substantial fuckin' time to his sentence.

"Yeah, he might," said Bill, *picturing his own father arresting him. He knew he should feel mortified, but didn't. After all, his dreams hadn't warned him of such a thing.*

"But we ain't big enough fish for my dad, man," said Bill. "He's got his

*hands full with all the shit that's goin' on. I'm more worried about other
dealers. They might try to rob us, or see us as competition they gotta get rid of.
Our own customers might try to fuck us over, too."*

"That didn't happen to my dad—"

*"Guess what, Charlie? We ain't your dad. We don't got the rep he does,
nor the connections he has. And he carried a gun on him, didn't he? Yeah, he
claimed he didn't use it, but he fuckin' carried it. So that says a lot."*

*Charlie took another nervous puff of his cigarette, running his fingers
through his hair—a new habit of his since the dream talk started.*

"Lemme ask ya a question, ese," said Charlie. "Did your dreams..."

A shadow of apprehension crossed his face.

"...did they warn ya about somethin'?"

Bill sighed.

"Yeah, I think so..."

*He hadn't planned on revealing so much to Charlie yet, as he wasn't
certain about everything he'd seen.*

("heard you boys like to sell coke...")

"...but it's not clear, man..."

("you know your daddy used to sell for us, right?")

"...just fragments..."

("hey, you boys like horses?")

"...fragments of bad people...and bad shit happenin'..."

("we got pretty horses y'all gonna love...")

"And me, you, and Skinny Kenny alone ain't enough to prevent it..."

(prettyhorsesprettyhorsesprettyhorses)

Bill trembled and took a puff of his cigarette.

"We need Graham," he said. "And we'll eventually need others, too."

"Others?" asked Charlie. "How many?"

"Just a few more," said Bill. "For our core group. The main members."

"Like who?"

"The Bedford Twins, for one."

Charlie's eyes widened. "The Bedford Twins?"

Bill nodded. "The Bedford Twins. But they'll come later. For now..."

"For now, we need Graham Riley the most."

*

Bill had plenty of classes with Graham, who, for some reason, always seemed impressed by him. They weren't as close as him and Charlie, never hung out on weekends, but they did shoot the shit a lot—and few guys could talk to Graham without a hint of fear in their voice.

Bill could, though.

From a young age, he had an uncanny knack for connecting with guys like Graham, as if guided by instinct or ancestral memory. Whatever the reason, he just knew how to talk to "bad dudes" who projected strength, fully aware they grappled with the same doubts as everyone else.

Bill understood that with guys like Graham, you showed respect—without showing fear.

Probably didn't hurt that Bill stood taller than most—big ol' boys tended to share an affinity, like they hailed from the same tribe. The fact that Bill's dad was Sheriff of Crow County endlessly fascinated the Graham-cracker, as well.

*

"Has your dad killed people?" asked Graham.

Bill and Graham smoked just outside the high school parking lot, watching other students pour into their cars.

"I think so," said Bill. "I mean, he cleans his work guns a lot. So they're gettin' dirty somehow."

Graham's eyes filled with awe and wonder. "Damn..."

"And he fought in Korea," said Bill. "So I'm sure he killed a bunch of Korean people and shit back then, too."

"Awesome..." said Graham. "...must be cool, havin' a dad like that..."

"Nope, not really." Bill spat on the pavement. "He's an asshole who beat the shit out of me when I was little."

Graham paused and looked out in the distance. "I bet he don't beat ya no more, does he?"

"Nah," said Bill. "Not once I got big and strong. Don't lay a hand on me now."

Graham's eyes met Bill's, a glimmer of understanding in them.

"That's when my dad stopped beatin' me, too."

1970s

CHAPTER XVI

RECRUITMENT, PART II

"That Skinny Kenny dude, he's alright

maybe, but Graham-fuckin'-Ri—"

"We need him."

"SO WHEN WE gonna rob this guy?" asked Graham.

Charlie glanced at Bill.

"When Bill's dreams tell us to," wasn't something he could quite say yet.

"Me and Charlie been scopin' the place," said Bill. "Figurin' out his schedule and shit. Once we know the right time, we'll let y'all know more details, then we'll make our move."

"What's his name?" asked Graham.

Charlie eyed Graham suspiciously. "His name ain't important, *ese.*"

"Hey guys," said Kenny, "I gotta ask, and I don't mean no disrespect or nothin', but just somethin' I'm curious about."

Graham's hand rustled inside his bag of chips.

"So far," said Kenny, "the way I'm hearin' it, I'm not real clear on why you need me and Graham."

Graham pulled a single chip out and held it right above his face, as if inspecting it.

"I mean," said Kenny, "I'm fuckin' pumped about this, don't get me wrong. Real thankful for the opportunity."

He flicked his eyes between Charlie and Bill, checking their reactions.

"But it sounds like robbin' this dude, is a two-man, maybe even a one-man job."

Charlie turned his gaze to Bill, communicating a message with his eyes: *"Told ya they'd fuckin' ask that."*

"That's a good question, Kenny," said Bill. "And I'm glad you asked that. Real glad. You're right, we probably could pull this off with one or two guys. But this ain't a one-time thing we're proposin' here."

Bill glanced at Graham, who continued holding the potato chip in the air.

"We wanna start doin' stuff like this on the regular," said Bill. "Keep a flow of steady money comin' our way. And if we do, we'll need a bigger crew."

"A bigger *Posse,*" said Charlie.

Bill nodded.

Good, Charlie...

Bring that positive energy in.

"The bigger we are," said Bill, "the less chance people'll wanna fuck with us."

"We already got random-ass dudes callin' me," said Charlie, "claimin' they wanna buy from me, random-ass chicks wantin' to party with us and shit."

"They hot?" asked Graham.

"I dunno, *ese*," said Charlie. "Ain't like they're fuckin', mailin' me their pictures or nothin'."

"You can tell if a girly's hot by her voice, Charlie-boy..." said Graham, still examining the chip he held in the air.

"Yeah, well..." said Charlie. "Some of 'em sound pretty fuckin' shady, to be honest with ya. So no, they don't sound so fuckin' 'hot', *ese*..."

Bill stroked his beard. "We don't know if these people are genuine, or lookin' to fuck us over. Steal our coke and shit. But if we're only two guys, we're pretty easy to fuck over."

"That's why you need me and Graham," said Kenny, nodding and looking pumped up. "'Cause we'll *fuck people up* if they try to pull that shit!"

"*Es correcto*, Kenny," said Charlie. "But we're lookin' for real bros to add to our Posse. Real *amigos*. Not just dudes who can fight."

"Real bros!" said Kenny, nodding. "And real *amigos!*" He punched his fist into his palm, bouncing in his chair. *"I'm fuckin' down with that, man!"*

Bill nodded.

Good, Kenny...

Good...

Graham dropped the potato chip into his mouth, staring at the ceiling as he munched with his mouth agape, kinda nodding in agreement, but only kinda.

"Graham," said Bill. "You cool with that, man?"

They needed Graham's affirmation. Didn't have to be the same, ultra-pumped level as Kenny, but at least some fuckin' affirmation on *some* fuckin' level.

"Yeah..." said Graham. "Guess I like what I'm hearin' so far..."

He rummaged through the bag of chips, which clearly only contained crumbs now.

"Hey Charlie-boy," he said. "You got any more chips?"

Charlie narrowed his eyes as a vein pulsed on his forehead. That marked Graham's *third fuckin' bag* he'd consumed entirely by himself since they started hangin' out.

"Dude eats like a human garbage disposal..." Charlie had said. *"Bet we can't even sell enough coke to feed the fucker."*

"Graham," said Bill. "We'll go rollin' in a bit. Maybe head to Dairy Queen, grab some real grub, not chips and stuff. Maybe holler at girls, too. That cool with you?"

"Can I have the rest of the Pringles?" asked Graham. "I know there's some left..."

Charlie sighed, stormed off to the kitchen, then returned, tossing the Pringles can across the room. The long, cylindrical container hit Graham's massive girth with a muted thud, then remained there, as if stuck.

"Thanks, Charlie-boy..." said Graham. He rummaging through the Pringles, gaze fixed on the ceiling.

"So, fuckin' anyway," said Charlie, glaring. *"De-todos-fuckin'-modos,* we could ause help with sales outside Crow, too. Diversify our customers and shit."

Charlie wasn't too keen on sellin' only to his dad's customers. Some of 'em—like Big Tits Nancy and Tiny Tina, the girls they'd double-fucked—were cool, hot, and fun to party with (and fuck), but others included people he claimed he didn't even wanna *interact* with.

*

"Sometimes my dad sold other drugs," said Charlie, "like this stuff called 'crystal meth,' when he got his hands on it. And he sold it for way more than coke. And it apparently gets you way, way higher than coke. Like, way higher, man. I'm talkin' fucked up. *So some of his old coke customers had switched to meth and they were the ones that actually scared him. The ones he'd tell me about and say, 'Now don't you ever start doin' meth, Charlie. Or you'll end up like them crazy fuckers.'"*

"Those are the motherfuckers that might rob us, man," said Charlie.

"The ones we need to be careful about."

*

"Kenny," said Bill, "you used to live in Hazard, right?"

"Yep," said Kenny. "Moved to Crow in middle school."

"You still got friends out there?" asked Bill. "Friends who might like to party?"

Kenny nodded like he fucking meant it. *"Oh yeah! I know just the guys who might be interested in buyin' coke. And I definitely know some hot-ass girls who'd be down, too!"*

Nice.

Kenny could be counted on.

"And Graham," said Bill, "you used to go to Zion, right?"

"For a year..." said Graham, snarfing down Pringles. "...'fore I got expelled..."

Bill and Kenny chuckled. The story of Graham's forced transfer from Zion to Crow ranked as legendary.

Kenny asked, "Did you *really* knock the vice principal out?"

"Yep," said Graham. "He grabbed me by the ear. I *hate it* when people touch my ears!"

Charlie raised an eyebrow, maybe noting one of Graham's weaknesses.

Bill asked Graham, "You think you know any Zion dudes who might wanna buy from us?"

"...it's like they say..." said Graham, cramming Pringles into his mouth. "...Zion County people are just a buncha bitches...goody two-shoes, stuck up bitches..."

"Es así?" asked Charlie. "You sure you don't know a single Zion motherfucker who likes to party? I'm sure even Zion's got a few rough boys who like to—"

"Yeah, yeah, might know a couple guys..." said Graham, wiping his greasy hands on Charlie's recliner. "...and maybe a girly or two..."

Okay.

That's a start.

Not as reliable, nor as proactive as Kenny.

But a start.

"There ya go," said Bill. "See, cocaine is like, *white gold,* y'all. And if we can get more to sell not only to people in Crow, but also to people y'all know in Hazard and Zion, *trusted* people—not these weirdos that keep callin' Charlie—then we can make some good fuckin' money."

"We can do some fuckin' business!" said Kenny, nodding and bouncing in his chair.

"That's right, Kenny," said Bill. "Some good fuckin' business..."

"But we still got more coke, don't we?" said Graham, his mouth full of Pringles. "So let's keep partyin', too."

"*Sí,*" said Charlie. "But *un poco, ese...*only a little left..."

Charlie lied—they had a *lot* more left. Cutting their stolen coke with a metric shit-ton of caffeine pill powder blessed it with long legs, but Charlie felt reluctant to share since Graham hogged it like he hogged their food. Probably took more to satisfy him on both counts due to his sheer size and all.

Big ol' boys required more of everything.

"Gotta be careful with what we got left," said Bill. "We're gonna rob this guy soon, though. Once we hit him up, it'll be—"

"Money in our pockets..." Graham shook the Pringles can into his mouth. "And candy up our noses..."

Bits of broken Pringles fell to his chest which he brushed onto the carpet, forming a pile of greasy crumbs.

Charlie sprang from his chair, pointing his finger at Graham like a knife.

"Now you listen *here,* motherfucker—"

1970s

CHAPTER XVII

NO LO SIENTO

"No lo siento, motherfucker.

Best watch your back, now."

"NOW YOU LISTEN *here,* motherfucker. Charlie stood with his finger pointed at a reclining Graham. "I done told ya not to get crumbs on my chair and carpet and shit! I got zero tolerance for that! *Zero-fuckin'-tolerance!*"

Bill and Kenny's eyes met, alarm flashing between them.

This ain't good.

"And wash your fuckin' hands!" said Charlie. *"You filthy, fat fuck!"*

The air snapped tight with unspoken tension. Graham didn't move a muscle, just reclined in his chair with his hands behind his head—still in beach mode.

"What'd you say to me, Charlie-boy?" he asked, as if he genuinely hadn't heard him.

"I said," said Charlie, *"wash your fuckin' hands, motherfucker!"*

A bead of sweat dripped down Charlie's now crimson face. His glare held traces of fear and revulsion, but mainly consisted of white-hot, righteous anger.

"Don't be fuckin' comin' here," said Charlie, "eatin' my fuckin' chips, doin' my fuckin' drugs and droppin' crumbs and shit everywhere and then wipe your hands off on *my* goddamn chair! I don't *tolerate* that shit!"

"Now, Charlie—" said Bill.

"I got zero tolerance for that shit!"

A long silence followed Charlie's screech—thick enough to cut with a knife.

Kenny's mouth hung open, as if watching a movie right before something big happened—

—something big and bad and terrible.

"Bill," said Graham. His voice stayed measured and calm. "Best tell little Charlie-boy to settle down, now..."

Graham popped his right-hand knuckles.

Crack!

Bill's mind raced.

Oh shit oh shit oh shit.

He had to act fast, but siding with one meant crossing the other. Charlie's anger was justified, but a little tact might've softened his approach.

You didn't talk that way to Graham-fuckin'-Riley.

Nobody talked that way to Graham-fuckin'-Riley, under any

circumstances—unless they wanted an old-fashioned Graham Riley head massage.

"Charlie," said Bill. "Can I talk to you outside, man?"

"Hablar conmigo, ese?" asked Charlie. "Why you gotta fuckin' talk to *me?* I'm fuckin' talkin' to this big dumb motherfucker right here named Graham-fuckin'-cracker, that's who I'm fuckin' talkin' t—"

"Charlie!" said Bill.

Graham popped his left-hand knuckles—*crack!*

Shit.

Bill had seen this before.

The *Graham Riley head massage* usually came next.

"Qué?" asked Charlie, never taking his eyes off Graham. "You think I'm scared 'cause you layin' there, poppin' your fuckin' knuckles like you some fuckin' badass? This is *my* house, motherfucker, *my* fuckin' *La Hacienda,* and you don't f—"

"Charlie!" said Bill *"Just go outside with me, man!"*

Bill grabbed Charlie and yanked him onto the back porch, slamming the door behind him.

***

Charlie's hand trembled as he brought his cigarette to his mouth.

He still looked pissed, but a portion of his rage had faded, maybe replaced by cold fear—

—fear of what he'd said, and *who* he'd fuckin' said it to.

But still mainly pissed.

"I can't stand that shit..." said Charlie, his voice cracking. "He's a fuckin' slob, man. I don't care how big or bad he is, ain't *no one* gettin' all them fuckin' Pringle crumbs on my fuckin' chair and carpet and—"

"Charlie," said Bill. "You've got to *chill,* man. About this OCD cleanliness shit. I mean, what're you gonna do when we start throwin' big parties?"

"Big parties?"

"That's what we talked about, dude," said Bill. "After we rob that Stevie Baker guy and get more coke and drugs and shit. We start throwin' bigger parties. Like, on a *legendary* level."

Charlie shook his head. "I thought you meant like seven or eight people. Max."

"Nah, man," said Bill. "Need at least thirty or forty! Probably more than that! Gotta make it *legendary,* man!"

"Thirty or forty people? In *La Hacienda?* Gettin' shit dirty and makin' a mess of things? Hell no!"

"C'mon, Charlie...think of how many hot girls'll—"

"How we gonna have have'em all follow The Rules, *ese?* Huh? *Charlie's Rules of Cleanliness!*"

"Okay, fine, twenty," said Bill. "Only twenty people."

"Fifteen, max," said Charlie. "And you're helpin' me clean up. And so are they. *Includin'* fuckin' Graham-cracker."

"Okay," said Bill. "But first, you gotta apologize to him."

"Qué?" asked Charlie. *"Me,* apologize to that fat motherfucker?"

"Yeah."

"But he's in *my* fuckin' house!"

"Yeah, but—"

"I told him before!" said Charlie. "I told y'all my Rules! *Charlie's Rules of Cleanliness!*"

Charlie *had* laid down his Rules of Cleanliness—multiple times, in fact. And if they kept ignoring Graham's mess, he'd likely explode again, and Graham wouldn't tolerate that.

In fact, today might've been the first and last straw.

***

"Think I'm gonna jet," said Graham. "Either that or give Charlie-boy a head massage. Tired of him bitchin' at me 'bout shit."

Kenny clasped his hands together, choosing his next words carefully. His time to shine had arrived—he could *feel* it.

"Graham," said Kenny, "Charlie was wrong talkin' that way to ya. But... it is *his* house man. And you did eat all his chips."

"So?"

"So," said Kenny, "I'm just sayin', everybody's got their own little thing that pisses'em off, and you know how Charlie is about cleanliness. You remember all those rules he told us when we first started hangin' out?"

Graham laughed. "Charlie's Rules of Cleanliness. That was some bullshit."

"It was kinda bullshit," said Kenny. "But it must drive him up the wall to talk to *you* that way, my man. Think about it from his perspective."

Graham sighed, rotating his head.

"I'll leave him a couple dollars," he said, "for the liquor and the drugs. And the chips. But I ain't rollin' with him no more. I ain't rollin' with people who bitch at me. *I'm so tired of people bitchin' at me!*"

Graham flung the empty Pringles can over his shoulder, eliciting a hollow *thud* as it hit the wall.

"People at work!" said Graham. "My parents! Everybody's bitchin' at me!"

Graham rose from the chair and stomped over to the Pringles can, the floor of *La Hacienda* creaking beneath his every step. With a look of desperation, he upended the can into his mouth, tapping it, but not a single crumb emerged. He shook his head and tossed the empty can onto the couch.

"I wanna give'em *all* head massages..." said Graham.

"Okay, okay..." said Kenny. "I understand how you feel, man. I do. I wanna beat the shit outta my parents too, sometimes. And all my brothers and sisters. And lots of other people. Nobody likes bein' bitched at."

Kenny leaned forward, lowering his voice.

"But think about what they told us today, man..." said Kenny. "About how much *money* we can make from sellin' coke. I mean, it's like Bill said..."

He surged from his chair.

"It's white fuckin' gold!"

Graham's eyes widened.

"White fuckin' gold for *all* of us, Graham!" said Kenny. "And I'm not even gonna do any, so that's even more for us to sell. More *big-time money* for us all!"

"Big-time money..." said Graham.

"That's right...*real* big-time..." said Kenny. "And what about this opportunity we got here, to have our own *Hacienda*? How many friends you got that have a whole house to themselves? Seven days a week?"

Graham's mouth fell open as he considered the question, then shook his head.

"That's what I thought," said Kenny. "And I think Charlie's dad'll be in jail for a good, long while…"

He sat back in his chair.

"Which means we could even use this place after classes, once school starts. To do *whatever* we wanted, *whenever* we wanted…"

"Whatever we wanted…" said Graham. "Whenever we wanted…"

"And imagine all the girls we could straight-up bang here, man…" said Kenny. "We could bring'em here after school and take'em straight to *bang-town,* man. For some after-school fuckin'. You know what I'm sayin'?"

"Bang-town…" said Graham, his mouth still agape. "After-school fuckin'…"

"Honestly, man," said Kenny, "this is the best thing I could imagine happenin' in my life right now. And I dunno know about you, but keepin' shit tidy around here and followin' Charlie's Rules of Cleanliness really don't seem like a high price to pay for all that."

He paused, gauging Graham's reaction.

"I don't like Charlie-boy bitchin' at me, though…" said Graham. "Worse than my parents…"

"Well," said Kenny, "if you follow his Rules of Cleanliness, then—"

"He needs to *chill* with those Rules," said Graham. "Don't wanna deal with that!"

"Graham, I got a question for ya, man." Kenny clasped his hands together. He liked doing that. Felt business-like. "Do you actually *like* workin' at Cracker Barrel? 'Cause I'm tired of flippin' burgers at Hardees, man."

Graham shook his head. "Nah, man. I hate washin' dishes at the Crackhouse. *I hate it!*"

"What I got from this conversation today," said Kenny, "is that not only do we have the chance to roll with these guys, party with'em, and bang hot chicks that come to our *Hacienda*, live like a badass Posse…"

Kenny looked Graham straight in his eyes.

"…but also start a fuckin' *business!*"

Kenny rocked back and forth in his chair, nodding and feeling *pumped up.* He bet he was pumpin' Graham up, too, especially when he'd said the word "business." Especially the way he'd said it—

—like he meant *fucking business.*

"And I don't know about you," said Kenny, "but I'm ready to make more than a few bucks an hour flippin' burgers. I'm ready to make some *real* fuckin' money! And do some fuckin' *business*!"

Graham nodded, slowly at first, then faster, nearly matching Kenny's fury.

Yep.

Sayin' "business" multiple times had clinched it.

Graham could get it.

He could get fucking pumped.

***

"Dime, hombre. Fuckin' *jódeme!"*

Charlie and Bill stood on the porch. "You fuckin' tell me what these dreams are showin' you, that're just fuckin' *demandin'* we recruit a dumbass like Graham-cracker into our fuckin' Posse."

Bill observed Charlie with caution and worry. The cold fear Charlie had started to (correctly) feel toward Graham had already melted, and now he seemed to be workin' himself into a righteous rage again.

The vein on Charlie's forehead throbbed. "'Cause I can name at least five other motherfuckers that I'd rather invite into our Posse than Graham-fuckin'-cracker, *ese."*

He slammed his fist on the porch table.

"Fuckers that can follow Charlie's Rules of Cleanliness!"

Bill nodded, lighting a cigarette.

Had to be careful with not only what he said to Charlie, but *how* he said it.

Real fuckin' careful.

Charlie crushed his cigarette into the ashtray, carefully wiping any ash that fell onto the table.

"And did you see what he smokes?" asked Charlie.

"No," said Bill. "Does it matter?"

"Camels." Charlie narrowed his eyes. "He smokes fucking Camels, Bill."

Bill sighed. "So? Kenny don't even smo—"

"Kenny follows the Rules!" said Charlie. *"Charlie's Rules of Cleanliness!"*

Bill nodded, taking a careful drag of his cigarette.

"And," said Charlie, "Kenny's positive as shit! And fuckin' listens!"

"Okay," said Bill. "But who gives a shit what Graham smokes—"

"It's another *sign,* man!" said Charlie. "First sign was he don't follow the Rules. Second was he don't smoke Marlboro's Mediums. He don't even smoke fuckin' Marlboros!"

"Charlie, him smokin' Camels ain't no 'sign' th—"

"Then what *are* the fuckin' signs, *ese?"* asked Charlie. "What's comin' up one day that we need Graham-fuckin'-cracker for?"

"I told ya, *amigo,"* said Bill. "It's bad stuff, but I can't really—"

"I don't care if you fuckin' see it clearly or not!" said Charlie. "You fuckin' tell me!"

Bill sighed.

Damn.

When Charlie got pissed, he got *pissed.*

"Alright, alright..." Bill took a long, slow drag of his cigarette and exhaled. The smoke obscured his view of the woods behind Charlie's house, then faded.

"I'll tell ya, man..."

("hey, y'all boys like horses?")

"But it ain't much."

("all little boys like pretty horses...")

"Just fragments."

("pretty, pretty horses...")

"It's somethin' about pretty hor—"

Kenny poked his head out the porch door.

"Hey guys, Graham's cool to talk now."

***

"Okay, y'all," said Bill. "Charlie has somethin' he wants to say."

All four stood in the living room. Bill and Kenny folded their arms, looking like parents who'd just negotiated a tough compromise with their kids. Graham shifted his gaze around the room, scratching his head occasionally while Charlie glared at him with slightly fearful, but mainly pissed-off, eyes.

"Charlie?" asked Bill.

Charlie shook his head.

"Charlie!"

"No lo siento, bastardo..." Charlie stuck his hand out toward Graham.

"Fuck's that mean?" asked Graham.

"Uhh," said Bill, "it means he's 'fuckin' sorry,' in Spanish. For explodin' and shit at ya just now."

"Didn't *sound* like no apology..." said Graham. "How 'bout he says it in *inglés?*"

Charlie looked on the verge of a stroke.

"How 'bout this, motherfucker?" asked Charlie. "How 'bout you start followin' *Charlie's Rules of Cleanliness* you fuck-faced piece of—"

"Charlie!" said Bill.

"Now, Graham..." said Kenny. "Charlie *did* apologize. And he did it in Spanish, or should I say, *español,* which means *even more* than in English. 'Cause Spanish is more *impactful.* And because Charlie loves Spanish."

Kenny raised a finger in the air.

"And, as you just heard, he speaks that shit real good."

"He does speak it real good," said Bill.

"Now, Graham..." said Kenny. "It'd be really cool, if you'd, ya know, *promise* to be a *little* more careful when eatin' chips and stuff..."

"Be more careful?" asked Graham.

"Yeah..." said Kenny.

Graham popped his knuckles.

Crack!

Kenny gulped.

"And, uhh..." said Kenny. "...not get crumbs and stuff everywhere..."

He gulped again.

"...as much..."

Graham popped his knuckles again.

Crack!

"Nah..." said Graham, "No can do..."

"Why not, brother?" asked Bill, poised to shield Charlie from a head massage at any moment. Deep down, though, he knew that if Graham wanted to hurt Charlie, nothing could stop him.

"Ya see..." Graham popped his knuckles again *(crack!).* "I don't think Charlie apologized in *español*...I think he talked shit..."

"De veras?" asked Charlie. "And why you think that, *ese?"*

"'Cause I took Spanish before..." said Graham.

He stepped closer to Charlie, towering over him like Goliath over David, his shadow stretching across half the living room.

"...and I know what *bastardo* means."

Bill sucked in air. He'd never taken Spanish, but even he could surmise what *bastardo* meant. Probably.

"Charlie," said Bill. "Did you say *'bastardo'*?"

"Nah, *ese...*" said Charlie. "I said *'retardo.'*"

Kenny snickered.

Bill didn't.

Graham's face turned a deep shade of red.

Oh shit.

This wasn't how shit should be goin'.

This wasn't how shit *needed* to be goin'.

"You feelin' brave, Charlie-boy?" asked Graham.

"I sure fuckin' am," said Charlie.

"You wanna *do* somethin', Charlie-boy?" asked Graham.

"I sure fuckin' do," said Charlie.

Bill's heart raced.

Quit tryin' to act badass, Charlie!

Just apologize!

In English!

"I got an apology for ya..." said Graham. "You ready?"

Charlie trembled, but stood firm.

"Ándale, ese," said Charlie. "Fuckin'. *Ándale.*"

Graham's whole body stiffened.

His face turned a deeper shade of red.

He cracked his knuckles again *(crack!)*.

"Well, then..." said Graham. "Here ya go..."

He closed his eyes and scrunched his face.

PFFFRRRRRRRRRRRT!

The loudest fart Bill had ever heard erupted from Graham, shaking the walls of *La Hacienda*.

A foul stench penetrated the room.

"Oh, God!" Kenny yanked his shirt over his face and rushed to the front door, swinging it open and closed, fanning out the room.

"Huh huh huh," chuckled Graham. "There's your apology!"

"Eso apestaaaa!" Charlie pinched his nose, swinging the side door back and forth.

"Huh huh huh..." chuckled Graham, "You like *that* apology, Charlie-boy?"

Bill gagged, yanking his shirt over his nose as he dropped to the floor, hoping the stench would rise. It didn't. He retched.

"Goddammit, Graham-cracker..." said Charlie, laughing now.

Kenny laughed, too.

Bill, retching on all fours, set off another round of laughter. Everyone doubled over, fanning the doors. They laughed and laughed until tears ran down their faces.

"Fuckin' *bastardo* motherfucker..." said Charlie, unable to stop laughing even while vacuuming crumbs around Graham's chair.

1970s

CHAPTER XVIII

CHARLIE'S RULES OF CLEANLINESS

Gonna write these down so fuckers don't forget...

TAPED TO LA Hacienda's *refrigerator:*

<u>YOUNG CHARLIE'S RULES OF CLEANLINESS</u>

1. Wash your hands after eating or shitting. *VAMOS!*

2. Do NOT touch the faucet with the same hand you ate with. OR that you wiped your ass with. *Asqueroso,* motherfuckers. *Asqueroso.*

3. Do NOT spill, ever, anywhere, but especially on the carpet. Y'all are buyin' me new carpet every time someone spills shit. *Prohibición!* Every fucking time!

4. Be CAREFUL with y'all's food and drinks in order to avoid violating Rule Number 3 (see above). *Ten cuidado,* y'all! *Ten*-fuckin'-*cuidado!*

5. Three strikes and you're out of the Posse. That goes for EVERYONE. Fuckin' *todos! (including you? - KM)*

6. Anything you get dirty, you make clean, except dishes. Only Young Charlie is allowed to wash dishes because only he can make them CLEAN. *Comprende? (I'll help you wash dishes, Charlie - BC)*

<u>EXTRA RULE</u> (not related to cleanliness, but *muy importante!*)

7. Y'all eat my food, y'all gimme some $$$. Real simple. I'm tired of <u>certain</u> fat dudes eating all my chips! *(Fuck you, Charlie-boy! - GR)*

1990s

CHAPTER XIX

DRIVE

"Daddy, what'll we do if a cop pulls us over?"

"Nothin'."

"But what if he opens the tr—"

"I said nothin'. He ain't gonna open the trunk."

"But how do you kno—"

"Because my dreams would tell me, Rhonda.

Now quit talkin' about killin' cops.

That's fucked up."

RHONDA MADE SURE to stay several miles below the speed limit on the drive to Daddy's. Didn't wanna get no ticket, and especially didn't wanna be on no cop's radar during their Quest for The Temple. *"We gotta keep a real low profile 'til we find The Temple,"* Daddy had said. *"Don't get in no trouble with the law, not even a speedin' ticket...and that means no fightin' at bars, either, and* especially *no rippin' no girl's eyeballs out!"*

"Gotcha, Daddy!" Rhonda had said, giving a mock military salute. But she took him seriously and had shit runnin' smooth now compared to when they'd first arrived. Stopped doin' drugs (mostly), passed her reference check to get hired at the local DQ (*"Don't tell 'em about the eyeball thing or I'll rip yours out, too,"* she'd warned her previous manager), got promoted within six months (owners noticed she had a real talent for tellin' people what to do) and had a few young bucks (like the Jaimey-Jimmy-Jim Bob boy or whatever the hell his name was) to satisfy her needs when called upon.

After she finally felt able to mess around again, that is.

And that took a while.

After him...

She cranked up the volume on her Toadies tape—her favorite song: "Possum Kingdom."

Gonna have a good fuckin' day today...

Hard rock, heavy metal. Only shit like that in the mornin'.

Shit that got ya goin'.

During childhood, Daddy played his heavy metal tapes for her over and over, teachin' her how to headbang and play air guitar. *"This is the real shit,"* he'd say. *"You don't need nothin' else."* Whenever he got too busy with "work" to visit on weekends like he was supposed to, she'd listen to those tapes, headbangin' 'til her neck hurt, pretendin' Daddy was right there beside her, headbangin' too. Back then, she took her little Walkman everywhere—on bike rides, strolls through the woods, journeys across fields. No matter where she wandered, as long as she had her Walkman and those heavy metal tapes, Daddy was right there with her, even when he wasn't.

("can't see ya this weekend, sweetie-pie...")

("but i'll make it up to ya, i promise...")

("you gonna keep practicin' with your bb gun and listenin' to heavy metal while i'm gone?")

("yes, daddy!")

("i'm gonna hit bullseye every time, just like you!")

Rhonda halted at a stop sign, the pile of cassette tapes in the passenger seat nearly sliding to the floor. Been meanin' to lend those to Daddy. He'd introduced her to the classics: Black Sabbath, Led Zeppelin. These days she returned the favor, gettin' him into the new shit: Nirvana, Alice in Chains, Toadies. Shit that went hard.

Her and Daddy had a good relationship like that—he taught her the old-school, she taught him the new. And since they began their Quest, they operated like a straight-up team—not just a family, but a *team*—gettin' closer to their goal, The Temple, with every new Clue.

After driving a bit further, she approached a four-way stop, bringing her car to a standstill. Even though she'd rarely seen another car on this road, best to play it safe. Wasn't no point in even havin' a four-way stop here—waste of tax dollars—but what-the-fuck-ever. She tossed her spent cigarette out the window, lit a new one, and drove forward.

Smokin' in the car remained one of the few rules of Daddy's that Rhonda willfully ignored. Too damn efficient not to—what else would you do when drivin' besides smoke and listen to music? Didn't make no sense to smoke a whole cigarette, *then* get in the fuckin' car, nor did it make sense to drive somewhere, park, step outside, *then* smoke. Waste of time, waste of life. Smokin' in the car was killin' two birds with one stone and Daddy was dead wrong on that one.

The wind in her face softened as she eased off the gas to round a sharp curve.

That was alright, though.

Ain't nobody perfect—not even Daddy.

She leaned back in her seat all relaxed, nodding to the chorus of "Possum Kingdom." Nice weather today. Real nice. Perfect for Temple Trainin'. Came not once but *twice* last night. Feelin' good. Gonna shoot, then go to work (as a manager), then meet with the girls to tear shit up at a bar or two. Jam-packed, solid day ahead. That was good. *Real* fuckin' good. Didn't like not havin' shit to do. Free time made her antsy. Started rememberin' things, usually unpleasant. Bad shit she did and bad shit done to her. She'd overanalyze and wonder why certain things happened the way they did and how it all could've gone differently.

("ohhh, abby myerrrrs...")

Stayin' busy helped her avoid that—

("where ya hidin', abby?")

that dark whirlpool—

(*"we ain't gonna hurt ya..."*)

of memories, regrets and what-ifs.

(*"we just wanna play with ya..."*)

She reckoned she was like a bicycle: always had to keep movin', or else fall over and cra—

"What the fuck...?"

Like a shark lurking behind a swimmer, the police cruiser emerged in her rearview mirror. The theme from *Jaws* played in her mind.

Shit shit shit shit...

She turned down her music.

Shit shit shit shit...

Nervously, she glanced at her speedometer—drivin' *exactly* the fuckin' speed limit. Not five miles below like she'd meant to, but not speedin', either.

Was I?

Was I fuckin' speedin'?

She let up off the accelerator.

This is the last fuckin' thing I need this mornin'...

Was the cop followin' her?

To Daddy's?

She took a nervous puff of her cigarette.

He's probably runnin' my license plate...

Lookin' my ass up.

No doubt the cop would find her record, dig up the Eyeball Incident and all that other stuff, and pull her over for some bullshit. Search her car for drugs and weapons and whatnot. Didn't have no drugs in the car, but she did keep her guns in the trunk.

Fuck...

Her right hand trembled.

Ain't got time for Johnny Law this mornin'...

Of course, the cop didn't have no right to search her trunk, but he could make up some "probable cause" bullshit and then she'd be in *real* fuckin' trouble. Technically, she wasn't even supposed to own no firearms 'til her bullshit semi-parole had finished, but this was America—land of the free—and she sure as fuck wasn't about to give up her God-given Second Amendment rights.

Reaching down, she felt for her Glock duct-taped to the seat's underside. Ol' Johnny Law wouldn't know about that one—not 'til it was too fuckin' late.

"Now Rhonda," Daddy had said. *"Don't you kill no cops. Even if they pull us over when we got one of them assholes in our trunk, don't* ever *kill no cop. You got that?"*

"Gotcha, Daddy..." But she didn't quite get it—after all, no one could be allowed to stop'em from findin' The Temple.

No one.

Cop or not—she wouldn't hesitate.

She touched the Glock under her seat again, loosening the tape. If need be, she could rip it out and blast a dude's face off in one smooth motion. *Smooth like butter.* If that happened to be a fuckin' cop's face, so be it.

The police cruiser turned onto a street behind her.

"That's fuckin' right!" She slammed her fist into the steering wheel. "You best be on your way! I ain't gonna let ya pull me over for no bullshit!"

She cranked up "Possum Kingdom" again, leaning back in the seat, nodding.

Cop or no cop—

Temple above all.

1990s

CHAPTER XX

CARDINAL

"It-is-a-sin to kill a cardinal!"

BY THE TIME Rhonda pulled into Daddy's driveway, she'd mostly stopped givin' a shit about the cop she'd seen. Still worth mentionin' to Daddy, though—just in case. Had never seen a cop in their neck of the woods before, and better to be *too* careful about shit than not enough.

Gravel crunched beneath her feet as she stepped out the car, stretching her arms. Behind her stood Daddy's house: two bedrooms, with both a living room *and* a dining room—twice as big as her place. No upstairs, though. None of the family had ever lived in a house with an upstairs yet, and Rhonda, for her part, nurtured a determination to try it one day—maybe after they found The Temple.

To her right, the garage held GB and the other assholes who needed keepin'. Ahead sat two small stand-alone rooms, about the size of storage sheds, linked by a short sidewalk under a roof overhang. Real lucky for little Zach and Taleiah to have their own mini-rooms like that. Almost like tiny apartments. Even had their own bathrooms and showers, but no kitchens— just as well, since the lil' Z-Man couldn't be trusted with anything involving heat or flames.

Both her siblings likely still slept, though Zach occasionally woke early to watch cartoons in Daddy's house. Daddy didn't allow no cable to be run out to their mini-rooms *("Y'all'd just watch TV all the time and rot your brains out!"),* but Rhonda reckoned he also wanted'em to keep comin' inside so he didn't get lonely. A reason other than food or askin' for money.

Daddy's bedroom blinds remained closed. No surprise—like her siblings, Daddy slept in late unless he had a mornin' shift. Rhonda hadn't done her Temple Trainin' with Daddy in a while, and she missed it, but wakin' him this early was only allowed in emergencies.

To wake Daddy now might interrupt his dreams.

To interrupt his dreams was to interrupt prophecy.

Temple above all.

She narrowed her eyes, turning her gaze to the garage.

Was GB still snoozin', too?

Wasn't sure about his sleepin' routines—figured it kinda didn't matter if you were tied up all the time. Maybe he still slept at night, when it got dark outside and cooler in the garage. Or maybe just slept all the time since he didn't have shit else to do.

Gave zero fucks, either way.

Leaning back against the car, she placed her hands on her hips, savoring the quiet morning calm. Felt so damn *good* hangin' around Daddy's property while everybody slept. Somethin' about it—a serene purity.

She popped her trunk to retrieve her guns and ammo bag, glancing at the garage again.

Maybe smoke another cigarette?

Lately, she fought urges to just stare at the garage and *think* about it for some reason, like a statue or a piece of art. Maybe if she stared at it long enough, she'd fi—

(what are you doing, rhonda?)

She shivered.

(what are you and your family doi—)

No.

Best to get a move on.

Slinging her bag over her shoulder, she strolled toward the woods.

Had to pay GB a little visit later.

No time for dilly-dallyin'.

***

A decent hike up a forest path stretched between Daddy's driveway and the Temple Training Range, or "TTR," as Daddy called it. Honestly, "shooting range" would've been just fine but Daddy went through a phase where he assigned codewords to everything. *"We gotta keep things real fuckin' secret, y'all,"* he'd said. *"I'm talkin' CIA-level secret, usin' codewords and shit, like they do. That way, ain't nobody know what we're talkin' about..."* Everybody tired of it fast, though, especially since Daddy changed the acronyms on the fly. Couldn't even remember half the ones he'd made up. TTR remained one of the few that stuck.

The morning hike always proved enjoyable. Soft dirt underfoot, birds chirping in the sunlit canopy, and rustling creatures in the shadows touched something deep inside her—primal, peaceful, zen-like.

How was her family okay with missin' all that?

Rest of 'em usually did their Temple Trainin' later in the day, so they could sleep late and avoid the midday heat. Wasn't the same as mornin's. *Mornin's were the best.* Fuck that afternoon-evening bullshit. Besides, the earlier you woke, the more you got from your day. The more you lived. And mornin's like today, when the sun shone just right and you hiked up the forest path to kick ass in Temple Trainin', those were the best parts of life right there.

She paused to catch her breath, absorbing the beauty of the forest. Never got old. Had been comin' out here almost every day since they moved from Crow, and it still felt fresh. God had truly blessed them with Daddy's property—bestowed under tragic circumstances, but a blessing from God all the same.

And once we find The Temple...

We'll be even more fuckin' blessed...

Hiking up the forest path, she glimpsed Daddy's house, the garage, and Taleiah and Zach's mini-rooms below, barely visible through the morning mist clinging to the forest's darker parts.

Now, how could them fuckers still be sleepin'?

How come their eyes didn't pop open like hers at the crack of dawn, ready to squeeze every bit of enjoyment from the day?

From life?

Thank God I ain't like them...

Thank God I actually wake the fuck up every—

She sniffed.

Wait a minute.

She sniffed again.

What's that smell?

Like a dog catching a scent, she sniffed rapidly, scanning her surroundings for the odor's source.

Did somethin' die out here?

Cautiously moving into nearby underbrush, she nearly stepped straight into it—

"*Eew!*"

"*Gross!*"

—the rotting carcass of a rabbit.

Tiny red ants swarmed the carcass, while maggots—or some kinda worms—wiggled in and out of a gaping hole in its torso. The rabbit's cold, dead eye seemed to track her every movement, as if the eye had died but the darkness within still lived.

She took a step back.

The carcass appeared deflated, like its insides—even the bones—had been ripped *clean out,* probably by a coyote or a fox. Those juicy parts likely got devoured first; no need to bother with the fur or skin, just went straight for the good stuff, then took the bones to chew on.

After saying *"Eew"* again, she kicked the carcass downhill. A swarm of flies erupted, but, thank God, seemed uninterested in her, instead chasing the carcass as it tumbled and finally hit a tree.

Rhonda surveyed her surroundings, making damn sure there weren't any other gross fuckin' carcasses nearby. Best to keep rotten shit like that away from the forest paths. Might attract unwanted critters. Smelled like shit and looked gross as fuck, too.

"Oh, shit!"

Something fluttered nearby.

"What the fuck is th—"

A bright red cardinal perched on the branch beside her.

Rhonda stood perfectly still, not wanting to scare it away. Had never been this close to a cardinal before.

Should she reach out to it?

Maybe it'd hop on the back of her hand, like a parrot?

Or fly away?

Maybe even peck at her?

Wish I had food to give ya...

The cardinal cocked its head, studying her. She extended her hand, silently willing the cardinal to hop on.

"Heeeeere little birdy-birdy-birdy..."

Didn't know what else to say to a bird.

"Heeeeere little birdy-birdy-birdy..."

It hopped to another branch near her face.

"I won't hurt ya, little birdie-bird...c'mon, now..."

What if it hurt *her,* though?

Pecked her face or somethin'?

Maybe had a nest nearby, saw her as a threat....

You better not peck me, you little shit...

I got guns in my bag, and I ain't afraid to use'em...

She'd hate to kill a cardinal, but, just like with the cop, she wouldn't hesitate.

"Heeeeere little birdy birdy-bird..."

Now, you gonna act up and start peckin' at me?

"Hop on my hand, now..."

Or be a good little bird, and do as I—

Rhonda locked eyes with the cardinal—only for a second—but in that second, time froze. Her surroundings melted away, leaving only her and the bird, bound by an inexplicable connection. A strange familiarity washed over her, as if she'd known the cardinal from long ago, and it tried to tell her something.

What you tryin' to tell m—

Like a wave shy of reaching rocks on a shore, for an instant she *almost* understood.

She *almost* felt it.

Something horrifying and pure.

And urgent.

Fucking urgent.

Almost as if—

The wave receded.

The cardinal flew away.

Rhonda exhaled, realizing she'd been holding her breath.

That was weird...

Cool, but weird.

Never had a cardinal come that close before.

Most birds, in general, didn't come that close.

Wonder why—

Rhonda froze.

She had the distinct feeling of being watched.

Goosebumps prickled her skin, every hair standing on end as if electrified.

The birds.

All the birds stopped chirpin'...

Standing perfectly still in the silence, she readied herself for something—anything—to jump out at her.

Rustling.

Rustling in nearby underbrush.

She calculated how long it'd take to unzip her bag and whip out her pistol. If she did it smoothly, only seconds—but if a rabid coyote or fuckin' bobcat charged, she wouldn't even have that.

Would have to fight the thing.

Mano a mano.

Slowly, she tightened her hands into fists.

I'll rip your throat out, motherfucker...

Like I ripped that bitch's eye out at the ba—

More rustling.

She steeled herself.

"C'mon, motherfucker!" she said. "I'm fuckin' ready for y—"

A small rabbit hopped onto the forest path.

Rhonda exhaled, letting the fight-or-flight response fade.

Just another rabbit...

The rabbit sniffed the air, then, perhaps detecting its dead brethren, hopped across the path.

Rhonda started up the path again. The birds remained silent and she still felt like someone or something was watching her, but whatever. A creature ready to attack should've made its move by now. Didn't have all fuckin' day.

Good thing she'd found the dead rabbit before Daddy did, though.

Any dead animal, even a dead dog on the side of the road, made Daddy so upset. About had a nervous breakdown when he'd discovered those dead robins that fuckin' Zach, *the little psychopath,* had murdered with his slingshot.

Thank God that shit had stopped.

And at least he never killed no cardinal.

That was Kentucky's state bird, after all.

1990s

CHAPTER XXI

TEMPLE TRAINING

"When the time comes, when we finally make The Run...

...y'all can't hesitate."

AFTER FINISHING THE hike to the Temple Training Range (TTR), Rhonda stopped to catch her breath, standing in a grassy clearing surrounded by dense forest. The air felt crisp and clear, with birdsong and the occasional rustle of leaves breaking the silence. Thankfully, she'd stayed mostly dry, avoiding that sticky, grody feeling before her DQ shift. Each summer seemed to get warmer, likely due to all that global warmin' shit her and Daddy had seen on the news.

"I swear to God," Daddy had said, *"if we don't start takin' better care of our planet, it's gonna straight-up fuck us in the ass."*

She rested her duffel bag on the picnic table under the canopy Daddy had built to shield it from the elements. A notebook and pen lay inside a Super Walmart plastic bag. *"Y'all make sure to record your Temple Trainin' in this here shootin' book,"* Daddy had said. *"Every fuckin' day. Ya know, for consistency, and transparency and shit."*

Flipping through the notebook, her heart raced—like it always did right before Temple Training. She reached for her gun-bag, but her right hand trembled, making the zipper hard to grasp.

My hand...

Why's it keep doin' that?

Right hand had been weird for months now, but lately seemed worse. Seizing it with her left, she squeezed, trying to stop the trembling.

C'mon, Rhonda...

You know the drill...

Her hand spasmed as she tore the zipper open. Slowly, she reached into the bag.

There it was.

There it was.

Just sittin' there, waitin' for her.

Her fingers pitter-pattered over the barrel like a tarantula, then *clamped* around the grip, like a copperhead's bite.

The cold familiarity sent a chill down her spine.

She closed her eyes and turned her face to sky.

It all melts away...

All my troubles melt away...

When I'm with you.

With a steady breath, she opened her eyes and drew the gun from the depths of her bag.

Colt 1911.

Nickel-plated.

Shiny as fuck and ready to blow a hole through anything she pointed it at.

The barrel caught the sunlight, glinting like King Arthur's goddamn Excalibur. Every inch sparkled, and that cold nickel-plating felt so damn good in her now steady hand.

Maybe it's that "gunlust" that Daddy talks about...

That's why my hand shakes sometimes...

And maybe...

Shootin' is my fuckin' medicine.

Next, she donned her pink earmuffs—same pair Daddy had bought her as a kid. They fit a little tight now and the guitar stickers had faded, but whatever. Still protected her hearin' and shit.

With a flick of her pistol's safety *("click!"),* she marched to the painted-white shooting line. Four target boards stood before her, each covered with fresh target sheets by the last shooter. A word, written in blood-red paint, topped each board. From left to right:

"ALL"

"FOR"

"THE"

"TEMPLE"

Rhonda tightened her grip on the gun, an invisible force taking hold.

God, she loved this.

The right before.

Just like right before sex, when it's hottest.

Not during, and not after—

—the right before fuckin' feelin'.

Gripping the gun with both hands, she aimed toward the heavens, eyes closing as a cool morning breeze blew from the east. Slowly, she opened them, taking it all in: the silver of the gun, the blue of the sky and the white of the clouds,

(the temple...)

absorbing everything,

(we're gonna find it, daddy...)

becoming one with the gun,

(all for the temple...)

and with the heavens above.

(temple above all.)

She rested the gun against her face, the long barrel extending from her nose past her hairline. Eyes closed, she centered herself, focusing on the rhythm of her breath, whispering prayers into the quiet morning wind:

(breathe in)

"God, grant me the love to shoot today..."

(breathe out)

"God, grant me the wisdom to shoot right today..."

(breathe in)

"God, grant me the courage to shoot without fear..."

(breathe out)

"God, grant me the power..."

(breathe in)

"...to shoot to kill."

In one fluid motion, Rhonda opened her eyes and brought the gun forward, aiming at the *"ALL"* target.

(breathe out)

She exhaled,

"ALL"

and squeezed the trigger.

"FOR"

Squeeze.

"THE"

Squeeze.

"TEMPLE"

Squeeze.

(breathe in)

Again—right to left this time.

(breathe out)

"TEMPLE"

Squeeze.

"THE"

Squeeze.

"FOR"

Squeeze.

"ALL"

Squeeze.

(breathe in)

The air crackled as eight rapid gunshots echoed around her. Shooting always bestowed a sharp clarity—like the kind felt after sex, minus the fatigue. A razor-sharp, Terminator-like focus priming her for everyone and everything.

She checked the targets—five bullseyes. *"THE"* and *"FOR"* hit slightly to the left, likely on the sixth and seventh rounds.

Marching back to her bag, she reloaded without thinking, an act as effortless as breathing. Back at the line, she closed her eyes and pressed the gun to her face once more.

Please God...

Grant me the love...

The wisdom, the courage, the power...

She fell to the ground,

Grant it all to me.

breaking her fall with her left hand,

(breathe in)

holding the gun steady with her right.

Like a lightning barrage, eight gunshots cracked through the air

(breathe out)

No controlled breathing between shots this time; "drop-shots," as Daddy called'em, had to be fired as fast as possible. *"Ain't nobody expectin' you to fall flat and start shootin' like that,"* Daddy had said. *"So the surprise outweighs your loss in fuckin' accuracy. Just fire real fast, and when they drop, shoot'em again. Ya know, to make sure they're dead and shit."*

"Daddy," she'd said, *"how many people you done 'dropped' with these drop-shots before?"*

A coldness fell upon Daddy's face.

"Can't remember..." He clicked his magazine into place.

But the look in his eyes gave her the answer:

Enough.

Enough to know it fuckin' worked.

***

Rhonda brushed dirt off her elbows while checking her targets. Drop-shots got ya dirty.

Good news: Six of eight hit the target circles.

Bad news: Only two hit remotely close to bullseye.

Not bad, though.

Now came the hard part.

After slamming in a fresh magazine and stuffing another in her pocket, she marched to the end of the shooting line, facing the target marked *"TEMPLE."* Pressing the gun to her face, she whispered her prayers *(pleasegod),* then—

(breathe in)

—sprinted across the firing line, unleashing a rapid volley of eight shots.

(breathe out)

Without missing a beat, she popped out the magazine, slammed the other in, and then—

(breathe in)

—sprinted to the other side, firing eight rapid shots.

(breathe out)

"Fuck!" She slowed to a walk.

"Stride-shooting," as Daddy called it, proved hard as hell. Keepin' your aim steady while you *ran across a field* felt like some cowboy movie bullshit. Daddy used to stride-shoot real good, though, before his Accident, so it was possible—just hard as fuck.

After retrieving her magazine from the ground, she replaced the target sheets and logged her score in the shooting book: twelve hits, four misses. Not bad, but not great. One hit surprisingly close to bullseye—slightly to the right on the *"TEMPLE"* target. If she ever nailed bullseye while stride-shootin', that'd be the one to hit.

She returned the pistol to her bag and grabbed the rifle.

Ruger 10/22.

Hardwood stock. Not that plastic shit.

Tenth birthday present from Daddy.

Her first gun ever.

Marching back to the line, she raised the rifle, aligned it with her nose and pressed it to her face, then kissed the barrel.

All for The Temple.

Gazing at the sky, she recited her prayers again.

1990s

CHAPTER XXII

I AIN'T NO SANTA CLAUS

BIG BOYS DON'T CRY

BIG BOYS DON'T CRY

BIG BOYS DON'T CR—

MR. STANNIS ROTATED THE sides of his Rubik's Cube, feet propped on his desk. Alabama sunshine from the open window glinted off his polished black shoes. Across from him, Bobby sat in silence, palms sweaty.

Oh boy...

Always so dang nervous when talkin' to this guy...

Mr. Stannis's desk and office stood immaculate—everything tidy, neat and clean. A gust of wind blew in through the window. No loose papers to be blown away, but if there had been, surely Mr. Stannis would've pounced on'em like a cat. Bobby liked things neat, too, but even he let things slide: a stray paper here, a pen there, pink and yellow sticky notes in random spots.

But Mr. Stannis didn't let *anything* slip.

Often, he'd even prowl amongst his employees and comment on their desks.

"Lookin' a little messy there, Jim."

"Yes sir, I'll clean it up, sir," Jim would say and shuffle things around.

"Mmm-hmm..." Mr. Stannis would say, lips pursed.

"Debbie, I don't see how you even function like this..."

"I'll clean it up today, sir," she'd say, trying to focus.

"Oh, I know you will. As a matter of fact, within the next five minutes I fucking know you will..." Debbie's eyes would widen, torn between fear and frustration as she frantically organized.

"Bobby, what's with these sticky notes? You're usually on top of things..." Then he'd shake his head in a way that made Bobby feel guilty.

"J-just got so m-much to k-keep track of..."

"Mmm-hmm..." And with that, he'd move to his next victim.

Mr. Stannis loved to say *"Mmm-hmm,"* inspiring imitations that even Bobby laughed at.

And there was his desk.

His *legendary* desk.

Crafted from African blackwood—the world's most expensive lumber—it exuded luxury and power. Mr. Stannis never missed a chance to mention it during orientation, claiming it was a client's gift.

"This is why we work so hard—every one of us—to give our clients the best service. This desk symbolizes that," he'd say, then rap his knuckles (*"knock-knock!"*) on the desk.

Bobby never forgot that sound. He'd spent hours calling lumberyards to calculate the desk's value, but none even dealt with African blackwood.

One supplier finally told him a desk like that would cost hundreds of thousands—less than Bobby's guess of a million, but still more than most people's houses.

The desk shielded Mr. Stannis like a fortress, resembling something fit for a head of state—only bigger, shinier, and pricier. Despite never smelling of polish, it always gleamed. The top of the desk maintained an austere, Spartan look: an oversized calendar under glass, a leather-bound notebook, a smaller planner and a black-and-gold Montblanc pen. Bobby had seen him use the planner, but never the notebook. Maybe he just liked having one nearby—in case he needed to write something down one day.

The desk lacked a computer—Mr. Stannis claimed his duties focused more on "managing and directing" than "mere computational matters," but Bobby suspected he'd never learned to use one.

A family photo—Mr. Stannis, his wife, two sons, daughter, and dog—faced outward. Beside it, a placard read: *BRETT STANNIS, PRESIDENT & CEO, M.B.A.* He always told new employees he earned his MBA from a school called Wharton, which, Mr. Stannis assured them, was the "best and most famous business school in all of America." Too bad he attended before they taught how to use computers.

Bobby scratched at the angry mosquito bite on his hand. Dang ol' thing wouldn't go away.

Mr. Stannis focused on his Rubick's cube. "What can I do for ya, Bobby?"

"W-well, M-Mr. Stannis, ya see..."

The first thing that had caught Bobby's eye today wasn't the desk, the Rubik's Cube, or the family photo—it was the view.

A *dang* good view.

The gray of the streets, the green of the leaves and grass, the yellow of the sunshine—all visible, all beautiful. Bobby's office overlooked a brick wall and a garbage-filled dumpster.

Mr. Stannis never even glanced out the window, though—just played with his dang ol' Rubik's Cube.

"I'd, uhh..." said Bobby.

He scratched his mosquito bite harder.

Should've never let that bugger bite him.

"...like to aaaask if...I c-can have the next W-Wednesday mornin' off..."

He gulped.

"...l-like I used to..."

The Barbie doll was better than nothing—satiating him like a bag of fries while waiting for a burger. Witnessing The Joining—the *real* Little Stacey projected over the doll—granted him a measure of solace. Peace.

But nothing compared to the real thing.

The *real* Little Stacey.

(littlestaceylittlestaceylittlestacey)

(not a doll!)

(the real little stacey!)

(she needs her FEED—)

"Did I used to give you Wednesday mornin's off?" asked Mr. Stannis.

"Y-yes, sir. You did."

Silence.

Bobby made an odd choking sound, something like *"Aack!"*

Mr. Stannis's eyes flicked up, then back to the cube.

More silence.

A cold drop of sweat ran down Bobby's forehead.

"...*a-and*...I-I more than made up for the l-lost hours...b-by workin' overtime everydaaay..."

Mr. Stannis rotated the cube's sides faster.

Bobby let out a slow, steady exhale, trying to release whatever tightened inside him. The urge to feed the real Little Stacey had grown, a beast clawing at his insides. He had to feed her, feed her, FEED HER—

(breathe, bobby, breathe...)

(ain't nothin' wrong with what you're askin' him...)

(just breathe...)

Breathe.

Just had to *breathe* and remind Mr. Stannis of all the valuable work he'd done. That's all.

"...a-and I *always* t-turn my work in on tiiiime, M-Mr. Stannis," he said. "I al—"

"Oh?"

Mr. Stannis paused, cube in hand.

"Not the Mabel account, you didn't."

The Mabel account!

Bobby's mouth dropped.

"Ah...ah..."

He rocked back and forth, searching for words—the dang ol' words!—saying *"Ah-Ah-Ah"* over and over again.

The Mabel account bordered on *insanity*—calling it complex was like calling dang ol' quantum physics "complex." A gargantuan mess of properties, companies, shell corporations, stocks, bonds, and enterprises, both legitimate and shady—every tax accountant's nightmare. And Bobby not only had to make it squeaky clean for the IRS but also find every dang ol' loophole possible.

"M-Mr. Stannis..."

A voice, desperate and feral, began to scream:

(I MUST FEED HER)

(YOU CANNOT STOP ME)

(YOU CANNOT STOP M—)

He squeezed his eyes shut.

Word word words—

—just had to find the words.

Words would convince him.

Words...

"...th-that was the most difficult a-account w-we ever handled—"

"We?"

Mr. Stannis looked at him.

"Was *I* on that account, Bobby?"

"...no, n-no, I mean..."

Bobby gulped.

"...the m-most difficult account..."

He yearned for a glass of water.

"...that I..."

A cold glass of water would be so *dang good* right now.

"...e-ever handled..."

Mr. Stannis nodded, turning back to his Rubik's Cube.

"And *when* did you say you'd have it done by, Bobby?"

"...b-by March 1st."

"And *when* was it done?"

"...A-April 15th."

"And *when* was the deadline to file?"

Bobby made another choking sound.

The walls closed in on him.

(YOU CANNOT STOP ME)
(I WILL FEED HER)
(I WILL FEED LITTLE ST—)
A weird, nervous laugh slipped out.
"Heh-heh-heh...A-April 15th..."
Mr. Stannis narrowed his eyes.
"Cut it reaaalll close, didn't ya, Bobby..."
Yes, but he'd made it.
It took sunrise-to-midnight, even on weekends, but he'd made that IRS deadline.
(I DID THE WORK)
(LET ME FEED HER)
Just hadn't grasped what he'd really signed up for when he promised March 1st. It felt like his first jigsaw puzzle—seemed simple at first, then a thousand pieces spilled out.
(I SOLVED IT)
(I DID THE WORK)
(I DID THE W—)
His voice almost slipped, and he snapped back to the room, hands trembling.
"...M-Mr. Stannis, there were s-so many irregularities...s-so many dang ol' shell companies...so many...s-so many—"
"Shhh..."
Mr. Stannis twisted the cube faster, his fingers a blur. The air in the room felt taut, stretched with each twist. Suddenly, he slammed the cube on the desk.
Bobby jolted, heart hammering.
"Look, Bobby..."
Mr. Stannis locked eyes with him and Bobby immediately dropped his gaze. Dread gnawed at his insides.
(DON'T LOOK AT ME)
(I HATE IT WHEN PEOPLE LOOK AT ME)
(THEIR STARES THEIR STARES THEIR ST—)
"The Mabel client is *extremely* valuable to us," said Mr. Stannis. "And you barely made the deadline. In fact, you cut it as close as someone can *fucking cut it.*"
Bobby winced.

(DIRTY WORDS)
(DIRTY WORDS ARE FOR DIRTY BOYS)
(DIRTY DIRTY DIRT—)

He felt Mr. Stannis's gaze bearing down on him, like a judge passing sentence on a guilty man.

(DON'T LOOK AT ME)

Like the people at the toy store stared at him.

(THEY ALWAYS STARE)

Like everybody did—

(EVERYONE ALWAYS ALWAYS STARES)

—every dang ol' day.

(STARE STARE ST—)

"Y-yes sir, I-I understand..." said Bobby. "*I'm sorry...*"

He glanced up, finding neither acceptance nor dismissal—only Mr. Stannis inspecting him, like one inspects roadkill on the side of the highway.

"*Mmm-hmm...*" said Mr. Stannis. "What's your question again?"

"Uhh..."

Bobby's stomach tightened.

(*"bar-fin' bo-bby!"*)

No.

He wouldn't puke.

(*"swea-ty bo-bby!"*)

He'd learned to control his pukin'.

"...it-it's just that..."

(THEY ALL MADE ME PUKE)
(THEY ALL MADE ME SW—)

He scratched his mosquito bite harder.

"I-I..."

Blood erupted, oozing like lava.

"...I-I was wonderin' if I could get the m-mornin's off...on Wednesdaaays again...buuut..."

Mr. Stannis's eyes widened.

Bobby sucked in air.

"...it doesn't...have to be...W-Wednesdaaays, actually..."

His eyes retreated back to his hands.

"...c-could be...any ol' w-weekdaaay..."

His voice shrank within itself.

"…I-I guess…"

He *vastly* preferred Wednesdays, though—hump day. But as long as it stayed in the morning, when nobody would see him, he'd compromise.

(I HAVE TO FEED-FEED-FEED HER)

(SOON)

Mr. Stannis's stare bore down on him, heavy and unyielding.

"And I *used* to give you the mornin's off on Wednesdays?"

"Y-yes sir. You did."

"For three months?"

"Yes."

"*Mmm-hmm*…Now, why would I do that?"

"W-well, y-ya see…"

(NOT THAT)

Did he really have to go through it again?

(NOT MY RUINING)

(RUINED-RUINED-RUI—)

"I-it's just that, my, my—"

Mr. Stannis held up his hand.

"I remember now."

A hint—only a *hint*—of shame and understanding crossed his face.

"And I have a heart, Bobby. Let me tell you…I have a heart…"

He stared past Bobby, lost in memory, perhaps recalling something that mirrored the partial Ruining-related lie Bobby had told to get Wednesday mornings off.

"*That's* why I let you take Wednesday mornin's off. Because I sympathized."

He shifted his eyes back to the Rubik's Cube.

"Even though I made'em mandatory for *everyone else*…"

He picked the cube up again, spinning its sides. Sunlight glinted off his black shoes as he adjusted them on the desk.

"Even for *me*, Bobby…"

The hint of understanding on his face vanished.

Bobby sensed the tide turning against him.

"Even for *me*…"

"Y-yes sir, I-I understand th—"

"That was a gift I gave you, Bobby."

"Y-yes, I know that, s-sir and I-I—"

"A *temporary* gift."

Bobby stopped scratching his mosquito bite.

Blood trickled down to his pants, staining them.

(I DID THE WORK I DID THE WORK I—)

"It was never meant to be permanent," said Mr. Stannis. "Do you understand that, Bobby?"

"Yes sir, I-I do and I-I—"

"There are temporary gifts, and there are permanent gifts."

Bobby couldn't move.

"It was never meant to be a *permanent* gift."

He yearned to scratch his mosquito bite, but couldn't.

"Now I may be nice, Bobby, and I do have a heart..."

The itch felt unbearable.

(SCRATCH SCRATCH—I DID THE WORK)

(ITCHY ITCHY—I DID THE WORK)

"...but this ain't Christmas..."

His eyes twinkled.

"...and I ain't no Santa Claus."

"B-but Mr. Stannis, I-I-"

Mr. Stannis held up his hand.

"Maybe *next* year," he said, "*if* you do a good job with the Mabel client, and *if* you finish well before the deadline, then I'll *consider* givin' you Wednesday mornin's off again."

(NO)

"But only once a month."

(NO NO)

"That's the best I can do, Bobby."

(NO NO NO)

Bobby felt queasy.

The room began to spin.

(NONONONONONONONO)

His breathing turned rapid and shallow.

(NONONONONONONONONONONONONONO)

Mr. Stannis glanced at him with pity, then back to the cube, like one glances at a homeless person before turning their eyes forward again.

"I know, Bobby, I know..."

(YOU DON'T)
"...I understand your situation..."
(YOU DON'T UNDERSTAND)
"...I really do..."
(YOU DON'T)
(YOU DON'T)
(YOU DON'T)
"...but it wouldn't be fair to give you the mornin' off one day and not everyone else...."
(I'LL MAKE YOU PAY)
"...and what if they *all* asked for mornin's off, too?"
(YOU'RE JUST LIKE THEM)
"Or the afternoons?"
(I'LL MAKE YOU PAY PAY PAY)
"It'd be insanity, Bobby."
(LIKE I MADE THEM PAY)
"This office would fall into chaos."
(I'LL MAKE YOU PAY PAY PAY PAY P—)
"Chaos!"
His fist came down with a thunderous crack, shaking the desk.
Bobby jerked upright.
"And then we wouldn't get anything *done*, Bobby..."
Leaning back, Mr. Stannis gazed at the ceiling and sighed.
"And there wouldn't be any company unity..."
He swiveled in his chair.
"You know how important *company unity* is, don't you, Bobby? Why, it's the glue that holds this place together..."
(NO NO NO NO NO NO)
Bobby stared at the view outside—
(NONONONONO)
—feeling like a comatose patient wheeled to a window.
(no...)
Mr. Stannis droned on. Chaos, he stressed, was the contagion that toppled empires. *("you know that, don't you, bobby?")* Constant vigilance, *("that means all the time, bobby...")* remained the only inoculation against chaos. *("the only one, bobby...")* Everyone had to do their absolute best, *("even me, bobby, even me...")* to maintain perfect harmony, so that...

Bobby stopped listening and gazed out the window.

Why did his view have to be of a dumpster?

***

At some point, Bobby rose, mumbled, *"I understand..."* and stumbled out.
One year...
He wandered the building as if lost in a bad dream.
One whole year...
Co-workers passed, greeting him.
And even then...
He said nothing in return.
Only once a month...
His ran his hand along the walls.
(*"bar-fin'-bo-bby!"*)
(*"bar-fin'-bo-bby!"*)
(*"bar-fin'-b—"*)
Vomit dribbled from his lips, acrid and sour.

Tonight he'd use the Barbie doll again.

Guess I should start goin' by "Wild Bill..."
And keep wearin' my cowboy hat, too, since it's my unique style and shit...

And 'cause it looks badass.

Blackbeard: The Man Who Scourged the Seas

By: Roberta Stevenson

CHAPTER 9

Blackbeard's Name

(pg.109) Now that you've learned about Blackbeard's most important crew members, it's time to examine what made him so famous. Let's start with his name—*Blackbeard.*

When Edward Teach decided to pursue fame and glory as a pirate, he knew he had to come up with a good nickname—something short and easy to remember. There was nothing wrong with his real name, but it didn't evoke anything, either, nor was it particularly memorable.

→ *Question Time: Do you remember the name of the French pirate mentioned earlier in the book? Probably not, since he didn't choose a cool nickname like Blackbeard. And because he's French!*

But *why* do you think Teach called himself Blackbeard?
Only because of the color of his beard?
While it's true his nickname partially derives from his enormous dark beard, it's not the *only* reason. If it were, any pirate with a similar beard could've used that name!

To achieve fame across the New World, Blackbeard tried something no other pirate had ever imagined. Before approaching enemy ships, he tied colorful ribbons around lit fuses and placed them in his beard. Smoke and ash from the fuses shrouded his face, granting him a dark, menacing appearance.

→ *Watch Out! Don't try this at home with your dad's beard. Only Blackbeard knew how to do that without getting burned!*

Imagine you're a peaceful merchant, minding your own business and doing peaceful merchant things. Suddenly, you encounter a pirate with a *gigantic smoking beard.* You'd likely think him crazy, and not to be trifled with. You might even run away or start crying! Now we can begin to understand why Blackbeard inspired such fear and holds such an enduring legacy.

But did you know Blackbeard *killed* lots of people, too?

→ *Did You Know? Killing someone is usually wrong. In fact, it's illegal in most countries!*

Yes, that's right—Blackbeard killed people.
But not because he wanted to.

Because he *had* to.

Read on to learn why Blackbeard killed people!

Discussion Exercises—Talk With Your Friends!

1.   Francis l'Ollonais was a French pirate who captured more ships than Blackbeard. Whose name is easier to remember? Why?

2.   Can you think of other famous people in history who have memorable nicknames? Try to list at least 5!

3.   When choosing nicknames, what do you feel is important?

4.   Do you have a nickname? If not, what would you choose that's memorable, like Blackbeard's?

5.   Does your group of friends have a nickname? If not, what would you call yourselves to gain fame and notoriety, just like Blackbeard?

1970s

CHAPTER XXIII

ROLLIN'

"We gotta play our music real loud when we roll through town.

It's how you let people know you're

badass, and don't give a fuck."

HEAVY METAL BLARED from Charlie's dad's black Camaro as Bill and his Posse cruised through the night on their way to Dairy Queen. Bill's cowboy boots gave his feet a satisfying weight, and he knew he looked badass as fuck in his aviator sunglasses. Tonight marked the first time he'd worn his boots, hat and shades together—the full getup. Sure, the sunglasses made it harder to see at night, and yeah, maybe it felt a little weird. But whatever. *It also looked badass.*

"We pickin' up girlies tonight?" asked Graham from the backseat.

"Hell yeah, we are!" said Kenny, nodding to a rhythm separate from the heavy metal. He tended to cruise on his own flow, marchin' to some kinda sick, awesome beat only he could hear.

"No smokin' in the car, Graham," said Bill.

Graham held his lighter to his cigarette. "Why not?"

Bill turned, his sunglasses catching the headlights of a passing car. *"We got fuckin' standards."*

"What's that mean?" asked Graham.

Bill didn't move.

Just stared at him.

"Fine," said Graham. He tucked his cigarette back in the Camels pack.

Charlie asked from the driver's seat, "How well can you actually see wearin' those at night?"

"Better than I thought," said Bill, adjusting his sunglasses.

Kenny leaned forward. "We should *all* get cowboy hats and sunglasses! And cowboy boots, too!"

Charlie nodded. "I'd be down with that. Like when we go to parties and shit, roll up like a *real* Posse. Like straight-up cowboys from hell."

"Ready to tear shit up!" said Kenny.

"Claro que sí, y'all!" said Charlie.

"Dunno about that," said Graham. "Rather spend money on food and booze than cowboy shit," He hocked a loogie out the window. "But that's just me."

"But think of the *impact,"* said Kenny, "that we'd have on people. When we rolled up to parties and shit. All wearin' the same badass cowboy getup. It'd be wild, man..."

"Impact, huh..." said Graham.

Bill kept quiet, careful not to push'em one way or another. Tough to admit, but part of him didn't like the idea of the other guys stealin' *his thing.*

It was *his* thing, after all.

He came up with it.

But if they only did it at parties and shit, maybe it'd be okay. And Kenny's claim rang true—it would have fuckin' impact.

(*"you tell your boys!"*)

Besides, his dreams had already shown him glimpses of 'em all wearin' the same getup one day.

(*"you tell 'em what we did!"*)

Glimpses and fragments—

(*"you tell 'em what wild bill and his posse did here today!"*)

of glory.

"And speakin' of impact, Graham-cracker," said Kenny, "I gotta say, that was the worst damn fart I ever smelled in my life."

"*Huh huh huh...*" chuckled Graham. "It was a good one, wasn't it?"

"I mean," said Kenny, "it was like a fuckin', nuclear bomb or somethin'. Might take days to get the smell out the *Hacienda*."

Bill chuckled. "I think even the walls and furniture absorbed it."

"God, I hope not," said Charlie. "Graham, you're buyin' air freshener if that's the case!"

The boys laughed.

"Always been real good at fartin'," said Graham. "It's like, one of my superpowers."

"*BRAAAAAAPP!*"

He belched.

"That's one of 'em, too," said Graham. "Huh huh huh..."

The other guys half-chuckled, half-groaned as the smell of Pringles tinged with *nastiness* infiltrated the car for a single, terrible moment. Luckily, they had their windows down and Graham's burps weren't even close to the military-grade lethality of his farts.

"Now Graham," said Charlie, "don't do that shit when we're chattin' up bitches. We'll be known as the fuckin', *Fart Posse* or shit like that."

Kenny slapped his knee. "I think bitches might die if Graham did that again. It'd be the Guinness World Record. *For killin' people with his farts!*"

He slapped his knee again and cackled like he'd made the funniest joke ever.

Really wasn't that funny, but the way he laughed made the other guys laugh, too.

***

"Look sharp, guys," said Bill, his laughter calming. "Pullin' into town."

Charlie cranked up the volume and let the heavy metal pound from the car speakers. Kenny yanked off his shirt and stuck his torso out the window.

"Crow County Posse motherfuckers!" said Kenny. *"Ow-owwwww!"*

Kenny always took off his shirt when they went rollin' or he got wild or when he fuckin' felt like it. It was his *thing*. With his shoulder-length wavy hair, dark complexion and smooth, hairless chest, he looked like a Cherokee warrior.

"The Posse is here, motherfuckers!" said Kenny, whipping his shirt like a helicopter. *"Ow-owwwww!"*

Bill chuckled. "Kenny, you're gonna lose your shirt one of these days."

"Callin' all hot girls!" said Kenny, "Come on down to our *Haciend-aaa!"*

All four guys yelled, *"Ow-owwwww!"*

They pulled up to a four-way stop.

"Check it out," said Graham, looking like he'd walked into an all-you-can-eat buffet. *"Girlies..."*

A blonde girl chewing gum in the passenger seat of the car beside them rolled down her window and winked. A slim, dark-haired girl drove, while a light brunette sat in the back, putting on lipstick.

"Pollitas calientes..." said Charlie.

"Wassuppp girrrrlllls," said Kenny, half his body jutting from the car window. "Y'all wanna come over to our *Hacienda?"*

"Come on over to *La Hacienda, mamacitas!"* said Charlie. *"Volvámonos, locas!"*

All four guys yelled variations of *"Ow-owwwww!"*

"Sounds fun, boys," said the blonde. She leaned out the front passenger window, her tank top showing off her not especially large, but beautifully shaped, tits to the world.

"But we're goin' to Dairy Queen," she said. "Get us some sweet stuff!" She winked, probably at Kenny, but every guy in the car felt special.

"That's where we're goin', too!" said Kenny.

"Coincidencioso!" said Charlie. *"Coincidencioso los mamacitaaaas!"*

Everyone laughed.

"You speak that Spanish shit real good," said the blonde. "You part-Mexican?"

"Nope," said Charlie, "but we got tequila back at *La Hacienda!"* He smiled bright enough to blind. "That's from Mexico! Y'all like that shit?"

"Hell yeah!" said the dark-haired girl driving. "We fuckin' like tequila!"

"We drink that shit up!" said the blonde.

All the guys hooted and hollered. Kenny started chanting, *"Te-qui-la, te-qui-la!"* but stopped when no one else joined.

"You supposed to be a cowboy or somethin'?" asked the dark-haired girl.

Bill narrowed his eyes. He'd prepared for this type of question: *"You supposed to be a cowboy?"* or *"You from Texas?"* or shit like that.

This time, he was ready.

"Why hell yes I am," he said. *"You wanna ride, girl?"*

"Ow-owwwww!" howled the guys.

"Giddy up, girls!" said Charlie. *"Vamos a La Haciendaaaa!"*

All the guys bounced in their seats like they rode horses and howled at the moon like wolves. Graham's bouncing shook his whole corner of the car which made Charlie cuss under his breath about the tires and suspension. The two girls in the front laughed, their eyes sparkling with amusement, while the light brunette in the back kept applying her lipstick.

"I'm Bill," said Bill, "and this is my Posse. What's y'all's names?"

"Bill?" asked the blonde girl. "You must be *Wild Bill* then, wearin' that cowboy hat!"

The girls laughed.

"See?" asked Charlie. "They called you 'Wild Bill,' *ese!* Now, what'd I tell ya earlier?"

Graham laughed. "Wild Bill! That's good!"

"Dude!" said Kenny. "We should start callin' you that! It fits your cowboy hat and everything!"

"Wild Bill! Wild Bill! Wild Bill!" chanted the guys. The blonde and the dark-haired girl laughed some more. The brunette in the back still didn't give a shit.

They pulled forward to another stoplight.

"Where y'all go to school at?" asked Bill.

"Hazard," said the blonde girl, sticking her chest out even further. Every guy in the car zeroed-in on her tits.

Damn...

Bill's pulse raced as he ran his fingers across the brim of his cowboy hat. Her tits weren't even that big, but they sure were shaped nice. She knew how to show'em off, too. *Real* good.

"Hazard County Hillbillies!" said Kenny.

"That's right!" said the blonde. "What about y'all?"

"Y'all ain't bitches from Zion, is ya?" asked the dark-haired girl driving.

Bill craned his neck for a better look at the dark-haired girl—couldn't see her tits, but she looked hot, too.

"Helllll no," said Charlie. "We ain't no bitches from Zion!"

"We're from Crow!" said Kenny.

All four guys flapped their arms like wings and yelled, *"Caw-caw!"*

***

The girls had to stop somewhere first but said they'd meet Bill and his Posse at Dairy Queen.

"The blonde girly had nice tits..." said Graham.

"Dude," said Kenny. "Her tits weren't that big, but they were real nice, man..."

"Did you know those chicks, Kenny?" asked Charlie. "From when you used to live in Hazard, back in middle school?

"Nah, must've been in a different grade from me," said Kenny. "Or they went to South Hazard instead of North."

"What was it like," asked Bill, "to go to school in Hazard? Like, how was it different from Crow?"

"There's a lot more Confederate flags, for one," said Kenny. "On their clothes and shit. And everyone's a lot more poor. But like, equally poor. And not as many cliques, 'cause they got a lot less people, so everybody kinda knows everybody, and don't really give a shit. Everybody just hangs with everybody kinda. At least, compared to Crow."

"So," said Bill, "it's more like, egalitarian and shit?"

"Yep," said Kenny. "More egalitarian. And more poor."

"What's 'egalitarian' mean?" asked Graham.

"It means 'equal'," said Charlie, adding under his breath, *"Ya fuckin' dumbass..."*

"I knew that," said Graham. "Just forgot."

"Sí, sí..." said Charlie. "I'm sure you did, Graham-cracker..."

"Ya know," said Bill, "that's how I imagined Hazard. People are more chill, but poorer, dumber, and got less class..."

Charlie nodded. "Hazard people really ain't got *no* fuckin' class. No wonder they're always fightin' Zion bitches. 'Cause Zion people got too much class, with fuckin' sticks up their asses!"

Everyone agreed that Zion bitches had sticks up their asses, and could go fuck themselves.

"But anyway," said Charlie, "those girls were fuckin' hot for Hazard girls. Hope they like candy..."

("my name's young ch-charlie...")

("and i'm the f-fuckin' candy man...")

Bill took off his sunglasses and rubbed his temples.

("y'all girls like c-candy?")

("i-i got some real *good c-c-can—")*

Why did he get cold chills whenever Charlie referenced drugs as "candy"?

Kenny pumped his fist in the air. "Hazard girls got no class, man! Of course they'll snort coke! They'll probably suck our dicks in the parkin' lot!"

Bill put his sunglasses back on. "Now Kenny, they ain't gonna suck our dicks in the parkin' lot. And if—"

"Nah, they might!" said Kenny. "Dude, when I went to North Hazard in middle school, you won't believe the shit that happened. I'm talkin' *redneck* shit."

"Like what?" asked Graham.

"Like, when I was in seventh grade," said Kenny, "four girls got caught suckin' dick! In the guy's locker room!"

The car erupted with disbelief, voices overlapping as everyone shouted and swore in shock.

*"No puede-*fuckin'-*ser!"* said Charlie. "You are shittin' me, Kenny!"

"Nope," said Kenny, "and durin' school hours, too!"

"Durin' fuckin' school hours?" asked Bill.

"Yep," said Kenny. "They were all in different classes and asked to go to the bathroom at the same time. And they almost got away with it!"

Graham's eyes grew wide and child-like. "You *serious*, K-Boy?"

Kenny continued. "It was a contest or a bet they made," said Kenny. "About which guy could cum the fastest, or which girl was the best at suckin' dick or somethin'. Anyway, after they got caught, it was a *huge* fuckin' deal. Everybody in the whole county knew about it. So, for a long time after that, teachers started bein' waaay more strict with people goin' to the bathroom and shit. Like a military lockdown, dude."

"Wow..." said Graham. "Wish I would've gone to North Hazard Middle..."

"So do fuckin' I!" said Charlie. "I knew shit got redneck over there, but that's fuckin' wild, man!"

Kenny continued. "Every girl who got in trouble for that became *ultra*-fuckin'-popular. Like, thirty different guys asked'em to the Hazard Hoedown and shit."

"Hazard Hoedown?" asked Graham.

"It's their biggest middle school dance," said Kenny.

Charlie cackled. "You're tellin' me, that them hillbillies and hicks up in Hazard actually got a school dance called the 'Hazard Hoedown'?"

Bill chuckled. "That's about as fuckin', stereotypical as you can get."

"I guess so," said Kenny. "But anyway, after that, every single guy in school wanted those chicks as their girlfriends."

"Heck yeah," said Graham. "That's every guy's dream...findin' girlies who suck dick like that in middle school..."

"And who was fuckin' *escandaloso* about it, as well!" said Charlie. "Fuckin' no shame, *ese!* That's what I'm talkin' about! Havin' dick-suckin' contests and shit!"

The car erupted in chatter about how awesome Kenny's story was and how they wished they'd gone to North Hazard Middle and if Kenny remembered those girls' names (he did, and they immediately decided to find'em in the phone book later) and then Kenny revealed that he'd actually negotiated a blowjob from one of those girls but she'd made him *swear to God* not to tell (though he figured it was okay by now) and the car erupted again with exclamations like *"No shit!"* and *"Are you fuckin' serious?"*

Bill had to quieten everybody down when they pulled up to Dairy Queen.

"Alright y'all," he said. "Play it *chill* from here on out."

Something about his cowboy hat, boots, and sunglasses imbued a sense of cool confidence. He remembered how Charlie had played it with those Nancy and Tina girls they'd double-fucked—now it fell upon him to lead by example.

"Now if y'all go out there," said Bill, "talkin' to them Hazard girls like you're expectin' some straight-up, *dick suckin'* or somethin', in the fuckin' parkin' lot, the way those girls did at Kenny's middle school, then they won't do shit with us."

He ran his fingers across the brim of his hat.

He liked doing that.

"We gotta play it cool, now," he said. "Y'all understand?"

Charlie nodded, looking impressed.

"*Es correcto,* y'all," said Charlie. "If we try too hard, those *muy caliente mamacitas* won't go back to *La Hacienda* or do nothin' with us. And then we won't get no dick suckin'!"

He raised his finger in the air, like a knife.

"*Con calma,* motherfuckers..."

"*Con calma...*"

1970s

CHAPTER XXIV

DAIRY QUEEN

"Best be careful of them Hazard girls.

They'll give ya somethin' Ajax can't scrub off."

THE DAIRY QUEEN sign cast a white glow from above, illuminating Bill and his Posse as they hung out near the outdoor tables. Charlie kept his car idling, heavy metal pounding from the speakers—not loud enough for the manager to bitch again, but a few decibels below that. Just loud enough to let the world know they were badass, and not to be fucked with.

"Dude," said Kenny. "We played it *con calma,* didn't we?"

Kenny had stayed shirtless since the car ride, only putting it on briefly at the manager's insistence when ordering inside.

"I mean, that's *con calma,* right?" asked Kenny. "That's how we played it, right?"

Bill leaned back against Charlie's dad's black Camaro, lighting a cigarette.

Yeah.

They'd played it *con calma,* alright.

For the most part.

Still hadn't worked.

"We sure fuckin' did, Kenny," said Charlie. "We played it *con calma* to the *muy* fuckin' *grande,* man."

Kenny said, "Can't get more *con calma* than we were!"

Graham snarfed on a triple cheeseburger. "It's that one chick that ruined it all. What was her name?"

"*Sí, sí!*" said Charlie. "What was that bitch's name?"

"Tracey," said Bill.

"Fuckin' Tracey..." Charlie shook his head, taking a drag of his cigarette and staring off, still trying to comprehend what the fuck had happened.

"*She* was the fuckin' problem, *ese.* That fuckin' Tracey bitch just kept checkin' herself in her little makeup mirror, lookin' like she had better places to be."

"Ain't no better place to be than the *Hacienda!*" said Kenny. "Ain't that right, boys?"

Everyone nodded, mumbling variations of *"Yep"* and *"Fuck yeah"* and *"Damn straight, Kenny."*

Charlie flicked ash onto the pavement. "I could tell she wasn't into us, even when they were drivin'. Them other two chicks, what's their fuckin' names?"

"Gina," said Bill. "And Sarah."

"*Sí, sí,*" said Charlie, "fuckin' Gina and Sarah. Them bitches loved us, *ese.* Had 'em eatin' out of our hands. And Gina's tits were so nice—"

"Weren't even that big," said Kenny, "but—"

"Weren't that small, neither," said Bill.

"Nope," said Charlie. "*Justo así. Justo perfecto.* And that Sarah chick, she was flat as fuck, but she had that cool, *dark* vibe to her, y'all know what I'm sayin'?"

Bill locked his eyes on the DQ sign, cigarette dangling from his lips. He took a drag.

"I know what you're sayin', man," he said.

Exhaling slowly, he blew the smoke upward, shrouding the sign's soft glow.

"She had that *vibe* to her," said Bill, "like a badass girlfriend of a Hell's Angel or somethin'..."

Charlie nodded. "*Así es.* We need to find more girls like that, man. Girls with attitude. And style. Those are the kinda girls we want at *La Hacienda,* I'll tell ya that right now..."

"Hell yeah, *amigo,*" said Kenny. "I liked her style, too. I don't say that about many girls, but I liked that Sarah chick's style."

"But that other chick," said Charlie, "fuckin' Tracey—"

"She didn't even wanna come to Dairy Queen!" said Graham.

The guys looked at Graham.

"Now," said Charlie, "why you think that, Graham-cracker?"

"'Cause she didn't eat no ice cream!" said Graham, holding his banana split tray to his lips. He crammed the entire contents into his mouth with a plastic spoon, eyes closed, moaning as he swallowed with minimal chewing, the way an anaconda swallows a bullfrog. Rivulets of ice cream and chocolate syrup dribbled down his chin, landing on his shirt.

"*Huh huh huh...*" chuckled Graham, his mouth overflowing with sweet goodness. "I *looove* banana splits..."

"*BRAAAAAAP!*"

He belched.

The guys watched Graham, transfixed, as he wiped his mouth and smacked his lips. Finally, Kenny broke the silence.

"That Tracey girl probably transferred from Zion to Hazard or somethin'." He crossed his arms. "That's how Zion bitches act. Like they got better places to be."

"Tracey was hot, though," said Bill. "I didn't realize how *hot* she was 'til she got out the car. I think she was the hottest out of all of 'em, to be honest with ya. Even if she was bitchy."

Some of the guys disagreed with that statement, and the conversation fell into a back-and-forth comparison of the girls for a while, taking into account not only their looks but their respective personalities and vibes as well. Amidst the debate, Graham took several long, slow licks across his banana split tray, leaving it spotless, then announced he had to take a massive shit. He stomped into the restaurant and barged through the bathroom door.

Kenny smiled. "Y'all think he's gonna buy even more food? After he takes a dump?"

Everyone chuckled.

"Might be him eatin' so much," said Bill, "that scared those girls away. I ain't ever seen a boy eat as much as him."

"Fuckin', *mucho apetito*," said Charlie. "Two chicken strip baskets, a triple cheeseburger, what else?"

"That banana split!" said Kenny. "He just swallowed the thing! Barely even chewed!"

Everyone laughed.

"He did get a fuckin'," said Bill, "what's that called? What's he drinkin?"

"Fresca," said Charlie. "'Cause it's sugar-free, said he had to watch his weight and shit."

They chuckled again.

"Dude," said Kenny. "I think we still got a good chance with those Gina and Sarah chicks. As long as that Tracey girl ain't with'em. Just wait a few days and call Gina, invite her and Sarah down to the *Hacienda* to party."

He stepped on top of a table.

"Just call'em up!" he said from atop the table. "And be like, *'Wassup girls? Y'all like RC? And tequila? And drugs? Then come on down to our* Hacienda! *Let's get fucked up!'* That's all ya gotta say! 'Cause we're the Posse!"

Bill stroked his beard. Charlie *had* managed to get Gina's number before she left—the only victory of the night so far. Luckily, he always kept a tiny notebook with a pen on him, and had written her number under the heading *"Chicas Que Necesito Follar."*

"I always write my stuff down in español *and shit,"* Charlie had said.

"That way, if anybody finds it, ain't nobody can figure it out. Like it's written in code, man..."

Bill said, "And maybe Charlie can speak Spanish real good to'em on the phone. They did seem impressed by that."

"Desde-fuckin'-*luego*, man, I can do that," said Charlie. "And of course all them *chicas bonitas* love it when Young Charlie speaks that sweet *español* to'em! That's how I get all my pussy, and half my dick suckin'!"

The boys laughed and talked about Charlie's Spanish and how it was real good and shit.

"I started studyin' German, y'all," said Kenny. "Been carryin' a German book with me all the time."

Bill said, "So that's why you brought your backpack."

"Ja," said Kenny. *"Das ist richtig."*

Bill whistled. "That sounded good, right there."

"Danke," said Kenny. "I'm just studyin' whenever I catch a chance. I wanna speak cool-soundin' shit to people, too. Like Charlie."

"That's just the attitude you need to have, Kenny," said Charlie. "That's how I got so damn good at *español, amigo.* Even back in elementary school, I just studied whenever I caught a chance, man. Every bit helps."

They talked about foreign languages for a while, and how they imagined Chinese and Japanese likely proved the hardest. *("All them symbols and shit,"* said Bill, *"don't even use no letters.")* As they spoke, a man with his wife and young son approached the DQ entrance, casting a wary glance at Bill and his Posse.

Bill tipped his cowboy hat. "How y'all doin' tonight?"

The father briefly locked eyes with Bill, then averted his gaze, pulling his family in close.

"Banana splits are good here," said Kenny, still standing shirtless atop a table. The young boy, caught between fear and awe, stared at him until his father hustled him inside.

They watched the family pass through the double-doors.

"Man," said Bill. "Must be bitches from Zion or somethin'."

"Fuckin' *sí*..." said Charlie. "Maybe the Zion Dairy Queen is closed tonight. They don't need to be up here, though. Best for Zion bitches to stay in Zion."

"Maybe it's the music," said Kenny. "Playin' heavy metal real loud like that outta Charlie's car might scare people."

"By people," said Bill, "you mean bitches from Zion."

Charlie shot a disapproving look at Kenny's feet. "Maybe it's 'cause you're standin' on the fuckin' table, Kenny. You ever thought of that?"

"Why's that matter?" asked Kenny.

"'Cause it fuckin' *does,* man," said Charlie. "Have some decency, for God's sake. People eat off that and shit."

"Nah," said Kenny. "Think I'm cool here, actually." He spat. "But thanks for the input."

Bill turned his gaze to the soft glow of the DQ sign. It flickered in a near-discernible pattern, like Morse code.

What ya tryin' to tell me, Dairy Queen sign?

You tryin' to warn me of somethin'?

The sign stopped flickering.

Bill shook his head. It'd be funny if the sign had been tryin' to communicate—maybe even warn him—but of course that wasn't the case. Even if it was, he didn't know fuckin', Morse code, so didn't matter.

"Now, Kenny," said Bill, "I do think Charlie's got a point. How would you feel if people—"

The sound of hippie music—maybe The Beatles, or bullshit like that—cut through the air as two pick-up trucks and a car pulled into a nearby parking lot. A dude in a cap stepped out first.

"Heads up," said Charlie. "Tommy Glick and his weedboys."

"You sure that's them?" asked Bill. His aviator sunglasses made it hard to see far away. "They don't usually hang around here."

"*Sí,*" said Charlie. "Glick with his *odioso* weedboys and his right-hand man, Longface."

They stared in silence as Glick and his weedboys poured from their vehicles. Bill lowered his sunglasses to get a better look.

Eight guys and two girls strong.

A few he recognized: Longface, that Muscle Man Mouse guy, that red-headed Jack-dude, and those Leslie and Lacey chicks that ran with'em. Didn't really know the others, though—probably underclassmen.

"Got their weedbitches with'em, too," said Charlie.

"Yep," said Bill. "Lacey and Leslie. They're fuckin' hot."

"*Sí, sí,*" said Charlie. "Fuckin' *muy bonitas,* ain't they? Too bad they run with weedboys."

"Dude," said Kenny, "that Longface guy is freakishly tall. Maybe even taller than Graham."

"Yep," said Bill. "Always lurchin' over and shit. Gotta have back problems when you're that fuckin' tall."

Bill rotated his neck. Even he had back problems, and he stood only kinda tall. Not *towering* like Graham or Longface.

Kenny bounced on the table. "You and Glick still got beef? I remember hearin' shit at prom."

"Nah..." said Bill. "...he should be over that by now..."

("you sure it's okay?")

("i thought you and glick were...")

Kenny narrowed his eyes. "I see'em at the Walmart parkin' lot all the time. Actin' like they're badass, playin' their music real loud." He shook his head. "Yellin' all that *'roll out'* and *'rally up'* bullshit..."

"That shit's obnoxious as fuck," said Bill.

"Mmm-hmm," said Charlie. "That's why I don't even like goin' to Walmart, *ese*. Don't even wanna see their asses. And definitely don't need to hear all their hootin' and hollerin' while they're playin' that hippie bullshit real loud. Who the fuck they think they are?"

"They *think* they're the kings of Tri..." said Bill. "But they ain't kings of shit. *'Hey maaan, wanna smoke some weeeeed, maaan?'*"

Charlie and Kenny laughed, but Bill watched Glick and his weedboys like a hawk.

Just in case.

1970s

CHAPTER XXV

THE RED GLOW OF MARS

"I always liked planets and shit," said Rhonda.

"Just thought outer space was cool."

("FIND IT, TOMMY...")

("the temple...")

Tommy Glick leaned back against his car.

Nope—none of that *"temple"* bullshit tonight.

Felt good tonight.

The Smoketown Boys rolled strong tonight.

Not only did he have his three main bros—Larry, Mouse and Jack—but also their four Possibles: Kevin, Grant, David, and...what was the other guy's name?

Oh yeah.

Wiley—Wilin' Wiley.

The newest Possible, but maybe the most promising. Recruited him 'cause he was good at fightin'—whipped the shit out of two bigger freshmen in the space of weeks. Seemed like he not only had balls, but actually *got* shit, too. Like he understood what the Boys were about, didn't just fake-ass copy. And he'd sold *all* he was supposed to—not what he could and claimed he did his best.

"Let's smoke a lil' Monkey before we go in," said Tommy. "More fun to eat when you're fucked up."

He'd meant it as a simple fact, not a joke, but of course Leslie and Lacey laughed and said, *"Fuuuuuuck yeah, Tommy."* They always laughed and said shit like that. They wanted him. He knew that. Didn't give a fuck.

Larry held out a tin of Monkey cigs. "If the cops roll up, we roll out."

Smoking Monkey proved not only more cost-effective than the pure stuff, but safer in parking lots and shit, as the tobacco blend helped conceal the telltale scent of marijuana. Even the Smoketown Boys had to be careful of Johnny Law.

"This is gonna be *awesome...*" said Kevin. "I *love* gettin' high..."

"Yeah, Kevin," said Tommy. "You sure do, don't ya?"

Kevin looked at him for a second, as if maybe he'd said something wrong, then returned to lighting his cig.

Fucking Kevin.

Rich boy Kevin.

Just had to announce he *"looooved gettin' high"* to make it crystal-fuckin'-clear for everyone in case they'd forgotten how cool he tried to be.

The weakest Possible, by far.

But his dad was rich and he chipped in a lot for the alcohol and parties and shit. Maybe every squad had to have one guy like Kevin in it.

"Man, this Monkey weed is *sooooo* good!" said Kevin. "I *looove* gettin' high..."

"Don't we all..." said Mouse, eyeing Kevin carefully. "Don't we all..."

Mouse didn't care for Kevin, either—mainly because Kevin went after Lacey the hardest. Despite Mouse's reminder at their last Smoketown Meeting that him and Lacey weren't "boyfriend and girlfriend and shit," a guy could still feel protective over a piece of ass. Especially when a rich boy freshman like Kevin repeated shit like, *"I looove gettin' high"* and *"I could smoke Monkey every day, it's sooo awesome..."*

In some ways, the Possibles were already part of the Smoketown Boys. More or less. They *rallied up* when called upon and *rolled out* when commanded to. They all sold Monkey (some better than others) and so far, there hadn't been any red flags—not any bright ones, at least.

Only Kevin actin' like Kevin.

"Man, I'm gonna eat like *two* chicken strip baskets," said Jack, exhaling smoke. "They're so fuckin' good."

"Ain't no way you can eat more than one," said Tommy. "One and a half, max. You always order too much."

"Yeah, well, this time I—"

"Dude," said Kevin, "I *love* chicken strip baskets here too, man!" He shot Tommy that dumbfuck need-to-please look. The other Possibles started yappin' about what they were gonna eat and how it'd taste *sooo* good because they were gonna get *sooo* high and that made everything taste *sooo* much better and gettin' high was *sooo* awesome.

Tommy and Jack exchanged a glance, narrowing their eyes, likely thinking the same thing:

Whaddaya know.

Kevin loves chicken strip baskets, too.

What a cool coinky-dink.

"I think chicken strip baskets are bullshit," said Tommy. "And guys named Kevin who eat'em, are fuckin' fags."

All chatter ceased.

Kevin's jaw dropped.

"I, uhh..."

Jack and Mouse sneered.

Larry chuckled.

"Did I...did I...uhh..." Kevin's hand trembled, now barely clinging his beloved Monkey cig. "Did I say somethin' wrong, Tommy?"

He gulped.

Mouse snickered. *"Did I-did I say somethin' wrooooong, Tommy?"*

The Possibles laughed nervously.

Larry grinned and reached in the car to lower the music.

"Hey..." said Kevin. "Why...why'd you turn the music down?"

Silence thickened the night air—thick enough to choke on.

Tommy stared at Kevin with neither malice nor friendship.

Just stared.

Leslie and Lacey got that *"Ooo, what's gonna happen next?"* look on their faces. Like they always did when shit got real.

Tommy stepped toward Kevin, never breaking eye contact, never blinking.

"Yeah...you said somethin' wrong..."

He blew smoke in Kevin's face. Eyes scrunched, Kevin coughed, then chuckled nervously.

"W-what did I do, man?"

He glanced at the other Possibles for support.

"Tommy, bro, just lemme kn—*URGGHH!*"

Tommy's fist blurred and slammed into Kevin's gut. Too fast for anyone to see.

"Ughhh...Goddd..."

Kevin bent over, clutching his sides. His balls probably hurt, too. When you got socked in the stomach, your balls hurt.

Leslie and Lacey giggled.

"W-why...?" asked Kevin. His cig fell to the pavement.

Tommy picked it up and took a hit.

Couldn't let good Monkey go to waste.

"Why you think, Kevin?" He spat on the back of Kevin's head. *"Huh? Why you fuckin' think?"*

Larry and Mouse snickered. The other Possibles looked like they'd witnessed slow-motion murder. Lacey and Leslie bit their lips with that "I wanna fuck Tommy" look while Jack observed the group with a scholarly gaze, like a professor about to quiz his students.

"Why do *you* guys think?" asked Jack.

The Possibles stood frozen, mouths agape.

"Jack asked y'all a question," said Larry.

"Y'all got ten fuckin' seconds to answer," said Mouse.

"Ten," said Jack.

"Nine," said Larry.

"Eight," said Mouse.

"B-Because," said Wiley, "Kevin ain't sellin' like he's supposed to..."

Tommy nodded.

Good, Wiley...

More bonus points for you.

"And?" asked Tommy, eyes fixed on Kevin.

"A-And..." said David, the quiet Asian kid with glasses, "b-because he acts like he does..."

Tommy smiled.

The quiet Asian kid actually spoke up for once.

Maybe he had promise, too.

Maybe.

Tommy ruffled his fingers through Kevin's hair. "You okay, buddy?"

Kevin rose, bent forward like a hunchback. Tears streamed down his cheeks. He sniffled.

Poor guy.

Lost some cool points with Lacey and Leslie. Not like he had much of a chance, anyway. Both girls fucked, but not the Possibles. They knew better.

Tommy pulled a still-trembling Kevin into a hug. "Come here, bro... come here..."

"I'm s-sorry, Tommy..." said Kevin.

"It's alright, man..." Tommy patted his back. "Just-be-*better.* Okay?"

He turned toward the other Possibles.

They had to see this.

"Be. Fucking. Better."

"I will..." said Kevin. "I promise..."

"And stop actin' like an asshat," said Mouse.

The guys chuckled.

"That's another way to put it, Mouse," said Tommy. He locked eyes with Kevin. "You cool? You understand why I did that, right?"

Kevin nodded, wiping tears.

Tommy returned his gaze to the Possibles, judging their reaction. They had to see both—the punishment, *and* the forgiveness.

They had to understand.

"Y'all know why I did that, right?" he asked. "Y'all fuckin' understand, don't ya?"

They nodded.

They understood.

***

After Rich Boy Kevin finally stopped coughin' and stood straighter again, Mouse cranked the music back up. Beatles, Beach Boys, Kinks. The good stuff. *Shit that got ya goin'.* Not that heavy metal bullshit that'd started to get popular. The other Possibles seemed shook up, like they'd witnessed a car crash, but the girls went back to talking like nothing had happened.

Larry and Tommy leaned against Larry's truck.

"How much longer we keepin' Kevin?" asked Larry.

Tommy craned his neck to look up at Larry. "Not sure..."

Larry had said he didn't trust the Possibles, either. Not fully. Still wasn't sure if they'd really be there, if they'd *rally up* when shit hit the fan. And eventually, it would—at least a few times before they graduated. Maybe with rednecks over in Hazard, preppies up in Zion, or more likely, with other squads in Crow who liked to talk shit and push their own (usually shitty) brands of drugs.

Sooner or later, him and his Boys would have to *fight* for their rep—just like Mikey and his Boys had.

Mikey...

He removed his cap and stared at the outline of the crow on the front.

Did you test your new guys, too?

How'd you know?

How'd you know if they were—

The Asian David kid asked the girls, "What kinda ice cream y'all like the most?"

"Good question, Asian David," said Mouse. "Maybe ask what their favorite colors are next."

The Boys snickered. Tommy put his cap back on and took a hit of Monkey, considering David.

Asian David.

Jack's protégé, pulled from chess club.

The only *ethnic* guy in their squad and one of the few non-white kids he'd seen in the Tri County, period. Adopted from Korea or Vietnam or wherever, by old folks without much money but driven by their Christian duty or something. Thick glasses, quiet as fuck, but listened well. Didn't spout stupid shit like Kevin. Rarely asked questions, even benign ones like that. Probably still got weak knees around girls. Might even have nightmares about Kevin gettin' socked in the stomach.

That was okay, though.

Meant he *learned* somethin'.

"I like banana splits," said Lacey, her eyes stoned and bloodshot. "One time, I ate like, *three* whole banana splits when I was all high and shit. And I swear to God y'all, I puked banana split *everywhere...*"

"Wow..." said David.

"Damn..." said Wiley.

"And you know what?" asked Lacey. "It tasted just as good comin' out as it did goin' in. *I swear to God, y'all!*"

The Possibles laughed, forming a crescent around the girls, nerves melting away. Only Kevin stood back, as if getting some no longer remained a priority in life.

"That is cra-zyyyy..." said Leslie.

"If you get sick tonight," said Wiley with a wink, "I'll take care of ya..."

"Me too," said Grant. "*I—*" He acted like he was gonna say more, but didn't.

Good Guy Grant.

Kevin's little sidekick. Probably sensed he'd jumped ahead in the race to get some. Grant wasn't special, just a *"good guy,"* but at least he wasn't annoying like Kevin. And sold his shit better, too.

Leslie swayed to the music, blowing smoke at the night sky.

"Y'all gonna take care of me, too?"

She shot the Possibles a pair of *fuck-me* eyes.

"Fuuuuuuuck..."

The Possibles said they would, tightening their circle around the girls, while Kevin hung back like a broken guitar string.

Fuckin' Possibles.

Might as well pull their dicks out, start circle-jerkin'.

No—didn't trust'em yet.

Too focused on pussy.

Mouse spat. "How many more chances we givin' Kevin?"

"Couple more weeks," said Tommy. "Let him prove himself or fuck off."

"I got other guys in mind," said Mouse. "Better than him."

Tommy nodded. Other dudes stood poised for consideration (*"Possible Possibles,"* as Jack called'em) but these were the main four so far. Couldn't take on too many at once, had to focus on quality over quantity. Didn't wanna start feelin' like an after-school club or shit like that. They were a real fuckin' *squad:* a money-makin', weed-smokin', ass-kickin' and bitch-fuckin' squad that didn't take shit from no one and would *rule* the fuckin' Tri County.

Not just Crow—*the whole of Tri.*

Tommy had a plan.

He had a *vision.*

For all he knew, the Possibles only wanted to smoke Monkey and try to get their dicks sucked—either by Lacey or Leslie or the other Smokehouse ornaments at their parties.

Fair-weather friends.

Didn't need none of those.

Not in the Boys.

"I'll tell ya who I'd like us to recruit next," said Jack, "is the Bedford Twins."

Mouse's eyes widened. *"The Bedford Twins?"*

"Yep," said Jack. "The Bedford Twins."

Larry and Mouse exchanged a look.

"What you think, Tommy?" asked Larry.

"Bedford Twins, Bedford Twins..." Tommy drew in a hit of Monkey and turned his gaze toward the stars.

The stars...

Some smaller stars shined brighter than others; some loomed larger but dimmer. Unless you knew the constellations, like he did, patterns proved hard to detect. But shapes and patterns existed everywhere—just as there was rhyme and reason to everything, even amongst the stars.

"Some of those stars," said Tommy. "Ain't even stars. They're planets. Hard to tell the difference sometimes."

"Bullshit," said Mouse. "You can't see other planets without a telescope."

"I bet ya can," said Larry. "Tommy knows his stuff when it comes to astronomics and shit."

"*Astronomy*," said Jack. "And it's true. Some planets just look like stars when viewed by the naked eye."

He pointed at a bright star.

"That bright one over there," said Jack, "is actually Venus."

"You're fuckin' kiddin' me," said Mouse. "That's the mornin' star!"

"Nope, he's right," said Tommy. "It's Venus. The morning star is actually Venus."

"Damn," said Mouse. "Always thought it was a star 'cause, ya know, it's the *morning star.*"

"Technically speakin'," said Larry, "it's the evenin' star, now."

"That's right," said Tommy. "Know any others, Jack?"

"Uhh..." Jack scanned the night sky, but after a few more *"Uhhs,"* Tommy pointed to a dull red star.

"That one over there, that's just barely glowin' red—that's Mars."

"Holy shit..." said Mouse. *"That's"* why it's red."

"Yep," said Tommy. "A whole other planet, my dudes. *The red planet.*"

"Fuckin' Mars, man..." said Larry.

They all stared at Mars for a while, smoking in silence. "Helter Skelter" by The Beatles drifted through the air.

Tommy pondered the planets, the stars—how it proved tough to tell 'em apart unless you'd done your homework. Nobody just "knew" the morning star was Venus; you had to learn it somehow.

"Bedford Twins, Bedford Twins..." he said, as if searching the sky for them.

What part do they play?

In the grand scheme of things?

"Let's hold off for now," said Tommy. "I'll talk to 'em this summer. Check their vibe and shit. Jack, you can go with me."

Best to proceed with caution.

They were the Bedford Twins, after all.

***

"All Day and All of the Night" by The Kinks played. The girls cheered and Leslie said, *"Fuuuuuck, I fuckin' love this sooong"* then danced while the Possibles nodded along, claiming they loved it, too. (They couldn't dance for shit, though, so just shuffled around.) Mouse called Lacey over and flexed his biceps for her.

"You like that, baby?" he asked. "Huh? You like that?"

Lacey traced her finger across the curve of his left bicep.

"Damn..." said Lacey. "You're gettin' so big..."

"Fuck yeah, I am..." said Mouse. "I'm gettin' real fuckin' big..."

He started making out with Lacey and squeezing her ass, making damn sure everyone saw it (especially Jack), then sent her back over to the circle jerk of Possibles.

Jack's freckled face turned red. "We need more girls rollin' with us. Not just Leslie and Lacey."

Tommy knew what he was gettin' at: *he needed new pussy.* Lacey was off-limits now, and while Leslie still fucked (and sucked), she was usually too high and stupid to be much fun. Kept sayin' *"fuuuuuck"* all the time, even while messin' around.

"Fuuuuuuuuck...that feels good as fuuuuuuuuck......."

"Fuuuuuuuuck...let's just fuuuuuuuuck..."

"Fuuuuuuuuck...I mean, fuuuuuuuuck..."

Over and over.

Just kept on sayin' it.

Annoyin' as shit, not to mention a boner killer.

"I'm cool with that," said Tommy. "Maybe talk with Larry about it."

Jack and Larry discussed which girls they deemed hot and worth callin' up. Plenty of cuties attended their Smokehouse parties, but they called upon only a select few to actually *roll* with'em. Outside of parties, Tommy never liked having too many girls around. Clouded judgment and distracted the Boys.

Two or three, okay—four or five, max.

Any more and the whole vibe changed.

Of course, he had Samantha, who stood leagues ahead of the Smokehouse ornaments like Leslie and Lacey, which made him feel differently about the issue.

Samantha...

He tried to relax his mind and clear it of all thought, to let the Monkey bring in that pleasant fog he liked to lose himself in. Tried to think of Samantha in a non-needy way, like how one loves and misses their dog but doesn't *need* the dog.

But, no.

He needed her.

She wasn't his pet or fuck buddy or some girl that occasionally sucked dick for Monkey—she was *Samantha-fucking-Henson.*

The smartest, coolest, hottest chick in all of Tri.

Cheerleader, but straight-A's.

Sexy, but cute and innocent.

Confident, but feminine.

Smart, but not a smartass.

And, most importantly—

fun to talk with.

Didn't have rocks for brains, like a lotta hot girls. Surprisingly fun to talk with about all kinds of things. Even more fun than his Boys— something he'd assumed impossible.

He needed Samantha.

He loved her.

Enduring summer break with her hundreds of miles away at Girl Scout camp, after they'd patched things up and she'd finally—

"Tommy," said Jack, "you cool if we call Deanna and Michelle to roll with us some?"

"What's up?" asked Tommy. "Oh..."

Deanna and Michelle.

Not half-bad.

No Samantha, of course, and not quite as smokin' as Lacey and Leslie, but not as obnoxious, either. Less *"One time I puked banana split, I swear to God, y'all!"* type stories and *"Fuuuuuck"* interjections. More semi-interesting talk.

And they fucked.

That was important, too.

Any chicks that *rolled out* with the Smoketown Boys and smoked their Monkey for free, on the regular, needed to fuck.

And suck.

Occasionally, at least.

"That's cool with me," said Tommy. "No more, though."

He took a deep hit of Monkey, letting the smoke burn his lungs and the high hit his brain, scanning nearby parking lots. Maybe send the Possibles to fuck with other squads tonight—test their resolve. That needed to happen soon. Especially with Kevin.

"Larry," said Tommy. "Is that…?"

He squinted. His vision had worsened this year—but no way would he wear glasses.

No fucking way.

"…is that long-haired jackass in the cowboy hat," asked Tommy, "who I think it is?"

"Yep," said Larry. "Bill-fuckin'-Cunningham. With a little crew. Playin' that heavy metal bullshit over there."

Tommy shook his head.

Fuckin' thought so.

"Mouse," said Tommy, "turn the music up. Don't even wanna hear that shit over there."

Mouse cranked up the music coming from his car. Lacey cheered. Leslie said, *"Fuuuuuck!"*

"Is he…" said Tommy, squinting, "is he wearin' sunglasses for some reason?"

"Yep," said Larry. "He's wearin' sunglasses for some reason."

"The fuck?" asked Tommy, blowing smoke. "Who the fuck wears sunglasses at night? Who the fuck does he think he is?"

Larry took a hit of Monkey and held it in, then released the smoke. "Dunno. Guess he thinks he's badass or somethin'."

"Badass, huh?" asked Tommy.

"More like retarded," said Mouse.

Mouse, Jack and Larry snickered.

Tommy didn't.

"Who's he with?" asked Tommy.

"Looks like Young Charlie," said Larry.

Young.

Tommy pursed his lips, like he'd tasted something bitter.

("you can smoke with me anytime, man…")

("we can be amigos…")

("i'll teach ya español, too...")

Young and him used to be cool, way back in the day, before he'd even formed the Boys. But then Young made friends with Bill-fucking-Cunningham, who Tommy never fucking liked, and when that bullshit went down at prom it was like him and Charlie had never even *been* friends.

("you fuck with bill, man...")

Like they'd never even smoked together.

("then you fuck with me.")

But what the fuck ever.

He had his Boys.

And Samantha.

That's all that mattered.

"Who's the other guy?" asked Tommy. "The dipshit standin' on the table?"

"Think that's Kenny Moser," said Larry.

"Moser?" asked Tommy. "That Skinny Kenny guy? Why's he on the fuckin' table? With his shirt off?"

"Dunno," said Larry. "Guess he thinks he's somethin' else."

"Huh," said Tommy. Didn't know that Skinny Kenny dude too well, only that he seemed kinda wild and eccentric, like he was pumped up about shit all the time. For no fuckin' reason. Didn't matter who that Bill shithead rolled with, though—still didn't like seein' his ass. Reminded him of—

("i swear we didn't do anything!")

("tommy, i swear!")

Tommy scowled. "Why the fuck they standin' near the entrance like that? Like they're top shit?"

"Tryin' to rep is what they're doin'," said Larry.

Jack blew smoke in the air. "Think they're sellin' coke here?"

"At *Dairy Queen?*" asked Mouse.

"Nahhh," said Larry. "They's just reppin'. Tryin' to be seen and shit."

"How you know that?" asked Jack.

Larry's eyelids drooped as he exhaled smoke. "For one, ain't nobody sellin' *cocaine* at fuckin' Dairy Queen. And two, apparently Young's got this rule that you can only buy at his house. They don't do deliveries."

"That's a smart idea," said Jack.

Tommy flicked ash, watching the flakes float slowly to the pavement.

Kinda was a smart idea, actually.

The Possibles made Monkey deliveries all the time, but Monkey wasn't near expensive as coke. Had to be careful with a product like that. People might kill a dude for enough coke.

"They still havin' little coke parties?" asked Mouse.

"Yep," said Larry. "Invitin' girls and shit."

Tommy's eyes narrowed.

Not *his* girl, though.

("tell me the truth, samantha")

("did you fuck him?")

("did you suck his dick?")

("fucking tell m—")

"Heard they call themselves a 'posse,'" said Jack. "Or some cowboy bullshit like that."

Mouse snickered. "A 'posse'?"

"A buncha cocaine-sellin', wannabe cowboys," said Larry. "That's some true bullshit, right there."

Everyone murmured in agreement.

True bullshit.

"But," said Jack, "I been workin' on some new line graphs for when *we* start sellin' coke. I'll show'em to y'all soon."

Tommy, Larry and even Mouse nodded. Everybody liked it when Jack drew line graphs. Made shit easy to understand.

Tommy returned his gaze to the Possibles circle-jerking around the girls.

They hadn't drawn line graphs yet.

They hadn't done *any* cool shit like that.

"I been meanin' to ask," said Mouse, "when we go to Nashville on our coke-findin' trip, can Lacey come with us?"

Jack folded his arms. "Why only Lacey?"

"Whatever," said Mouse. "Invite Leslie, too, then. Or whoever you want. Just no dorky-ass bitches from your chess club."

Jack stepped toward Mouse. "Why you always talkin' shit about chess club, *Mitchey Mouse?*"

An argument ensued, and Larry stepped between them, trying to calm shit down. The Possibles remained oblivious, still guided by their dicks. Tommy took a hit of Monkey and held the smoke in, considering Mouse's question.

Girls could be a liability.

Might have to check out some scuzzy-ass places to find new suppliers. Especially if they were lookin' to buy hard shit, like coke.

But girls could also add an advantage.

All dudes—even and especially scuzzy dudes—loved talkin' to hot chicks.

He returned his gaze to the DQ entrance.

Didn't give a shit about the Nashville trip either way, though.

Not now.

Not when Bill-fucking-Cunningham wore a gay-ass cowboy hat and sunglasses at night, leanin' back against that black Camaro like he was the king of the Tri.

("did you do somethin' with him?")

Bill Cunningham wasn't king of shit.

("tell me if you did somethin'!")

Never was, never would be.

("fucking tell me!")

He had to fuck with him.

("swear to me!")

("swear it!")

Honor demanded it.

***

"I just don't understand why Graham smokes Camels," said Charlie. "If we're gonna be a *real* Posse, unified and shit, we should at least smoke the same brand."

Bill glanced inside the Dairy Queen. Graham was still in the bathroom, likely takin' a monster shit that'd stink up the whole place. Good. Didn't need him attendin' Professor Charlie's lecture on Marlboros vs. Camels. One conflict today was enough.

"No disrespect, Charlie," said Kenny, still standing on the table. "But what's the difference?"

"What's the difference?" Charlie stared at Kenny like he'd asked the Stupid Question of the Year.

"They're all cigs, right?" asked Kenny. "Who cares? I mean, if he drank

Pepsi instead of RC, would you really care? I personally prefer RC, for a variety of fuckin' reasons, but if someone preferred Pepsi, I wouldn't..."

As Bill listened, he observed Glick and his crew eat their food in the neighboring parking lot. They'd mad-dog eyeballed him as they slow-motion walked in and out the side doors, probably high as fuck on their bullshit "Orangutan Weed" or whatever they called it, but hadn't actually started anything.

Good.

Didn't want no bullshit tonight.

Bill still felt good about tonight, and he knew those Hazard chicks had been impressed with his style. His vibe. Except for Tracey, the bitchy one—who might've actually transferred from Zion, so didn't count. Still the hottest, though, maybe *because* she was so bitchy. Maybe that's what made him want her more. Like how walkin' by hot-ass, preppy Zion chicks who wouldn't give him the time of day made him want'em even more.

To really give those girls some deep, *powerful* fuckin'.

The kind that Zion boys couldn't deliver.

(what if you get another girl pregnant?)

(another one...)

Nope, nope.

Got his pull-out game real good, now.

Didn't even wanna think about that shit.

(her name is rhonda...)

(and she's your daught—)

He grimaced.

Anyway, other chicks would probably roll up soon, and he just wanted to focus on takin'em back to the *Hacienda* to snort coke, drink liquor, and hopefully get some fuckin' on, too.

Didn't need no drama—especially from weedboys.

That was all in the past, now.

Glick should be over that shit.

"Now see, Kenny," said Charlie. He stared at Kenny perched on the table as if he were a misbehaving child. "You don't even smoke, so, *no fuckin' offense, ese,* but gettin' your input on this ain't even real valid. Like gettin' somebody's input on Pepsi, or fuckin', RC, when they ain't even drank neither before."

"Actually," said Kenny, "I think my input is still pretty valid."

"Oh yeah?" asked Charlie.

"Yep," said Kenny. "Even if somebody hasn't drank Pepsi or RC before, they can still say it don't matter which one ya like. 'Cause it don't."

"Now Kenny," said Charlie, "you was the one goin' on about us dressin' up like cowboys, for fuckin' *impact*."

"That's different," said Kenny.

"How's it different?" asked Charlie. "Think about the fuckin' *impact*, if we're all smokin' the *same* brand of cigarettes with our cowboy hats. The cigarettes would be like the cherry on top."

He pulled out his pack of Marlboros.

"Look here. Marlboro's—fuckin' Medium. The red and white label kind."

Kenny shrugged. "So?"

"So, don't these look *cool*, man?" asked Charlie. "I mean, way cooler than Camels..."

"Why?" asked Kenny.

"You didn't see'em, man?" asked Charlie. "You didn't see Graham's Camels?"

"Nope," said Kenny. "Didn't give a fuck."

"Well, Kenny, next time," said Charlie, "how about you use your goddamn eyeballs, 'cause that's what God gave'em to ya for. *How about considerin' that for a motherfuckin' second?*"

Bill and Kenny chuckled. Charlie probably hadn't meant it as a joke, but it was funny how worked up he got about shit.

"Now Camels," began Charlie. He seemed unsure why Bill and Kenny laughed, but not bothered by it, either. "They got a fuckin' *cartoon camel* on the pack. Now, what're we tryin' to be, *ese?* The Looney Tunes Posse or somethin'? *Mierda!* We don't smoke that shit!"

Just as Bill prepared to change the subject, a chicken strip smacked him in the face. He turned to see Tommy-fucking-Glick with Larry-fuckface lurching close behind, gawking at him with shit-eating grins.

"Oh, look, Larry!" said Tommy.

"It's a gay-ass cowboy..."

1970s

CHAPTER XXVI

RALLY UP

"What's that 'rally up' bullshit they do, anyway?

How'd they come up with that?"

"Dunno...but I sure wouldn't fuck with 'em..."

"YOU DROPPED SOMETHIN'. Best come on over here, now, and pick it the fuck up," is what Tommy expected Bill to say after he hit him square in the face with Jack's leftover chicken strip. Or, at least something *like* that. That's what he would've said if he were Bill, then followed it up with a cowboy boot to the face.

But Bill hadn't said that.

In fact, Bill hadn't said shit.

Just stared from behind his scraggly-ass beard and those fucking aviator sunglasses.

"I knew cowboys liked to suck dick," said Tommy. "I didn't know they wore sunglasses at night, though."

Charlie spat on the pavement. "Now you listen *here,* motherfucker, you wanna—"

"Tsst!" Bill held his hand up.

Charlie and Kenny's faces seethed with cold hatred, as if Tommy had defiled a shrine, but Bill's face showed all the emotion of a stone.

"You deaf, Bill?" asked Tommy. "I knew you was retarded, but you deaf on top of that?"

A cool wind blew. Unusually cool for a summer night.

Kenny stepped off the table and stood beside Bill.

Every muscle in Tommy's body tightened in preparation for Bill and his Posse to charge at him. Bill stood taller and was likely stronger, but he couldn't match Tommy's speed—once the cowboy charged, he planned to punch him hard and fast right in his goddamn sunglasses.

Come on, Bill...

The DQ sign above flickered.

Step up to me...

Lemme break those sunglasses.

Bill brushed chicken strip crumbs from his beard and finally spoke, his voice raspy and hoarse, like he'd been breathing desert air.

"You ever throw somethin' at me again, Glick," said Bill, *"I'll shove it down your goddamn throat."*

A silence followed.

For a moment, a twinge of fear seized Tommy—the kind of dread that hits when you realize you've pushed too far, like poking a grizzly bear. But he reminded himself Bill wasn't a bear, just a bitch-ass, gay-as-fuck wannabe cowboy, and that *he* was the leader of the Smoketown Boys.

And the Smoketown Boys feared no one.

Good one, Bill...

I'm real scared.

He mock-gasped in surprise.

"Look, Larry!" said Tommy. "The gay cowboy! It speaks!"

Larry snickered. "I was worried he might be deaf on top of bein' blind. I mean, why else would a gay cowboy wear sunglasses at night?"

Tommy grinned.

Good one, Larry.

Good...

Tommy didn't wanna be the only one shit-talking—teamwork trumped solo efforts. *Always.*

"Well, Larry, I can think of a reason..." said Tommy, maintaining his faux-awestruck expression. "...maybe it's 'cause he's fucking retarded. Bill Cunningham is a fucking gay-ass, cowboy retard."

He stared at Bill with an unblinking grin.

C'mon, cowboy...

Giddy up.

"Unless..." Tommy stepped forward with Larry close behind. "Billy-boy wants to...*do* something about it..."

He cocked his head, still grinning, never blinking.

"No?" he asked. "Billy-boy's not gonna...*do* something about it?"

An awful silence followed.

Charlie and Kenny looked ready to throw down, like they'd resolved to *do* something about it, but Bill's expression remained still as stone.

"Well, then," said Tommy. "Guess the gay-fuckin'-cowboy don't got nothin' to say..."

He shot one last look at Bill, straining to peer past the mirrored lenses of his sunglasses, instead finding only his own warped reflection.

"C'mon, Larry," said Tommy, turning around. "I guess Cunningham's not only a *retard* who wears a cowboy hat, but a pussy, as well..."

"Pussssayyyyy!" Larry turned to join Tommy.

They sauntered away, slowly at first, then picking up speed.

Bill's voice rang across the parking lot like a gunshot, clear and true:

"I fucked your girlfriend after prom."

Tommy froze.

No.

He whipped around. *"What'd you fuckin' say?"*

Bill leaned back against the car like he hadn't said anything.

Tommy's lower lip quivered.

"What'd you fuckin' say, Cunningham?"

He squeezed his hands into fists.

"After prom," said Bill, "I took her fuckin' cherry. And then we fucked four times after that, before y'all got back together."

Charlie and Kenny snickered.

Tommy felt the blood drain from his face.

No.

"And even when we first fucked," said Bill, "on Prom night, she told me to bust on her face."

No.

"And in her mouth."

No.

"I didn't even ask for that," said Bill. "But she told me that's how she wanted it."

No.

"And I didn't tell her to swallow, either," said Bill. *"She just did."*

No.

Kenny keeled over, slapping his knee while howling.

"Did you *kiss* her after that, Tommy? You didn't *kiss* her after that, did ya?"

No.

Charlie's grin spread from ear to ear.

"I hope that bitch brushed her teeth!"

No.

Charlie and Kenny howled like hyenas while Bill just stared from behind those fucking sunglasses.

No.

No.

No.

Tommy's stomach tightened.

("i swear we didn't do anything, tommy!")

("i swear!")

"He's lyin' dude," said Larry. "He's fuckin' lyin."

("did you do anything with him?")

Was he?

(*"fucking tell me if you did!"*)

Was he fucking lying?

(*"tell me!"*)

She'd never looked him in the eyes when she answered.

(*"we just went as friends, tommy..."*)

She'd *sworn* she hadn't done anything,

(*"we didn't do anything!"*)

but she never looked him in his fucking eyes.

(*"i swear, tommy!"*)

(*"i swear!"*)

"She got better at fuckin', each time," said Bill. "And she liked ridin' on top the best."

(*"i wanna ride on top, tommy..."*)

(*"it feels the best..."*)

"Liar!" said Tommy. *"You're a fucking liar!"*

"Nope," said Bill, his face devoid of emotion. "I ain't lyin', Glick. I took her cherry and done loosened it up for ya."

Kenny and Charlie cackled.

"And each time I finished," said Bill, "I made sure to bust on her face and in her mouth, too. *Real good,* just like she wanted it."

He took a drag from his cigarette.

"And each time," said Bill, "she fuckin' swallowed."

Kenny and Charlie's cackling hit a fever-pitch, like they'd inhaled laughing gas. Cackling so hard they could barely fucking stand.

"And she swallowed every fuckin' drop," said Bill. "And I never once asked her to swallow, man. I was cool with just bustin' on her face and shit. I mean, to be real honest with ya, I was surprised she even wanted that. Not somethin' I imagined a girl like Samantha askin' for."

No.

(*"give it to me on my face, tommy..."*)

He lied.

(*"on my face...and in my mouth..."*)

But how could he know?

(*"that's how I want it every time..."*)

How could he fucking *know* that?

(*she lied, tommy...*)

Bill flicked his cigarette at Tommy, landing just short of his shoes.

"She made me swear not to tell," said Bill. "Like swear to God and shit. But..."

He shrugged.

"Liar!" said Tommy. *"You fucking take that back, Cunningham!"*

The knot in his stomach hardened. He saw Mars, the red glow of Mars, growing brighter and brighter and—

"He's just fuckin' with you," whispered Larry.

—brighter.

No!

Everything around Tommy melted—the Dairy Queen sign, the restaurant and the customers inside, the blacktop and the stars in the sky, *even Mars, even fucking Mars melted into fucking Venus* and he sank into an abyss of lies *(you bitch!)* and deceit *(you whore!)* and betrayal *(you fucking whore!)* and at the center stood Samantha, his precious, sweet, innocent Samantha, still just a freshman, riding naked atop that motherfucker Bill, mewing and moaning and looking into Bill's sunglasses while she bounced and grinded on his cock, and then the abyss swirled and she got on her knees, *on her knees like a fucking whore,* swallowing every drop without Bill asking, just like she had for *him* even though she'd sworn that *he* was the first, that she'd *never* done it before, and she looked at Bill and saw herself reflected in his sunglasses all warped and distorted like *he* saw himself in those fucking sunglasses and—

(she lied, tommy...)

He squeezed his eyes shut.

(she gave it to bill...)

(her virginity...)

No.

She swore to me.

(she lied to you, tommy...)

No.

Bill's fucking with me.

(you knew she lied...)

No.

(she lied she lied she fucking LIED)

No!

(she's a whore!)

(you always fucking knew!)
He opened his eyes, still seeing nothing but Samantha,
(what you gonna do?)
warped in the reflection of Bill's sunglasses,
No!
He's fucking lying!
cum dripping down her chin,
(what you gonna do now, *tommy?)*
gazing up at Bill and smiling.
(what will y—)
Tommy raised his fist, his mouth opening before his mind even formed thought:

"SMOKE-TOWN-BOYS, RALLY-UUUUUUUUP!"

Every single Smoketown Boy—even the Possibles, even Kevin—bolted across the parking lot, eyes ablaze with readiness. Out of the swirling abyss of doubt and jealousy and rage, *burning rage* emerged a singular clarity, sharp as crystal:

Time to fuck up a cowboy.

1970s

CHAPTER XXVII

ROLL OUT

"I'll only do this with you, Tommy..."

"I'LL KILL YOU!" said Tommy. *"I'll fucking kill you, Cunningham!"*

Tommy had never killed before, but he felt ready. He'd smash Bill's sunglasses to pieces and use'em to cut off Bill's face, *his fucking face with that goddamn beard* and send it to Samantha in a package along with that fucking cowboy hat *so she could kn—*

"Not here, Tommy," said Larry. "Everybody's lookin' at us."

Tommy's surroundings sharpened back into focus. Everyone in the whole fuckin' Dairy Queen gawked from the windows like it was the Kentucky version of *West Side Story*.

"High school baseball field!" said Tommy.

"We'll fuckin' settle this!"

***

All eight Smoketown Boys glared at Bill and his Posse, awaiting their response. Bill lit another cigarette, appraising the weedboys before him.

Tommy Glick, frothin' at the mouth.

Larry Longface, lookin' strangely wounded, as if Bill had hurt his feelings, too.

That red-haired, freckle-faced Jack-dude, seemin' slightly confused, but determined.

And that Mitchell-Mickey-Mouse-motherfucker—lookin' excited, like a kid about to ride a roller-coaster.

The four underclassmen standin' behind'em—three dudes he didn't know and one Asian kid he'd seen in the halls a few times—looked both proud and terrified, like soldiers confident in their advantage but still afraid of battle.

"Four on eight," said Charlie. "Ain't really fair, now, is—"

"Life's not fair, bitch," said Mouse.

"Get over it."

***

Tommy raised an eyebrow. Amidst his rage, a tiny voice pointed out that Bill only had *three* guys, not four.

Why had Young said *four?*

"I like those odds," said Bill. "We'll meet y'all at the baseball field. Gimme two hours, though."

He tipped his cowboy hat.

"Need time to fuck Samantha again."

Charlie and Kenny busted out laughing.

"Think I'll try doggystyle this time," said Bill. "But I'll still blast all over her fa—"

Tommy's lips pulled back into a snarl. *"Don't you even say her fucking name, Cunningham! I'll k—"*

"What's goin' on at the baseball field now?" a deep voice asked.

The double-doors of the DQ swung as Graham Riley stepped up behind Bill, looming like a mountain.

"Was takin' a dump," said Graham. "But heard y'all yellin' from inside."

Tommy and his Boys stood frozen, eyes wide and mouths agape.

Graham?

Graham-fuckin'-Riley?

Graham-fuckin'-Riley is hangin' with these *motherfuckers?*

"Grahaaaam," said Tommy. "What up, man? You ain't hangin' with *these* losers, are ya?"

Graham spat. "What if I am, weedboy?"

Tommy paused—he had to choose his next words carefully. If it'd been anybody else but Graham, he would've kept up with the shit-talkin'—maybe said something like, *"Just didn't think you liked to take it up the ass, that's all."*

But this was Graham Riley.

The guy who—

"BRAAAAAAAPPPP!"

Graham belched.

"'Scuse me..." Graham patted his chest. "So what's goin' on at the baseball field, now? Couldn't hear the rest."

Tommy exhaled slowly, reassessing the situation. Even with their advantage in numbers, taking on Bill's little gay-ass posse with *Graham-fucking-Riley* in the mix posed a huge gamble.

But he couldn't back down, either.

Not in front of the Boys.

He glanced around. Jack, Larry, and Mouse—the Originals—would

still fuckin' throw down, even *with* Graham in the mix, but they'd almost
certainly lose, too.

Not unless they had an edge.

...the Possibles?

Maybe they could swarm Graham? Like ants?

He studied their faces: fear, raw and unfiltered.

Nope.

They ain't swarmin' shit...

No surprise—Graham fucking terrorized the underclassmen. Got
like fifty bucks a week in "tribute" from takin' their lunch money and shit.
Motherfucker needed only *walk* toward'em and they'd piss their pants.

Except Wiley.

Wilin' Wiley might hold his ground.

Maybe.

And if word got out that *eight* of the Smoketown Boys lost against *four*
of Bill's Posse? That *half* his squad ran away?

The damage to their rep would be lethal.

No, they weren't ready for this.

They needed an edge.

His focus turned to Charlie.

("you can smoke with me anytime, man...")

("mi casa, fuckin' su casa...")

An inkling emerged,

("just be careful with droppin' ash and stuff...")

only a mere shadow of an idea,

("like, make sure you get it all in the fuckin' ash tray...")

not yet fully formed.

For now, he had to neutralize Graham.

"Hey Graham," said Tommy, attempting to sound respectful but
unafraid. "We ain't got no problem with you, man. We're *cool* with you. In
fact, been meanin' to invite you to our party next Saturday."

"Oh, yeah?" asked Graham. "You're invitin' *me*?"

Tommy paused.

Was Graham fucking with him?

"Yeah, man," said Tommy. "You and us, we're always cool. We'll all get
high together."

"Wow..." said Graham. "Get high together...*sounds real cool, dude...*"

Bill and his Posse snickered.

Tommy clenched his jaw.

Graham *was* fucking with him.

"Graham, man," said Tommy, "I don't—"

"AAAAAAAAAAAAAAAAAHHHHHH!"

A shrill male voice pierced the air.

"What the...?" asked Tommy.

"AAAAAAAAAAAAAAAAAHHHHHH!"

Kevin rushed toward Graham, screaming like a Comanche warrior, fist reared back like a tomahawk.

"AAAAAAAAAAAAAAAAAAHHHHHH!"

He leapt, fist hurtling toward Graham's face, and—

"AAAAAAAAAAAAAAAAAAAAAAAA—

—aaaaggh! Aaaaaaaggh!"

—Graham caught him by his throat.

"Aaaaagh! Aaaaaaggh!"

"Shit..." said Tommy.

"Huh huh huh..." chuckled Graham.

Kevin squirmed, kicking his legs out like a cockroach.

"...can't...bre...athe..." He pulled at Graham's grip around his neck.

"Let him go, man!" said Jack.

"Graham," said Tommy, "let Kevin go. We ain't got no problem with you, man."

*"Huh huh huh...*seems like *he* had a problem, though..."

Kenny and Charlie sneered.

Bill's lips twisted into a dry smile.

"He was actin' stupid!" said Tommy. "Let him the fuck go!"

"Aaaaaaaaaaaggghh!"

Kevin's face turned a deep shade of crimson.

"You're gonna kill him!" said Tommy.

"Aaaaaaaaaaaaaaaaaaaaaaaagh!"

Kevin's eyeballs looked like they might pop out.

"Aaaaaaaaaaaaaaaaaaaaaaaaaaaaaggggh!"

His face turned from crimson to purple.

"Let him go," said Bill.

"Aaaaaaaaaaaaggh! Aaaaaaaaaaaaaggggh!"

"You sure?" asked Graham.

Bill nodded.

Graham released his grip.

"Aaaaaaaagggh-umff!"

Kevin fell to the pavement like a lifeless doll, wheezing as his lungs struggled for air.

"Ugggghhhh..."

David and Grant ran forward to help him. Leslie's voice echoed in the distance: *"Fuuuuuuck..."*

"Desaparece, motherfucker!" Charlie kicked Kevin from behind, propelling him forward. David and Grant flinched, staring as if he'd kicked a wounded dog.

Bill and his Posse cackled.

"Any other challengers?" asked Graham, cracking his knuckles.

"BRAAAAPPPP!"

He belched.

Kenny slapped his knee.

Bill and his Posse cackled even louder.

"Nah..." said Tommy, keeping a steady eye on Graham. Sweat moistened his palms.

"...we'll save it for the baseball field..."

He meant to come off as cool and confident, but his voice had cracked.

"Sí, motherfucker, *sí!"* said Charlie. "Graham's gonna throw y'all for a home run!"

Bill and his crew laughed like he'd said the funniest thing.

Blood pounded in Tommy's ears.

How had he even been friends with Young?

("you can come by and smoke with me anytime...")

How'd they used to smoke together?

("mi casa, fuckin' su casa, man...")

Tommy's eyes widened.

("just be careful about ashes on the table and shit...")

Previously only a shadow, a brilliant idea now glimmered into form.

"We'll see y'all in two hours..." said Tommy, turning to leave. "Got shit to smoke before then."

Tommy and his Boys sauntered toward their vehicles. Kevin's arms clung around David and Grant.

"Oh," Tommy turned back to Bill. "If y'all wanna coke up beforehand, go ahead. You'll fuckin' need it."

Mouse cackled. "And tell your little fag-friends to wear cowboy hats, too!"

"I've always wanted to beat the fuck outta cowboys!"

***

Bill and his Posse watched the weedboys return to their cars, where those two weedchicks, Leslie and Lacey, waited. They huddled up for a while, discussin' somethin' real fuckin' intently, then one of 'em shouted, *"SMOKE-TOWN-BOYS, ROLL-OOOUUUT!"* and they all yelled and screamed like monkeys as they peeled out the lot.

"See ya soon, cocksuckers!" said Mouse, as he and Jack flipped the bird.

Bill glanced at the DQ sign.

A moth fluttered into a web woven across it.

He tightened his hands into fists.

"Charlie?" he asked.

"Yeah?" said Charlie.

The moth struggled to escape the web.

"You still got some coke in the car?"

A spider rushed forward, eager to consume its prey.

"I sure fuckin' do."

I wouldn't ever kill nobody...

But I can understand why guys like Blackbeard had to.

Blackbeard: The Man Who Scourged the Seas

By: Roberta Stevenson

CHAPTER 11

Why Did Blackbeard Kill People?

(pg.112) When Blackbeard approached a target, he gave the crew a choice: surrender their cargo, *or else.* If they complied, he showed mercy, leaving everyone unharmed. If they resisted, he killed them without hesitation.

"*That's awful!*" you might be thinking. "*Why couldn't he just beat them up?*"

That's a great question!

To understand, try *imagining* yourself in Blackbeard's shoes, facing the same situations he did.

→ **Use Your Imagination!** *Your imagination is a powerful tool. Pretending you're someone else can help you understand their reasons for doing things that might seem bad at first.*

Imagine: You've decided to pull off your first bank robbery. Like Blackbeard needed his crew, you'll need loyal, trusted friends to help you with this exciting *(and dangerous!)* adventure.

But *what else* would you need to pull it off?

→ **Fun with Your Friends!** *Round up your buddies and brainstorm what you'd need to rob a bank. But don't let anyone hear—they might call the police!*

What did you come up with?

Hopefully, you realized you'll need a getaway car, masks to protect your identity, bags for the money, and—most importantly—*guns.* After all, no one's scared of bank robbers with knives!

→ **Did You Know?** *The last known instance of knives used in a bank robbery occurred in 1960 in New York City. Customers tackled the robbers, stabbing them to death with their own knives! Not such a "sharp" idea, after all!*

Now, imagine you and your friends have *masked-up* and stormed the bank, guns drawn.

"*Everybody on your knees!*" you yell. "*Hands behind your head! No funny business!*"

Your heart races.

You can *feel* the adrenaline in your veins.

It feels good. Powerful.

The excitement *pumps you up.*

"Put the money in the bags!" you command. *"Or we'll shoot!"*

The bank clerks look terrified, stuffing your bags with cold, hard cash.

But while they're filling the bags, what do *you* do?

Tap your feet and look at your watch?

After all, you need to keep everyone *afraid.* You can't have anyone trying to be a hero.

So...

What do you do?

That's right—keep your guns pointed at people! Even without shooting, the *threat* of getting shot makes people comply.

→ **Did You Know?** *Often, it's the threat of action that keeps people in line more than the action itself. You don't always have to hurt people to scare them—they just need to* underline*believe* underline *you might.*

Now, what if the bank clerks *didn't* comply?

What if they weren't afraid of you? And refused to put the money in your bags?

What if they tried to *fight* you?

In this situation, you'd have two options:

Option 1) Try and subdue them without shooting.

Option 2) Shoot them.

If you choose Option 1, you can beat the clerks up instead of shooting them. You definitely might feel better about yourself! After all, you just want the money, right? And you probably don't like to hurt people, much less kill them.

But by *not* shooting, you show everyone in the bank you might *not* use your guns—and that they could resist you without fear of being shot.

But what if you choose Option 2?

If you *shoot* the uncooperative clerks, *you show everyone you mean business.* You show the world you aren't afraid to use your guns, and that everyone had better comply—

—or else.

<u>Tolerating Disrespect – A Big No-No</u>
Blackbeard had another good reason to kill people—to show he *never* tolerated disrespect.

→ *Vocabulary Question: Do you know what "tolerate" means? It means to allow or accept something, even though it's bad.*

When you *tolerate* disrespect from someone, you let people know you're okay with it. This usually results in further disrespect, as your *tolerance* only invites more.

Imagine if someone in a tavern said to Blackbeard, *"Hey, man! Your beard sucks! It looks so ugly! You should call yourself 'Poopbeard!'"*

Publicly insulted, Blackbeard would face two choices:

1) Do *nothing.*

This would signal he tolerates disrespect, inviting others to insult him, too.

2) Do *something.*

He could harm that person, or perhaps kill them in a dramatic fashion—so people would *think twice* before disrespecting him again.

Given these options, it's clear why Blackbeard always took action. If people thought they could disrespect him, he'd become "Poopbeard," the joke of the pirate world!

→ *Thought Question: Has anyone given you a disrespectful nickname? Did you tolerate it? If so, what happened?*

Blackbeard showed <u>*zero tolerance*</u> for disrespect. He understood that tolerating it would only lead to more.

→ *Vocabulary Tip: The phrase "zero tolerance" can be a powerful tool in your vocabulary. It lets people know you mean business! The next time someone* *disrespects you, tell them you have <u>zero tolerance</u> for it. Get close, look them in the eye, and say it confidently.*

<u>Blackbeard – No Choice But to Kill People</u>

Now you understand why Blackbeard killed all who resisted without a drop of hesitation, nor an inch of mercy. *He had no choice.*

But did you know he didn't *just* kill people?

Sometimes he committed unspeakable acts of brutality!

Turn the page to learn more about Blackbeard's brutality!

Discussion Exercises—Talk With Your Friends!

1.   Blackbeard never tolerated disrespect. Can you imagine what would have happened if he did?

2.   Have you ever been disrespected by someone? What did you do to that person to punish them? If you didn't do anything, what do you _wish_ you'd done to them?

3.   Killing people is wrong. But sometimes, it's okay. Can you think of situations where it's okay to kill people?

4.   The police and the military kill people all the time. Why is that okay?

5.   Imagine you have to kill someone tomorrow. Who would you kill, and why?

1990s

CHAPTER XXVIII

YOU SO PURTY AND SWEET AND SPECIAL

"OPEN YOUR MOUTH, BOBBY!

YOU'VE BEEN A BAD BOY!"

BOBBY SMEARED HIS penis across the Barbie's face.

"You so p-purty..." he said. "...and sweeeeet a-and..."

He slurped up his drool.

"...speciaaalll..."

Pale moonlight caressed his back as he gazed into her eyes.

"...s-so...so...purty..."

He'd fed her so much today.

"...so s-sweeeet..."

And she *ate it all*, every single drop, like a good girl.

"...so...speciaaallll..."

Neither the doll, nor the real Little Stacey ever blinked during this part.

"...you ate it aaaallll uppp..."

This was the most important part—

"...like a g-gooood girrrllll..."

—when she gazed up at him with her grateful, unjudging eyes.

"Ahm a gud gurlll, Bawww-byyy..." he said in her voice. A strand of drool dangled from his mouth.

It was only right before The Feeding, and for a precious few moments after, when the *real* Little Stacey appeared, projected over the doll.

When they became one.

When they *Joined*.

"Tss!"

He winced.

Scabs had peeled off again, leaving his bloodied foreskin sensitive to touch. Was gettin' harder and harder to feed Little Stacey her late breakfast, and the past three weeks had rubbed him raw. Tonight took longer than ever—nearly a dang ol' hour—but, *thank God,* he'd finally fed her.

And he'd entered it and *touched* it—The Void.

And he'd *witnessed* it—The Joining.

"You so p-purty...and sw-sweet..."

His drool dangled down again.

"And speciaaalll..."

The Void and The Joining remained the only things he looked forward to in life. Seeing the *real* Little Stacey, rubbing his pecker across her face, staring into her eyes, seeing himself in them, everything he was and could be, past, present and future—her *eyes* held it all.

"Ah wub you, Bawww-byyy..."

Sometimes she'd say it while gurglin' her breakfast, which he adored, but couldn't imitate.

"I l-love you, too...L-Little S-Stacey..."

"See ya next taaa-iiime..."

She faded away.

Only the doll's plastic eyes peered back at him.

"S-see ya...next t-time..."

A glob of her breakfast fell to the ground.

"L-Little...S-Stacey..."

He looked up from the doll, feeling calm and satisfied. Woods felt good tonight. Not too muggy. Pleasantly warm. Mosquitoes had stopped botherin' him once he used the spray, and he'd grown comfortable with this little spot. Felt special now. His secret hideaway; his new Good Woods. Had a certain magic to it, like the enchanted forests in fantasy books he'd read as a child, the ones he imagined while playing in the Good Woods behind his house. Had himself some good times back then. Nobody could bother him, and he found safety from the other kids.

Stayed safe from his momma, too.

("wash your hands before you eat!")

("you little shit!")

("you're a dirty little boy!")

("dirty! dirty! dirty!")

No, he wasn't dirty.

("momma...")

He was clean.

("i'm sorry!")

And he was safe here, back in his Good Woods.

("i'll wash my hands!")

("i'll be a good boy!")

Branches, leaves, and tree trunks enveloped him. No one bothered him out here—not with their words or their looks or their dang ol' laughter. Here, he was safe and sound, able to feed her in privacy, certain that nobody on the highway could see him thanks to the magical veil that kept him and Little Stacey hidden from the world.

I'm safe out here...

Safe and sou—

Something rustled nearby.

What's that?

A critter?

He sucked up his drool like a vacuum, part of it latching to his shirt.

I ain't gonna let no critter hurt Little Stacey!

Come on out!

More rustling—this time from a bush.

He squeezed Little Stacey *real* tight, her breakfast sliding down his closed fingers.

I ain't afraid of you!

He'd faced plenty of critters before, even in his Good Woods.

Just had to scare'em off, that's all.

I'll protect you, Little Stacey...

Something hopped from a bush—

—a bird?

A red bird.

A cardinal.

Bobby exhaled, letting his whole body relax. His eyelids drooped as his mouth fell open again.

A little birdy-bird...

Drool pooled back under his tongue.

Purty red cardinal...

A big one, too...

The cardinal hopped toward Bobby, chirping as it studied him.

I ain't here to bother you, purty birdy-bird...

Just feedin' Little Stacey...

He reckoned it was like birds feeding their chicks when they're y—

WHOOP-WHOOP!

A high-pitched siren cut through the air.

Oh no...

Oh God, no...

Red-and-blue lights flashed from the parking lot.

(think fast, bobby!)

(think fast!)

Within seconds, he weighed his options—drop Little Stacey, shove her in his pocket, throw her deeper into the woods, or—

(your pants, bobby!)

(your pants!)

(pull your dang ol' pants up and walk out!)

He flung Little Stacey into the branches above. Seemed the least conspicuous way to hide her.

(hurry!)

(don't get caught with your pants down!)

After tucking his penis back inside his underwear, he yanked his pants up. A car door slammed. A police officer strode across the parking lot.

(get your belt on your belt on your belt!)

Bobby's hands shook as he tried to push the prong through the belt hole. He kept poking at it and missing it and his hands shook and shook *and shook* and he knew he faced big trouble and his hands shook more and more *and more* and they just kept shakin' and shakin' and sh—

"Excuse me, sir?" asked the officer. "Could you step outta them woods?"

(ohshootohshootohshoot)

"J-just a second!"

(ohboyohboyohboy)

He kept poking the prong at the belt holes.

Any hole.

Any dang ol' hole would do.

"Sir, may I ask you to step out here, please?"

"Just a m-minute!"

Just a dang ol' minute!

His mind raced.

Maybe he should run.

Wasn't guilty of no crime, and it'd be mighty tough for the cop to chase him through the woods. But there might be critters out—and what if he tripped on somethin'? Then the officer would catch him, or worse, he might impale himself on a dang ol' branch. Besides, his car was in the parking lot— they could look him up from his license plate.

(quit bein' a weenie!)

(just buckle your dang ol' belt and go out there and talk to him!)

Finally, he pushed the belt prong through the loop and tightened it.

(you can do this...)

(stay cool, bobby...)

(stay cool...)

"S-sorry officer." He stepped into the gravel parking lot with his hands up, feeling like a bank robber who'd been caught.

The officer narrowed his eyes. "Sir, what were you doing out there?"

"Ohhh, I-I was j-just...uhh..."

He let out one of his weird chuckles.

"...t-takin' a dang ol' leak..."

"Uh-huh," said the officer, studying him.

There ain't nothin' wrong with takin' a leak, is there?

He's gotta let me go...

This is America, and I got my dang ol' rights...

"Are you carrying a weapon on you, sir?"

"N-no sir," said Bobby.

The officer smirked.

"You can put your hands down, then."

Bobby put his hands down.

He exhaled, feeling his stress slip away.

Maybe this cop was one of the nice ones.

1990s

CHAPTER XXIX

BULLY

(he's just a dang ol' bully...)

(ain't he, bobby?)

BOBBY IMAGINED HIM and the policeman would have a nice little chat and it'd all be over. Would even have time to stop by DQ and get one of them tasty Blizzards.

After all, it wasn't no crime to take a dang ol' leak in the dang ol' woods, was it?

The officer narrowed his eyes. "So, if you stopped here to relieve yourself, why didn't you stop at one of the restrooms over there—"

He pointed at a glow in the distance.

"—where there's restaurants and stuff?"

Bobby shuffled his feet on the gravel. "Ohhh, shucks...m-maybe I-I sh-should've..."

He chuckled, putting his hands on his hips.

"I-I'll do that next t-time, officer."

"You got some stuff," said the officer, "on your shoulder there."

"Huh?"

Bobby brought his hand to his shoulder, felt something slimy and pulled away.

Little Stacey's breakfast...

Must've landed on his shoulder when he flung her up.

"Oh, shoot!"

He glanced at his breakfast-covered hand.

"G-guess I got bird p-poop on me..."

A series of weird, nervous chuckles burst forth as he wiped his hand on his pants.

"Got some on your head, too," said the officer.

"Huh?"

Bobby wiped his forehead, sticky wetness clinging to his fingers.

"Ohhh, shoooot..."

He flung Little Stacey's breakfast onto the gravel and wiped his hand on his pants again.

"Guess I g-got it all over me, then...sh-shoot..."

He chuckled.

The cop stared at him with a look that screamed, *"I know that isn't bird poop on your shoulder, it's your own dang jism."*

Bobby stared back.

Another weird chuckle escaped him.

He patted his hips. *"Yep, yep..."*

"Do you stop here often, sir?" asked the officer.

"N-nope..."

He started whistling, then stopped. Whistling was what guilty characters did in *Looney Tunes*.

"No, s-sir..." said Bobby. "...it's my first d-dang ol' time up in these parts..."

(you idiot)

(he knows it's a lie)

(you've gotta tell him at least some *truth)*

"I-I mean...uhh..."

He coughed.

"I don't, I don't *think* I have..."

"*Uh-huh...*" The officer locked his eyes onto Bobby like laser beams. "We've gotten reports of someone parkin' out here and goin' into that woods you just walked out of, maybe shootin' drugs or somethin'."

"Oh...w-well it ain't me, officer," said Bobby. "I d-don't do no, no... *druuugggs...*"

Bobby grinned like a schoolchild—one of the slow ones—standing before his class, promising he'd *"just say no to drugs."*

The officer's stare intensified.

"You *sure* you haven't been here before, sir?" he asked. "You *sure* you haven't been in those woods before?"

Bobby kept smiling his stupid grin.

He knows.

He knows I been comin' out here.

He knows...

Bobby chuckled.

There was no reason to chuckle.

No reason at all.

"N-now that I think about it...I *m-might've* came here a-a...*f-few* times before..."

"*Uh-huh...*" The officer's expression grew graver by the second.

"Shucks..." Bobby looked at the moon and the gravel and the highway as if he found them all extremely fascinating now.

The officer asked, "May I ask you what you were doin' here *the other times,* sir?"

"...well, uhh..."

Bobby glanced down, shuffling his feet on the gravel.

(*think*)

"...it's-it's kinda embarassin'..."

(*think, think!*)

"Heh."

The cop's tone sharpened. *"What were you doing here, sir?"*

"Ya see..."

(*medical condition!*)

(*medical condition!*)

"I-I mean, this is k-kinda embarassin'..."

(*tell him you got a dang ol' medical cond—*)

"b-but I got a...dang ol'..."

He gulped.

"...overactive bladder."

He flicked his eyes up, then back down.

"I mean, *r-real* overactive! It's *real* dang b—"

"And you always come here to relieve yourself?"

"Well, yeah!" Bobby nodded furiously.

"I-I mean!"

He gulped.

"S-sometimes..."

"And why don't you go over there?" The officer pointed again at the glow in the distance. "At one of those restaurants or gas stations?"

(*you got this, bobby*)

(*you can do this*)

(*stay cool...*)

"Well-well now, I-I have before...but those places can be real, real crowded...g-gotta wait in a dang ol' line and I...uh..."

"You what?"

"Well...I-I...uhh..."

(*think bobby, think!*)

"I-I pee my dang ol' pants sometimes!"

He cleared his throat.

"Officer."

"Uh-huh..." said the officer. "And why don't you take any medication for that?"

"What?"

"Medication. For your condition."

"Well-well now, I-I'm *supposed* to be takin' pills for it...

(insurance!)

(side effects!)

(lost the pills!)

"...b-but my dang ol' insurance d-don't cover it."

Bobby clenched his jaw.

Please believe me...

Please...

"Uh-huh..." The officer nodded in a way that showed he clearly didn't believe him. "And why doesn't your insurance cover it?"

(now he's gettin' nosey!)

"H-how am I supposed to know?"

Bobby attempted to laugh, but it sounded like choking.

"Y-you'll have to c-call them and ask!"

Oh, shoot!

What if he actually calls 'em?

"Uh-huh..." The officer fell silent, studying Bobby like a doctor might study a bump on a patient's skin.

Bobby's stomach tightened.

Oh boy...

The full moon cast a cold glow over them both. Bobby had avoided looking at the woods behind him *(Little Stacey...)*, but in the silence, he couldn't help but sneak a quick glance back.

The officer asked, "Is there somethin' in those woods?"

"W-What?"

Bobby tried to laugh.

It sounded like choking again.

"N-no...I-I mean, I d-don't *think* so..."

"Then why you keep lookin' back at the woods?"

"W-Was I?"

Bobby choke-chuckled again.

"N-no reason..."

Cold sweat rolled down Bobby's forehead and streamed from his armpits. The officer craned to his left, peering past him.

(he saw you lookin'...)

(you gotta say somethin'!)

Bobby laughed again—this time it came out like a squeeze horn. The kind clowns use.

The officer placed his hand on his holstered gun.

"Stay where you are, sir. *Do not move.*"

The officer marched to the perimeter of the woods and pulled out a flashlight, shining it into the darkness.

"You here by yourself?" he asked.

"Y-yes, sir..."

Actually, I'm here with Little Stacey...

"Did you throw anything out there?" asked the officer. "Or leave anything behind?"

"N-no, sir...sure didn't..."

The officer stepped into the woods, flashlight sweeping as his hand rested on his gun. Several times he passed right below Little Stacey, tangled in the branches above.

(please-don't-find-her-please-don't-find-her-pl—)

The officer asked, "You sure you didn't leave anything out here?"

Bobby's stomach tightened.

What if Little Stacey falls on him?

And gets her breakfast all over him?

"P-pretty sure, officer..."

Then he'd take her as evidence...

And they'd do lab tests and stuff...

A gust of wind blew; the branch holding Little Stacey swayed. Bobby pictured her falling on the officer, who'd then pick her up and say, *"Well, well, well...what do we have here?"*

No no no.

Can't allow that.

Can't allow him to take Little Stacey.

After searching a bit longer and occasionally flicking his flashlight at Bobby, the officer marched back to the parking lot. He switched his light off and studied Bobby, like he'd nearly solved a puzzle but lacked one final piece. Translucent white liquid dribbled from his shoulder behind his badge.

Little Stacey's breakfast...

"Find a restroom next time," said the officer. "And don't use this spot anymore."

Bobby expelled a cubic ton of air from his lungs.

Thank God...

"Y-yes, sir. I will."

"You see that highway?" asked the officer. "With all the light from the traffic, everybody can see you clear as day, *even when you're in the woods.*"

Bobby's mouth dropped.

Oh boy.

"That's public urination," said the officer. "And that's a misdemeanor."

There was no...

No dang ol' magical veil...

"I'm gonna let you off with a warning this time," said the officer. "Use the bathrooms from now on."

"O-okay...I-I will, officer..."

Can't leave without Little Stacey, though...

Might be some dang ol' critters out there!

Gotta rescue her!

Bobby wasn't sure what to do next, so he just stood there, patting his hips and saying *"Yep, yep"* several times. Leftovers of Little Stacey's breakfast dripped down his forehead, pooling above his eyebrows. He wiped it away, then smeared his hand on his pants.

"You're free to go now, sir," said the officer.

"O-oh. Okay. Okay."

He reached for his keys but they fell to the gravel with such a *crash* that even the stars seemed to blink and cringe in astonishment.

"Oops..."

After retrieving his keys, he tried unlocking his car in the smoothest, least-conspicuous way possible.

I'm home free...

Just gotta stay cool, unlock my car, and drive away...

Stay cool...

That's all I gotta d—

"Just one more thing, sir."

Bobby froze.

(tell him no and get the heck outta there)

(you ain't been charged with nothin'!)

(just drive away!)

"You weren't bringin' a *Barbie doll* out here, were you?"

(no!)
(say heck no!)
(tell him you wasn't playin' with no barbie doll!)
"A *w-what*, officer?"
"A doll. You weren't bringin' *a Barbie,* or some kinda doll out here, were you?"
Oh boy...
"Because we have reports of an individual matchin' your description standin' in those woods holdin' something. With his pants around his ankles."
Ohhh boy...
"And some reported it looked like a doll, or a *Barbie doll...*"
Oh boy oh boy oh boy oh boy oh boy...
Bobby wheeled around. A torrent of words escaped him in an uncontrollable flow:
"H-heck n-no officer I wasn't out here p-playin' with no, *hehe* dang ol' Barbie doll that's the c-craziest dang ol' thing I ever heard, *hehe* p-people like that n-need to be p-put in the d-dang ol' looney bin, *hehe* I-I tell ya what!"
He sucked in air.
"I mean!" he said. "They, they *sound*...l-like they do..."
His voice grew smaller, shrinking within itself.
"I-I'm a dang ol', full-grown man...I don't p-play with no, no..."
He swallowed his spit, wetting his lips.
"...no Barbie doll..."
The heat around Bobby intensified, as if he boiled in a stew—a stew of his own making.
Oh boy...
The officer shot him a cold, no-bullshit stare.
Oh boy, oh boy....
"You sure about that?" asked the officer.
Ohboyohboyohboy...
The chorus of nearby crickets rose.
"You *absolutely* sure about that?"
The chirping grew louder.
"That you weren't out here with a Barbie doll?"
Louder.
(now he's startin' to bully ya, bobby...)

Louder.

(*just a dang ol' bully...*)

The chirping hurt his ears.

(*like them bullies who tied you to the tree...*)

Something *clicked* inside Bobby, something which hadn't clicked in a long time. He spoke with a sharpness that could cut through steel:

"*No, officer, I was not. May I ask if I'm free to go now?*"

The officer's eyes widened.

He returned his hand to his holstered gun.

"Before you go, I'd like to check your license and registra—"

"*And why would you need to do that?*"

Something lurked behind Bobby's voice now—something that didn't wobble or stutter or chuckle. Something that said, "*Don't fuck with me anymore.*"

"I've committed no crime, officer," he said. "You best let me go."

The crickets chirped even louder, their chorus vibrating the night air.

"Sir," said the officer. "Public urination is a crime, and I could arrest you right now if I wanted to. I won't, though, as long as you coopera—"

"My wallet's in my car," said Bobby.

Now was *his* chance to lock eyes with the officer, to show *his* gaze devoid of fear or falter.

How you like me now?

When I stand up for myself?

The officer tilted his head, seeming to reappraise Bobby.

(*bullies never like it when you stand up to'em...*)

(*do they, bobby?*)

The crickets' chirping rose to a crescendo.

(*and that's what he is...*)

(*just a dang ol' bully...*)

"May I turn around and open my car to get it?" asked Bobby. "*Is that alright with you, officer?*"

The officer sighed, exhaustion etched into his face. Now he looked like a man ready to go home.

"Sure," he said. "Go right ahead."

Bobby unlocked his car door, reached inside, and opened his glove compartment.

The crickets fell silent.

A pair of scissors fell to the passenger seat, glinting in the moonlight.

1990s

CHAPTER XXX

PLAYTIME

"Always do what I say, Abby...

...always do what I fuckin' say..."

RHONDA STOOD IN the center of Strawberry Fields savoring the calm, *the clarity* she felt after shooting.

It felt better than sex.

Better than gettin' her pussy eaten.

It made her feel *one with God.*

She could've shot for hours, losing herself in the zen that Temple Training provided, but bullets cost money, and money was tight. Plus, Daddy stressed that consistency outweighed the actual time spent trainin'. *"Practicin' an hour a day's better than twice a week for four,"* he'd say. *"Y'all gotta stay consistent with this shit to get ready for The Run."*

Rhonda agreed. Consistency kept her, and the gun, as one fluid engine.

(pleasegod)

And her prayers kept her straight.

(god, grant me the love to shoot today...)

Reminded her that God was on *their* side.

(grant me the power to shoot to kill...)

And with God's help, they'd find The Temple and make The Run.

(temple above all.)

Strawberry plants surrounded Rhonda, but she chose the oldest, longest vine—the first they planted. Always tasted best from that one. She plucked the ripest strawberry and popped it into her mouth, savoring the burst of juice.

Mmm...

Good today.

Real good.

Tart, with the right amount of sweet.

As juice squirted from her lips, trickling down her chin, an idea crept in. Something to try with GB today.

Something *kinda* fucked up, that she'd only tried with a few of the assholes before.

But she could try it again.

Today felt like a good day for it.

Yanking another strawberry off its stem, she held it in the sunlight, admiring its plump size and crimson hue. Daddy let 'em eat one strawberry a day, and only if they did good during Temple Training. Poor little Zach and Taleiah only got a strawberry once or twice a week, if that—but *she* helped herself almost every fuckin' day.

Includin' today.

She'd shot good today.

Not real good, but good enough.

Much better with the rifle than the pistol (they always started with the pistol—made the rifle seem easy in comparison) but lately she'd kinda hit a plateau. Wasn't gettin' worse, but wasn't gettin' better, either.

And she *had* to get better.

Every shot had to hit its mark during The Run.

Straight-shots.

Drop-shots.

Stride-shots.

All of 'em.

They all had to hit their fuckin' mark.

Every single one.

She strolled in the direction of the garage, strawberry in hand.

GB could get a treat today.

If he didn't act up.

*　　　***

Rhonda peeked through the garage's side door, holding it open *just enough* for GB to glimpse her radiant smile—if he hadn't been blindfolded.

He was, though.

Fuckin' blindfolded.

After the MB Incident, they blindfolded *all* the fuckers with the same Kentucky state flag bandannas they used to gag 'em. Daddy had a bunch of those for some reason, so that's what they used.

"How ya doin', GB?"

Sunlight crept in behind Rhonda, shining right on GB's bucket.

"You need to go potty?"

She closed the door, her grin bright as the morning sun.

GB let out a *"nnn"*-like sound.

"GB…?" she asked.

She set the strawberry on the counter and moseyed over. In only a few weeks, he'd already gotten so skinny. Unlike most of the assholes, GB had the fit build of a young buck with just a slight beer belly—but that had melted away fast once they tied him up.

She ran her fingers over his blindfold.

"Huh? You need to go potty?"

His blonde stubble bristled under her touch as a solitary tear slid past the blindfold's edge.

"Lemme help ya out..."

She pulled his blindfold up and tugged the bloodstained Kentucky state flag bandanna from his mouth, draping it around his neck like a dirty necklace. Still hadn't opened his eyes. Maybe still scared and shit.

"It's okay..." she said. "Ain't no need to cry, now..."

Daddy must've roughed him up lately. Couldn't be helped, though— had to get that Clue sooner or later.

"Now." Rhonda's voice dropped. "I'm gonna ask ya again. Last time."

She squeezed his face.

"Do you need to go potty?"

A fat teardrop descended from GB's chin, landing on the concrete floor with a *plop.*

"...n-no..."

Rhonda nodded in a sympathetic way—how a therapist might nod at their patient.

"Okay, okay...just checkin'..."

She scooted his bucket away, careful not to spill the mess inside. Despite the newspaper on top, the stench always managed to seep out. *"We don't wanna clean their bucket too often,"* Daddy had said. *"Else they might think they're at the Holiday Inn or somethin.'"*

Sunlight sparkled on yellow snot running from GB's nostrils. A wedding band glinted on his finger. Most fuckers they kidnapped were married. Usually had kids, too. In the movies, guys in their situation said shit like, *"Please! I have a family! A wife and kids!"* Few of these assholes ever did, though. Maybe they sensed that neither she nor her family gave a fuck.

GB sniffled.

"Ohhh..." said Rhonda. "Don't you worry, boy..."

GB's left eye struggled open, then his right.

"Ain't gonna be rough with ya..." said Rhonda. "Not this time..."

She pushed his chin up.

(lookatme)

He fixed his gaze on the floor.

"Look at me, GB," she said.

GB flicked his eyes up, then down again.

(isaidfuckinglookatme!)

Rhonda gripped his chin, pushing her nails into his face.

(LOOK)

(AT)

(ME)

GB's eyes darted before finally meeting hers, as if squinting at the sun.

(there ya go, boy...)

(there ya go...)

As their eyes locked, a pleasant chill ran up her spine.

(always do what I say, now...)

So much fear, weakness in those eyes, now.

(always do what I fuckin' say...)

Where was the good ol' country boy now?

(obey)

What happened to his swagger?

That country confidence?

(obey me like the dog you are)

Not for the first time, Rhonda admitted that GB, *all things considered,* proved a handsome young man. Blonde, beach-boy type—like Zach from *Saved by the Bell,* but with a rugged "I like to hunt and fish" vibe.

"You like to hunt? And fish, GB?"

GB's lower lip trembled. Through weak moans, he uttered something like *"...yeah..."* but it sounded so garbled she couldn't be sure.

"Yes or no, GB," she said. *"Do you like to hunt and fish?"*

Rhonda wrapped her hand around his neck and *squeezed*—not tight enough to cut off his windpipe, but enough to let him know she meant business.

GB's voice barely rose above the phlegm in his throat.

"...y-yes..."

"What fish you like to catch?"

He swallowed, his throat pushing against her palm.

"...c-catfish..."

He cast his brown puppy-dog eyes at her with a sad, pitiful expression—probably rememberin' better days, like when he caught his first catfish or bullshit like that. Thank God he didn't have blue eyes *(did he? did he? no—brown),* or else she couldn't even *look* at his eyes.

("you gon' be my bi—")

Rhonda glanced at the bloody hammer and baseball bat on the counter, the morning sunlight catching each blood fleck. Daddy liked'em fine, but swingin' those wore her the fuck out. Needed something with more *finesse,* that cut rather than bludgeoned—

—but what could *cut* without makin'em bleed too much?

Maybe stop by Walmart later.

"Please..." said GB. "Please don't hurt me..."

Rhonda opened her mouth wide.

"What?" she asked. *"Me?* Hurt *you?"*

Keeping her right hand around his throat, she wiped GB's tears with her left thumb, pressing hard against his face.

"Done said I ain't gonna be rough with ya..."

She licked her thumb.

Mmm...

Salty.

Should've snuck another strawberry—salty taste would go real good with'em.

"Brought ya a little present..."

She ran her saliva-coated thumb across his dry, cracked lips. He shook his head, mouthing *"No, no..."*

Sauntering back to the counter, she picked up the strawberry, then, after a moment of consideration—the hammer.

GB squirmed. *"No, no!"*

Despite the blood flecks, the hammer still gleamed in the sunlight. Daddy cleaned it regularly, so the blood must be fresh—maybe from yesterday or somethin'. Hadn't visited GB in a while; didn't know and didn't give a fuck, either.

Sauntering back across the garage, Rhonda held her closed hand before GB's face, then opened it, revealing the strawberry like a magic trick.

GB squeezed his eyes shut, flinching away.

"I don't want it!"

He coughed.

"I don't want it! I don't want it!"

He twisted against the ropes, rough fibers chafing his raw skin, dotting his arms with pinpricks of blood.

"I'm sorry!" he said. "I'm sorry, I'm sorry, I'm so—"

He coughed, the sound breaking into sobs as tears streamed down his cute little cheeks.

"I'll tell ya The Clue..." he said.

His whole body shook, as if shocked by an electric current.

"...the Clue...to the puzzle..."

"The puzzle?" she asked. "We ain't playin' no jigsaw, GB."

"I mean!" he said. "To the...shrine..."

"Shrine?" asked Rhonda. "What fuckin' 'shrine,' you dumbfuck?"

She shoved the strawberry in his face.

He squealed.

"What's wrong, GB?" asked Rhonda. "You don't like strawberries?"

She glanced at him, then the strawberry, then back at him.

"Ohhh, I see now...my bad, GB..."

She lowered the strawberry.

"Didn't even think, ya know..." she said. "...that you might have...a few..."

Her eyes wandered, searching for the right word.

"...unpleasant...memories...related to—"

She thrust the strawberry forward.

"—fuckin' strawberries!"

He yelped, as if it might sting him.

Rhonda sighed.

"GB..."

(you still don't fuckin' get it)

She switched the strawberry to her left and the hammer to her right.

(gonna have to hurt ya)

"...we done talked about this..."

(teach ya a lesson)

"...we don't *'find'* The Clue, GB..."

(teach ya real good, now)

"You tell it to us," she said. "You *tell us* the fuckin' Clue."

Shaking her head like a disappointed mother, she raised the hammer high.

"You still ain't gettin' that, is ya, boy..."

"I get it!" he said. "I underst—"

THWACK!

She slammed the hammer onto his shoulder.

He screamed.

"Stop actin' up!" she said. *"And eat the damn strawberry!"*

She shoved it against his lips, his bare teeth, raising the hammer again. "Don't make me hit ya again!"

GB sobbed, his lips parting just enough to take the strawberry's tip.

"Nope." She leaned in. "Put it all in. *Now.*"

She pressed the hammer's flat end against his skull.

"Take it deep, boy..."

Slowly, GB relaxed his jaws, accepting the entire strawberry into his mouth.

"Good...take it deep, now...like a good little boy..."

She shoved the strawberry past the back of GB's tongue, touching his throat.

"Gaack!"

He gagged.

"...keep it in *deep,* boy..."

"Gaack!"

He gagged once more, then calmed.

Good...

Just let it happen, GB...

Just let it happen.

She withdrew her hand.

"...now, chew and swallow..."

GB closed his mouth around the strawberry, squishing it.

"Goooood boy, gooood boy..." she said. "...strawberries taste *real* good, don't they..."

GB sobbed. Strawberry juice trickled from his mouth.

"Don't they?"

He sobbed again, nodding.

"Now," she said, "how many times I hit you today?"

"...o-once..."

"That's right, only once..."

She caressed his face, savoring the friction of his blonde stubble.

"...and I ain't gonna hit ya again, neither..."

Leaning forward, she licked his chin, catching the trickle of juice with her tongue.

"...not today, and not tomorrow...."

She smacked her lips.

Mmm...

Salty *and* sweet.

"...and maybe not for a whole dang week, GB..."

She kissed his forehead, then pulled back, as if surprised by her own action.

("playtime...")

("let's have playtime together...")

("will you play with me?")

Playtime.

She used to have playtime a lot, back in school. Sometimes with the older boys, sometimes with the younger girls. Sometimes with whoever would play. Always enjoyed it, though. Playtime.

The good ol' days.

Sauntering back to the counter, she set the hammer down with a satisfying *thud*.

"You like tits, don't ya, GB?"

Her Dairy Queen uniform made a soft stretch as she lifted it off.

"You really liked Taleiah's..." she said. "I remember that..."

She unhooked her bra, letting it drop to the floor, then turned to face him.

"...you remember when you squeezed my little sister's tits?"

Morning sunlight bathed her half-naked body in a warm glow.

She grasped the hammer with her right hand.

"...and slammed her into the wall?"

Moving with lithe confidence, she sauntered back to GB and seized his face with her left, forcing his gaze to her breasts.

GB swallowed the last of the strawberry.

"...slammed her into the wall..." she said. "...and started squeezin' her tits real hard..."

She moved her hand to his throat, clasping it.

"...as soon ya walked into the hotel room..."

"I'm sorry," he said. "I didn't mean to—"

"Shh..."

With her right hand, she raised the hammer.

"Do ya like *my* tits, GB?"

She tightened her left around his neck.

"...yes...yes..." he said. "...I-I like'em..."

"But you really liked Taleiah's, didn't ya?"

He looked unsure of how to answer.

"Didn't ya?"

"...yeah..."

"Whose you like better? Mine, or Taleiah's?"

GB's throat tightened, then bulged as he swallowed.

"...yours...yours..."

"Ohhh..." she said. "Why, that's so nice of you to say, GB..."

She stepped forward, pushing her breasts close to his face.

"Ain't as big as Taleiah's..." she said. "...but nice, ain't they?"

"...y—"

"Ain't they?"

"Y-Yes! Yes!"

Rhonda ran her fingers through GB's pretty blonde hair. Not as oily as the other assholes usually got. Surprising, since Daddy probably hadn't washed him in a while. Must be the dry-skinned type.

"I like your pretty blonde hair..."

She'd tried this a few times before, with the half-decent lookin' ones (definitely *not* FB—the fuckin' weirdo), but why did she want it so *badly* today? Bearded guy had ate her good last night, *real* good, and that usually satisfied her for a while.

Maybe a little *too* fuckin' good?

Maybe that's what got her all revved up?

Or maybe it was the coke he'd brought?

That good ol' party powder always made her horny as fuck, but should've left her system by now. Besides, coke didn't have no long-term side effects—not like them cancer sticks did.

"C'mon, boy..."

She guided him to his knees, the ropes binding his torso sliding against the pillar, and poked her left nipple against his dry, cracked lips.

"Lick."

She pressed the hammer's flat end against his cheek.

(don't start actin' up, now...)

"And you best be gentle," she said, "or I'll bring this fuckin' hammer down on ya, real hard-like..."

Like a snail's slimy head poking out, GB extended his tongue, licking her left nipple.

"Ohhh...that's *gooood,* GB..."

She unbuttoned her jeans.

"...just like that..."

GB licked up and down at first, like a cat, then took her whole nipple into his mouth and really started suckin' on it.

Mmm...

Young buck knows what he's doin'...

She licked her middle finger and shoved it down her underwear.

There it was.

There it was.

Wet, ready and waitin' for her.

"Good, GB...good..."

(don't you fuckin' stop, now...)

Fuckin' with GB like this was probably wrong on some level. She knew that. She wasn't crazy. Daddy definitely wouldn't approve *(oh, if only Daddy could see me now...),* but GB was too damn cute. Cutest piece of shit they'd ever kidnapped, in fact.

Besides, that's what made it hot—

—that it was so fucked up.

And wrong.

Sinful.

"You ain't gonna tell my Daddy about this..."

GB smacked and licked her other tit now, really gettin' into it.

"...is ya, GB?"

A muffled sound—maybe *"No,"* wasn't sure.

"Is ya?"

"...no..."

"Good...don't you tell Taleiah or Zach, neither..."

She moved her finger faster.

"...don't you tell nobody, GB..."

Tilting her head back, she gazed at the blue lightbulb above.

("you gon' be my b—")

No.

You can't hurt me, now.
I'm the one with the goddamn power now.
(blue-eyed boy can't touch me he'll never touch me ag—)
"I'll...I'll h-hurt you if you tell somebody, GB..."
(i'll hurt you so fuckin' bad)
(you piece of shit)
"Keep it our secret, now..."
Oh, what would lil' T or Z say if they saw me?
What would...
GB licked faster, sucked harder.
...Daddy say?
They'd say she was crazy—fucked up—but on some twisted level she *wanted'em* to see her,
"...oh God, GB..."
doin' naughty things,
"...now you're *really* suckin'em..."
that felt so fuckin' good.
(always do what i say...)
Daddy wouldn't approve *(why do i want him to see me now? why?)*, but she didn't care: top-tier titty-suckin' only came from a guy with a hammer held to his face.
"...that's so fuckin' good, GB..."
Gradually, the visage of a young girl *(not abby—darla!)* appeared before her.
("always do what i say...")
Darla—where she was supposed to be,
(don't fuckin' stop, darla...)
where she was *meant* to be,
(don't ever stop...)
and she held Darla's little head down while she licked and licked and tried to get away *("i said don't stop!")* and—
"If you tell us the Clue...we'll let ya go...I promise we'll let ya go, GB...I promise!"
Her left finger moved faster.
("always do what i fuckin' s—")
She bucked her hips.
"I promise!"

"Just be a good boy!"

"Don't act up!"

"Be a good boy!"

"Don't you fuckin' act—"

"AH-CHOO!"

Cold, slimy wetness sprayed across Rhonda's chest.

She opened her eyes.

"Eew! Gross, GB!"

Thick strands of green and yellow snot plastered her breasts.

"I'm sorry!" said GB. "I'm so sorry! I'm—*KHAAF-KHAAF!*"

He coughed and wheezed.

"That's fuckin' gross, GB!" she said. *"You got snot all over my tits!"*

Her tits jiggled as she stepped back, strands of snot falling to the floor.

"I'm sick!" said GB. "I need medici—"

She swung the hammer in a shining arc.

THWACK!

"—*AAAGH!*"

"Goddammit!" she said. "Are you gonna sneeze or cough again?"

GB sobbed and cried like a baby.

"Huh?" she asked. "Is ya?"

"I'm sorry! I'm—*AH-CHOOOO!*"

"Goddammit, boy!"

Rhonda stared into GB's eyes—they shined *blue* now, not brown like Darla's but *blue,* blue blue blue blue blue but blue but blue blue blue bluebluebluebluebluebluebluebluebluebluebl—

("you-gon'-be-my-bitch?")

"I told you to stop actin' up!"

("you-gon'-be-my-bitch?")

"I told you!"

("you-gon'-be-my-bitch?")

"I knew you had blue eyes!"

A banjo twanged, warping the world around her.

Pleasure in the left.

Pain in the right.

Every time she saw blood or got close to cummin' she heard *music*— this time a lone fuckin' *banjo* strummin' amidst an orchestra and it twanged harder and harder and each note, each drop of blood made it better, *the music and blood made everything better* and she needed to *see* it, to see the blood, fucking *see* it—

"I'm sorry!" said GB.

("do ya hear music before ya cum, abby?")

"I'm sick!"

("I do...")

"I need medicine!"

("every single time...")

And then it appeared—

"I don't got blue eyes!"

—the first glimmer of a brilliant wave of light.

Rhonda raised her hammer, claw-end out.

(I KNEW YOU HAD BLUE EYES)

1970s

CHAPTER XXXI

HUDDLE UP

"...that Bill dude took Tommy's girl to prom. As friends and shit."

"Ohhh..."

"That Samantha Henson chick? Why didn't she go with Tommy?"

"'Cause they broke up or somethin'.

'Cause she wouldn't fuck him."

"Wouldn't give him no blowjobs, neither?"

"Dunno. Guess not."

"FUUUUUUCK..." SAID LESLIE. "What happened over there, y'all?"

The customers inside Dairy Queen had mostly stopped gawking and returned to their meals. Bill and his fucking Posse hadn't budged from their spot by the entrance.

"You alright, Kevin?" asked Lacey.

"Kevin's fine," said Tommy. "We gotta huddle up for a bit. This is Boys' business."

He snapped his fingers.

"Boys, huddle up."

"What're y'all gonna do now?" asked Lacey.

"Fuuuuuuck..." said Leslie. "Y'all gonna fight?"

Tommy turned to say, *"Shut the fuck up, sluts,"* but Mouse saved him the trouble.

"Girls," said Mouse. "This is Boys' business. Back up."

Lacey and Leslie sighed, then sauntered out of hearing range.

The Smoketown Boys formed a huddle. A serious air enveloped them, like generals handling a military crisis.

Tommy looked Kevin straight in the eyes.

"Kevin," said Tommy. "That was impressive, what you tried to do back there."

"Fuckin' stupid," said Mouse.

"Maybe a little stupid," said Tommy, "but also showed he's got balls. So fuckin' impressive, too."

He glared at Mouse.

"Wasn't it, Mouse?"

Mouse shrugged. "Yeah, alright. Kinda. Until you got choked out mid-air."

Tommy almost said, *"Mouse, I didn't see you charge at Graham,"* but thought better of it. Not in front of the Possibles.

"See," said Tommy, "that's what I'm talkin' about. What Kevin did just now. *Showin' initiative.*"

Kevin's eyes ignited with zeal.

"But we gotta be smart," said Tommy. "We can't be afraid of 'em just 'cause they got Graham, but we gotta be smart, too. Gotta have an edge."

He took a long look at his Boys.

His plan, though risky, seemed a hell of a lot smarter than a straight-up fight at the baseball field against *Graham-fuckin'-Riley.*

"I got a plan, boys," said Tommy. "But first, we're goin' to Piggly Wiggly."

"*Piggly Wiggly?*" asked Mouse. "We buyin' country ham?"

"I'll tell y'all more when we're there," said Tommy. "For now, we gotta act like we're real pumped to fight those fuckers at the baseball field. So when we roll out, we gotta be *wild* about it, yell at'em and shit as we're drivin' off. Y'all got me?"

"So we *are* throwin' down tonight?" asked Mouse. "Or we ain't? I just wanna know what the fuck we're doin', Tommy."

"*We're throwin' down, Mouse,*" said Tommy. "But we're gonna fuck with'em some. I'll explain later. We'll drop the girls at the Smokehouse on the way. Gotta move fast."

He turned to Kevin.

Poor guy—not only had he been socked in the stomach, but also nearly choked to death.

I was wrong about you, Kevin.

Tonight proved that.

"Kevin," said Tommy, "can you breathe okay, now?"

"Yeah," said Kevin.

"Can you yell?"

"Yeah."

"You sure?" asked Tommy. "You can yell?"

"Yeah!"

"Then I want you to be the one to call it."

Shock and awe fell across Kevin's face. Outside of emergencies, typically only the Originals held that privilege.

"*What?*" asked Mouse. "That's bullshi—"

"Mouse!" said Tommy. Mouse shut his trap.

Tommy put his hand on Kevin's shoulder.

"Chargin' at Graham like that..." said Tommy. "That takes balls, man. You showed initiative. You got better. You showed us, and them, that you ain't just a rich boy. That you just might be...a *real* Smoketown Boy."

Tears welled in Kevin's eyes. Mouse shook his head with a *"What the fuck?"* look, while Larry and Jack nodded in reluctant acceptance. The other Possibles looked stunned.

"Th-thank you, Tommy..." said Kevin.

Tommy kept his hand on Kevin's shoulder for a moment longer, then spoke again.

"Alright, say it."

Kevin gazed at his trembling hand and clenched it. He shut his eyes, raising his fist in the air.

"SMOKE-TOWN-BOYS, ROLL-OOOUUUT!"

1970s

CHAPTER XXXII

SHIT THAT GETS YA GOIN'

"I fuckin' love history, man...

It's the only subject I really liked at school.

That, and español."

GRAHAM SAT IN the backseat behind Charlie, nodding to the heavy metal pounding from the speakers. Whenever they rolled out, he always sat behind Charlie, and Kenny behind Bill. Didn't know why. Just did. He pulled a chicken strip from his pocket, brushed off sediment, and popped it into his mouth.

Cold.

But good.

Still tasty and good.

Charlie glanced back. "Where'd you get that chicken strip?"

"Found it," said Graham, smacking on chicken deliciousness. "Before we left."

Kenny pulled a book from his backpack. "That's the one Glick threw at Bill."

"So that's how it started..." Graham swallowed the chicken strip after minimal chewing. "A food fight."

Leaning his head out the window, Graham opened his mouth to let the cool night air in. Ever since he was a kid, he liked doing that. Something about the air going in his mouth. *Felt good.*

Kenny flipped on the overhead light. "You know you look like a crocodile? They just lay there with their mouths open."

"You look *estúpido, ese,*" said Charlie. "Kinda like a dumbass. I mean, no fuckin' offense or nothin'..."

"None taken, Charlie-boy..." Graham leaned forward and thumped Charlie's head with his finger.

"*Oww!* Motherfucker, I am drivin' here!"

"Huh huh huh..."

"Alright now," said Bill. "Charlie, don't be rude to Graham. Graham, don't be fuckin' with Charlie when he's drivin'. Might get in a wreck."

"That hurt, motherfucker!" said Charlie.

"Huh huh huh..." Graham reached forward to thump Charlie again, but Bill grabbed his hand.

"*Graham.* That's enough, man."

Graham caught his reflection in Bill's sunglasses. Something about the way he saw himself in them, warped and distorted—

—slowly, he withdrew his hand.

"Can we snort coke now?" he asked.

"Not in the car!" said Charlie. "You crazy?"

"Why not?" asked Graham.

"Let's save the Columbia marchin' powder for later," said Bill. "Bet those weedboys'll be late. Too high on their gorilla grass to keep track of time."

"Kenny," said Charlie. "I can't believe we're about to get in this epic fuckin' fight, and you're studyin' German."

"Why not?" asked Kenny. "You can speak *español,* I wanna speak cool shit, too."

"*Sí,*" said Charlie. "But I didn't study it before no epic fuckin' fight."

"If I can say somethin' cool," said Kenny, "somethin' real badass, in German, right before I knock a dude out, it'd be *awesome.* Add some impact, ya know what I'm sayin'?"

"It would add impact," said Bill.

"*Sí, sí,*" said Charlie. "But I'm already teachin' y'all *español* and shit. That's enough, ain't it..."

Bill narrowed his eyes. Earlier at Dairy Queen, Charlie had sounded supportive of Kenny studyin' German, but now he was gettin' all ornery about it. Probably 'cause speakin' another language was *his* thing, and he didn't wanna lose that—*his thing.*

"Now Charlie," said Bill. "If Kenny wants to learn a different language and speak it real good and shit, that's his right, now. Don't try to stop his learnin.'"

"Yeah, Charlie-boy," said Graham. "Quit tryin' to stop Kenny's learnin.'"

"Graham," said Charlie, "you ain't learned nothin' since you learned the alphabet! And you barely learned that shit, *ese,* so don't be talkin' shit to me, now! Not in *my* fuckin' car!"

"Now listen here, Charlie-boy—"

"Settle down, now," said Bill. "Now Charlie, just let Kenny study what he wants."

"Well, in case y'all didn't know," said Charlie, "it's illegal as fuck to drive with your interior light on. At least in the state of Kentucky. And the last thing we want is to get pulled over before this epic-fuckin'-fight for epic bullshit and get arrested when they find our coke."

"Fine..." said Kenny.

He flipped the light off.

"Ein zeich, ein leiss..."

***

Everyone nodded quietly to the heavy metal for a while. Charlie drove more carefully than usual, halting completely at four-way stop signs even in the absence of other vehicles. Cops loved to get ya for shit like that.

"So," said Graham. "Why German?"

"BRAAAAAAAP!"

He belched.

"Just always thought it sounded cool," said Kenny. "Especially when we watched those videos in class of Hitler and that other dude, Goebbels, givin' epic speeches and shit. I mean, I know they were bad dudes and all, but man, they knew how to fuckin' speak."

"Them dudes were good at public speakin'," said Bill.

"Hell yeah, they were," said Kenny. "I mean, say what you want about'em, maybe like the worst mass murderers in history and all that, but man...they knew how to give speeches."

"They just said shit that got ya goin', right?" said Bill.

Kenny nodded. "Shit that got ya goin'."

"Those guys sounded powerful," said Graham.

"Yep," said Kenny. "And I mean, I ain't down with all that Holocaust shit and all—"

"Nah," said Bill. "Me neither."

"But," said Kenny, "dudes did almost take over the world."

"They didn't play around, did they?" asked Bill. "Them Germans."

"Helllll no," said Charlie. "Not in Dubya-Dubya Two, and not in Dubya-Dubya One, neither."

"And ya know what?" asked Kenny. "If they'd just *chilled* on that racist bullshit, against Jews and whatnot—"

"I never even met a Jew," said Bill.

"Me neither," said Graham.

"I think they all live in New York and stuff, big cities," said Kenny.

"Ain't none in Kentucky," said Charlie.

"Probably not," said Kenny. "But anyway, if they'd just *chilled* on that shit, they could've had a way bigger army. Badass Jews fightin' for'em, man."

"I think you're right, Kenny," said Bill. "Then Albert-fuckin'-Einstein might've been on *their* side, man. Think about that."

"Einstein was German?" asked Graham. "And a Jew?"

"Yes, he was, Graham," said Bill. "Albert Einstein was a German Jew."

"Thought he was 'merican," said Graham.

"Maybe he was," said Bill, "maybe he switched his citizenship and shit, I don't fuckin' know. But I tell ya what, Hitler done blocked himself from gettin' one of the smartest motherfuckers on his team. Like the Babe Ruth of geniuses."

"Dude," said Kenny. "If Albert-fuckin'-Einstein would've been on the Germans' side, they would've *fucked shit up,* man."

Everyone agreed the Germans would've absolutely fucked shit up.

"What German you learned so far, Kenny?" asked Bill. "What you keep repeatin' back there?"

"Ein zeich, ein leiss," said Kenny.

The words hung in the air.

"Mmm-hmm," said Charlie. "And what the fuck's that mean?"

"I dunno," said Kenny. "Just sounds cool."

"Just *sounds* cool?" asked Charlie.

"Ja, das ist richtig," said Kenny. "I just looked through the dictionary and found words that sounded cool. And powerful. And I switched the letters and shit to make'em even better. And then when I say'em, when I'm knockin a dude's teeth out, it'll add so much *impact* to everything, ya know. If I say that shit, when I hit him."

"I like it," said Graham.

"Sounds cool to me," said Bill.

"Estúpido!" said Charlie. "I mean, no fuckin' offense, *ese,* but ya gotta know what that shit *means,* right? You can't just be spurtin' nonsense German words as ya—"

"Why not?" asked Kenny.

"Well, 'cause ya can't," said Charlie.

"Why can't I, Charlie?"

"'Cause it's bullshit."

"Why's it bullshit?"

"'Cause it fuckin' is, Kenny."

Bill shook his head. "That ain't no reason, Charlie."

Graham nodded. "Gotta give him a reason, Charlie-boy."

"Charlie don't need no reason," said Kenny. *"He just likes to bitch!"*

Graham and Kenny guffawed, slapping their knees.

"That's a good one, Kenny," said Graham. "Charlie-boy does like to bitch..."

Charlie's face darkened.

"Check this out, y'all," said Kenny.

He raised his index finger.

"Ein schliebben, ein fliebben!"

A moment of silence passed.

"That sounded cool," said Graham.

"That legitimately sounded cool," said Bill.

"Cool as fuck, right?" asked Kenny. "And I just made it up. But *sounds* German, don't it?"

"It does," said Bill. "And that's all that fuckin' matters."

"Just needs to *sound* cool," said Graham.

"Estúpidos, estúpidos..." said Charlie. "Y'all are talkin' like straight-up *idiotas.*"

Kenny scrunched his face. "Don't be callin' nobody no fuckin', *idio... idio-datas.*"

"Kinda rude, Charlie," said Bill. "Be nice, now."

"Oh, my bad!" said Charlie. "Fuckin', *lo siento,* y'all! *Lo siento!* I'm real fuckin' sorry if I hurt y'all's feelin's and shit..."

He glanced at Kenny in the rearview mirror.

"...especially yours, Kenny..."

"You didn't hurt my feelin's," said Kenny. "I just don't get why you're actin' like a bitch."

"'Cause y'all ain't *bi-fuckin'-lingual,* like me!" said Charlie. "So y'all don't fuckin' know, man!"

"Don't know what?" asked Kenny.

"What it's like," said Charlie.

"To be what?" asked Kenny.

"To be a bilingual," said Charlie. "The fuck you think I'm talkin' about?"

"Now, Charlie," said Bill. "Ain't like no fuckin' Germans, nor anybody who even *speaks* fuckin' German gonna be around tonight, so—"

"It's the goddamn principle, Bill!" said Charlie. *"Es-el-fuckin'-principio!*

I just—I can't believe this shit right now. I'm in fuckin', disbelief. Straight-up *sorpresa.*"

"Ya know what?" asked Kenny. "I don't think my German's got nothin' to do with your *sorpres-iana.* Or your *sorpres-ioso,* either."

His seatbelt creaked as he leaned forward.

"I think you're just mad, cause Bill's takin' *my* side..."

Graham nodded. "Yep."

Kenny leaned back. "You gotta learn to *chill* about shit, Charlie. Don't get so worked up ab—"

"Now you listen *here,* motherfucker," said Charlie. "I studied my *ass* off to learn *español,* and I'll be *god-damned* if—"

"Charlie," said Bill. "Just calm the fuck down, *amigo.* If Kenny wants to speak nonsense German while he's beatin' ass, that's his God-given right."

"As an American," said Kenny.

"First Amendment, Charlie-boy," said Graham. "Even I know that."

"Well, I'm glad you learned somethin' in school, Graham-cracker!" said Charlie. "I'm sure your parents'll be real proud and shit!"

"Charlie-boy..." Graham leaned forward, placing his heavy hand on Charlie's shoulder. "You're just nervous."

"Nervioso?" asked Charlie. "Me?"

"Yep." Graham leaned back. "'Cause we're 'bout to get in a fight."

"I ain't *nervioso, ese,*" said Charlie. "But, I mean, this *is* gonna be—"

"—*legit,*" said Kenny. "This'll make us, or break us, as a posse."

Everyone fell silent.

Bill ran his fingers across the brim of his cowboy hat, shifting his heavy cowboy boots on the floorboard. The boots would come in handy tonight—he planned on stomping Glick's face into the ground with them.

He tapped a steady rhythm on his knee, counting down the minutes.

"Ya know," said Bill, "I'd like to meet a German one day."

"Me too," said Kenny.

"And just, ya know, really talk to him and shit," said Bill. "Find out what he thinks about Dubya-Dubya-Two, and how it *feels,* as a German, to belong to a nation that almost took over the world..."

"Twice," said Kenny.

"Fuckin' twice," said Bill. "I mean, I'd wait a while before I asked him that. I wouldn't be like, fuckin', *'Hey, name's Bill Cunningham. By the way, how's it fuckin' feel, ya know, to lose Dubya-Dubya Two?'* or shit like that."

Kenny nodded. "You'd break the ice a lil' bit. At first."

"I would," said Bill. "I'd shoot the shit with him, break the ice a lil' bit, then once I sensed we're cool, I'd fuckin' ask him."

"I bet a lot of Germans," said Kenny, "not *all* of 'em, maybe, but a lot of 'em, they just spend days lookin' at the sky, wonderin' what it'd be like if they'd succeeded in their plan, ya know, to take over the world and shit."

"I would," said Bill. "If I was them. I would sure as fuck look at the sky and think about that. Hell, it'd be all I'd think about sometimes."

Graham hocked a loogie out the window. "Germans didn't play around."

"Yep" said Bill. "They did *bad shit,* that's undeniable—"

He turned to Kenny and Graham.

"—but did they ever fuck around?"

"Nein," said Kenny. *"Nein,* they didn't ever fuck around."

Bill raised an eyebrow. Almost forgot the number nine meant *"No"* in fuckin' German.

"If there's one thing them Germans knew," said Charlie, "it's how to take care of business."

"Like we're gonna tonight!" said Kenny.

The heavy metal tape clicked to a stop.

Charlie pressed rewind.

A long silence ensued.

***

Charlie made another complete halt at a four-way stop, despite no other vehicles present.

Graham asked, "Why'd Glick start talkin' shit, anyway?"

"It's all that prom stuff, right?" asked Kenny.

"Yep," said Bill. "Claimed he was gonna beat my ass at prom. For takin' Samantha Henson as my date."

"But didn't do shit, did he?" asked Charlie.

"Nope," said Bill. "Just mad-dog glared at everyone the whole night, like a fuckin' dipshit..."

"I told ya," said Charlie, "you should've stepped up to him on the dance floor and said, *'Why ya eyeballin' me, motherfucker?'"*

"And then ripped his fuckin' eye out!" said Kenny.

The car erupted in laughter.

"That's a good one, Kenny!" said Charlie, cackling. "Ask him *'why ya eyeballin' me,'* and then rippin' his fuckin' eyeball out!"

"Huh huh huh..." chuckled Graham.

"Even I wouldn't do that."

1990s

CHAPTER XXXIII

EYEBALL

"You keep eyeballin' me, girl...

I'll rip that eyeball right-the-fuck-out."

RHONDA STARED INTO Daddy's bathroom mirror, pulling her right eyelid down.

("my eye!")

("you fucking bitch!")

("you ripped out my eye!")

She pressed her finger against her eyeball, pushing it deeper inside her skull.

("oh my god!")

("somebody call 911!")

("i told ya to stop eyeballin' me, bitch!")

She didn't think about the one-eyed bitch much; in fact, hardly at all. But when she did, she felt good about herself—happy she'd taught the bitch a lesson.

("what did you do, rhonda?")

Gave her a gift that kept on givin', in a way.

("you're insane!")

("you're a fucking animal!")

Who knows, maybe even saved her life?

("stanch the blood!")

("stanch the blood comin' outta her eyesocket!")

By rippin' that bitch's eye out, maybe saved her from talkin' shit to a *real* mean bitch—one who would've killed her ass without hesitatin'.

("there's too much blood!")

("grab more napkins!")

Betcha now she wasn't talkin' shit, though.

("stuff 'em in there!")

("stuff 'em in her eyesocket!")

Rhonda pushed her eye in deeper, briefly losing vision.

("i told the bitch to stop eyeballin' me!")

("now look what happened!")

The one-eyed bitch probably wasn't *eyeballin'* nobody, either.

1970s

CHAPTER XXXIV

NAPOLEON

"The real genius of fuckin', Napoleon, is that he always surprised his enemies, ya know?

He always made 'em say, 'Holy shit!' and 'What the fuck?'"

"ALRIGHT, MOTHERFUCKERS," SAID Charlie. *"Estrategia.* Let's fuckin' talk about it."

Bill and his Posse stood before the headlights of Charlie's dad's black Camaro as it illuminated the baseball field before them. A sudden gust of wind blew a cyclone of dirt from home base, carrying it halfway to first.

"Estra-wha?" Graham popped his knuckles in his right hand.

Crack!

"Estrategia, hombre," said Charlie. "Fuckin' *strategy.* We can't go into this shit without a plan."

Bill agreed—even *with* Graham-cracker, they faced eight weedboys. Odds weren't in their favor.

"How about I just give'em all head massages?" Graham popped his left-hand knuckles.

Crack!

"There's your strategy," he said. "Huh huh huh..."

"You ever gone up against *eight* guys, Graham?" asked Bill.

Graham paused, his mouth falling open as he combed through memories.

"Don't think so," he said. "But those little underclassmen don't count."

"Those underclassmen might be pussies," said Bill, "but them other weedboys can scrap. You know that, right?"

Graham shrugged.

"Glick can fight," said Kenny. "Remember when he whipped that one Eric-dude's ass after school? Right here on the baseball field."

"Yeah..." Bill strained to peer past the infield lit by Charlie's headlights. Sunglasses made it hard to see, and he considered takin'em off, but no.

Would add more *impact* when he stomped Glick's face in.

"Probably why he chose this place to fight us," said Bill. "It's his fuckin', power spot or somethin'."

"Glick punches real fast," said Charlie. "I'll give him that."

"That he does..." said Bill.

Fast was an understatement, though. Glick's fists had moved with liquid speed when he wrecked that Eric-dude. *Moved like liquid, struck like lightning.* Fortunately, Bill stood taller, and he intended to deliver a cowboy boot into Glick's fucking face before he got close.

Then he'd pin the weedboy to the ground and introduce him to Wild Bill.

"That Mitchell Mouse guy's pretty ripped," said Charlie.

"Probably 'cause he's short," Bill kicked dirt with his boot. "Got an inferiority complex or some shit, so ol' *Mitchey Mouse* gets ripped as fuck to compensate for it."

He kicked dirt again—this time toward moths fluttering in Charlie's headlights. They scattered, then returned.

Charlie nodded at Bill's boots. "Think I'll buy me some cowboy boots, too. Probably help when you're in fights and shit, give ya a little extra kickin' power."

"Oh, they'll help ya kick alright," said Bill. He stomped his boot on the ground, imagining it was Glick's face. A cloud of dust flew up.

And make ya feel badass, too.

"I'll buy some too," said Kenny. "If they got cheap ones at Walmart."

He extended his arms, rotating them like they'd learned in P.E.

"And by the way, *I'm* takin' Mitchey Mouse tonight. He's mine."

"You sure?" asked Bill.

He didn't doubt Kenny's ability to fuck shit up, not one bit, but he was "Skinny Kenny," and Mouse was "Muscle Man Mouse."

"*Jawohl.*" Kenny winked, then bobbed his head like he was listening to music.

Bill nodded. Something about Kenny's wink, that beat he marched to, his *rhythm*—both impressed and disturbed him.

"You got Mitchey Mouse, then," said Bill. "And make sure to yell some cool-soundin' German while ya beat his ass."

Kenny's face lit up.

"That Larry Longface guy is real fuckin' tall," said Charlie. "Maybe even taller than Graham."

"Longface ain't shit," said Graham.

"He can fight, though," said Charlie. "I seen him in the Walmart parkin' lot once. Some Zion dude looked at him wrong and they got into it. He actually stopped the rest of the weedboys from helpin' him and fought the guy one-on-one, like they was in a duel, like gladiators and shit."

"How'd he do?" asked Bill.

"Beat his face in real good," said Charlie. "Enough so the Zion bitch swore he wouldn't come to Walmart no more. Like, publicly swore it, as an oath, right there in Walmart parkin' lot. I watched it all from a distance, just smokin' my Marlboros."

Bill stroked his beard.

Maybe he could make Glick swear somethin', too—

—in front of everyone.

("you tell your boys!")

"The only one who can't fight," said Charlie, "is that red-headed, freckle-faced dude. *'Jack,'* or whatever his name is. Ain't he in the chess club or somethin'? Winnin' tournaments and shit?"

Graham spat. "Why's a nerd like him runnin' with weedboys?"

"Probably the brains of the group," said Bill. "The one who's fuckin', strategizin' shit right now."

"He can fight, too," said Kenny.

"You seen him?" asked Charlie.

"Back in freshman year," said Kenny. "A senior gave him a monster wedgie in the cafeteria, right in front of some hot girls, and he went wild on the guy. I mean, *wild.* Grabbed a lunch tray and wouldn't stop wailin' on him."

"I remember that now," said Charlie. "And when the teachers tried to stop him, he fuckin' hit *them* with the lunch tray, too, right?"

"Huh huh huh..." chuckled Graham. "I remember that. Even I wouldn't hit no teacher or nothin'."

"But you did hit a principal once," said Charlie.

"That was different," said Graham. "He touched my ears. I hate it when people touch my ears!"

An insidious smirk crept across Charlie's face. Bill sensed it wasn't long before Charlie used Graham's weakness against him.

Don't do it, Charlie...

Whatever you're plannin', don't fuckin' do it.

"Now, if I remember correctly," said Bill, "didn't both Jack *and* that senior who gave him a wedgie get put in A-School?"

"Yep," said Kenny. "That's when he started hangin' with Glick, 'cause Glick was in A-School at the same time. For beatin' that Eric-dude's ass."

"To be fair," said Bill, "I don't think that Jack guy, fuckin' wailin' on people with a lunch tray, all pissed 'cause he got a monster wedgie in front of girls, means he's good at fightin'. Just means he flipped the fuck out once."

He spread his arms wide.

"And I don't see no lunch trays 'round here, do y'all?"

"I sure fuckin' don't, Bill," said Charlie. "And as long as we don't give him no wedgie, we'll avoid ol' Jack-in-the-box springin' out."

"Huh huh huh..." chuckled Graham. "I wanna give him a wedgie now..."

Kenny grinned. "That'd be real nice, wouldn't it, Graham?"

"Huh huh huh..." chuckled Graham. "To see how mad he gets..."

Bill spat, then gazed at the stars. One of them glowed a dull red.

"Let's just focus on beatin' their asses first. Keep it nice and simple."

He patted Graham on the back, assured by his large presence.

Glad we got ya on our side, Graham-cracker...

Gonna need ya.

"Charlie," he said. "You got any strategies and shit you thinkin' up yet?"

"I sure fuckin' do, Bill," said Charlie. "I think we should get *real* strategic on their asses, like Napoleon. I'm talkin' *estrategia*-fuckin'-*brillante*."

Bill nodded. "I'm all about goin' Napoleon on these motherfuckers. Whatcha cookin'?"

"Well, uhh..." said Charlie. "...like, we could..."

He stroked his mustache as his eyes darted left to right.

"...fuckin', *ambush* their asses and shit..."

"Ambush?" asked Graham.

Charlie narrowed his eyes. "That means, surprise-fuckin'-attack their asses, Graham-cracker."

Graham thumped Charlie's forehead.

"Oww! That fuckin' hurt!"

"Huh huh huh..." chuckled Graham. "I done *ambushed* your forehead."

Everyone laughed except Charlie. "Now you listen *here,* motherfucker—"

"Nope, nope," said Bill. "You deserved that one, Charlie. Best stop runnin' your mouth to Graham, now."

"Huh huh huh..." chuckled Graham. "...I like thumpin' your head..."

He raised his hand to thump Charlie again, but Charlie hopped back. More laughter ensued. Charlie rubbed his head, glaring at Graham's right ear.

"Anyway," said Bill. "So, are y'all down to epically ambush their asses and shit?"

They discussed it for a while and agreed that an epic ambush was just what the doctor ordered. Even Graham said, *"I'm down with that."*

"So we leave my car runnin'," said Charlie, "doors open so the interior lights are on, with the heavy metal playin'—"

"We *gotta* have the heavy metal playin'," said Bill. "Can't beat no ass without it."

Graham nodded. "Music makes stuff more fun."

"It sure does, Graham-cracker," said Charlie. "So anyway, when they check my car out, wonderin' what's goin' on, we fuckin' run out, from all fuckin' directions..."

"It can't be from the *same* direction, y'all," said Bill. "This is key. It's gotta be from *all* different directions. That's what makes it like Napoleon."

Kenny looked pumped up. "That *is* what Napoleon would do, y'all. It'd be just like him. I know my history, too."

"Sí, I'm sure ya do, Kenny," said Charlie. "So anyway, we fuckin' run out, from all fuckin' directions, fuckin' screamin' and shit..."

"Why we gotta scream?" asked Graham.

"For *impact,* man," said Charlie.

"Like when that kid screamed at Graham earlier?" asked Kenny. "He was like, *'Aahhhhhhhhh!'* Like a Comanche warrior or somethin'!"

"Huh huh huh..." chuckled Graham.

"And then he was like, *'Aaagh! Aaagh! Can't breathe!'"*

Kenny fell to his knees, grasping his throat.

"...can't...breathe..."

Everyone laughed, enjoying the playful reenactment.

"Aaaaaagh! Aaaaaaaaaaaaaaaaaagh!"

Charlie cackled, slapping his knee. "That was some good shit, wasn't it?"

"He...lp...meeee..." said Kenny.

"Huh huh huh..." chuckled Graham. "I done choked him real good."

"Y'all remember," said Bill, laughing, "how Glick was gettin' all upset? How he was like, *'Hey maaaan, stop that shit, maaan, you're gonna kill him, maaaan!'"*

Their laughter grew to a roar, and Kenny collapsed to the ground, clutching his sides.

***

"Ya know," said Bill, his laughter fading. "They're probably gonna charge at ya, Graham. All at once."

"Who?" asked Graham. "The weedboys?"

"All them little freshman and sophomore weedboys," said Bill. "They'll try to overwhelm you with their numbers and shit. I mean, that's what I'd do, if I were them."

Bill studied Graham, calculating how well he'd defend himself if ambushed from different angles—like if he was *cross-attacked* or some shit.

"I'll fling'em across the baseball field." said Graham. "Four home runs."

"Babe Ruth style," said Kenny. "I like that."

"Huh huh huh…" chuckled Graham.

"I don't know those underclassmen weedboys really," said Charlie, "but I talked to that little Asian boy once. Y'all know he can't even speak no Asian shit?"

"Even though he's Asian?" asked Kenny.

"*Sí,*" said Charlie. "Even though he's fuckin' Asian. Ain't ever figured that one out, *ese.* I mean, even if I was just *part*-fuckin' Mexican, I'd sure as fuck be speakin' *español,* even better than I do now."

"Probably adopted and shit," said Bill. "From Korea or Vietnam or whatever. War orphan."

"Don't matter," said Charlie. "Should still speak that shit."

He spat.

"But anyway, *de-todos*-fuckin'*-modos,* them weedboys, they'll be like, *'What the fuck? Why is Young Charlie's car just sittin' here? With the music playin' and the doors open?'* And they'll just *have* to investigate, man. And then we run out, attackin' and screamin' and shit. Now, I don't mean we gotta scream like that one kid did, like a little bitch—"

"I honestly thought it was epic," said Kenny. "I mean, the kid had balls to charge at Graham like that."

"It *was* epic," said Bill, "until he got epically choked out mid-air. And I agree with Charlie, we do gotta yell shit as we run out. Really put the fear of God in'em."

"*Sí, sí,*" said Charlie. "Yell like this, y'all: *'RAAAAAAAAAAAAAH! MOTHERFUCKERRRRRS!'*"

Kenny and Graham snickered.

"What's so funny?" asked Charlie.

"You want us to yell, *'Raaaaah! Motherfuckerrrrrs'?*" asked Kenny.

"Bueno, fuckin' *sí."* Charlie put his hands on his hips. "And what's wrong with that, Kenny?"

"I think what he's sayin'," said Bill, "is that we should yell somethin' with more *impact.*"

"What's got more impact than yellin, *'RAAAAAAH! MOTHERFUCKERRRRRS!*" asked Charlie. "That's about as, fuckin', *impactful,* as you can fuckin' get, man..."

More snickering.

"How about we yell somethin' in Spanish, Charlie?" asked Bill. "You know, good ol' *español...*"

"Sí, sí..." Charlie stroked his beard. *"Bueno, amigo,* fuckin' *bueno...*I like that, I do. Might really strike fear, ya know. In their fuckin' hearts."

"How about we yell somethin' in German?" asked Kenny. "How about—"

"Fuck your German bullshit, *ese,"* said Charlie.

"Good ol' *español* will do us just fine..."

***

"Hey, y'all!" said Kenny. "Look what I found!"

A metallic clatter echoed as Kenny dropped four aluminum baseball bats to the ground.

"Baseball bats..." He took a practice swing.

"Muy excelente." Charlie picked one up. "We *are* outnumbered four to eight. Baseball bats might help even the fuckin' odds a little."

"But it's even more badass," said Bill, "if we beat'em outnumbered *without* the bats. And if we do use'em, it'll kinda taint our victory. They'll just say we cheated and shit."

He picked one up and took a swing.

Felt good, though.

Real fuckin' good.

"Maybe," said Charlie. "But I bet nobody would fuck with us, either. Not after that."

"Not after we beat the livin' fuck out of'em!" said Kenny.

He swung the bat upward in a shining arc.

"Ein zeich, ein leiss..."

"But if we lost," said Charlie, "if we fuckin' lost, despite usin' the fuckin' bats—"

Graham ruffled Charlie's hair. "Ain't nobody gonna lose, Charlie-boy. Stop with the pussy-talk."

Graham picked up a bat and took a practice swing. It looked tiny in his hands, like a giant wielding a toothpick. "I'm cool with or without the bats. Either way."

Bill nodded.

Graham seemed more like a *hands-and-fists* kinda guy.

"Let's hide 'em for now," said Bill. "And if shit hits the fan, maybe we can use 'em."

"As a last resort."

***

"BRAAAAP!"

Kenny laughed from his hiding spot in the home team dugout. "Did you just fuckin' burp, Graham?"

"Huh huh huh..." chuckled Graham from behind a tree. "Y'all heard it over there?"

Charlie's voice rang from the away team dugout. "Fuck yeah, we heard it! Motherfucker!"

"Huh huh huh..."

Bill stood behind a tree near Graham, nodding to the heavy metal playing from Charlie's car.

"Now Graham," he said. "Don't be burpin' and shit when they get close."

"I'm hungry," said Graham. "And I wanna snort coke."

Bill felt for the coke baggies in his pocket, reassured by their presence. Snortin' off the back of his hand might prove tricky, but not impossible. Just had to be careful when pourin'.

"I done told ya," said Bill. "I'll toss ya a bag when they drive up."

"Why not now?" asked Graham.

"Because you'll fuckin' snort it all before—"

"Hey, Graham!" called out Charlie. "You best not be burpin' or fartin' when Glick and his boys roll up! Or you'll spoil the ambush, *ese!*"

"I already told him that!" said Bill.

"This sucks!" said Graham. "I'm tired of waitin'!"

"Me too!" said Kenny.

Bill sighed.

He was tired of waitin', too.

Graham scratched his head. "What're we supposed to yell in Spanish again? I forgot..."

"Estúpido! Estúpido!" said Charlie. "We spent ten fuckin' minutes practicin' that shit!"

"Well, I forgot!" said Graham.

"I swear to God, Graham," said Charlie, "you are the anti-fuckin' Napoleon, man!"

"You're the anti-Napoleon, Charlie-boy!" said Graham.

"You got the patience," said Charlie, "and the brain, of a bird that's—"

"You're...you're *stupid,* Charlie-boy!" said Graham.

Charlie fell silent, then snickered.

"That was good, Graham-cracker!" said Charlie. "I'm talkin' *muy brillante, ese!* How long it take you to come up with that? A couple of days, while you was eatin' all my fuckin' chips?"

Kenny and Bill laughed.

"While eatin' me out of my goddamn house and home?" asked Charlie. "I ain't got no more food left n—"

"Guys, guys!" said Kenny. "We been waitin' too long, y'all! I mean, this is rude of them! To challenge us, and be this fuckin' late!"

A frog hopped toward Bill, then away, as if sensing danger.

"It is rude," said Bill, watching the frog hop into darkness. "Makin' us wait like this..."

He squeezed the coke baggies in his pocket.

Rudeness deserved to be punished.

"I changed my mind about the baseball bats," he said.

"Fuckin' arm up."

1990s

CHAPTER XXXV

BREAKFAST WITH YOUNG ZACHARY

"Zach," said Daddy. "How in God's name could you do this?"

AFTER DOIN' HER business in Daddy's bathroom, Rhonda removed
her shirt and bra before applying soap and water to one of his oversized
Budweiser towels. Her tits still had an *icky, grody* feeling even after she'd
wiped GB's blood and snot off with his shirt.

She examined herself in the mirror and scrubbed and scrubbed *and
scrubbed* so hard her breasts turned bright red, making sure to clean under
them, as well—where the sun didn't shine. Even after more soap, more water
and more scrubbing, they still didn't feel *quite* clean,

("please stop!")

not really,

("i don't have blue eyes!")

but she'd done her best.

(I KNEW YOU HAD BLUE EYES)

She shrugged and put her clothes back on.

***

A shirtless young Zachary lounged before the living room TV, clutching his
Teenage Mutant Ninja Turtles pillow, fully immersed in cartoons. Rhonda
ruffled his hair as she passed.

"How's it goin', lil' Z-man?" she asked.

"Good..." said Zach, his voice still heavy with sleepiness.

On the TV screen, people in costumes yelled dramatic shit while lasers
flew around, and then a dude with long-ass metal claws started *slicin' and
dicin'* a bunch of robots.

"Is this *X-Men?*" she asked.

"Yep," said Zach. "Just started..."

Nice. Could watch it with him while enjoyin' her breakfast.

"You already ate, lil' Z?" she asked.

"No," said Zach, "and I told ya to stop callin' me that..."

"Mmm-hmm," said Rhonda. "One day when you're big and strong, and
not little anymore, I'll stop callin' ya that..."

Maybe.

But probably not.

In the kitchen, she whipped up breakfast—brown sugar-flavored
oatmeal (never blueberry, *never blue)* and eggs fried with a touch of extra

virgin olive oil. *"The only oil y'all ought to use is olive oil, the extra virgin kind,"* Daddy had said. *"It's got that alpha-delta-omega in it. Good for your brain and shit."*

She wolfed down everything at the dining table, saving her frosted strawberry Pop-Tarts for last. A balanced breakfast—oatmeal for carbs and fiber (*"Fiber's real important,"* Daddy always said. *"Keeps ya regular."*), eggs for protein, and Pop-Tarts for a sweet, well-deserved dessert. Pretty sure Pop-Tarts had vitamins and minerals and shit, but she *always* took her Flintstone chewable after breakfast, so didn't really matter. Daddy had taught her that vitamins fuckin' *ensured* she got her nutritional needs met, no matter what the fuck she ate. *"Vitamins are like magic pills that give ya a hundred percent of what your body needs,"* he'd said. *"Except for fiber, protein, and some other shit."*

That's why she never skipped her eggs and oatmeal—for the fiber and protein and other shit, too.

"Where's the Flintstone vitamins?" asked Rhonda, her mouth stuffed with eggs.

"In the cabinet they're always in..." said Zach.

"I checked, they ain't there."

"I dunno, then..."

Rhonda scooped up another mouthful of eggs and sighed. She didn't relish diggin' through cabinets just to find the fuckin' Flintstone vitamins.

Inefficient.

Fuckin' inefficient and a waste of time.

She sipped orange juice to wash the eggs down. "Can't y'all keep the vitamins and shit in the same fuckin' place without movin'em around all the time?"

"Think Daddy moved'em..."

"Mmm-hmm," she said. "Either Daddy, you, or Taleiah—doesn't matter. Somebody should've moved'em back."

Zach stayed silent, the back of his head motionless as he watched *X-Men.*

"Ya hear me?" asked Rhonda.

"Yeah...I hear ya..." said Zach.

Rhonda shook her head.

Patience...

I need so much goddamn patience with this family sometimes...

She asked, "Did you already take yours today?"

"Not yet..." said Zach. "...I will after I eat..."

"Mmm-hmm," she said. "Don't forget..."

Lack of vitamins'll probably make ya even more messed up...

Little fuckin' psychopath...

"You shoot good today?" asked Zach.

What do you think, pipsqueak?

"Yep." She savored a spoonful of oatmeal. "Shot real good today."

Well, not "real" good...

But better than you ever have, and ever will, either...

"How's *your* shootin' goin', lil' Z?"

"Good..." said Zach. "...gettin' better at stride-shootin'..."

"Stride-shootin's *real* hard, ain't it?"

"Yeah..."

Rhonda almost added *"even for me,"* but Daddy taught her to be humble about shit, so she exercised restraint.

"How about Princess T?" she asked. "How's her shootin'?"

"...doin' alright, I guess..."

"Doin' *alright,* huh..."

Now, that was some bullshit, right there: Taleiah fucking *sucked* at shootin'.

Oh, she likely shot better than most girls her age—a perk of practicin' for The Run everyday—but in the family, she sat at the bottom of the totem pole. Lil' T just didn't love shootin' like the rest of 'em. Okay, maybe Zach didn't either, but he didn't *dislike* it—just preferred his pocketknives and slingshot for some reason. But at least he shot half-decent for an elementary schooler. Not as good as *she* did in elementary school, of course. Not even close. Probably 'cause Daddy hadn't started him nor Taleiah shootin' as early as he'd started her. Or maybe they just lacked that *gunlust* her and Daddy shared.

(is it gunlust that makes your hand shake, rhonda?)

(or somethin' el—)

Rhonda shrugged, savoring another bite of oatmeal.

"Ya know, lil' Z," she said, "I don't even count how many times I hit bullseye no more. Just how many times *I don't.*"

Zach yawned.

"Because the times *I don't* hit bullseye are pretty fuckin' few," she said. "So just easier for me to count that."

Zach scratched his head, yawning again.

"Ya hear me?" asked Rhonda.

She held a spoonful of oatmeal to her lips, focusing on the back of his head.

"I hear ya..." said Zach. "...that's cool, Rhonda..."

***

Rhonda whipped up more eggs and oatmeal for herself, keeping an eye on the TV. Some dude wearin' a blue costume shot a big-ass laser from a gold visor coverin' his eyes, knockin' a buncha robots down like they were bowlin' pins. Rhonda nodded in satisfaction, scooping up more eggs. The *X-Men* cartoon overflowed with action. She liked that stuff way more than that kiddy-ass, *Tiny Toons* bullshit.

"I am so hungry this mornin'..." she said.

"Don't eat all the eggs and oatmeal," said Zach. "Ain't had breakfast yet..."

Rhonda had already fixed herself the remaining oatmeal and eggs, but whatever—little man would do just fine with SpaghettiO's or shit like that. Kids ate anything.

She opened the fridge. "Y'all got any more Tabasco? Or hot sauce?"

"That was all we got..." said Zach. "Probably get more from Walmart today..."

"Fuck!" She slammed the fridge-door shut.

"We got Mrs. Dash, though..." said Zach.

"Did I say I wanted *bullshit* on my eggs, Zach?" she asked. "Because if I wanted bullshit on my eggs, I'd say so. I'd be like, *'Hey Zach, you got any bullshit? 'Cause I'd like some on my eggs.'*"

"Taleiah eats it on her—"

"Newsflash, little man," said Rhonda, "My name's not fuckin' Taleiah, nor do I want any Mrs. Fuckin' Dash on my eggs. *I want my fuckin' hot sauce, and that's why I fuckin' asked for it!*"

"Okay..." said Zach. "Chill..."

Rhonda clenched her jaw.

Don't start that "chill" bullshit with me, boy...
I ain't above whippin' a midget's ass.

"Y'all got any chili powder, at least?" she asked. "Or spicy shit like that?"

"Daddy keeps on forgettin' to buy more..."

"Well, you help him remember next time," said Rhonda.

She sat down and sighed, resigned to finish her eggs *without* any hot sauce or spicy shit. Bland as fuck without'em, but driven by hunger (likely from cummin' both last night *and* this morning), she shoveled'em down, anyway.

"I been tryin' to help Daddy remember stuff..." said Zach. "But he's gettin' worse...like, even worse than normal..."

Rhonda paused, holding a spoonful of oatmeal. Daddy's memory shifted in waves—sometimes clearer, sometimes worse—but lately, it was like he drowned at the bottom of Lake Gilead.

"He still goin' on about that Young Charlie dude?" she asked. "And that, uhh, what's-his-fuckin'-face, Skinny Jimmy and—"

"Skinny Kenny."

"Yeah, and that Graham-cookie fucker?"

"Graham-*cracker*, yeah..." said Zach. "...and all the rest of'em...almost every day now..."

Rhonda raised an eyebrow.

Almost every day now?

Damn...

"Gotta be patient with him..." said Rhonda, but a knot of worry tightened in her stomach.

What if Daddy kept on gettin' worse?

Like them senile old folks? At those creepy nursin' homes?

Then what would they do?

(the temple)

(the temple)

(all for the temple)

The Temple.

The Temple would make Daddy better.

The Temple would make *everything* better.

"I'm sure his memory'll improve," said Rhonda. "Once we find the Temple."

She narrowed her eyes.

"Until then, lil' Z, you best remind him about the hot sauce."

Zach yawned.

Rhonda slammed her fist onto the table.

"Ya hear me?"

***

While Rhonda finished her breakfast and watched *X-Men,* Zach shifted to a different position, then twirled the thin tail of hair down the back of his neck—a "rat tail," as the kids called it, but a better name for it was *"a bitch-ass ponytail that made dudes look like pussies."*

"Zach, move your head, please," said Rhonda. "You're blockin' the screen."

Zach sighed, shifted back, and twirled his bitch-ass ponytail.

"...this okay?" he asked.

"You're good now."

Zach yawned. "Why're you eatin' breakfast here today'?"

"'Cause I fuckin' want to," she said. "Problem?"

Zach said nothing *(good)* as she shoveled oatmeal into her mouth, washing it down with a swallow of coffee. The bitterness of the coffee contrasted real nice with the sweetness of the oatmeal. Now, how would her oatmeal taste if she'd have used *coffee* instead of water when microwavin' it? Had to try that next time. If it was good, she could tell everybody and claim recognition as the one who came up with such a badass, innovative fuckin' idea.

"What's on after this?" she asked.

"Another episode of *X-Men...*"

"Oh, good," she said. "There's two episodes on today?"

"Two every mornin' since summer started..." he said. "Then two of *Spider-Man...*"

That *Spider-Man* cartoon was alright. Music pumped her up and the New York City setting excited her, but didn't care much for the Spider-Dweeb himself. Just a geek in blue and red spandex, yellin' smart-ass quips like he was somethin' else, spurtin' his little web-shit everywhere, makin' a mess.

Actin' up is what he was doin'.

And a little ass-kickin' is what he needed.

Just what the doctor fuckin' ordered...

Speakin' of doctors, she wouldn't mind seein' that Dr. Octopus guy rip the ol' Spider-Dweeb limb from limb. Now, *that* was a guy she could get behind—that fuckin' Dr. Octopus. Knew how to take care of business. Real smart, too, but not a smartass about it—just took care of business.

"You know," she said, "I never liked *Spider-Man* as much as *X-Men*."

"Me neither..." said Zach.

"I do remember that one time," she said, "when Spider-Man got that black costume, you remember that?"

"Yeah..."

"That's the only time I really liked the show," she said. "He looked a lot cooler wearin' that and his personality changed, too. Started actin' more *badass,* like he really didn't give a shit, ya know?"

"Yeah," said Zach. "Made him stronger, too..."

"Hell yes, it did," said Rhonda. "I remember when he picked up that big-ass rhinoceros-lookin' guy over his shoulders and was about to throw him off the edge of some tower and straight-up kill his ass. You see that episode?"

"Yeah..." said Zach. "That was so awesome..."

"And then, he said to the rhinoceros dude, somethin' like, *'I ain't gonna take your shit no more, you dumb, piece of shit!'* and I was like, *'Holy shit!* Now this show's gettin' fuckin' good! 'Bout time he starts takin' care of business,'* and I think he threw that fucker off the tower and straight-up killed his ass, but I had to go to work so couldn't finish it."

She sipped her coffee.

"And next time I watched it, he didn't have his black costume no more."

"BRAAAP!"

A belch escaped her.

"Excuuuse me..." She patted her chest. "And I was like, *'What the fuck? I thought this show was finally gettin' good!'* because he was back to actin' like a limp-dick smart-ass again."

"Yep," said Zach. "Shouldn't've given up that costume..."

"He gave it up?" she asked. "Why the fuck would he do that?"

"Can't remember..." said Zach. "...but another guy got it, and tries to kill him with it now..."

"What's that guy's name?"

"Venom..."

Venom. Now that sounded like a cool-ass guy—one who didn't take shit from nobody. *Just took care of business.* Maybe if they had more episodes with that Venom dude in it, she'd like the show better.

A gorgeous, real strong-lookin' woman in yellow and green spandex flew across the screen, slammin' straight through a shit-ton of gigantic robots. She cackled, called the robots *"tin cans,"* then proceeded to obliterate a fuck-ton more.

"Which one's that?" asked Rhonda.

"What do ya mean?"

"The bitch flyin' around!" she said. "Slammin' straight through them giant-ass robots!"

"Oh..." said Zach. "...that's Rogue..."

Rogue...

The character named Rogue spoke with a distinct Deep South drawl—more robust and melodic than Rhonda's Mid-South Kentucky twang. *"These tin cans might be big,"* said Rogue, *"but they're no match for a Southern belle that can fly!"*

Rhonda smiled. That Rogue chick was a badass bitch, alright.

Bet no one fucked with her.

After cackling again, Rogue flew off, crashing through a wall on her way out.

Didn't give no fucks about that wall, did she?

Just kept on flyin'...

"That's the character I like the most," said Rhonda. "Rogue."

"Why?" asked Zach. "'Cause she's a girl?"

Rhonda rolled her eyes. "No, not just because she's a girl, Zach. Because she's the one that's most like me."

And I bet she don't take shit from anyone or anything...

Just takes care of business...

Like somebody else I fuckin' know...

Rhonda winked at her reflection in the adjacent window, smiled, then shoveled down the last of her oatmeal. Now time for those sweet, sweet strawberry Pop-Tarts.

"I think you're more like Wolverine..." said Zach.

"Which one's that?"

"The hairy guy with metal claws..."

"The hairy guy with metal claws? Now why the *fuck* would you say that, boy?"

Zach shrugged.

Rhonda wrapped her entire mouth around the Pop-Tart, cramming it in as deep as possible, then bit down. White crumbs sprayed forth, landing on her jeans and floor.

"That was rude..." she said, her voice muffled by chewing. "I ain't no hairy guy..."

She bent over to pick up the crumbs and pop'em in her mouth. Couldn't let Daddy's carpet get dirty.

"I'm a Southern belle..." she said, spraying more crumbs everywhere. "Like that Rogue bitch..."

Zach stayed silent, the back of his head motionless as he stared at the TV. Rhonda crammed the remaining half of the Pop-Tart into her mouth, her mind formulating the words she yearned to say:

You know what, Zach?

I think you're *the one who's like Wolverine...*

You're *the one who cuts up all them poor animals and shit...*

Little psycopath...

Zach said, "You got blood on your jeans, by the way..."

She glanced down.

Fuck.

Why didn't he tell her earlier?

When she walked past him?

Had to get that shit out before she headed to work.

"Well, shit..." She jammed the second Pop-Tart into her mouth.

"Thanks for tellin' me."

***

Rhonda sipped her post-breakfast coffee while munching on Cool Ranch Doritos, enjoying the next exciting episode of *X-Men* with young Zachary.

She'd scrubbed and scrubbed *and scrubbed* that damn bloodstain with Dawn liquid detergent, but a pale orange afterimage remained. Needed to ask Daddy how to get that out.

"Y'all got more chips and shit?" she asked, tilting the Doritos bag to her mouth. All that scrubbin' made her hungry again.

"...those were the last of our Doritos, Rhonda..."

"Yeah, but y'all got any *more* chips and shit?"

She opened the pantry.

"Mmm, y'all got Tostitos? Where's the dip?"

Snatching the Tostitos, she shoved a handful in her mouth.

Mmm...

Crunchy with a light, salty taste.

Just needed dip.

"Zach!" She threw open the fridge door. "Where's the fuckin' dip?"

"Ain't got no more..."

"How y'all got Tostitos with no fuckin' dip?" she asked. "Somebody's hoggin' that shit!"

"Probably Taleiah..." said Zach. "She hogs all the good stuff..."

Rhonda narrowed her eyes.

Taleiah.

That bitch *did* hog all the good stuff. Didn't help wash or feed the assholes in the garage, either. Didn't even clean their buckets! That "special treatment" she got from Daddy wasn't fair—not to her, not to Zach, not to the whole damn family. Everyone had to work equally hard in their Quest for the Temple.

Fuckin'.

Equally.

"Where is lil' T this mornin'?" she asked. "Still gettin' her beauty sleep?"

"...I guess..."

"Still sleepin', huh..."

Little Princess Taleiah, gettin' her much-needed beauty sleep. Wastin' her day away without a care in the world. At least lil' Z was up and about.

After cramming one last handful of Tostitos in her mouth, she sat back down and pulled GB's tooth from her pocket, rolling it between her fingers. Popped right out the first time she hit him.

("...good, that's real good, GB...")

Kind of a cool little keepsake.
(*"...lick it up and swallow..."*)
Maybe start a new tradition?
(*"...like a good little boy..."*)
Start takin' a tooth from each asshole they kidnapped.
(*"...get'em nice and clean..."*)

Somethin' to remember'em by.

***

On TV, the X-Men battled against a bald, blue, semi-robotic lookin' dude with metal tubes comin' out his arms. The dude yelled somethin' epic, like, *"I am more powerful and superior! To all of y'all!"* then got big—real fuckin' big—swattin' the X-Men away like they were flies.

"I like that big blue guy," she said. "He knows how to take care of business. Ain't that right, Zach?"

"Heck yeah..." said Zach. "He's so powerful..."

"What's his name?" she asked.

"Apoca...Apocal..."

"Apocalypse?"

"Yeah..."

"Well," she said. "That's an intimidatin' name."

"I think it's stupid..."

"Why?"

"His name should have somethin' to do with his powers," said Zach. "Not his lips..."

Rhonda scrunched her face.

"What the fuck his *lips* gotta do wi—"

BEEP-BEEP-BEEP-BEEP!

An alarm clock buzzed.

Rhonda sprang from her chair.

"Daddy's awake!"

1970s

CHAPTER XXXVI

SORPRESA DESAGRADABLE

"This'll make Young Charlie have a fuckin' meltdown…"

"WE GOTTA TELL *everybody* what happened tonight," said Charlie. "Every-fuckin'-body we know."

Bill let his hand drop from the car window, drumming his fingers to the rhythm of Charlie's heavy metal tape.

"Still can't believe they didn't show up," said Bill. "I mean, Glick was pissed. Frothin' at the mouth and shit."

"I'm callin' twelve different people tomorrow," said Charlie. "People who love to talk, to spread it around that Glick and his weedboys are just a buncha shit-talkin', pussy-ass hippies who hang out in the Walmart parkin' lot, actin' like they're the Kings of Tri, but—"

"—they ain't kings of shit," said Bill. "More like court jesters, is what they is."

"Absolutamente fuckin' *cierto,"* said Charlie.

He stopped at a four-way. Baseball bats clattered in the backseat.

"Alright," said Charlie. "I'm always lost on the way back from droppin' Kenny and Graham-cracker off. Which way I turn to get to back to *La Hacienda?"*

"Make a right," said Bill, "and keep goin' 'til you see Piggly Wiggly. Then turn left to get on the road leadin' to your house."

Bill liked advising Charlie on directions—made him feel cool and competent. Didn't know why, but he'd always been real good at roads and whatnot. Not like Charlie. Without help, he'd probably drive around 'til mornin' and end up in Tennessee or some bullshit like that.

"Sí, sí, ahora recuerdo..." said Charlie, making a right. "Man, I can't wait until Graham and Kenny get their licenses so I don't have drop'em off all the time. I swear to God, I think Graham's sheer body weight is messin' up my back-left tire. Or the fuckin', axis and balance of the car and shit."

"A boy as big as Graham-cracker," said Bill, "probably brings down your gas mileage, too."

The full moon dominated the night sky. Something felt *off*—a strange, anti-climactic lull hung over everything.

Bill stroked his beard.

Feels like I'm missin' somethin'...

If Kenny and Graham didn't have morning shifts the next day, he would've insisted they crash at the *Hacienda* with him and Charlie.

Just in case.

"Anyway, *de-todos*-fuckin'-*modos,"* said Charlie, "I'm even gonna call people I know up in Hazard and one dude in Zion. Ain't talked to'em in a while, but I'm sure they'd just *love* to hear how Tommy Glick and his Smoketown Pussyboys challenged *us* to a fight—"

"—and didn't even show up," said Bill.

"Didn't even fuckin' show up!" said Charlie. "Even though they out-fuckin-numbered us—"

"—eight to four," said Bill.

"Eight to fuckin' four!" said Charlie. "And they *still* pussied out!"

As they drove down a road flanked by dark forest, Bill peered out the window at the treeline. Part of him felt relieved the fight never happened—his dreams had never even hinted at it. An epic-fuckin' brawl between his newly-formed Posse and the Smoketown Bullshit Boys should've shown up, at least in fragments. Shards of images from a shattered mirror—like most things he dreamt.

Maybe that's why I didn't dream about it...

It was never gonna happen.

"Still wonder *why* they pussied out, though," said Bill. "Like, what made'em fuckin', decide that..."

"It is kinda weird..." said Charlie.

"Probably smoked too much gorilla grass," said Bill. "That's why I don't like smokin' weed, man. Makes you dumb and lazy as shit."

"*Sí, sí,*" said Charlie. "But, ya know, as much as I hate to admit it, I bet the Graham-cracker-factor might be what scared'em off."

"You think?" asked Bill.

"I sure fuckin' do," said Charlie. "Glick changed his tune once he saw him with us. *'Hey Grahaaam, we ain't got no problem with you, maaaan.... we're so cool with you, maaaan...'*"

Bill laughed. "He did 'bout shit his pants when Graham walked up behind us."

"They *allll* fuckin' did," said Charlie. "They all shat their pants so hard and fast they didn't even feel it, *ese.*"

Bill laughed again.

"And then," said Charlie, "what was that bullshit Glick said? Somethin' like, *'Hey Grahaaam, I was meanin' to, fuckin' invite you, maaan, to our next lame-ass, gay-ass Smokehouse Party, maaaan...'*"

"Now see," said Bill, laughing, "that is one good thing they got goin'.

If they're holdin' big-ass parties on the regular, we need to have our own big-ass parties, too. Like I been sayin'—"

"I know, I know..." said Charlie. "I'm just worried people'll get *La Hacienda* all dirty and shit..."

He turned to pull in his driveway.

"I mean, what if people spilled on the carpet?"

"If you're really worried about that," said Bill, "we could make a rule, where people can only drink clear—"

Charlie halted the car.

"Holy shit..." said Bill.

They sat in stunned silence.

Charlie's lower lip trembled.

1970s

CHAPTER XXXVII

THE SPARK

"I'm just askin' one fuckin' thing of y'all:

Keep shit clean."

"I CAN TAKE a dump on command," said Mouse, unzipping his pants. "It's like my superpower."

The night's darkness made it hard to see how badly the Smoketown Boys had egged Charlie's house so far, but it didn't matter. Eggs weren't enough. Mouse's little present on his doorstep would be the extra step that pushed Bill and his Posse to where they needed 'em to be.

Jack turned away from Mouse. "That's a pretty gross superpower."

"Well," said Mouse, "it's pretty useful now, ain't it..."

Mouse squatted over the welcome mat. The laughter and chuckles of the Boys surrounded the house as they rotated their assault, making sure to egg it equally on all sides.

"Hey," said Mouse. "Did y'all know that poopin' like this, when you're squattin', is actually better for—"

"Wait!" said David. *"Don't poop yet!"*

Mouse got a look on his face that said, *"Did the Asian kid just tell me not to poop yet?"*

"What's up, David?" asked Jack.

"Mouse." David shielded his eyes. "Don't poop there yet."

"Why the fuck not?" asked Mouse. He'd felt the nudging of a turtle head already, but retracted it and stood up. Asian David rarely spoke, but when he did, he usually said something at least half-way intelligent.

"Wouldn't poopin' inside be better?" asked David. "Like on his carpet and stuff?"

"Sure," said Mouse. "But his doors are locked and—"

CRASH!

The living room window shattered.

"Holy shit..." said Mouse

"David," said Jack. "What the hell are you doin', man?"

David picked up another brick from the shrubbery bed.

"Showin' initiative."

***

"The fuck was that?" Tommy rushed into the front yard with the rest of the Boys.

Jack stood open-mouthed, eyes fixed on a brick-wielding David.

Mouse pulled his pants up. "Asian David made an entrance for us."

"David," said Jack. "What are you doin', man? You crazy?"

David stared at Tommy with sheer determination—the first time Tommy had seen that look on him.

It suited him well.

"Wouldn't it be better," asked David, "if Mouse pooped inside, on his carpet?"

"Maybe," said Jack, "but you don't break his windows, man!"

Tommy locked eyes with David, whose thick glasses intensified his stare.

Good, David...

Good...

This is what I wanna see.

"This is good," said Tommy. "This is takin' initiative. Nice work, David."

David's eyes widened behind his glasses. He hurled his brick at another window, shattering it. The sound of glass breaking into a thousand pieces—

("i hope that bitch brushed her teeth!")

—made Tommy smile.

Hope you enjoy livin' in a windowless fuckin' house, Young...

He turned to the other Possibles.

"See, that's what I'm talkin' about," said Tommy. "David just showed *initiative*, like Kevin did. Now let's knock all his other windows out, too. And clear the glass off the edges of the back one, so we can go inside."

Larry, Mouse, and the Possibles began collecting bricks from the shrubbery beds around Charlie's house.

Jack pulled Tommy aside. "You sure about this, man?"

"What do ya mean?" asked Tommy.

"I mean," said Jack, *"twenty* cartons of eggs. Ain't that enough?"

("i fucked your girlfriend after prom")

"Nope..." said Tommy.

("she got better and better each time we fucked")

"...just throwin' eggs is middle school shit..."

("and I didn't tell her to swallow, either")

("she just did")

"...it ain't enough..."

("i hope that bitch brushed her teeth!")

"...not even close."
(*"i hope that bitch br—"*)

"We gotta do more."

***

"I'll go in first," said Tommy. "Everybody keep an eye out. If the cops come, stick to the plan."

The plan dictated they'd scatter from the cops in different directions—that way, in even a worst-case scenario, the cops would only catch one or two of 'em, max.

Tommy pulled himself over the back window into Charlie's dad's bedroom. Broken glass crunched beneath his shoes with each step. Going in first felt empowering, like a conqueror's first steps into an enemy castle. He slinked through the dark rooms, savoring the thrill of trespassing. It'd been a long time since he'd visited Young's house, but not much had changed. Still immaculate. Still held an undertone of allure, like a secret hideout. He flipped on the Christmas lights—*nice.* Added ambiance. Might wanna buy some for the Smokehouse, too. The little coke parties Young and Bill held here probably did lead to some fun nights.

(*is this where bill fucked her, tommy?*)

He shook his head.

No.

Bill was just talkin' shit.

(*you sure about that, tommy?*)

(*maybe he fucked her here...*)

(*right on this bed...*)

The bed did indeed appear made for fucking: a silky crimson comforter enveloped it, with furry tiger-print pillows on top.

(*"i hope that bitch brushed her teeth!"*)

Tommy scowled.

I could burn this place down, Young...

Ruin your fuckin' life...

And then you and Bill wouldn't even have a little "Hacienda."

Tommy had almost decided to fuck up Bill's house instead, but lucky for Bill, he wasn't stupid enough to mess with the house of the sheriff of Crow County.

"Tommy," said Larry from outside. "They could come back, dude. We better hurry up."

Tommy returned to the window. "Everybody come in one-by-one. Be careful, there's glass."

"And bring the rest of the eggs."

***

"That'd be a good spot." Mouse pointed to the center of the living room. "That way, when they open the door, they'll smell it right away, and when they turn on the light, they'll fuckin' see it. *Double* the fuckin' impact."

Tommy nodded in approval.

That kind of *double-fuckin'-impact* would make Young flip his shit. Nobody liked walking into their house to find a huge pile of poop on the carpet, but Young got his panties in a wad over even a little ash on a table. He'd go *nuclear*, demanding immediate retaliation. Then Cunningham and his dumbass Posse would charge straight to the Smokehouse. *And then...*

Kevin returned to the living room with the other Possibles. "We're finished," he said. "Left the egg cartons in the bedroom, figured no reason to take'em back with us. And we found a notebook and pen, so maybe you could write a message or somethin'."

"Nice," said Tommy. Kevin already spoke with more authority now—less like "Rich Boy Kevin" and more like "Leader of the Possibles Kevin."

"Hadn't thought of writin' a message..." said Tommy. "But that'd be a nice touch..."

"And Wiley's got an idea," said Kevin.

"What's up, Wiley?" asked Tommy.

"What if we like, uhh..." said Wiley. "...stole all his shit? And fucked up the shit, ya know, we couldn't steal."

Mouse's face lit up. "Let's steal his coke!"

Larry's long face twisted with excitement. "We *need* to find their fuckin' coke, y'all! We can cut it with baby laxative and sell that shit!"

"And let's bust his TV!" said Mouse. "No, steal it! Then we can have *two* TVs at the Smokehouse!"

Everyone erupted in chatter about what they could steal or destroy and how cool it'd be to have two TVs at the Smokehouse—everyone except for Jack. He pulled Tommy aside.

"This is too much, man. We gotta stop now."

"As long as we don't take too long," said Tommy, "I think it's okay."

"Dude," said Jack. "It's one thing to egg their house and poop inside it, but to break all his windows *and* steal his shit? *And* destroy what we can't steal? That's too much, man. Too much for just talkin' shit in the DQ p—"

"*It wasn't just talkin' shit!*" said Tommy. "I told you on the way over here th—"

"Okay, I gotcha," said Jack. "And I see the big picture. Like you said in the car, we can't let even *one* squad disrespect us. I get it. And the shit that Cunningham said about Samantha, that's mad disrespect, man. But stealin' all of Young's shit, *and* their squad's cocaine, too? Feels like an old-fashioned ass-whoopin' is all they need."

"Oh," said Tommy, "they're gonna get that, too. But—"

"Okay," said Jack, "and what if Bill goes cryin' to his sheriff daddy about this? And what if they *are* gettin' their coke from his dad? What you think'll happen then?"

Tommy began to speak, but halted.

(don't listen to him, tommy...)

(he doesn't understand...)

He sighed and rubbed his temples.

("you're the only one i'll let do this, tommy...")

("only you...")

He covered his eyes, clenching them shut.

("i love you, tomm—")

("i hope that bitch brushed her teeth!")

("i hope that bitch br—")

"*Fuck!*" Tommy slammed his fist on the living room table. Only Jack noticed—everyone else rummaged through drawers and closets, chattering in excitement while searching for Charlie's cocaine, as if hunting for a mythical treasure. Mouse lugged Charlie's TV to the bedroom window.

"Listen, dude," said Jack. "Isn't beatin' the living shit out of Cunningham and his Posse all that's important?"

Tommy glanced around, lost in a haze, seeing nothing but Bill and his Posse, leering and laughing like hyenas.

("did you kiss her after that, tommy?")

("you didn't kiss her after that, did you?")

("i hope that bitch br—")

"They all gotta pay..." said Tommy. "They all gotta f—"

"I understand that," said Jack. "But goin' overboard, like stealin' his shit, could pull us into some huge *bullshit* that drags over the entire summer. Destroy our sales. And who knows, Bill's dad just might make it his mission to arrest us and take all our Monkey. And he fuckin' could, too. Super fuckin' easily."

Tommy turned his gaze toward Jack, noting the sincerity and intelligence in his eyes, remembering when he drew line graphs for everyone.

("check out these line graphs I drew, y'all...")

("these show how we can straight-up maximize our profit by...")

A calm washed over Tommy.

This felt like another line graph moment.

"Put the TV back!" said Tommy.

"What?" asked Mouse.

"Everybody put everything back!" said Tommy. "We're not stealin' his shit!"

"But the coke!" said Larry. "Fuckin' *cocaine,* man! That's easy money for us, and—"

"No," said Tommy. "We're leavin'. No more."

Disbelief etched across everyone's faces, especially Larry's; his long face looked like it might drop to the ground. Tommy felt shitty, like he'd invited them to a party only to cancel it just as the fun began.

"We don't wanna do *too* much," said Tommy. "Not so much that Billy-boy goes cryin' to his sheriff daddy. Especially if we fuck with their coke and it turns out his dad *is* their supplier."

Jack nodded, looking satisfied.

"Tommy's a hundred percent right, guys," said Jack. "We've done more than enough. Now it's time to let *them* come to *us* so we can beat their asses to the ground."

Larry shook his head, but he and the Possibles began putting everything back, slowly, like scolded kids returning toys to the shelf. Only Mouse stood still, holding the TV, glaring at Tommy in disbelief.

"Mouse," said Tommy. He walked over to help him carry back the TV.

"Sorry about bein' a bummer, man. But you understand why we gotta stop, right?"

"No..." said Mouse, almost pouting. "...not really..."

They both carried the TV back to the living room.

"Can you still lay down your present?" asked Tommy. "A big fat one, right here in the middle of the living room."

"I guess..." said Mouse. "...got a turtle head pokin' out, anyways..."

***

As they returned to their vehicles parked a few streets over, Tommy felt thankful for Jack's wisdom. A leader should know when to be ruthless, and when to show restraint. He could be ruthless later—later tonight, when he'd beat the fuck outta Bill Cunningham's fucking face and smash it into a bloody, sunglasses-wearing pulp.

But now marked the time for restraint.

And not just because of Jack's warning about Bill's dad.

Tommy wanted Bill and his bitch-ass Posse pissed enough to fight, pissed enough to slip up and come straight to the Smokehouse where him and his Boys would be waitin' with a few surprises—but not so pissed they'd take it to another level.

Not so pissed they'd do something *crazy*.

1970s

CHAPTER XXXVIII

CHARLIE'S DEMAND

"Dales de su

propia

medicina."

"I'M SORRY THIS happened, Charlie," said Bill. He pondered the best way to remove the gigantic pile of poop on the carpet. A solitary fly landed on top.

Now, how did that fly know how to get in here so fast...

"I'm gonna clean all this up for ya," said Bill. "The *Hacienda's* gonna be just fine, *amigo...*"

Charlie sat on the porch, head buried in his hands.

Shit...

Not fuckin' good...

At least he'd stopped hyperventilatin'. Bill had never seen anyone have such a gut-level, *visceral* fuckin' response before.

"*...my...my God...*"

"*...what...*"

"*...what happened...*"

They'd walked through the house like journalists touring a bombed-out city. Charlie clutched his shoulder the entire time, lookin' ready to have an aneurysm, stroke, or heart attack—all at once, if possible.

"*...this...*"

"*...this...can't be real...*"

As they inspected the damage, Bill kept having to seat Charlie, hand him a glass of water, and tell him to "just breathe."

"*...breathe, Charlie, just breathe...*"

"*...deep breaths, now...*"

Several times Bill even weighed the idea of calling the ambulance.

"*...Bill...*"

"*...tell me this ain't real...*"

"*...tell me this is a nightmare,* amigo...*"

The massive pile of poop had hit Charlie the hardest. He'd glanced at it, then away. Over and fuckin' over. Then he started hyperventilatin', stammerin' nonsense in *inglés* and *español,* and cried. Cried like a kid who'd found his dead dog in the street. *"I don't feel good, man, I don't feel good..."* Bill finally walked him to the porch for fresh air. *"Don't worry, Charlie...we'll get our revenge on'em..."*

"We'll fuck up their precious Smokehouse real fuckin' good."

Bill first focused on cleaning up the heap of poop in the middle of the living room carpet, carefully scooping it with a plate and spoon. After placing the spoon and poop-covered plate into a Walmart bag, he tied it up good and tight.

Whoever pooped had clearly eaten corn.

The little note left on top was not cute.

Next, he poured soap on the carpet, scrubbed it hard with a rag, sprayed it with every cleaning solution he could find, and scrubbed it again with another rag.

Nothing removed the stain, though.

Not entirely.

Thankfully, Charlie's begonias and shrubs around the house had been spared. Just lots of glass in'em. Bill had almost said, *"At least your begonias are okay,"* but he imagined Charlie's likely reply: *"Oh, well goddamn Bill, I'm so glad my motherfuckin' begonias are okay! I guess shit ain't so bad after all!"*

The whole time Bill cleaned, he reassured Charlie in a loud but calm voice that he'd make everything good and clean again, and that everything would be alright. He even promised they'd get revenge by having Graham poop all over *their* precious Smokehouse—and cover it with *rotten* eggs, not fresh ones.

"And I'm gonna call somebody about the windows," said Bill. "First thing tomorrow..."

Didn't know who to call, though.

Had never heard of "window repair-men" before, nor was he sure such a profession existed.

"Dunno who I'll call," said Bill, "but I'll start with the *W's* in the phone book. For windows and shit. I'm sure we'll find somebody..."

Silence.

"And I'll pay for *all* of it," said Bill, wondering just how much window repairs cost. "I'll do more chores for old people and start applyin' for jobs around town. Maybe at the deli over at Piggly Wiggly."

More silence.

"I'll pay for it *all*, Charlie," said Bill. "This is my fault..."

Still fuckin' silent.

Charlie had never remained silent, ever, for any extended period of time in their friendship.

Not a good fuckin' sign.

***

Bill called out from inside the house. "Gotta wash your underwear, man! And your socks! They crushed up eggs in your dresser!"

He opened cabinets near the washer, searching for detergent and shaking his head.

Fuckin' weedboys...

"Where's your detergent, Charlie?"

Silence.

"Charlie?"

God, I hope he didn't have a stroke or nothin'...

Bill stepped onto the front porch to find Charlie gazing at the moon, smoking a cigarette.

"Hey buddy," said Bill. "If you want fresh underwear and socks tomorrow, ya gotta let me know where that detergent is."

Charlie's cigarette trembled as he took a slow pull, his eyes reflecting the moon's glow.

"I know you're upset, *amigo,*" said Bill. "But ya gotta talk to me."

He studied Charlie's moonlit face. It seemed to hold both sorrow and rage now, in equal measure.

"Charlie?"

But something *else* lurked within his expression.

Something Bill hadn't seen before.

"Hey *amigo,*" said Bill. "I know you're real upset and all, but you gotta—"

"What did the note say?" Charlie's voice, though soft, carried a hint of iron.

"The note?" asked Bill. "Uhh, nothin' man, just some bullshit, don't worry—"

"What did it say, Bill?"

Bill sighed. The note read: *"BILL AND CHARLIE'S FAGGOT ASS POSSE SUCKS DICK,"* something Charlie didn't need to know.

But he told him anyway.

Charlie nodded, staring at the moon as if it spoke to him. A look of pity crossed his face.

"Bill?"

"Yeah?"

"We gotta...we gotta..."

Charlie's voice cracked. He swallowed, then took another slow pull from his cigarette.

"We gotta *what,* Charlie?" asked Bill.

"We gotta go..."

"What do ya mean?" asked Bill. "We gotta go wh—"

"We gotta go Blackbeard on them bitches."

I understand why Charlie wants to get brutal with them weedboys...
But I don't like his idea...

That's too fucked up.

Blackbeard: The Man Who Scourged the Seas

By: Roberta Stevenson

CHAPTER 12

Blackbeard's Brutality

(pg. 116) Why is Blackbeard so famous, despite capturing fewer ships than other pirates?

To answer this question, we first must accept that success alone doesn't guarantee fame or legendary status. It's also about *how* you achieve success—your personal branding.

Blackbeard had a keen sense of personal branding. His memorable nickname, along with the smoke rising from his enormous beard, set him apart. He could have looked like any other pirate, but then you wouldn't be reading about him today.

But were those the *only* secrets to his success?

Just a nickname? And a smoking beard?

Nope!

Blackbeard's success required one more special ingredient:

brutality.

→ ***Vocabulary Question:*** *Do you know what "brutality" means?*
Brutality is when someone acts harshly or violently, causing pain or suffering to others. It involves extreme cruelty, often using physical force or harsh words to hurt someone. It can leave a lasting impact on those who experience it.

Let's look at a few times when Blackbeard wielded *brutality* against his enemies:

- In one famous incident, an enemy captain failed to follow orders, so Blackbeard sliced off his ears! He didn't stop there—next, he fried and salted them, then slowly fed them to his parrot. Salty sea dog, indeed!
- Once, Blackbeard asked a captured sailor, *"Need a hand?"* When the sailor said no, Blackbeard cut off his hand and tossed it into the ocean, laughing. *"Haha! Now you do!"*
- In another brutal act, Blackbeard ripped out a man's heart and forced him to eat it—*while he was still alive!* Not a tasty treat!

Those examples may shock you, but they're just the beginning. Blackbeard liked to *flay* those who resisted him, as well.

→ *Vocabulary Question: Do you know what "flay" means? To flay someone is to remove their skin, usually while they're still alive. Ouch! That sounds worse than scraping your knee!*

"*But why did Blackbeard do those things to people?*" you might be wondering.
"*Why didn't he just kill them?*"
"*Isn't killing people brutal enough?*"

Those are all great questions!

Turn the page to learn why killing people wasn't enough!

Discussion Exercises—Talk With Your Friends!

1. Have you ever wanted to get revenge on someone? Did you? Why or why not?

2. Has anyone ever gotten revenge on you? If so, how did it make you feel?

3. Revenge can fuel an endless cycle of conflict. How can you exact revenge in a way that prevents this?

1970s

CHAPTER XXXIX

MIRACLE

POWER.

PURE POWER.

THE MIRACLE GIVES ME POWER.

JACK STARED AT the red liquid-filled water gun in his hand. It felt good and heavy, like a real gun.

"This here water gun," said Jack, "is filled with the hottest Kentucky Blood sauce money can buy. The *extra*-hot kind. Y'all tried it before?

The Possibles sat on the Smokehouse living room floor before the Boys, eyes wide and attention rapt.

"I tried it once," said Wiley. "It's real good, but...I shat for hours..."

Jack gazed at the water gun. "So you know the power, then..." He looked up. "The power of this stuff. I mean, I love Kentucky Blood sauce, but this kind is fuckin' hot, y'all. *Like melt-your-dicks-off hot.* Can't imagine what it'd feel like in your eyes..."

He aimed the gun at the Possibles, sweeping it slowly across their faces. They all squirmed—

—except David.

"David," said Jack. He pointed the water gun at David's face. "You ain't afraid? Afraid of *the power* of this stuff?"

"Not really," said David. "My glasses would probably block it from gettin' in my eyes."

"Hmm..." said Jack. "Nice point. Good thing Graham don't wear glasses."

He pulled the gun back, pointing it upward.

"So after I squirt Graham's eyes, y'all go for his legs."

"Go *straight* for his fucking legs," said Tommy.

"Don't hesitate!" said Mouse.

"Surround him first," said Larry. "Then aim for his kneecaps. These'll fuck him up real good."

He pointed at the four jet-black crowbars before them.

"Don't waste time goin' for his arms," said Jack. "Or his body. You go for his arms, he'll just grab your crowbar like he grabbed Kevin's throat. And if you go for his body, the crowbars won't do shit."

"Probably just bounce off him," said Larry.

Tommy nodded. Even a solid swing with a crowbar wouldn't even dent Graham's massive torso.

"That's the plan, guys," said Tommy. "Jack'll lead y'all with the crowbars to fuck up Graham. Once he squirts him in the eyes, go straight for his legs—*don't fucking hesitate.* Me, Larry and Mouse'll handle Bill, Young, and

Skinny. We'll split into two groups, hide in the woods, and ambush'em when they get outta their cars."

The ambush excited Tommy the most—the *Napoleon-like* part of their plan. Mouse had pointed out that attacking Graham inside the Smokehouse gave him the advantage, making it hard to surround him—and surrounding Graham was *key*. Then Larry's long face had lit up. *"We should fuckin' ambush their asses! As soon as they get outta their cars!"*

They all agreed: an epic ambush was just what the doctor ordered.

"Any questions?" asked Tommy.

David raised his hand. "Why don't y'all use crowbars, too?"

"That's a good question, Asian David," said Mouse. "And honestly, I ain't above beatin' ass with crowbars, but—"

"It's about *honor*," said Tommy. "Those guys are our age, so we're gonna beat their asses the old-school way."

"Unless," said Larry, "Bill and his guys show up with, like, baseball bats or somethin'. Then we'll fuckin' arm up, right, Tommy?"

An image flashed in Tommy's mind—Bill and his Posse marching toward him in cowboy hats and sunglasses, wielding—

Tommy squeezed his eyes shut.

"We got bats, too," he said. "And won't hesitate to use'em if Bill's bitch-ass Posse wanna play that way. But I doubt they'd—"

The image, cold and clear, flashed again.

Baseball bats—aluminum ones. Sunlight glinted off the metal.

("glick...")

"Tommy," said Larry. "You okay, man?"

("desayunaste?")

"Earth to Tommy?" asked Mouse.

("ya desayunaste?")

"...yeah..." said Tommy. The living room sharpened back into focus. "...but just in case, we'll..."

*("ya desa-*fuckin'*-yunaste, glick?")*

"...we'll get our bats ready, too..."

Tommy shook his head.

The fuck was that?

Gotta stay focused...

For a moment, he saw his dead brother Mikey and that *"temple"* he'd dreamt of, but only for a moment. He pushed the strange thoughts away.

"...but we're only gonna use 'em if they do," he said. "Smoketown Boys fight with honor."

Jack nodded. "With y'all, it's different. Y'all are younger than Graham and like a tenth his size. So it's okay to use crowbars, and that I'm gonna blind his ass with the water gun. Rules of honor don't apply when you're up against Graham-fuckin'-Riley."

The Possibles nodded.

"Any more questions?" asked Larry.

Grant raised his hand. "But won't we, like...*really* hurt him? If we hit his kneecaps with these?"

The Boys sighed.

"That's the fuckin' point, dumbass!" said Mouse.

Larry shook his head. "What the fuck, dude..."

Tommy narrowed his eyes.

Good Guy Grant...

Afraid to hurt people...

Minus one point for you.

"If you're afraid to hurt people, Good Guy Grant," said Tommy, "then you shouldn't be runnin' with the Boys. We only fight people who fuck with us, but when we do, *we don't hesitate.*"

"Nah, I'm-I'm *cool* with that, Tommy!" said Grant. "I'm so down with that!"

"Better be," said Larry.

"Better fuckin' be," said Mouse. "'Cause you're startin' to sound like a—"

"—a pussy," said Tommy. "The opposite of what Kevin showed us in the DQ parkin' lot."

Kevin's eyes ignited with zeal.

"Boy Scout meetin's are on Tuesdays!" said Larry.

Everyone laughed.

"I'm just tryin' to ask!" said Grant.

"Ask what?" asked Larry.

"Can't we, like..." He lowered his voice. "...go to jail and stuff?"

"Go to jail?" asked Larry.

"Ya know..." said Grant. "...if we like...*really* hurt Graham?"

"Helllll nooo," said Larry. "We can't go to no jail!"

"First off," said Jack, "we'd only get in trouble if they file a police report, which I highly doubt they'd do. That'd be the pussiest move in the universe."

"And see," said Tommy, "that's the beauty of them comin' to our turf. They're trespassing, so it's self-defense. Ain't that right, Jack?"

Jack nodded. "Damn right. Laws on our side."

"But Bill's dad is the sheriff," said Grant.

"So what?" asked Larry. "Law's the law. People have shot motherfuckers for trespassin' before and didn't get in no trouble."

"Yep," said Jack. "Seen it on the news. Technically, we're within our right to shoot 'em, even. So bustin' Graham's kneecaps ain't shit compared to that."

"And I highly doubt," said Mouse, "that Graham-fuckin'-Riley is gonna squeal to the cops over a busted kneecap. He'll just say he fell or some shit."

The Possibles fell silent, looking uneasy.

Tommy furrowed his brow.

It wasn't just the *legal* aspect that bothered them, was it?

It was the *moral* aspect, too.

The Possibles needed more convincing.

They needed to get *riled up*.

"Guys," said Tommy, "if y'all *really* wanna be one of the Boys, y'all gotta think long term, about our squad. And a squad's only as strong as its rep. Y'all get that, right?"

The Possibles mumbled in agreement, their nods uncertain.

"And just talkin' shit," said Tommy, "recruitin' more guys and havin' numbers ain't gonna protect our rep. There's squads out there with two, three times our numbers. Hazard's got that one squad, what do they call 'em?"

"Hazard Mafia," said Larry. "They roll like twenty fuckin' deep sometimes."

"And the Zion soccer team," said Jack. "They roll hard and deep, too."

"Yep," said Mouse. "And try to push their own brand of weed."

Tommy had sampled the Zion soccer team's weed before; not half-bad. If they ever started pushin' hard in Crow, they'd need to be dealt with— especially if they claimed their shit was more "pure" since they didn't cut it with tobacco.

"And that Hazard squad," said Tommy, "that Hazard Mafia or whatever the fuck they're called, they're huge. They don't really start shit in Crow now, but—"

"They do in Zion," said Larry.

Tommy nodded. "And I'm all for Hazard rednecks beatin' the fuck outta Zion preppies, but eventually they're gonna rep more in Crow. Hangin' out in *our* parkin' lots and shit. Or might show up at a Smokehouse Party, ready to throw down."

He paced before the Possibles, meeting each of their eyes.

"And what's the only thing that'll stop'em from fuckin' with us?"

"Our rep," said Kevin.

"That's right," said Tommy. "Our rep."

Kevin gets it...

But do the rest of'em?

"And if we take down Graham-fuckin'-Riley," said Tommy, "and Bill's little coke-dealin' Posse, that'll be *huge*."

Mouse's eyes blazed. "Fuckin' legendary..."

Larry asked, "Y'all think Graham's gonna mess with underclassmen after tonight? After y'all fuck him up with these crowbars? He'll be *afraid* of y'all."

"Y'all'll be heroes," said Jack.

Mouse nodded. "Fuckin'. Heroes."

"My dudes," said Tommy. "Nobody likes the shit that Graham does. Smoketown Boys never do that. Do we, boys?"

His Boys answered with variations of *"Hellll no,"* and *"We're above that shit."*

"We ain't the Smoketown Bullies," said Tommy. "We'll fuckin' fight, but we got better shit to do than take underclassmen's lunch money."

Kevin raised his hand.

"Kevin," said Tommy.

Kevin rose, looking at the other Possibles.

"Graham Riley fucking deserves it. He took my lunch money almost every day last year. Had to bring double and tell my parents I was eatin' two lunches. He choke-slammed me on the wall in front of hot girls. He's a bad guy. *I hate him.* He deserves to be hurt."

He picked up a crowbar, staring at it.

"Graham has to pay..."

Tommy allowed a silence, then spoke. "Thanks for sharin', Kevin. Anybody else?"

Kevin sat down, still gripping his crowbar.

David raised his hand.

"Asian David," said Tommy.

David stood, pushing his glasses up his nose. "Graham broke my glasses once. My mom had to sell her wedding ring to buy new ones."

What?

Tommy's mouth dropped.

He'd heard David's parents were old and poor, but *that* fucking poor? Probably livin' off Social Security.

No wonder he wanted to sell Monkey and roll with the Boys.

"I'm sorry that happened, man," said Tommy. "You can borrow from me if your glasses break again. Just pay me back by sellin' Monkey or somethin'. Don't worry about it."

David's eyes widened behind his glasses. "Th-thanks, Tommy..."

"*Or*," said Mouse, "you can borrow money from Rich Boy Kevin. Since his dad's loaded."

Kevin looked up from his crowbar. His face darkened, but he shrugged.

Tommy glared at Mouse.

He still has it out for Kevin...

Need to talk to him about that...

"There ya go," said Tommy. "Stealin' y'all's lunch money...choke-slammin' y'all in front of hot girls...breakin' David's glasses and makin' his mom sell her wedding ring to buy him new ones..."

He paused, allowing the weight of that particular grievance to linger.

"You guys know why we gotta go *hard* on these bitches," said Tommy. "But especially Graham. No fuckin' mercy."

He scanned the Possible's faces:

Kevin looked ready to shatter kneecaps.

Atta boy...

Asian David looked somber, like he finally understood.

Wilin' Wiley stroked his chin, likely still weighing things.

And Good Guy Grant looked constipated.

The weak link.

And if Grant pussed out, so might Wiley. Only Kevin, and maybe Asian David, would stand their ground. But even *with* crowbars, no way two Possibles could take on Graham-fuckin'-Riley—even *if* Jack blinded him with the Kentucky Blood-filled water gun, which was still a big fuckin' *if*. The gun didn't have much range, and he'd have to get close to hit his eyes...

He looked at Larry, who met his gaze.

You see it too, don't ya, Larry?

They still ain't ready...

Not riled up enough.

Larry and him had a bond like that: often knowing the other's thoughts before saying a word.

"Maybe we should give 'em *the stuff*," said Larry.

Tommy nodded.

Good idea.

"What 'stuff'?" asked Mouse.

Larry's long face lit up.

"The stuff we bought in Alabama."

***

"Is it...cocaine?" asked David.

The glass vial felt solid and heavy as he rolled it between his fingers. Inside, the white powder sparkled in the moonlight, revealing hints of pale blue. He squeezed the vial, sensing an almost tangible power; the chirping of nearby crickets seemed to swell in response.

"It's, uhh..." said Larry. "...maybe got *some* coke in it..."

"It's like Heinz 57," said Tommy. "Got a little of everything."

Wiley removed the lid from his vial, peering inside. "Can we snort it now?"

"*No*," said Tommy. "It's powerful shit. *Do not* snort any 'til you see Graham."

"What's it...gonna *do?*" asked Grant.

Tommy and Larry looked at each other.

"It'll get ya goin'," said Larry, smiling.

Wiley's eyes filled with hunger.

"It *will* get you goin'," said Jack, eyeing Wiley. "So don't like, snort it all or somethin' crazy like that. One good hit should be enough."

"Where'd you get it?" asked Wiley. He gazed at the vial as if hypnotized.

"Bought it from a dude in Alabama," said Tommy. "We were lookin' for weed suppliers, but this one guy..."

"He was somethin' else," said Larry.

"Definitely somethin' else," said Tommy. "Didn't have no weed, but sold us this stuff real cheap. I did a bump once, to test it, and..."

Larry grinned. "You got fuckin' wild."

"Don't even remember half of it," said Tommy.

"Like a rabid fuckin' animal," said Jack.

"And I didn't feel no pain, either," said Tommy. "Started punchin' trees and walls and shit..."

He gazed down at his hands, squeezing them closed, then open.

Even now, they still kinda hurt.

But part of him *ached* for that feeling again.

Power.

Invincibility.

"What's it called?" asked Kevin.

"Miracle," said Tommy. "The dude called it Miracle."

Wiley stared at the vial in awe. "Miracle..."

"Do we *have* to snort this?" asked Grant.

"Quit bein' a pussy, Grant!" said Kevin. "If we're gonna take down Graham, we need this stuff!"

Tommy nodded.

Good, Kevin...

Now you're talkin' like a leader.

"Grant," said Tommy. "You don't have to do anything you don't wanna do, my man. But if we get fuckin' *stomped* by Graham, and you didn't snort that shit, then it's your fuckin' fault."

"Yep," said Larry. "Then you can fuck off and hang with your mom the rest of the summer. Go to Boy Scout meetin's and shit. Smoketown don't need no pussies."

"Or join the Girl Scouts," said Jack. "So you can sell cookies like a bitch."

Tommy and Larry cackled, throwing Jack high-fives.

"Why don't y'all snort it then?" asked Grant.

"'Cause we don't need to," said Tommy. "Y'all do, 'cause you're younger, smaller and afraid."

"And I can't snort it," said Jack. "'Cause of my heart condition."

Wiley eyed Grant's vial like he might snatch it. "I'll snort yours, if you don't want it."

"No," said Jack. "You don't need two vials. Don't even need a full one. This shit'll—"

Mouse yelled from across the lawn. *"Lights comin' down the street!"*

A nervous energy charged the air.

"Get ready!" said Tommy. "When I call the *rally up,* y'all fuckin' charge! Not a second before! Y'all got me?"

Jack and the Possibles nodded.

"We'll trap those motherfuckers between us," said Tommy, "and teach'em not to fuck with the Smoketown Boys!"

He glanced at Larry, a flicker of worry in his eyes.

They'd have *one* shot.

As he ran to his hiding spot, Tommy turned back. "David, take your glasses off, man!"

"Oh," said David. He placed them on a nearby bush.

"Get down!" said Jack, crouching in a James Bond-like pose, water gun aimed at head level. The Possibles knelt, gripping their crowbars and vials of Miracle. Wiley opened his vial and—

"Not yet!" said Jack. "Wait 'til we know it's them..."

Gritting his teeth, Wiley capped the vial, staring at the powder inside.

He really wanted to snort that shit.

1990s

CHAPTER XL

GOOD MORNING, DADDY

"I love you, Daddy…"

"I love you, too, girl…just stop bein' so wild, alright?"

"…no can do, Daddy…"

RHONDA MADE SURE to slip GB's tooth back in her pocket before knocking on Daddy's door. He wasn't too *keen* on stuff like that.

"Daddy?"

Sipping her coffee, she gave his door two gentle raps *("knock-knock!")*. Nothing.

Only the chatter of cartoons off in the living room.

She didn't stop by Daddy's room every morning; even someone as badass as her had occasional maybe not-so-good Temple Training days. Days when she didn't shoot well for whatever fuckin' reason and felt too ashamed to face him. Pretended she had the breakfast shift on those days. On *actual* breakfast shift days, he'd still be asleep when she finished, likely deep in The Ethereal, searchin' for the next instructions from God—

("we follow your dreams, daddy...")

("tell us what to do.")

—seekin' His guidance toward the next Clue to the Temple.

"Daddy, you awake?"

She knocked again *("knock-knock!")*, shuffling her feet. They did have an emergency knockin' code—four rapid knocks—to tell Daddy they'd met *trouble*. Trouble meant either the police had arrived, or an asshole had escaped and gone crazy, maybe with a knife to their throats. Either way, four knocks meant one thing: *"Daddy, get your gun."*

She'd lost track of Daddy's guns. He kept his revolver under his pillow, a sawed-off under his mattress, another sawed-off under the couch cushion, and likely several more pistols and shotguns *(maybe one in the bathroom?)* that she didn't know about. Didn't matter—they'd probably never need those secret guns, nor the secret knockin' code, despite Daddy's reminders.

"Don't y'all forget that emergency knockin' code!" he'd said. *"I swear to God, it's gonna save our asses one day..."*

His alarm clock *had* rung, though, so it should be okay to talk to him now, as stipulated in the Family Rules.

"Good morninnnnn', Daddyyyy...."

She considered opening the door but knocked again. Just in case. Didn't wanna catch Daddy naked again—an incident that had traumatized'em both for a fuckin' week.

"Daddy," she said, "are-you-alive-in-th—"

A muffled *"yeah"* came from the other side of the door, akin to yelling from a cave.

Slowly, Rhonda turned the doorknob.

"...Daddy?"

Amidst the soft shadows of his bedroom, Daddy lay entirely covered by his red-and-white Marlboro comforter, his long hair barely peeking from the top.

Why did he sleep like that?

Like a kid afraid of the dark.

Did he see scary shit at night?

Or in his dreams?

"Daddy...you awake?"

A hoarse voice answered: "Yeah..."

Should've brought him some coffee. That'd be nice, to put a cup of coffee on his nightstand when he woke up. Always forgot to do that. Oh well.

"You doin' alright, Daddy?"

Daddy flipped his covers off and stared at the ceiling.

"Yeah..."

He sat up, sighed, then muttered *"fuck"* under his breath.

Since childhood, Rhonda had often likened Daddy's morning rise to that of a grizzly bear emerging from hibernation. Hard to imagine they were even kin sometimes. Morning vigor must come from her momma's side.

Daddy scooted across the bed to his blinds and yanked'em open with a *"snippt!"* Sunlight flooded in, prompting him to shield his eyes. He strained to peer at the garage.

"D'you see GB this mornin?" he asked.

"Yep."

Rhonda glanced at the bloodstain on her jeans—now an orange splotch after her scrubbing attempt.

"He seem okay?" asked Daddy.

("I knew you had blue eyes!")

("I'm sorry I'm sorry I'm sorr—")

(I KNEW YOU HAD BLUE EYES)

She sipped her coffee.

"Seemed normal to me."

Daddy leaned closer to the window, eyes narrowed like he could see through the garage walls.

"What kinda dreams you see this time, Daddy?"

He shook his head, letting out a long, tired sigh.

She knew what that meant: not the kind he wanted to share.

Silence passed as Daddy scratched his head and looked around, occasionally burying his face in his hands, as if still processing something. Maybe an unresolved thought, or maybe still half-lost out there—in The Ethereal.

She asked, "Notice anything different about me today?"

Daddy glanced at her, then back at the garage.

"Change your hair?"

Rhonda frowned, giving him the look she always gave when he didn't notice obvious shit.

"Try again, Daddy..."

He started kicking his right leg out, part of his morning routine before stretching.

"Did you, uhh..." He glanced at her again.

"...change your makeup and shit?"

Her frown expanded.

Not a good mornin' for ya, is it, Daddy?

Here's a hint...

She tilted her face to the right, cupping her left ear.

"Huh?" He glanced up. "Oh..."

He turned his eyes back to the garage.

"You're wearin' those guitar earrings I bought ya...for your birthday..."

"That's right, Daddy."

And I love them.

Just like I love you.

A faint smile appeared on Daddy's face, as if he'd heard her thoughts.

"Glad you like'em..." he said. "You ever think of playin' guitar?"

He always asked that.

"You know," she said, "other people ask me that when I wear'em, too. Maybe I should..."

"Lotta guys like a girl who plays guitar," he said. "One of the reasons I fell for T and Z's mom..."

Rhonda clenched her teeth.

If I ever do start playin' guitar...

It won't be 'cause of that bitch.

"Was his poop okay?" asked Daddy.

"What?"

"Was GB's shit lookin' good?" he asked. "Or did it look...ya know..."

Daddy, a self-proclaimed *"stool-analyzer,"* often requested reports on the poop status of the assholes after they went potty in their little buckets. Something she and Taleiah found disgusting, but Zach found "kinda cool."

"You can tell a lot about someone by their shit," Daddy had said. *"In terms of their health and stuff. It's all ya really need to know."* Then he went on about the different types of poop (the color, shape, and texture) and whether it comes out in long turd shapes or in bits and pieces. But Taleiah, in a rare moment of open fuckin' defiance, said *"Daddy, please do not tell us about those disgustin' things,"* and Rhonda agreed they didn't need to hear about that from Daddy, nor from anyone else, for that fuckin' matter.

"I mean, I *think* it was okay..." said Rhonda. "...didn't study it like it was a book or nothin'..."

Daddy shook his head, still gazing at the garage. "His poop's been kinda strange lately..." He stroked his beard. "Somethin' might be wrong with him..."

"He was coughin' and sneezin' some," said Rhonda.

"Been doin' that for a while now..." said Daddy. "Might've caught a cold or somethin'. I'll get Zach to give him some orange juice. And a Flintstone vitamin, for his immunity and shit..."

"Might as well start givin'em *all* Flintstone vitamins, every day," said Rhonda. "Can't hurt nothin', and ain't that expensive."

And we don't want one of them fucker's croakin' on us...

Not before they tell us a Clue.

"That's a good idea..." said Daddy. "Oughta start doin' that..."

He chuckled.

"Ol' Charlie Young...he's the guy that got me started on vitamins and shit...did I ever tell ya about him?"

Only about a thousand times, Daddy...

"Wonder what happened to him...what ol' Young Charlie is up to these days..."

Shit.

Not that bullshit again.

Gotta change the subject...

"Did I ever tell ya about my Posse?" asked Daddy. "This *wild* group of boys I used to hang with back in the Tri. I tell ya what, we—"

"*Yep,*" said Rhonda, sharpening her tone. "*You told me, Daddy. Lotsa times.*"

Daddy nodded, a pang of disappointment on his face.

Rhonda sighed.

Sorry, Daddy...

Don't got time for that this mornin'.

"How's trainin' lil' T and Z goin'?" she asked. "For The Run?"

Daddy shot her a blank stare.

"For the *what?*"

"*The Run, Daddy,*" she said. "*The Run on The Temple.*"

Daddy's vacant gaze sent a shiver down her spine, reminding her of the haunting stares of the human vegetables she'd seen in nursing homes. After a few terrible moments, recognition *(thank God)* finally dawned on his face.

"Oh, *yeah...*" said Daddy. "The Run...The Run on The Temple..."

"That's right, Daddy..." She forced a smile—the same smile she gave clueless old folks.

"Sorry..." he said. "...was thinkin' about Young Charlie, and my Poss—"

"*How's trainin' T and Z goin', Daddy?*"

Daddy looked confused, then nodded, slowly gettin' with the program.

"It's goin' alright, goin' alright..." he said. "Zach's gettin' better at stride-shootin'...Taleiah's doin' her best..."

Her "best."

Rhonda almost scoffed.

Princess T needs to do better than her fuckin' "best..."

"How's it goin' with you, sweetie pie?" asked Daddy. "How'd it go at, ya know...*TPR* today?"

His eyes expanded when saying "*TPR,*" as if to emphasize its secretiveness.

"You mean TTR?" asked Rhonda.

"What?"

"You said it's called 'Temple Trainin' Range', Daddy," she said. "And that we should call it TTR."

Daddy ran his fingers through his long hair.

"Thought we called it *TPR*...short for 'Temple fuckin' Practice Range'..."

Rhonda tried to hide the worry on her face. Zach was right—Daddy's memory fuckin' *sucked* lately.

Had it gotten *any* better since The Accident?

Or only worse?

"Now, Daddy," she said. *"You're* the one who said we should call it 'Temple Trainin' Range.' *I'm* the one who came up with 'Temple Practice Range,' but then *you* said you didn't like 'TPR' 'cause it made you think of 'TP,' which made you think of toilet paper."

"Oh..." said Daddy. He stretched his other leg. "Sounds 'bout right, I guess..."

Rhonda sipped her coffee, letting the revelation sink in. Daddy could be sensitive about his memory; usually best to ask a series of questions that made him realize his mistake on his own.

"So," she said, "should we call it, 'TTR' or 'TPR?'"

"Well," said Daddy, "fuckin' *trainin'* sounds cooler than *practicin',* don't it? Like more hardcore and shit..."

Rhonda shrugged. "I guess."

Daddy's heavy gaze returned to the garage, like the world weighed on him.

"Lemme think about it..." He ran a hand over his face, looking worn. "Got a lotta shit to think about today..."

She nodded.

You need to think about what to do with GB...

He still ain't given us no Clue yet, and if you don't make him—

—then I will.

Daddy yawned and resumed stretching, scratching that weird mark on his arm. She'd always assumed it was a birthmark, but one day decided to ask. *"Can't remember..."* he'd said. *"Think an Asian boy bit me or somethin'..."*

A statement so ridiculous she decided it was, in fact, probably just a birthmark.

Daddy yawned again. "Still fuckin' sleepy..."

Rhonda shook her head, recalling all the shit she'd gotten done before her family even woke the fuck up: made coffee, sat on her porch and drank a cup *(real slow-like),* shat, showered, shaved her armpits, put her makeup on and got ready, fuckin' *eloquently* talked the bearded pussy-eater out of fallin' *too* madly in love with her but also *(eloquently)* kept him in the pipeline for future pussy-eatin'. Then she drove to Daddy's, did her Temple Trainin', ate a strawberry, enjoyed playtime with GB, came real hard, cleaned GB's mess off her titties, used the bathroom again, then fixed and ate breakfast while watchin' almost two full episodes of *X-Men* with Zach. Then had another cup of coffee.

And her day had just fuckin' started.

But no point in sayin' shit. Some people, like Daddy, just liked to stay up late and sleep in later.

Like sloths, in a way.

Nocturnal-ass sloths.

But that was okay.

As long as Daddy witnessed his dreams, their Quest for The Temple could continue.

"How was your shootin' this mornin'?" asked Daddy.

"Good, Daddy," she said. "Real good."

"That's my girl," he said. "Bullseye every time?"

"Yessir," she said. "Almost."

"Bulls-to-the-fuckin'-eye," he said. "That's my girl..."

Rhonda's face lit up with a smile.

"Even on the stride-shootin'?" asked Daddy. "And the drop-shootin'?"

Her smile dropped.

"No, not on that yet..."

Daddy grinned. "Not even once?"

Rhonda lifted her chin, as if her honor had been challenged.

"No, but I'm gettin' there."

"Mmm-hmm..." Daddy bent over for a stretch.

"Besides," she said, "you said with stride and drop-shootin' just hittin' the target is the most important th—"

"I know," said Daddy. "I know..."

He turned to look at her.

"But *I* used to hit bullseye drop-shootin' *and* stride-shootin'..."

He winked.

"Daddy, you only did that like three times that I've s—"

"That's three times more than you." He shot her his *"What ya gotta say to that?"* look.

Rhonda couldn't help but grin. Daddy liked to fuck with her like that. Keep her sharp. Competitive. Taleiah and Zach weren't even close to her level (and never would be), but if she always compared herself to them she'd never get off the plateau she was stuck on. Might even start shootin' shittier.

"You at least hit the target every time?" he asked.

Daddy, why you even gotta ask that...
My name ain't Zach or Taleiah.

"Hell yes, I did."

"That's my girl..." He eased himself to the floor for a butterfly stretch.

"Saw a cop this mornin'," said Rhonda.

"What?"

Fear washed over Daddy's face.

"On the way here," said Rhonda. "He was followin' me."

"Did he fuckin' pull ya over?"

"Nope, turned down another road. But I bet he ran my plate."

"And he *didn't* pull ya over?"

"Nope."

Daddy sighed, looking relieved.

"Surprised he didn't," he said. "They usually come up with some bullshit to pull over people who got records. Fuckin' discrimination is what it is."

"Think they know somethin', Daddy? About our Quest? About The Tem—"

He held out his hand, shaking his head. "If they did, they'd already be stormin' this place with SWAT teams and shit."

"What if we're bein' watched? Under surveillance or somethin'?"

Rhonda wasn't sure, but she reckoned cops would scope out their targets before a big operation.

"Nah," he said. "Dreams would tell me if they were doin' shit like that..."

He closed his eyes, mumbling something inaudible, like an incantation.

"At least...I *think* they fuckin' would..."

Goosebumps rose across Rhonda's arms. Sometimes Daddy's dreams didn't quite tell the whole story—occasionally he interpreted'em wrong, too. What he *did* see usually turned out to be true—it's what he *didn't* that caused problems.

After a moment of silence, he opened his eyes again.

"You was drivin' careful, right?"

"Always," she said. "Always stayin' below the speed limit, just like you told me, Daddy."

"Good girl..." He resumed stretching. "Well, if they pull ya over, just talk to'em real innocent-like, like I taught ya. Ain't nothin' ya can do..."

Rhonda thought of her Glock taped under the driver's seat.

Oh, there's somethin' I can fuckin' do...

"Maybe cops ain't bad over here," she said. "So far they ain't gave us no trouble."

"Yeah..."

He glanced back at the garage, a worried frown emerging.

"So far..."

Daddy likely thought the same she did: *Cops were the same everywhere.* But no use in worryin' now; just had to keep her Glock good, warm, and ready.

"Why you got blood on your jeans?" asked Daddy.

Shit.

He noticed.

She switched to her innocent voice. "I, uhh, meant to ask you about that, *Daddy...*"

Maybe he'd mistake it for her period.

"How can I get this out?" she asked. "I tried scrubbin' but—"

"What'd you use?"

"Water," said Rhonda. "And Dawn liquid dish—"

"Did you use cold water, or hot?"

Fuck.

"Hot," she said. "But I was supposed to use cold, wasn't I?"

"Yep," said Daddy. "Taught you that about fifteen times, now. *I* fuckin' remember that. Maybe *you're* the one who got memory problems, girl. Not me."

Fuck.

Didn't make no sense why cold water got bloodstains out easier than hot. She liked these jeans, too, and didn't have another clean pair ready.

"I'm gonna ask you one more time, Rhonda," said Daddy. "*Why* you got blood on them jeans?"

"I, uhh..."

"And don't tell me it's that time of the month, either," said Daddy. "You always say that shit when you got blood on ya."

Shit.

Why did Daddy's memory suddenly turn good whenever she needed it to stay bad?

"I had to, uhh..."

She shifted her feet, bringing the coffee mug to her lips.

"...get a little rough with GB..."

Daddy's eyes widened.

"And you made him *bleed?*"

"Maybe..." she said. "...just a little, from his mouth..."

And he lost a fuckin' tooth, too...

Best not to show Daddy the tooth, though. He'd probably call her "crazy" or "fucked up," like he did after the Eyeball Incident.

Daddy's tone sharpened. "Why'd you have to 'get rough' with him, *Rhonda?*"

Uh-oh.

Daddy sayin' her name like that meant one thing:

Trouble.

Trouble on the horizon.

But she'd prepared for this.

"He kicked his bucket over again, Daddy!" she said. "Made a *real* nasty mess on the floor..."

Daddy scowled.

Rhonda took a nervous sip of coffee, unsure if the scowl was meant for her, for GB kickin' his bucket, or maybe both.

"You clean his mess up?" he asked.

"Yep. Cleaned his bucket, too."

Daddy's face relaxed.

"Good girl..."

He gazed out the window again, then whirled around, glaring.

"How 'rough' d'you fuckin' get with him, *Rhonda?*"

"Just, uhh..." she said. "...hit him once or twice..."

"With what?"

"...the hammer..."

"Where?"

"...the mouth...."

"You didn't knock any of his teeth out, did ya?"

She bit the edge of her coffee mug.

"No, I don't...*think so*..."

"You better not have..." said Daddy. "You know how fuckin' hard it is to feed'em when they got a tooth knocked out. And they bleed a fuck-ton, too. He ain't still bleedin', is he?"

Rhonda glanced down the hallway and said, *"Idunno,"* really fast, like it was one word.

"Rhonda Jean Cunningham," said Daddy.

Oh shit.

Her full name.

Mega trouble.

"I asked you a question, now," he said. *"Is GB bleedin' a lot, or fuckin' not?"*

"I don't *think* so, Daddy, geez..." she said. "Listen, I cleaned out his bucket real good and finished my Temple Trainin' already, and now I gotta go work a double-shift at Dairy Queen."

She said the next part carefully: *"Daddy, I'll give ya your money at the end of the week, okay? After I get paid."*

Daddy's face melted into embarrassment.

Whenever he nagged her about some bullshit, Rhonda could always leverage the fact that she out-earned him and contributed more to the FTF *(Family Temple Fund)* than he did. In reality, most of her money didn't go to the Temple Fund, but to cover T and Z's basic livin' expenses, a fact Daddy hated. After all, no father worth his salt liked dependin' on his own daughter for financial aid.

"Well, I'm just askin'..." said Daddy. "Best not be bleedin' too much..."

She shot him her *"Whatever, Daddy"* look. "What time you go into the deli today?"

"No deli today," he said. "Goin' to Super Walmart."

His face turned grave.

"Family Mission."

Rhonda nodded, sipping her coffee.

Among the Family Missions they'd undertaken since moving to Raven, the Super Walmart one ranked the most critical. *They'd save so much goddamn money it wouldn't be funny.* Money for their food, clothes, guns, ammunition.

Money for The Quest.

Money for *everything.*

But she had her doubts about the chances of success—ones she'd keep to herself. Last time she offered advice, Daddy got real sensitive. *"I know how to talk to women, Rhonda,"* he'd said. *"Back in my Wild Bill days, just about every girl in the whole damn Tri was fuckin', madly in love with me!"*

Sure, Daddy.

That was then.

This is now.

And we ain't in the Tri no more.

"Well, good luck," she said. "I believe in you, Daddy."

Daddy nodded, rose, and pulled his right leg back for a quad stretch.

"And don't forget," she said, "you need to pick up some Tabasco while you're at Walmart today."

"Yeah, I'll get'em..."

"And you need other spicy shit too," she said. "Like chili powder, cayenne pepper, and—"

"I gotcha...I know what we need..."

Daddy switched to pulling his left leg back, leaning on the wall for support.

"Still got Mrs. Dash, though," he said.

Rhonda shook her head.

"*Fuck* that Mrs. Dash bullshit, Daddy! I'm talkin' about Tabasco and shit, *real* shit, not—"

Daddy held up his hand. "Okay, I heard ya. We'll pick some up today..."

He plopped back onto the bed, looking exhausted. Poor Daddy. Even stretchin' took a lot out of him. But if he stretched real good every mornin', he'd be a hell of a lot more limber the rest of the day. On good days, he could even walk like normal—for a little while, at least.

"Why'd you eat breakfast here?" he asked.

Rhonda shrugged. "Just wanted to catch up with the Z-man. And see you."

Daddy nodded in a way that showed he neither believed, nor disbelieved her statement. Just fuckin' nodded.

"That okay with *you,* Daddy?"

"'Course it's okay, sweetie pie..." he said. "You can eat breakfast here anytime..."

Rhonda slurped up her remaining coffee and placed the empty mug on his dresser.

Damn fuckin' straight, I can.

I contribute a third of my fuckin' paycheck to this family and to our Quest so I do believe I have the right to eat whatever the fuck I want here.

"How 'bout you?" he asked. "What you got planned today?"

"Just workin'," said Rhonda. "Then hittin' the bars with some friends. Tear shit up a little."

Daddy narrowed his eyes. "Don't get in no trouble or nothin'."

"I won't, Daddy..."

"Don't start no shit, Rhonda..."

"I won't..."

"Don't get in no fights, now..."

"I won't, Daddy..."

"Promise?" he asked. *"You promise you won't get in no fights tonight?"*

"I promise, Daddy." She crossed her fingers behind her back. "I promise I won't get in no fights tonight."

As long as no one starts shit with me...

"Gotta get goin', now..." She bent down to give him a hug, closing her eyes as they embraced.

"Have fun..." said Daddy, patting her back. "Be careful, now. And be safe."

"I will..." she said. "Love you, Daddy."

"Love you, too, girl."

"See ya!"

She bounded down the hall.

Daddy yelled from his room, *"And don't rip no girl's eyeball out, neither!"*

Rhonda shot Zach a grin as she passed, pulling her eyelid down.

"Eye can't hear you, Daddy!"

1990s

CHAPTER XLI

DADDY'S DREAMS

Bill's dreams tended to come in four types:

dreams that revealed the future,
dreams haunted by his past,
dreams that demanded action,
and fucked-up dreams that made no sense.

Sometimes they blurred together, and he
couldn't tell one from the other.

GB.

    Why are *you* here?

    Where's Charlie?

    I was talkin' to Charlie, now.

    Lemme talk to Charlie.

    Or, how about you tell us the fuckin' Clue, GB?

    Then we'll let ya go.

    I promise we'll let ya go, GB, we just want the—

    —no.

    Somethin' ain't right.

    Gotta get that Clue from ya soon, 'cause somethin' ain't right with y—

    (is he sick?)

    Maybe.

    Snot runnin' out his nose.

    Coughin', too, but ain't no big deal.

    (did somebody hurt him?)

    Nah, ain't nobody hurt him.

    Not too much.

    Not more than we got to, in order to—

    (what if he died?)

    (what if he died before we got a clue?)

    Nope, nope, ain't had any of them fuckers die on us yet.

    Not before they gave us a Clue.

    Keepin' my nose to the ground now.

    Don't do more violent shit than I got to.

    (none of that blackbeard-cowboy-bullshit no more)

    Just gotta finish The Quest.

    For my family.

    For Wayne.

    Sure would like to see him again, I—

    Charlie.

    Young Charlie.

    Quit lookin' at me like that, now.

    You ain't my friend no more.

    (i mean it, charlie)

    (you ain't my fuckin' friend no more)

    No, don't be pullin' that *mejores amigos* shit on me, now.

You were *always* a bad influence on me, Charlie.

My dad was right about you.

Nothin' but trouble.

You're the one who got me into drugs.

You're the one who got me into all that cowboy bullshit.

You're the one who—

Nope, nope, you can't see'em.

I don't want you near Rhonda.

I don't want you near Taleiah.

And you stay the hell away from Zach, *you stay the hell away from him,*

you—

Cornfields.

("charlie?")

("you out here?")

That fuckin' Cornfield Party.

("we gotta leave, we gotta leave before the cops—")

(tap-tap!)

(tap-tap!)

Peanut butter.

I used to love peanut butter, but you ruined it for me and now—

(tap-tap!)

(tap-tap!)

just the fuckin' smell, the *smell* of that shit ma—

("y'all got peanut butter?")

("oh, i think ya do...")

("everybody's got peanut b—")

No.

No.

(that wasn't my fault, charlie)

(them girls didn't give us no choi—)

I'm done talkin' to ya now, Charlie.

Gonna talk to someone else now, gonna t—

Wayne.

("daddy, what happened to uncle wayne?")

No.

No.

("why don't you ever talk about him?")

It wasn't my fault it wasn't my fault—
("did he see dreams too, daddy?")
it—
wasn't—
my—
("did he see the f—")
Taleiah.
Taleiah grippin' that arrowhead pendant of hers.
Always so distant.
Why can I see her, but not talk to her?
Sweetie, what are you goin' through?
I just want you to talk to me, like—
"Taleiah, don't grip that arrowhead too tight, now—"
Zach.
My little young Zachary.
Sleepin' in bed.
He's a good boy, yes he is.
Real good, and real smart, too.
Does what he's told, feeds them assholes in the garage on a regular basis, like he's supposed to, and—
("zach!")
("what have you done?")
("i didn't do it, daddy!")
("i swear!")
No, no, no.
Zach's a good boy.
Plays with his Game Boy a lot, but he don't bother nobody.
Not like Rhonda.
She's *always* startin' shit.
But not young Zachary.
He's a good boy.
Maybe a little messed up, but that ain't his fault.
No sir—that's his momma's fault.
That's his *(meth-whore momma's fault)* because she did that bullshit when she was pregnant with him and *(that's Charlie's fault that's not my fault that's Charlie's fault)* I can always get the doctor to prescribe Zach some *new* medicine, that'll calm him down, just needs some—

Charlie.

My best friend.

Mejores amigos.

Where ya been, *amigo?*

Donde estás?

Or was it, *donde has estado?*

Always got that shit mixed up, brother.

Sí, sí. Still remember that good ol' *español.*

You taught me *real* good, ya did.

Muy bueno.

I try to speak some at Mexican restaurants and shit.

No, not at Taco John's, but at *real* Mexican restaurants.

You know what I'm talkin' about, *amigo.*

Quit pullin' my leg.

(you always made me laugh, charlie...)

(no matter how bad shit got you always made me l—)

But I tell ya what, when I do speak that *español,* it impresses my kids a lot.

Sí, fuckin' *sí.*

I tried to teach'em, too, Charlie, to *tell'em* about you but—no, no.

Forget I even said that.

(i don't talk with my kids about you, charlie)

(they don't need to know about you)

But I tell ya what, whenever I eat Mexican or hear somebody speakin' Spanish, it makes me think about ya.

Of course, brother.

Of course, I wanna see ya.

Mejores amigos.

We'll always be *mejores amigos.*

Charlie, I—

—don't look at me like that, now.

Stop shakin' your head and fuckin' say what you wanna s—*now Charlie,* don't be makin' *me* feel guilty about all *that* bullshit, now.

You was the one who got me into that shit.

You.

All them drugs, all that drama and fucked up shit we did, actin' like the fuckin' Blackbeards of Tri County, that was all *you, you're* the one who—

(who, bill?)
(who really did all that?)
—stop shakin' your head, Charlie.
No, no, don't *you* shake your fuckin' head at *me,* Charlie!
Like *I'm* fuckin' guilty!
That was all *you!*

I just went along with that shit because *you* pulled that *mejores amigos* shit on me like you *always* fuckin' did, but even I got my limits, even I got my fuckin' limits about what's fuckin'—

Charlie?
You still here?
Char—
—hey, I didn't mean to get all pissy with ya, man.
Lo siento, amigo.
Fuckin' *lo siento* about that shit.
I'm sorry.
(i'm not sorry charlie i hate you i hate y—)
My mind ain't good no more, brother.
Not like it used to be.
Not since The Accident *(it's not my fault it's not my fault it's not my f—).*

Let's just let the past be the past, now.
Can't remember half that shit, anyway.
(i don't wanna remember, charlie)
(rememberin' makes me sick...)
I still wanna hang out.
I miss ya.
I really miss ya, man.
(i hate you i hate you and i hate what we did because of y—)
Ain't got no friends out here in Raven.
Not real ones, like I did in the Tri.
(everybody knew me back then)
(i was wild bill and i had a posse)
(i was somebody...)
I know, I know.
Hard to believe, ain't it?
Cool guy like me without no friends.

Sí, sí.

I still got my Rob Zombie-look.

Or, should I say, *he's* still got *my* fuckin' look.

(you know he copied off of me, right?)

(gonna have to sue his ass one of these days...)

But out here in Raven, it's different.

Ain't like the Tri.

(you're why we moved out here, charlie)

(to get away from your bullshit)

I miss my life back then.

The good ol' days.

("we follow your dreams, bill...")

("just tell us what to do")

Hey, what's goin' on with Skinny Kenny?

And ol' Graham-cracker? And the rest of 'em?

(why ya look at me so strange, charlie?)

(whenever i mention them?)

Hey, I got an idea, *amigo,* why don't y'all come over and visit next weekend?

Sí, sí.

You call up Kenny, tell him I got a bottle of tequila and a case of RC with his name on it.

(what happened to kenny, charlie?)

(that was your fault, charlie, that wasn't m—)

Let's put on our cowboy hats, get *wild* and tear shit up like we used to, let's—

—well, alright, let's call up *all* the old Posse, then.

All of 'em.

Huh?

Why the fuck not?

Why you lookin' at me like that, Charlie?

(NO)

(NO)

(it's not my fault it's not my fault it's not my f—)

I told ya my dreams don't show me *everything,* now, I fuckin' told ya th—whose idea was it to be like Blackbeard, huh?

Who read that book first?

Who got everybody in our fuckin' Posse to read that fuckin' book?

That's how it all started, Charlie, that's how it all fuckin' started.

Even Graham read it, and I swear that's the only book that big ol' boy ever read, I fuckin' tell ya that right n—

—now wait a minute, Charlie, wait a fuckin' minute.

I can't go back to that life, man.

All them drugs.

All them bad things we done.

(lemme see that mouth charlie open that fucking mouth charlie open th—)

Ain't nothin' worse than what we did, Charlie.

(gimme your mouth charlie I'll open your fucking mouth I'll do somethin' worse to you than what we did to—)

And ain't nobody worse than us.

(why'd you make me do that, charlie?)

(why?)

(i never wanted to hurt nobody, i never w—)

But I got Taleiah and Zach to think about now.

And Rhonda.

Rhonda's out here, too.

Oh, she's still wild.

Gets it from her Daddy, I guess.

Sí, sí.

She did rip a chick's eyeball out once.

She did, indeed.

That girl's a handful, lemme tell ya.

But I tell ya what, she's manager of the Dairy Queen out here now, and she quit them drugs and she's—

Wayne.

("bill?")

("why won't you play dungeons and dragons with me?")

Wayne, who was I talkin' to just now?

Was that *you?*

Or someone else?

Why can't I see your face?

Why can't I *ever* see your face?

("find it, bill...")

Why's it always blurry and swirlin'-like?
(*"temple above all."*)
It looks like your face but not your face and—
Charlie?
Where's Wayne?
(*LEMME SEE THAT MOUTH CHARLIE OPEN THAT FUCKING MOUTH*)
Ain't nothin' worse than what we did, Charlie.
(*GIMME YOUR MOUTH CHARLIE I'LL OPEN YOUR—*)

And ain't nobody
worse

than us.

"Good morninnnnn', Daddyyyy..."

1990s

CHAPTER XLII

VISION

"...pl-se...hel-hel-me..." said the piece of shit.

You still sayin' that, AB?

Even after all this time?

BOBBY SAT IN his car outside the Dairy Queen in Maplefield, Alabama. The sun shone bright in a cloudless sky.

"Boy, last night was s-somethin' else...w-wasn't it, Little Stacey?"

His mouth barely moved as he answered in her voice:

"*Suurrre waasss, Bawww-byyy...dat was a kwooossse one...*"

He darted his eyes to the passenger seat.

Empty.

Empty, except for a small briefcase.

She ain't there.

The real Little Stacey wasn't there, and neither was the Barbie doll.

He squinted at the parking lot.

"*I missss youuuu, Bawww-byyy...*"

He touched his forehead to the steering wheel, closing his eyes.

I miss you, too...

Wasn't the same talking to her now. Not without the Barbie. Like a priest needed his cross, he needed the doll as an intermediary, a conduit to commune with her.

Communion.

He needed the doll for communion.

Without it, he was just talkin' to his dang ol' self.

Like a crazy person.

He buried his face in his hands.

What do I do now, Little Stacey?

What do I do now...

Until recently, he'd spent Saturday afternoons with Little Stacey, snug as a bug in her briefcase beside him. They'd talk all day as he drove around town, sampling treats from fast-food places, always in the parking lot to commune in private, safe from eavesdroppers.

They wouldn't understand.

He knew that.

He wasn't crazy.

But Saturdays belonged to him—to spend the way *he* wanted to.

America was still a free country, after all.

Last time he dang ol' checked.

Sundays belonged to church, weekday nights revolved around her feedings, but Saturdays remained exclusively for Little Stacey.

They loved enjoyin' each other's company.

"A-almost got in a p-pickle last night..." he said. "...d-didn't we, L-Little Stacey?"

"We suuure diiid, Bawww-byyy..."

He glanced at the briefcase.

"...but we're s-safe and s-sound, now..."

Safe and sound...

He breathed in, then out, slowly.

("you sure about that, sir?")

("you sure you weren't out here with a barbie doll?")

Best to wait a while to retrieve her.

Too dangerous now.

Dangerous...

His lungs expanded and contracted, inhaling and exhaling the artificially chilled air.

Was she okay out there?

All by herself?

I'm sorry, Little Stacey...

I didn't mean to abandon you...

I'll get you back soon...

He slammed his fist on the steering wheel.

I promise!

He leaned back and sighed, trying to control his breathing.

That cop.

He'd handled him good.

Better than anyone else in a long time.

But *how?*

The cop stood as the biggest threat he'd faced in recent memory—bigger than the KB toy store girl (who he still suspected knew why he *really* bought the doll), bigger than Mr. Stannis (who he *hated* with a passion), and even bigger than his Ruining. By all rights, he should've been reduced to Jell-O the moment the cop questioned him.

But he'd held his own, especially at the end.

Maybe because he'd dealt with the cop right after feedin' Little Stacey. That always helped calm his nerves, deflate that nasty anxiety and tension inside him, like a balloon ready to burst.

But there'd been somethin' *else.*

Post-feedin' calm might've been a factor, sure, but somethin' *clicked* when the cop just kept pesterin' him, *actin' like a dang ol' bully.* After that *click,* he'd spoken the way he'd always wished he could; the way he'd seen others and longed to imitate.

What triggered that?

That *click*?

He released his breath in a slow, steady stream, reliving the moment.

"No officer, I was not. May I ask if I'm free to go now?"

The way he'd said it.

With sharpness.

Power.

Like he wasn't messin' around no more.

That bully didn't like it when I stood up for myself, did he?

(they never do, bobby...)

(they never do...)

He balled his hands into fists.

("we was just playin', bobby!")

("bobby, stop!")

("stop!")

("st—")

If only he could talk to Mr. Stannis—no, to *everyone* like that.

(what happened after that, bobby?)

(after you stood up to him?)

Staring into the parking lot, Bobby felt his eyes glaze over as a distant, unplugged sensation washed over him. Drool trickled from the corner of his mouth.

"The-the officer...s-said he didn't n-need my license..."

(that's right...and then?)

"...and-and thennnnn..."

(this is important, bobby...)

"...thennnn...he...he g-gave me a warnin'..."

(that's right, bobby...)

(a dang ol' warnin'...)

(...and after that?)

"...and thennnnn...he...he let me gooo..."

(good, bobby...)

(good...)

Bobby slurped his drool and turned on the radio.

"...and in a recent update regarding BDK..."

Nope, didn't wanna hear the dang ol' news, just some dang ol' *music*.

He switched the car off. Good to save gas. Besides, his sweat had dried, and a strange coldness enveloped him. Something felt *off*, like he'd almost recalled something *nasty*, but couldn't quite—

(ain't ya hungry, bobby?)

His stomach rumbled. Saturday afternoons usually began with his usual: a chicken strip basket, double cheeseburger, and one of them tasty Blizzards.

Oreo and cookie dough type.

Always.

He glanced at the small briefcase he'd bought to conceal Little Stacey. Almost went with a backpack, but a grown man wearin' one risked lookin' *mighty* suspicious. Glad he chose the briefcase. She fit nice and snug inside, and they enjoyed such fun lunches together in the DQ parking lot. Of course, sometimes he yearned to take her out—*of course he did*—so she'd sit beside him proper, like a real lady, and he could gaze upon her perfection.

Little Stacey...

But what if he ran into someone from work?

Or church?

Risky...

Besides, she needed her rest after a week of feedin'.

All that eatin' made a girl tired.

"H-havin' your belly full makes ya sl-sleeeeepy..."

He reached his trembling hand over to the brieface and stroked it.

"...d-don't it..."

God, I miss you...

"...L-Little S-Stacey?"

Sometimes he'd pet her a little. Hold her. Stroke her while driving. Had to give her love and affection throughout the day, let her know he was *always* there for her.

He slid his clammy hand inside the briefcase, yearning to rub her little nubs for boobs. Stroke her and squeeze her *real tight*—as tight as he could— whispering, *"Everything's gonna be alright, now..."* and *"I love you, Little Stacey..."*

He opened and closed his hand inside the briefcase, grasping at air.

Empty now.

Hollow.

Didn't feel right eatin'.

Not without Little Stacey beside him.

A heaviness in his chest made it hard to breathe.

Maybe he should go back?

Go back *right now* to the woods and look for her.

That dang ol' cop should be—

(*not a good idea, bobby...*)

He shook his head.

But if another cop caught him there again...

Maybe wait a few weeks? And then—

No.

The risk remained.

His secret haven, his Good Woods, could never be used again. Wasn't as hidden as he'd thought—*no dang ol' magical veil, after all*—and cops might slap him with a misdemeanor for public urination. Or worse, they might figure out what he was *really* doin' out there. He wasn't no lawyer, but he had a hunch jerkin' off near a public highway constituted a heavier crime than peein' beside one. And what if they put it on the news?

"MAN CAUGHT MASTURBATING ON BARBIE DOLL BESIDE HIGHWAY I-65"

He shuddered.

It'd be worse than his Ruining.

Could go back to KB Toys and buy another Barbie—one of them cute little blonde ones. Didn't relish seeing that register girl again, (and maybe—*just maybe*—the same mean momma with her finger-pointin' brat) so best to check other toy stores, first.

But *where* would he feed her then?

Other woods and empty parking lots dotted the area. Could scout for a new spot.

(*but what if they catch ya again, bobby?*)

The police likely had him in their system now. If he was caught with his pants down again, it'd look mighty suspicious...

He shifted his legs, wincing as his bloodied foreskin rubbed against his underwear. Scabs had peeled off again, probably in the shower from scrubbin' *real hard* down there, makin' himself clean.

(*"you dirty, dirty little boy!"*)

(*"i'm not dirty, momma!"*)

("yes you are, dirty boy!")

("i'm gonna make you clean...")

Feedin' Little Stacey at home—the place of his Ruining—was unthinkable.

No way.

Couldn't even *fathom* it, nor muster the focus it required.

Couldn't touch The Void or witness The Joining, either.

(which are you feedin', bobby?)

(little stacey?)

(or the void?)

He shrugged, considering other possible feeding locations, and held out a chubby finger—

Option One: his car.

Nope. Her breakfast went *everywhere* that first time. Even splattered on the dang ol' speedometer. Tough cleanin' all that up, especially from the crevices of the steering wheel. Besides, he needed to do it standin' up; her breakfast always *flowed better* standin' up.

His hand trembled as he extended a second finger—

Option Two: office bathroom.

That *might* work—he'd jerked it into the toilet a few times before, pretendin' it was Little Stacey's mouth—but only after the other guys cleared out, which could be pretty late. Some of 'em even worked past midnight thanks to those dang ol' deadlines Mr. Stannis liked to set. Feedin' her that late would prove *mighty hard*...besides, the bathrooms stank like crap and that'd ruin it all.

He held out three sweaty fingers—

Option Three: restaurant or gas station restrooms.

Gross.

Even worse than the office restrooms.

Akin to feedin' Little Stacey with a dirty plate.

He sighed and rotated his head, glancing at the surrounding cars, the pavement, and the sky, now an oppressive gray. Hadn't the sun been shinin' earlier? Oh well.

Slowly, he extended a fourth finger—

Option Four: his office.

His little office room, overlookin' the dumpster.

If nobody worked late on his floor, that *might* work. But Mr. Stannis's dang ol' *"door-free policy"* presented a risk if anybody returned. Not to mention the rumors of Mr. Stannis's secret cameras hidden throughout the building.

No.

Too dang risky at the office...

"Ohhh, Little S-Stacey, L-Little Stacey..." he said. "What in the w-world am I g-gonna dooo..."

He laid his head on the steering wheel, the rubber grip cold to the touch.

The doll was supposed to be a *temporary* solution, anyway.

("...there are temporary gifts...")

Never meant as a *permanent* replacement.

("...and there are permanent gifts...")

Besides, he was tired of beatin' off on a Barbie!

Was rubbin' his ding-dong raw!

He needed *the real* Little Stacey—and soon.

("...you understand that, don't you, bobby?")

("...this ain't christmas...")

("...and i ain't no santa claus.")

He pounded the steering wheel with both fists.

Dang—

ol'—

Mr.—

Stannis!

Dang ol' Mr. Stannis with his shiny black shoes propped up on that dang ol' African blackwood desk, always playin' with his dang ol' Rubik's Cube. He'd been messin' with that for years now and probably hadn't solved it once. No surprise—he couldn't begin to understand the complexities of everyone's day-to-day jobs, and especially not the Mabel client.

Mr. Stannis is the dang ol' problem!

Not the doll, not the woods, and not the police!

Dang ol' Mr. Stannis!

Dark fantasies played out before Bobby; of teachin' Mr. Stannis a lesson, just like he taught those kids who tied him up to that tree.

("there he is!")

("barfin' bobby!")

("let's get him to barf everywhere!")

Children laughin', their dang ol' laughs fillin' the air.
("if we poke him enough, he'll puke!")
The girls—the girls always had that guilty look in their eyes,
("hurry up and puke, bobby!")
and so did one or two of the boys.
("he's about to barf!")
But they all did it.
("i can see it in his eyes!")
They all poked him with sticks.
("it's dribblin' out his mouth!")
("gross!")
They were all guilty.
("keep pokin'em!")
("don't stop!")
("make him puke more!")
Even the girls.
("bobby, stop!")
("we was just playin'!")
But they couldn't make him cry.
He never cried he never CRIED.
Momma said big boys don't cry and he NEVER did.
("bobby!")
("stop!")
Instead, he made'em *pay.*
("stop!")
("stop!")
("st—")
They all paid.
(what'd you do, bobby?)
"...I-I...m-made'em..."
(made'em what?)
"...paaayyy..."
(that's right, bobby...)
(bullies always gotta pay...)
Dang ol' Mr. Stannis was just like them.
A dang ol' bully!
He hit the steering wheel again—

HONK!

"Shoot!"

Shrinking into his seat, he scanned his surroundings, making sure he hadn't attracted attention.

What?

A bird—a *red* bird—landed on the hood of his car.

A cardinal!

Easily the biggest he'd ever seen. Almost the size of a young crow, or raven.

Well, hey little birdy-bird...

Are you the same birdy-bird I saw in the woods?

The cardinal cocked its head sideways.

You're a big birdy-bird, ain't ya...

It pecked at the windshield, staring at him with expectant eyes.

Ya hungry, birdy-bird?

He touched the glass, longing for the barrier to vanish.

Wish I had food for ya...

Then I could feed ya, just like I feed Little Sta—

With a flutter of its wings, the cardinal flew off.

What the...

Suddenly, everything felt *blurry.*

What's goin' on?

His surroundings took on an *ethereal* quality, as if he'd drifted into the dreamworld itself.

Is this a dream?

Am I still awa—

A girl emerged from a nearby car—the meanest-looking girl he'd ever laid eyes upon.

Oh boy...

She slammed her door shut and took a long drag from her cigarette, projecting a cold confidence surpassing even the hardest of men.

Oh boy, oh boy...

Clad in a DQ uniform, she sported wild blonde hair and crazy tattoos up her arms, like a female rock star.

Now that girl's nothin' but trouble...

Like a lion crossing the savannah, she strode across the parking lot with confidence and power.

Don't think I wanna order no Blizzards from her...

After one last hit of her cigarette, she flicked it away and blew smoke, turning toward Bobby with a look that dared the world, *"You got a problem?"*

Nope.

Sure didn't.

Didn't want *nothin'* to do with a girl like that.

Looked mean as a snake—and probably bite ya like one, too.

She turned back and marched toward the DQ entrance, then halted and bent over, clutching her head.

What the...

Why'd she stop?

A tremor jolted through her, forcing her back to arch.

What's wrong with her?

Probably on dru—

She whirled around, scanning the parking lot, slowly, like a predator searching for prey.

Bobby froze.

What's she lookin' for?

Her scanning eyes swept past Bobby, as if unable to see him but still *sensing* his presence.

Can she...sense me lookin' at her?

Time slowed to a crawl. Bobby cowered in his seat, afraid to move, every instinct screaming that the girl *hunted* for someone.

Is she...

Huntin' for me?

He gulped.

A shiver ran up his spine.

With a scowl, the girl spat on the pavement and turned toward the entrance.

Oh boy...

She headed inside. Bobby exhaled, relief washing over him as his surroundings sharpened into focus.

Boy, oh boy...

They'll hire just about anybody at the Dairy Queen these days...

Didn't wanna have to interact with *her* at the drive-through.

Maybe Taco John's would be better today.

Girl like that's liable to rip your dang eyeball out, shove it in your—

A haunting note cut through the stillness. Bobby jerked his head to the right, spotting a young Black man beside his passenger door, violin in hand.

"Jesus!" said Bobby.

The sound twisted in his ears, raw and unnatural, as if the instrument were alive.

What the...

The man stared at him through the window—

Do I...

—with the most soulful eyes Bobby had ever seen.

Do I know you?

Eyes like whirlpools that sucked you in.

Those eyes...

The violin's eerie wail emerged not from the instrument, but the man's eyes.

"I don't g-got any money!" said Bobby. "Leave m-me alone!"

The man's stare intensified.

Why you lookin' at me?

Everything darkened.

How do I know you?

He gasped for air.

How do I know that song you're playin'?

Something about the melody,

("i got him, daddy!")

that girl he'd seen,

("tell us the fucking clue!")

this man's eyes staring into him,

("to the goddamn temple!")

and the violin screaming from his *eyes.*

That violin!

I've heard it before!

That vio—

Bobby gasped as a vision, horrifying and pure, spilled across his mind.

No!

He started his car and peeled onto the highway.

1990s

CHAPTER XLIII

DROOL

"Why do you drool sometimes, Bobby?

What are you thinking about?"

BOBBY'S HANDS TREMBLED, eyes fixed on the road.

Boy, oh boy...

Now, who plays a dang ol' violin at Dairy Queen?

He slurped up his drool.

A dang ol' weirdo, that's who.

1990s

CHAPTER XLIV

THE SHAPE OF THINGS TO COME

"You ever get the feelin' that a cat walked over your grave?"

RHONDA LOUNGED IN her car at the Raven County, Kentucky, Dairy Queen. Windows down, tattooed arm hangin' out, cigarette between her fingers like she didn't give a fuck. Part of her routine once she'd ascended to manager. Every day before headin' inside, she'd lean back, way back, and listen to metal, hard rock, shit like that. *Shit that got ya goin'.* Shit that pumped her the fuck up to become Boss Rhonda—the best goddamn Dairy Queen manager in the whole wide world.

"Man in the Box," her favorite Alice in Chains song, blasted from the speakers. She cranked the volume up. Had to play that shit *loud.* Let the world know she was badass, and not to be fucked with.

As the first chorus began, a feeling of raw and gritty toughness washed over her. Wasn't sure what the lyrics meant, but it sounded hard. Hard and badass. A tad mournful, too. Like the tale of someone burdened by regrets but didn't give a *fuck* no more.

She could identify with that.

Didn't give a *fuck* no more.

Nodding to the chorus, she took a deep pull from her cigarette, focusing on looking tough and badass. It was all in the facial expression: narrow your eyes, release all emotion—let your face die, *like you gave zero fucks*—and you could pass for a hardened criminal, or one of them Nirvana boys on MTV.

Maybe I should start playin' guitar...

Already got that badass metal look to me...

A father, accompanied by his wife and child, exited the restaurant, casting her a wary glance.

Cranking the volume higher, she narrowed her eyes at the family and leaned back, *way back,* cigarette dangling out the window. The father locked eyes with her *(look at me),* then glanced away, pulling his family in close.

"Little square ass bitch..." she said. "Actin' like you ain't seen a girl with tattoos smokin' and listenin' to loud music..."

The family settled in their car, fastening their seatbelts.

Look at me, little bitch...

Narrowing her eyes to tiny slits, she emptied her face of all emotion,

Look at me...

making it devoid of everything but *toughness,*

I dare you to fuckin' look at me...

raw and gritty toughness,

I fuckin' dare you, bitch...
of the don't-give-a-fuck variety.
(LOOK)
(AT)
(ME)
The family pulled out of their parking spot.
The father hadn't looked at her.
Not even once.
That's what I fuckin' thought...
She flicked ash into the air.
Little pussy ass bitch...
Blowing smoke out the window, she tracked the bitch-family's car as it pulled onto the highway.
So many square-ass bitches out here...
I swear to God, people actin' like they're from Zion and shit...
She glanced at the clock. Fifteen minutes 'til clock-in. Best go in early, set a good example. As a manager, that shit mattered.
Striding across the parking lot, she took one last drag of her cigarette, blew a plume of smoke, and flicked it away.
("who's the bully now?")
She halted.
A sudden *pulse* in the air sent a jolt up her spine, forcing her to arch her back.
("who's the dang ol' b-bully now, huh?")
The fuck was that?
That weird *pulse*—it came from behind her.
("you ain't g-gonna hurt me again!")
She whirled around, scanning the parking lot.
Hardly any cars around, but—
("you ain't g-gonna hurt n-nobody again!")
—was some weirdo watchin' her?
From inside his car?
("how does it feel?")
One of them pervert types, like the assholes they kept in the garage?
("how does this f-feel?")
("huh?")
Except this one felt familiar, like she knew him from her past,

("i'll k-kill you!")
or her future.
("and the rest of your d-dang ol' crazy family!")
Rhonda clenched her jaw, scanning the near-empty parking lot.
Where ya at, little weirdo?
I know you're watchin' me...
I can feel your beady little eyes st—
A violin's melody whispered through the air, carried by the wind.
A violin?
Who's playin' a fuckin' violin?
A feeling of dread—terrible dread—gnawed at her stomach.
Sounds familiar...
But wh—
She spat and turned back toward the entrance.
Ain't got time for this shit...
Flinging the door open, she swore she heard the violin again, that fucking vio—
(why's it sound so familiar?)
(why?)
—but she shrugged it off.
Just somebody playin' classical music and shit...
Don't give a fuck...

It's Boss Rhonda time.

PART III

WE USED TO SMOKE TOGETHER

1970s

CHAPTER I

WITH BLOOD ON HER FACE

"I wanna ride on top first, Tommy…"

"I LIKE IT when you're inside me..." said Samantha.

Headlights from distant vehicles glinted in the rearview mirror, but Tommy paid them no mind. He focused on her eyes—*his* Samantha's eyes.

God, she's so tight...

He let her ride him nice and slow, so gently she barely even moved. Any faster might push him over the edge.

"It feels good..." said Samantha.

He squeezed her ass. "You like ridin' on top?"

"Yeah...I like ridin' on top..."

She kissed his forehead.

"With you inside me, Tommy..."

("she liked ridin' on top the best...")

"It doesn't hurt?" asked Tommy. "It feels good now?"

"...it feels good now..."

("after prom...")

("i took her fuckin' cherry...")

"...it feels good now, Tommy..."

("and then we fucked four more times...")

"...I wanna go slow..."

("before y'all got back together...")

"...and look at you..."

Damn fine with that.

Damn fine and happy if she rode him nice and slow, all fuckin' night. Their first time needed to be *special,* and he wanted to make it last as long as he could.

"When you're ready..." she said. "...ready to cum...I..."

Tommy's penis stiffened.

"...I-I want you to..."

"What?" asked Tommy. "You want me to what?"

("i hope that bitch brushed her teeth!")

No.

("i hope that bitch brushed her t—")

No.

("on prom night...")

("when I took her cherry...")

"...I want you to..."

("she told me to bust on her face...")

"...cum on my face..."

(*"and in her mouth..."*)

"...and...in my mouth..."

(*"did you kiss her after that, tommy?"*)

"...promise me, Tommy..."

(*"you didn't fuckin' kiss her, did ya?"*)

"...promise me you'll give it to me like that..."

(*"i hope that bitch brushed her teeth!"*)

"...every time we do it..."

Why?

Why'd she ask for that?

Why'd she make him promise that?

(*"i thought..."*)

(*"i thought all guys liked that..."*)

Why'd she say "all guys?"

Why *"all?"*

(*"she made me promise to give it to her that way..."*)

(*"every single time..."*)

—then Tommy fell on top of her, thrusting and thrusting and pounding away at that little fucking body of hers, about to give it to her the way *she* wanted, the way *she'd made him promise,* and she looked up at him with those eyes, slut's eyes, WHORE'S EYES and he fucking knew his precious Samantha was just a little freshman slut, she wasn't special, she wasn't pure, just a fucking WHORE, and he never should've loved her and he should've just fucked sluts like the rest of his Boys and he should never *feel* anything for a girl, not ever, *ever—*

(*"i love you, tommy..."*)

(*"you're the only one i'll let do this..."*)

—and then Bill appeared, that piece of shit Bill-fuckin'-Cunningham wearin' his fucking cowboy hat and sunglasses just poundin' and poundin' away at that little body of hers while she stared at her reflection in those fucking sunglasses all warped and distorted and *she liked it, she liked seeing herself all fucked up and broken,* and then Bill busted on her face with blood on his dick from her hymen (*"why don't you have a..."*) (*"i lost it in gymnastics, tommy..."*) and then smeared his bloody dick all over her cum-covered face and *she likes it, she likes it, she likes the blood on her face* and she sticks out her tongue and licks up the cum and the blood and the blood and the blood AND THE BLOOD around her lips and looks up into his FUCKING SUNGLASSES with those eyes, WHORE'S EYES and sees herself and—

("i said no!")

("we didn't do anything, tommy!")

("stop asking me about it!")

("please!")

"Tommy?"

("i love you, tommy...")

"Tommy?"

("you're the only one i'll let do this...")

"Tommy!"

("i love you, tomm—")

("you're the onl—")

1970s

CHAPTER II

SCARECROW

Did you really fuck her, Bill?

Did you really rub your bloody dick across her f—

"*TOMMY?*"

"*Tommy!*"

(*"you're the onl—"*)

"Tommy!" said Mouse. "Snap out of it, man!"

Late morning sunlight brought Tommy's surroundings into focus. Amidst the yellow rays and green of the grass, Samantha's face emerged, dripping cum and blood, warped in the lenses of Bill's sunglasses.

Smiling.

Licking the cum and blood off her lips and—

just

fucking

smiling.

(*"i love you, tomm—"*)

(*"you're the onl—"*)

Gradually, her visage dissolved into a scarecrow. Fashioned with iron bars for limbs, the scarecrow bore a piece of paper labeled *"GRAHAM RILEY"* on its chest.

"*HA-YAAAAAAH!*"

Kevin rushed forward, slamming his crowbar onto the scarecrow's left leg.

DONNNG!

"*Aah, fuck!*" said Kevin. "It hurts my hand!"

"Means you hit him real good," said Larry. "Asian David, you're next. Go for his right this time."

"*Earth to Tommy!*" said Mouse.

"I'm here..." said Tommy. Samantha's cum and blood-smeared face had vanished, but he knew it would return.

He saw it everywhere now.

Every fucking day.

"Were you listenin' to what Jack said?" asked Mouse. "Because he said some bullshit, man."

"It's not bullshit," said Jack. "It's called bein' careful. We have to—"

"It's called bein' a *pussy-ass-bitch!*" said Mouse.

"Mouse, you d—"

DONNNG!

David clutched his hand. "*Aaah!*"

"Can't we wear gloves or somethin'?" asked Grant.

Larry's long face drooped in disapproval. "Fuck no, you can't wear no gloves. Quit bein' a puss. Now Grant, you go for his left leg, but come from behind, and Wiley, you go for his right, but come from his front. Y'all need to get good at attackin' him from *all* directions, fuckin' simultaneously. Like, *cross-attack* him and shit."

"Mouse," said Jack, "take a second and *think* about things for once."

"*Think* about things?" said Mouse. "I *am* fuckin' thinkin', and what I'm thinkin' is that your dick has—"

"Alright guys," said Tommy. "Alright..." Jack and Mouse had been bickering all morning, both repeating the same fucking arguments. No wonder he'd zoned out.

"*RAAAAAAAAAAAAAH!*"

DONNNG!

"*AAAAAAAAAAAAAAH!*"

DONNNG!

Grant and Kevin dropped their crowbars, crying out in pain.

"*My hand! It stings!*"

"*Let us wear gloves, y'all!*"

"There's definitely somethin' up," said Tommy. "I agree with Jack on that. Doesn't make sense that Bill and his bitch-ass Posse didn't show up that night."

"Here's an idea," Mouse tapped his forehead. "Maybe...they're...just... *pussies!*"

Jack shook his head. "Graham Riley ain't no pussy, man."

"Neither is Young Charlie," said Tommy. "Not when it comes to his OCD cleanliness and shit. Motherfucker would fight a crocodile if it spilled coffee on his carpet..."

He drummed his fingers against his leg.

Bill should've come at us...

They all should've come at us by now...

"Dude," said Mouse. "You guys are so fuckin' paranoid! They just pussed out, that's all!"

"I'm tellin' ya," said Jack, "they're *plannin'* somethin'. And if I was them, I'd do it during our next Smokehouse Party, where they got a big-ass audience and can unleash as much chaos as possible."

"Then we fuckin' throw down!" said Mouse. "We beat their asses in front of everybody! And it'll be even *more* epic! *More* fuckin' legendary!"

"If they're comin' at us during our party," said Jack, "then they probably got a plan, dude. They're the ones who'll have the drop on *us*. So not only did we lose the best part of our plan, the epic fuckin' ambush, but—"

"The epic ambush was never the best part!" said Mouse. "The crowbars, and the Kentucky Blood sauce in Graham's eyes were the best parts!"

Jack folded his arms. He always did that shit when he thought they were wrong or didn't see "the big picture."

"I disagree," said Jack. "The ambush part was essential. It's the kind of move genius military leaders, like Napoleon, would make. And also—"

DONNNG!

"Aaah! Fuck!" said Wiley.

"Wilin' Wiley," said Larry. "You hit like a bitch. Even Good Guy Grant hit harder than you. Go for his right leg again. Aim for the kneecap area."

"Can we snort that Miracle stuff?" asked Wiley. "Just a little, to see if it helps us hit him better?"

"Maybe it'll make our hands sting less," said Grant.

"Nope," said Larry. "That's for when the real show starts."

Wiley's eyes pleaded. "Can you at least give us the vials to keep on us? In case, ya know, we run into—"

"Nope," said Larry.

"Wait a minute, wait a minute," said Jack. "Maybe they *should* keep a little on'em, just in case. What if they run into Bill and his Posse?"

Larry shrugged. "Then they fight or run. But they're with us most of the time, anyway. What's the big risk?"

"If I was one of Bill's crew," said Jack, "I'd go after one of the Possibles, and use'em as leverage somehow."

"Leverage?" asked Larry. "What you think they're gonna do? Kidnap a Possible or somethin'? Tie him up in a garage and torture him and shit?"

"I dunno..." said Jack. "Seems like givin'em a *little* Miracle for self-defense ain't a bad idea..."

"No," said Tommy. He'd only tried Miracle once, but the way it'd made him feel...

Powerful.

Invincible.

Hungry.

Rabid.

If they snorted that shit without supervision...

"They get their vials the night of the party," said Tommy. "And they don't snort *any* unless trouble starts."

He looked at the Possibles.

"You guys got that?"

They said they did.

"Let's huddle up," said Tommy, "and make a decision about this shit. Larry?"

Larry turned back to the Possibles. "Asian David, Wilin' Wiley, after y'all's hands stop pussy-throbbin, attack him diagonally, from the front and back, different legs. Cross-attack him, like I been teachin' y'all. And fuckin' yell that shit when you do."

"Yell what?" asked Kevin.

"*Cross-attack!*" said Larry. "The fuck you think?"

Larry's lanky frame cast a long shadow as he approached the rest of the Boys. He tilted his head down as if peering over a ledge.

"Gonna be honest with ya," said Larry. "I don't think we should cancel the party."

"*See?*" said Mouse.

"But Jack might be right," said Larry. "Cunningham and them, they might be plannin' somethin'..."

His long face grew somber, like a beardless Abraham Lincoln.

"Somethin' big..."

"That's why we got the Possibles practicin'!" said Mouse. "They're gettin' better with the crowbars, and we'll be even more prepared on Saturday than we were that night!"

Jack folded his arms again. "We definitely won't be, for a multitude of fuckin' reasons, that I've already fuckin' expl—"

"So we cancel it," said Mouse, "and then what? Wait all fuckin' summer for'em to come at us, and never have any Smokehouse Parties? A Smokehouse Party-less summer?"

"I'm tellin' ya," said Jack, "I got a bad feelin' about this..."

"No offense, Jack," said Mouse, "but I think your bad fuckin' feelin' is that your dick has magically transformed into a..."

While Jack and Mouse bickered, Tommy turned his gaze to the sky, its clouds a canvas for his thoughts.

What to do, what to do...

Birds chirped nearby.

He fixed his gaze on one cloud in particular.

That cloud...

Looks different...

Why?

He narrowed his eyes.

The birds stopped chirping.

The cloud resembled a hat—

—a *cowboy* hat.

He shook his head.

Fuck.

Didn't wanna admit it, but he had a bad feeling, too. Deep down in his gut, the kind he couldn't ignore.

But hey, maybe Mouse was right? Maybe they were paranoid about shit.

Probably not.

But maybe.

Still, even if Bill and his Posse *did* have shit up their sleeves, it didn't make sense to endlessly cancel Smokehouse Parties 'til they made a move.

Besides, what if Mouse was right?

And they never did shit?

Or what if they had another plan entirely—

—one that had nothin' to do with the Smokehouse Parties?

"No offense, *Mitchey Mouse*," said Jack, "but I think your mom did drugs when she was pregnant with you, because your—"

"Don't bring my mom into this!" said Mouse.

"Settle the fuck down," said Tommy. "I'll tell y'all what we're gonna do..."

All eyes turned to Tommy, and the weight of leadership pressed down on him. He glanced at the sky, yearning to stare at it for a minute longer—

—but that fucking cowboy hat-shaped cloud *(again again FUCKING again)* dragged his gaze back to his Boys.

"We're still gonna have the party."

"*Yes!*" said Mouse.

"But we ain't gonna smoke."

"*What?*" asked Mouse.

"We ain't smokin'," said Tommy, "nor doin' any other dr—"

"But it's a Smokehouse Party!" said Mouse.

"I fucking know that, Mouse," said Tommy. "But we can't be high off our asses if they show up ready to throw down."

"But we're the Smoketown Boys!" said Mouse.

Jack raised a finger. "But we'll be the Smoketown Bitches if they kick our ass."

"Dude," said Mouse. "I can fight high as a kite, man. You know me. I beat that one dude's ass no problem when I was high. You remember that, right?"

"Yeah, yeah…" said Tommy. "That Freddy dude, or whatever his name was. From Zion."

"I beat the shit out of that little Zion bitch!" said Mouse.

He flexed his muscles and pounded his chest.

"I was so high my head was in the clouds, man! And I *still* whipped him!"

He struck different poses, showcasing his muscles from every angle.

"Shit," he said, "I think I fight *better* when I'm high!"

"It's also about alertness, Mouse," said Jack. "Not just about how strong you are, or how good you can fight."

He paced like a professor mid-lecture.

"We have to stay alert, on our guard, ready for *anything* they might—"

"I'm alert as fuck when I'm high, dude!" said Mouse. "I ain't like Leslie, sayin' *'fuuuuuuck'* all the time. I'm sharp as shit, man!"

Larry furrowed his brow. "Sorry, Tommy, but I'm with Mouse on this one."

Tommy clenched his jaw. This pattern of *Larry and Mouse vs. Tommy and Jack* had been comin' up more and more.

Didn't used to be like that.

Larry looked at Tommy, then away, embarrassed. "I'm just sayin', it'd be weird if the fuckin' Smoketown Boys, didn't even, ya know, fuckin' smoke at their own Smokehouse Party."

"How about this?" asked Mouse. "You and Jack—y'all don't gotta smoke. But me and Larry, we'll fuckin' smoke. How's that?"

Tommy sighed and rubbed his temples.

Larry had a point.

And maybe Mouse's proposal seemed okay, too.

But what about—

"CROSS-ATTAAAAAAACK!"

DONNNG!

DONNNNG!

"Oh, God!"

"My hand!"

"Quit bein' little bitches, y'all!" said Larry. He marched over to the Possibles. "And y'all gotta get into the fuckin' *stance,* first!"

"What 'stance'?" asked David.

"The stance!" Larry yanked David's crowbar from his grip and held it high, adopting a battle-ready stance. "Lock your eyes forward, then fuckin' aim at his leg. I mean *lock-the-fuck-on-it,* and charge at him! Don't just run at him like a dumbass! Charge at him! With your eyes *locked-on* his fuckin' kneecaps!"

He handed the crowbar back to David.

"Y'all got me?"

The Possibles said they did.

He marched back over.

"Tommy," he said, "I get where you and Jack are comin' from. So how 'bout this—we ban *the Possibles* from smokin' and drinkin' that night. And use'em as our lookouts. Let'em call a rally-up if they see trouble."

"That's a good compromise," said Mouse. "I'm down with that. Is that cool with you, Tommy?"

Jack's freckled face darkened with worry. "That's a really bad idea, for multiple reasons, but mainly because—"

"I'm askin' Tommy," said Mouse.

Jack narrowed his eyes, muttering something.

Tommy turned from his Boys, removed his cap and stared at the lone crow etched on the front.

What would you do, Mikey?

Tell me...

Guide me...

He drew in a breath and held it, the sights and sounds around him melting away.

In that instant, he felt it—as if Mikey spoke to him:

Compromise.

He'd agree to a compromise.

Use the Possibles as sober and alert lookouts, granting them the emergency privilege to call a rally-up if needed. And—just in case—he'd go easy that night and keep a sharp eye out, too. Him and Jack both.

He turned to face his Boys.

"We go with Larry's idea. A compromise."

"*Yes!*" Mouse and Larry exchanged high-fives.

Jack shot Tommy a worried glance.

The cowboy hat-shaped cloud passed before the sun, and for a moment, everything around the Smoketown Boys darkened.

***

After their debate, the Boys passed around a Monkey blunt and watched the Possibles take turns cross-attacking the Graham scarecrow.

"*CROSS-ATTAAAAAAACK!*"

DONG!

DONNNNNG!

"*Oh God!*"

"*My hand!*"

"*Fuckin' stings!*"

Tommy took a deep hit from the blunt and passed it to Jack. He flicked his gaze from the scarecrow, to the Smokehouse, then to the scarecrow again, fighting a sense of dread. No matter how much he smoked, a nagging worry remained:

Their position.

Their position fucking sucked.

On the defense, with zero intel.

Missing something.

And endlessly fucking waiting for a retaliation that might or might not happen—but if he knew Young like he thought he did, then that retaliation would likely happen.

Not a question of *if,* but *when.*

And when the cowboy bitches did make their move, they'd bring their walkin'-fuckin'-tank, Graham-fuckin'-Riley, with'em and—

Graham.

"Hey Larry," said Tommy. "Doesn't Graham work at Cracker Barrel?"

"Yep," said Larry. "In the back, as a cook or dishwasher or somethin'."

Tommy scanned the sky. The cowboy hat-shaped cloud had vanished, but his nagging worry remained.

"Then let's go talk to him."

1970s

CHAPTER III

CRACKER BARREL

"That grilled Colby cheese is so fuckin' gooood, y'all!"

"FUUUUUUCK, Y'ALL..." LESLIE surveyed the Cracker Barrel menu. "I'm gonna eat so fuckin' muuuch..."

Mouse had wanted to fuck Lacey and eat at Waffle House afterward (their little ritual—they smoked, fucked, smoked again, then ate a shit-ton at Waffle House) and Grant and Wiley had to make Monkey deliveries so they rolled short of those three.

Not a problem, though.

They just planned on *talkin'* with Graham.

Nobody intended to throw down at a Cracker Barrel.

"Your oatmeal's not enough?" asked Kevin.

"Fuuuuuuck no..." said Leslie. "This is my fuckin' appetizer..."

She laid the menu down and stirred butter, sugar, and milk into her oatmeal.

Kevin scrunched his face. "Does it taste...better that way?"

Leslie stuffed a heaping spoonful into her mouth. "Fuuuuuuck yeah, it does...this is the only way I eat my fuckin' oatmeal..."

When they'd stopped at Leslie's place to pick her up she'd said, *"Fuuuuuuck, I don't got no money, y'all,"* so they almost went without her, but then Kevin offered to pay for her shit, so she shrugged and said, *"Fuuuuuuck, guess I'll go, then."*

Tommy looked around, scanning for Graham, or maybe even Bill and the rest of his Posse. He'd always had a soft spot for the southern cooking and rustic, country-store vibe of this place. Lanterns flickered softly, while old-timey Coca-Cola bottles, vintage signs and antique knickknacks adorned the walls. Nearby, two checkers tables, each draped in checkered tablecloths and framed by mismatched chairs, invited customers to a game. The entire restaurant bustled with energy; they'd waited twenty minutes just to get seated.

"Man, it's crowded," said Larry. "I wonder if Graham can actually come out and talk to us."

Jack glanced up from his menu, eyes still bloodshot from smoking Monkey.

"If he does talk to us, and wants to start shit..."

He pulled his Kentucky Blood-filled water gun from under the table.

"...I got this baby, ready to fire."

"Jack!" said Tommy. "Put that away!"

"What?" asked Jack.

"Do *not* use that here, man." Tommy shook his head. Whenever Jack smoked Monkey, he turned stupid—fast.

"I'm just sayin'," said Jack, "if he starts shit, I won't hesitate..."

"Fuuuuuuck," said Leslie, gobbling up oatmeal. "What's inside that?"

"Good question, Leslie," said Jack. "This here water gun is filled with the most powerful, hottest type of Kentucky Blood sauce ever made. Like melt-your-pussy-off hot."

"Fuuuuuuck..." said Leslie. "Can you squirt that shit on my fries?"

"No," said Tommy. "He fuckin' can't."

"Why not?" asked Jack.

"Because the water gun is part of the plan, Jack," said Tommy.

"I got more than enough for our food," said Jack, "and to squirt ol' Graham-cracker in his ey—"

"*Shh!*" Tommy looked nervously at Leslie. He trusted her—more or less. But she wasn't one of the Boys. Didn't need to know everything.

"Fuuuuuuck," said Leslie. "Y'all gonna squirt that shit in his *eyes?*"

"No," said Jack. "I'm just...uh..." He cleared his throat and returned the water gun to his lap.

"Asian David," said Larry, "Kevin, what y'all gonna order?"

"Umm..." said Kevin. Both him and David tapped their butter knives anxiously on the table.

"Y'all ain't nervous, is ya?" asked Larry.

(*"aaaaaagh! aaaaaaaagh!"*)

"No..." said Kevin.

(*"can't...bre...athe..."*)

"It's just, that, uh..."

(*"huh huh huh..."*)

"Fuuuuuuck..." said Leslie. "...y'all looked scared as shiiiit...."

"Boys, I'm tellin' ya," said Tommy, "ain't nothin' gonna happen here. What's he gonna do, beat the shit out of us in the middle of Cracker Barrel?"

The moment the words left his lips, though, Tommy felt a twinge of fear:

Is Graham stupid enough to start shit at a fucking Cracker Barrel?

Leslie scraped the remaining oatmeal from her bowl. "Why didn't y'all just call him on the phone? Graham's the biggest dude in Bill's little posse-group. What if he tries to fight y'all and shit? While we're eatin'?"

"He's not gonna try to fight us here," said Tommy, feeling less and less certain of that. "He'd lose his job, for one. And two, he might be the biggest fucker in Bill's Posse, but he's also the dumbest. I'll know if he's lyin', but it's easier to tell in person than on the phone."

He darted his eyes to a long-haired bearded guy—

—was that?

Cunningham!

He rose from his chair.

"Tommy," said Larry, "what's up?"

Tommy squeezed his hands into fists.

"It's Bill-fuckin-Cunnin—"

Wait.

No—

—not Bill.

Just another dude into that heavy metal bullshit.

Slowly, he sat back down.

"...thought it was Bill or somethin'..."

"Fuuuuuuck..." Leslie's eyes returned to the menu.

"...this is some dramatic shit here, y'all..."

***

They ate their food in silence. The powerful, unseen presence of Graham Riley oozed across the table, seeping into everyone except Leslie, who'd ordered more than everyone else. Conversation around them mingled with the clinking of dishes from the kitchen.

"Everything alright with y'all's meal?" asked the waitress. She had a natural, no-fuss beauty to her. Maybe just a few years out of high school.

"Fuuuuuuck," said Leslie. "These grilled Colby cheese sandwiches are *so* fuckin' goooood..." She bit into the corner of her grilled cheese and closed her eyes.

"I'm glad you like'em," said the waitress. "That real sourdough bread adds a lot, don't it?"

"Fuck yeah, it does..." Leslie stuffed half the sandwich into her mouth, closing her eyes again.

"Mmm...fuuuuuck..."

The waitress stared at Leslie. "Y'all need anything else?"

"Naaah," said Larry. "We're good here, but thank you so much. Appreciate all your help today."

Larry's long face betrayed his emotions like an open book. He obviously had a thing for the waitress, usually drawn to girls with her simple kind of beauty. Not slutty or sexy or sophisticated-looking—just simple beauty.

"Just checkin' on y'all," said the waitress. "And if y'all need anythi—"

"Actually," said Tommy, "we asked earlier about one of our buddies in the back, Graham Riley? We just wanna holler at him real quick, we know he's busy and all, but—"

"Oh, Graham-cracker!" said the waitress. Her eyes widened. "He's the biggest boy we got here!"

Larry's long face erupted into a smile. "He is a big ol' boy, ain't he?"

"He sure is!" said the waitress. "I ain't ever seen a boy as big as him! I'll tell him y'all wanna say hi, now!"

"Thank you, ma'am," said Larry. He watched her head to the next table.

"You should ask her number, dude," said Jack.

"What?" asked Larry.

"You obviously like her," said Jack. "You should go for it."

"I dunno, man," said Larry. "She's older, probably in her twenties and shit..."

Tommy nodded, not saying anything. He didn't wanna discourage Larry—in fact, he didn't wanna *ever* discourage his Boys from steppin' up to the plate—but the chance of that chick turnin' him down felt pretty high, and he hated seein' his best bro get bummed out by that shit.

"Oh," said Tommy. "Forgot to tell y'all. Horse People got new stuff for us. Some new strain, it's purple and shit."

"Purple?" asked Jack.

Tommy nodded. "Purple weed, man."

"Duuude," said Larry. "That sounds fuckin' raaaaaw..."

"Fuuuuuuck," said Leslie. "I want some of that shit..."

Kevin gripped his butterknife like a weapon. "That...that sounds pretty good..."

"Hell yeah, it does," said Tommy. "And it's been dusted, too."

"Dusted?" asked David. "What's that mean?" Almost the first words he'd said the whole meal.

"Dusted," said Tommy, "means like, sprinklin' pill powder and stuff on it. Apparently, this shit's real fuckin' strong. The purple strain itself, and what they dust it with. Called it *Purple Dream.*"

Leslie's eyes glazed over. "Purple Dreeeeeam..."

David asked, "What kinda pills did they...dust it with?"

"Who gives a fuuuuuuck?" asked Leslie. "Just smoke that shiiiit..."

Tommy shrugged. "Maybe muscle relaxants or somethin'."

"Sometimes people dust weed with painkillers and shit," said Larry. "I smoked weed dusted with codeine once. At least, that's what I think it was. Fucked me up real good."

Jack stroked his chin. "Purple stuff sounds good. The color alone could drive sales."

"Purple shit will sell, y'all!" said Leslie. "I don't even want green shit now that I heard about that purple shit." She savored another bite of her grilled cheese. "*Fuuuuuuck...*"

"That's good input, Leslie," said Jack. "I agree, and the dust could be the icin' on the cake, a differentiator that sets it apart from competin' products."

Larry, Jack, and Leslie buzzed excitedly about Purple Dream for a while. Jack said he wanted to draw up new line graphs, then went on a long spiel about *"differentiators."* Kevin and David stayed silent. Leslie said *"Fuuuuuck"* a lot. Tommy tried to follow the conversation, but his eyes kept drifting to Leslie's remaining oatmeal—

("i like it when you're inside me, tommy...")

—seeing Samantha's cum-covered, blood-smeared face inside the bowl.

("i love you, tomm—")

("you're the onl—")

"When we goin' to Nashville?" asked Leslie.

"Huh?"

Tommy squeezed his eyes shut.

Gotta stop thinkin' about that shit...

"Nashville!" said Leslie. "Nashville-Cashville! So y'all can find coke and shit. I wanna see live country music, and I wanna—"

"We delayed the Nashvillze trip," said Tommy, opening his eyes. "Too risky for that shit. Don't wanna leave the Smokehouse undefended for that long..."

He glanced around for signs of Bill and his Posse.

Something didn't *feel* right.

"I'm okay with delayin' the trip," said Jack, "but, like I said earlier, we should make diversifyin' our procurement a top priority. I don't like relyin' on the Horse People so much..."

"You talked to *him* again?" asked Larry. "Did he—"

"Nah, not *the* Horse Guy," said Tommy. "One of his lackeys."

"You ask him about us sellin' coke?" asked Larry.

"Yep," said Tommy. "Said he'd bring it up with the main dude, but chances were slim he'd go for it. Said we had a long way to go before they'd trust us with coke. I told him other kids in school were sellin' it, and he didn't give a shit at first, but then he said he wanted us to find out who their supplier was, if we could."

Jack twirled his fork. "I'm all about product diversification, especially expandin' into higher margin stuff, like coke. But, like I said earlier—"

A shadow darkened the entire table.

Everyone froze.

A voice, deep and slow, rumbled through the air:

"Heard y'all was askin' for me?"

1970s

CHAPTER IV

CRACKER BARREL, PART II

*Graham had never lost a fight, though
he rarely needed to fight at all.*

*He merely glanced at those less powerful
and commanded them with a word.*

THE HAIR BRISTLED on the back of Tommy's neck.

Time froze as Graham loomed over the table like a mountain blocking the sun.

Leslie held her grilled cheese mid-bite.

"Fuuuuuck..."

Silence reigned. Graham's shadow stretched over them all.

"Ain't got all day, weedboys," said Graham. "Y'all got somethin' to say?"

Tommy closed his hand into a fist.

Mikey wasn't afraid of nobody.

And neither am I.

"Grahaaam," said Tommy. "What's up, maaan?" He rose and attempted a bro-hug, barely able to wrap his arms around Graham's massive torso.

Like huggin' a goddamn boulder...

Graham stood still as a statue. "Glick. Longface. What y'all want?"

Larry's face darkened.

He hated being called Longface.

"Duuude," said Tommy. "We ain't here to start shit. We come in peace, man."

"Yeah?" asked Graham.

"Yeah," said Tommy. "Our beef is with Cunningham and Young. And that Skinny Kenny guy. We just came here to tell ya that."

"Could've just called me," said Graham.

Tommy looked straight into Graham's eyes.

"I wanted to talk to ya face-to-face, man," he said. "Are we cool, or you with them?"

Graham opened his mouth to speak, then halted. Something—intelligence?—flickered in his eyes, but only for a moment.

"I dunno if we're *cool* or not, weedboy," he said, "but I don't roll with those bitches no more. In case ya haven't heard."

"Oh really?" asked Tommy. "Why's that?"

"'Cause Young Charlie's a bitch."

Tommy laughed and then, as if on cue, Jack, Larry and Leslie laughed, too. Kevin and David gripped their forks and knives.

"That Young Charlie," said Tommy, "he really *is* a bitch, ain't he?"

Graham nodded. "Bitched at me all the time for bein' messy, like my mom. And stopped sharin' his coke, so I peaced out."

He flicked his eyes to David.

"What ya gonna do with that knife, four-eyes?"

"David," said Larry. "Drop the knife."

"Huh huh huh..." Graham flung one of Tommy's fries toward David's face. In a seamless blur, David deflected it with his butter knife.

"Fuuuuuck..." said Leslie.

Kevin and David sprang from their seats, clutching their utensils like weapons.

"Whoa, whoa, whoa!" said Larry.

Nearby customers quietened and stared.

"Settle down, now," said Tommy. "Settle down..."

Both Possibles began breathing rapidly, as if bracing for battle.

("let him the fuck go!")

("aaaaaaaaaaaagh!")

("huh huh huh...")

"Sit the fuck down," said Larry.

Kevin looked at David.

("aaaaaaaaaaaaaaaagh!")

They shook their heads.

("you're gonna fuckin' kill him!")

("...can't...bre...athe...")

Slowly, they descended back to their seats,

("huh huh huh...")

never taking their eyes from Graham.

Gradually, nearby customers resumed eating and chatting.

"Sorry about that," said Tommy. "They're just a little nervous, after what ya did to Kevin and all."

"Huh huh huh..." Graham tossed one of Larry's fries into the air and caught it in his gaping mouth. "Your boy charged at me," he said, chewing with his mouth open. "What was I supposed to do?"

Jack gripped his water gun.

A cold drop of sweat rolled down his forehead.

He wouldn't hesitate.

"Fair enough, fair enough..." said Tommy.

Graham shoved a handful of fries into his mouth. "They end up goin' after y'all that night? After y'all fucked up Charlie's house?"

"They never showed up, man..." said Tommy, staring into Graham's mouth full of half-chewed fries.

So that's why they didn't show...

Lost their star quarterback and got afraid to play the game...

Tommy studied Graham's expression, searching for any trace of a lie.

"So you ain't seen'em since?" he asked. "Not hangin' with'em at all?"

For a moment—just a moment—something flickered in Graham's eyes again.

"Nope," he said, swallowing. "Charlie threw a hissy fit and Bill took his side. That *always* happened. I'm done with that!"

He glanced at Jack.

"Why ya got a water gun?"

Oh shit.

Everyone's mouths dropped.

"Uhh..." said Jack.

Tommy's heart pounded.

I fucking told you to put that away, Jack...

You always get sloppy when you're high.

"I...uhh..." said Jack. "...ya see..."

"See what?" Graham grabbed a handful of Larry's fries. "I asked you a question, freckle-face."

Kevin and David's hands glided back to their forks and knives.

Jack coughed. "It's actually because, uhh..."

Leslie dropped her sandwich on her plate. "We're gonna have us a water gun fight after eatin'. Wanna join us?" She stuck out her chest, fixing Graham with the most *"fuck me"* eyes Tommy had ever seen.

"I'll be wearin' my bathin' suit..."

Graham's face turned crimson. "Huh huh huh...really?"

Tommy breathed a sigh of relief.

Fuck yes...

Nice save, Leslie...

Thank God...

"But I gotta, uh..." Graham scratched his head. "Work 'til close today..."

Tommy alternated his gaze between Leslie and Graham.

Interesting...

Even the great Graham Riley fell prey to the charms of a hot girl with big tits.

"Let's hang out sometime soon, then..." said Leslie. "Wanna smoke with you...get fucked up together..."

"Huh huh huh..." chuckled Graham. "I'm cool with that..."

He stared at her cleavage, mouth agape.

Leslie swayed side-to-side. "...*fuuuuck*..."

After an awkward silence, Graham shook his head like a dog shaking off water.

"Gotta get back now."

As he stomped toward the kitchen doors, Tommy leapt from his chair.

"Hey! Wait up!"

Graham halted, peering back at Tommy over his shoulder.

"I wanna invite you again," said Tommy, "to our Smokehouse Party this Saturday. Leslie'll be there, and a bunch of other hot chicks, too. You can smoke with'em, get high together and shit. Who knows..."

He winked.

"...somethin' might happen, man."

Graham's eyes widened, likely thinking of Leslie's tits. He opened his mouth, almost ready to agree, but stopped.

"Can't," he said, "Goin' to a party in Hazard."

"Hazard?"

"Yeah," said Graham. "Hazard Mafia or whatever. Got invited."

Tommy raised an eyebrow. "Didn't know they let Crows in."

Graham nodded as passing customers stared up in awe.

"Guess I'm special."

1970s

CHAPTER V

CONFIDE

"Shh..." Charlie raised a finger across his mouth.

"...cállate...silencio..."

"WOULDN'T IT BE awesome," asked Larry, "if I fucked that Cracker Barrel waitress, right in front of the dumpster?"

Leslie waved goodbye as Jack drove her and the Possibles back to the Smokehouse. Larry gripped his steering wheel, staring at the dumpster behind Cracker Barrel.

"Like," said Larry, "straight-up *dumpster-fucked* her..."

"Kinda gross, dude," said Tommy. "Why would you wanna do that?"

"I don't mean *in* the dumpster, dude," said Larry, "I mean in front of it.

"I get it," said Tommy. "Still seems kinda messed up."

"Just somethin' dirty..." said Larry. "And cool about it..."

Tommy stared out at the Cracker Barrel parking lot. The sky, previously blue, had darkened into a cold Kentucky gray. Thunder rumbled in the distance.

("desayunaste, glick?")

Something still didn't *feel* right.

*("desa-*fuckin'*-yunaste?")*

Something about—

"Dude," said Larry, "if I did get to fuck that Cracker Barrel girl, I would *only* dumpster-fuck her. Right over there, in front of that one. Like, that's how we gotta fuck. Ain't no other place to do it."

"You really think so?"

But the more Tommy thought about it, the more he admitted there might be a certain *allure* to fuckin' a Cracker Barrel girl in front of the Cracker Barrel dumpster.

Kinda epic.

Poetic, even.

Larry turned his long face toward Tommy. "I really do think so, man. Unless it was cold outside and shit."

He turned his misty-eyed gaze back to the dumpster.

"Only dumpster-fucked once, man."

"Who?"

"Leslie."

Tommy nodded.

No surprise there.

"Was it like you thought it'd be?"

"Yes and no," said Larry. "It was hot as fuck when we were doin' it, but she kept on sayin' *'Fuuuuuck'* and shit, like *'Fuuuuck, I can't believe we're fuckin' in front of a dumpster, this is gross as shit, y'all, fuuuuuck...'"*

"She said that? While y'all were fuckin'?"

Larry nodded. "And while she was suckin', too. And at first it was hot, 'cause it was like, *'Oh man, we're doin' this dirty dumpster-suckin'-and-fuckin','* and her complainin' about it made it even *more* hot. I mean, at first, at least. But then she told me to hurry up and nut, and after I busted she got all upset and was like, *'I am never fuckin' here again!'* Like she felt fuckin' *dirtied* by it or somethin'. And then, I dunno, felt weird drivin' her home, dude. She was cryin' and shit."

"Dude," said Tommy. "You probably made her feel dirty as fuck. That's why she fuckin' cried. What made you even think of bangin' in front of a dumpster?"

"It was my brother," said Larry. "Heard him talkin' about it with his friends when I was little. He was like, *'Dude, you ain't fucked 'til you dumpster-fucked!'* And it's always stuck with me since then. Knew I had to make it my thing."

"Your thing, huh?" asked Tommy. "Guess I can get that..."

On some level, he could relate—when your older brother did shit you thought was cool, you wanted to try it, too.

Mikey.

He removed his cap and stared at the crow on the front. Never knew much about Mikey's love life—only the drugs, the violence, the fame—the Boys' side of him. He'd thought about looking up Mikey's old girlfriends, hoping to learn more about that part of him, maybe even find a clue as to why he—

He shook his head.

Never got around to that shit, though...

Larry continued. "...and it's different from fuckin' beside a trash can or somethin'..."

Tommy leaned back in his seat and sighed. Normally he'd enjoy this kinda bro-talk with Larry, but his thoughts still haunted him.

Thoughts of Mikey,

("find it tommy...")

and that "temple" or whatever,

("the temple...")

and Samantha,

("i love you, tommy...")
with her fucking blood-smeared, cum-covered face.
("you're the only one I let do this...")
Just—
("the temple...")
couldn't—
("desayunaste?")
concentrate.

Larry finally stopped talking about dumpster-fucking and turned his gaze to the rearview mirror.

"Tell me the truth, man. Is my face really *that* long?"

"No," said Tommy. "It's not."

"You sure?" asked Larry. "You ain't just sayin' that, are ya?"

"I mean," said Tommy, "okay, it is *kinda* long. Like, a little. But not *that* long. It's just 'cause your name is 'Larry,' and starts with *L*. If your name had been Mark or Adam, nobody would call ya that."

"Why you think the Cracker Barrel chick turned me down, then?" asked Larry. "She ain't got no boyfriend, man. You could tell that was bullshit."

"Dude, she was *smokin'*," said Tommy, even though she wasn't. Not really. "And she's older than us. Maybe even early twenties? If you were a hot chick in your twenties, would *you* date a fuckin' high schooler?"

"Guess not..." said Larry. "...so you don't think it was, ya know, 'cause my face is long?"

"Naaah, dude," said Tommy. "Fuck no. She would've turned down anybody that's still in high school. I'm just proud you had the balls to ask her, man. I sure wouldn't."

He bro-punched Larry's arm.

"Now quit worryin' about how long your face is. That's pussy shit."

Larry nodded, looking satisfied. He leaned back and patted his stomach. "Man, I'm sooo full now..."

Outside, the sky continued to darken.

("desayunaste, glick!")

("desa-fuckin'-yunaste!")

"Hey," said Tommy, "you know what *'desayunaste'* means?"

"Desa-what?" asked Larry. "That Spanish?"

"Think so..."

Tommy peered out the window. The first heavy raindrops splattered on the glass, blurring his view of the outside world.

"Nah, don't speak no spic," said Larry. "Anyway, when we pickin' up that purple stuff? From the Horse People? What's it called again?"

"Purple Dream," said Tommy. "Said they'll tell me soon."

"I'll roll with you, dude," said Larry. "I know dealin' with them is always kinda weird."

"Yeah..." said Tommy. "...hope we don't gotta meet with the main guy again..."

"Dude," said Larry, "if we meet with the main guy again, we better not have to—"

"Don't even say it," said Tommy.

Didn't even wanna remember that shit.

("y'all boys like horses?")

("pretty, pretty little hors—")

Larry asked, "We bustin' that shit out at the party?"

"Could sample a bit," said Tommy. "Probably put us the fuck to sleep, though. I mean, I assume that's why they call it Purple Dream. Good to smoke at the end of the party, maybe. When the sun is comin' up..."

Tommy stared out the window in silence. The first few raindrops still clung to the pane, defying gravity.

"Hey," said Larry, "is somethin' botherin' you, man?"

"You could tell, right?"

Larry could tell.

Larry could always tell.

"Dude," said Larry. "I been waitin' for you to open up to me all week. You ain't acted the same since that Bill Cunningham bitch—"

"—talked shit," said Tommy.

("i fucked your girlfriend after prom...")

("i took her fuckin' cherry")

"Larry, my man..." said Tommy. "You're my boy. My brother."

"Always," said Larry.

"I need you to tell me somethin'," said Tommy. "Honestly."

"What's up?"

"Do you think...."

Tommy paused.

Didn't even like *talkin'* about this shit.

("i hope that bitch brushed her t—")

"...you think Bill was tellin' the truth?" asked Tommy. "About him and Samantha? After prom?"

"Naaah, man," said Larry. "He was just talkin' shit. Tryin' to get a rise outta you. Why you even think he was tellin' the truth? Samantha's square as shit. Everybody knows that. She won't even fuck you."

("i love you, tommy...")

("you're the only one i'll let do this...")

"We fucked, Larry."

"What? *Y'all fucked?*"

"It's why we got back together."

"But you said—"

"'Cause she made me swear to God not to tell anyone, man. Not any of the Boys, not even you."

"Dude..." Larry looked as if his world perception had shifted. "How many times?"

"Just twice," said Tommy. "Before she went off to work at Girl Scout camp."

"Was it awesome?"

"Fuck yeah, it was."

("i like it when you're inside me, tommy...")

("it feels good...")

"That's the thing, man..." said Tommy. "...it was...*too* good..."

"Too good?" asked Larry. "What do ya mean?"

"Like she was...experienced, man," said Tommy. "Or seemed like it."

"Dude, that's how all them square girls are," said Larry. "Once they actually start fuckin' and suckin' and shit, most of 'em turn real slutty, real fast. Square girls are actually *more* horny than slutty girls, and do more freaky shit. They just make you work harder for it. World's weird like that."

"That's not all, man," said Tommy. "She didn't have her hymen."

"What?"

"Said she lost it in gymnastics."

"She didn't have no fuckin' cherry, dude?"

Tommy shook his head.

"That *does* happen, though," said Larry. "I mean, I heard it does. Like in gymnastics and shit. Don't know if it's true or not. But you really think she gave up her V to Bill Cunningham? When they just went to prom as friends? Barely even knew each other?"

"See," said Tommy, "it's also what Bill *said,* man..."

(*"she liked ridin' on top the best..."*)

"The shit he knew..."

"Like what?" asked Larry.

"Like, that she likes ridin' on top the best," said Tommy.

"So?" asked Larry. "That don't mean shit. Lucky guess, man. A lot of girls like ridin' on top."

"And that..." said Tommy.

(*"i want you to..."*)

"...that she wanted it on her face..."

(*"promise me, tommy..."*)

(*"promise me you'll give it to me like that..."*)

"...and in her mouth..." said Tommy. "...like, that's how she *had* to have it..."

"What?"

Tommy turned his gaze back to the window.

Didn't even wanna *look* at Larry when talkin' about Samantha like this. Not his Samantha. She was perfect.

At least—

—he *thought* she was.

"Samantha-fuckin'-Henson," said Larry, "one of the most *ideal* girls in Crow, possibly in the whole of Tri, like the type that's on the cover of *Teen* magazine and shit, said she wanted you to cum on her face? And in her fuckin' mouth?"

"I couldn't believe it either, dude," said Tommy. "And we'd never even talked about that kinda shit before. I mean, I wore a condom, so I was just gonna bust inside the—"

"She made you wear a condom?"

"Yeah."

"And then she said *'When you cum, I want you to cum on my face, and in my mouth'*?"

"Yep..."

"And she swallowed, too?"

"Yep..."

"Dude, she's a nympho-maniac-sl—"

"Hey!"

Larry fell silent, looking sheepish.

"My bad, man..." he said. "...but she said she was a virgin, right?"

"Yeah..."

"Dude," said Larry. "That ain't what virgins ask for. Ain't no virgin girl in the world ever asked for that shit. Not in the whole history of mankind."

"I know..." said Tommy. "And after we fucked, I kept on askin' her why she wanted that, but she got upset, like she'd done somethin' wrong. She said she thought that's how all guys liked it. And I thought it was weird, how she said '*all* guys'..."

He sighed and looked away.

"But I didn't think much of it," he said. "Until Bill-fuckin'-Cunningham said that shit..."

Larry nodded.

They both gazed into the parking lot for a while.

Thunder rumbled—closer this time.

"You can't call her, right?" asked Larry. "'Cause she's at Girl Scout camp."

"Nope," said Tommy. "No phones in their cabins. She's been writin' me letters every week, though."

"Don't ask her in a letter."

"I ain't gonna ask her in no fuckin' letter," said Tommy. "*Dear Samantha, did you let Bill Cunningham fuck you, and then cum on your face, and in your mouth, after prom? And did you swallow his jism? Love, Tommy.*"

"Don't mention it 'til you meet her, dude," said Larry. "Don't give her any warnin'. And when she comes back, you get her alone and look her straight in the fuckin' eyes, and you ask her."

Thunder crashed overhead—so violently it shook Larry's truck.

"You'll know..." said Larry. "You'll know if it's true or not."

Tommy sighed. Heavy raindrops splashed against the pavement.

Would I?

Samantha was smart—smart as fuck. Maybe even smarter than Jack, even though she was three years younger. Lyin' required intelligence—the higher one's intelligence, the better one lied.

(she lied, tommy...)

(she fucking li—)

"What you gonna do if it *is* true?" asked Larry. "Break up with her?"

"Fuck yeah, I'm breakin' up with her," said Tommy. "I ain't datin' no fuckin' slut that's fucked Bill Cunningham. And not only that, we'll *destroy* her reputation, man. Me, you, and the Boys, we'll tell everyone—everyone in the whole damn school, in the whole damn Tri is gonna know how she *begged* for me and Bill to blast on her face and in her mouth like that, and then they'll know what a fucking slut, what a whore she is, and she'll have to transfer schools it'll get so fuckin'—"

"Okay, okay, man," said Larry. "If that's how you wanna play it, we can do that. Destroy her rep. Make her switch schools and shit. Because she'll fuckin' have to after that shit gets out. But—"

"But what?" asked Tommy.

Samantha's visage appeared before him—her *face,* her fucking cum-covered and blood-smeared fa—

"But," said Larry, "like I said back then, when her and Bill went to prom..."

"I know, I know..." Tommy squeezed his eyes shut, pushing her visage away. "I'm the one who broke up with her...so it's fair game when you're broke up...anything goes..."

A jagged streak of lightning lit up the distant sky. Tommy wondered, not for the first time, why it always seemed to strike far away. Maybe one day it'd strike closer—when God decided.

"I hate to say this, man," said Larry, "but maybe her and Bill already had somethin' goin' on? Even before prom?"

Fuck.

Tommy clenched his jaw.

Was she lyin' about that too?

Was there more to them goin' to prom together?

"Okay," said Tommy. "That's somethin' else to think about...but she swore up and down about that shit, man..."

("i swear we didn't do anything, tommy!")

("i swear!")

"...swore they were just friends, that they barely knew each other..."

("please stop asking me about it!")

("please!")

"She swore up and down, man..."

(but she didn't look you in the eyes...)

(did she, tommy?)

A wave of bitterness crept into his mouth.

If she fucking lied...

"Man, that's fucked up," said Larry. He shook his head. "Anyway, at least we know shit ain't gonna happen at our party this Saturday. That's one problem fuckin' solved."

The sky cracked with thunder again. Rain pelted the truck like machine gun bullets. Amidst the barrage, Graham's stupid, slow chuckle pushed through.

("huh huh huh...")

That flash...

What was that *flash* he'd seen in Graham's eyes?

Intelligence?

Like he was—

Nah.

Dumbfuck's too stupid to lie that good.

"Glad they don't got Graham no more," said Tommy. "Still got three guys, though..."

"Who cares?" asked Larry. "They ain't shit without Graham. And we'll not only be eight guys strong, but have lots of people backin' us up, too. Friends of the Boys. And Possible Possibles."

He started his truck.

"They'd be *insane* to attack us without Graham. Besides, what could three guys do?"

As they pulled out of the parking lot, Tommy drummed three fingers against the dashboard:

One—Bill Cunningham.

Two—Charlie Young.

Three—Kenny Moser.

What *could* three guys do?

Lightning flashed again, creeping ever closer.

1970s

CHAPTER VI

LA BAMBA

"You know I can speak, fuckin', español?

That's Spanish, for fuckin' Spanish, man…"

YOUNG CHARLIE WALTZED out of Walmart into the balmy evening air, whistling "La Bamba." Still hadn't memorized all the lyrics yet, but he'd resolved to within a week or so. Surely, singin' the whole song in straight-up *español* would impress a whole lotta bitches.

"Yo no soy marinero..."

If that couldn't, what would?

"Yo no soy marinero, soy capitán, soy capitán..."

As he pushed his cart across the parking lot, he imagined himself in Mexico surrounded by a shit-ton of *mamacitas*, all sippin' margaritas and snortin' *la cocaína* together. Sometimes on a beach, occasionally beside a swimming pool.

"La, la, bamba..."

Mexican *mamacitas* of all ethnicities and colors.

Young Charlie didn't discriminate—no sir, he would fuck them all.

"La, la, bamba..."

As he sang,

"La, la, bamba..."

he lost himself in fantasy,

"La, la, bamba..."

not seeing the Asian boy wearing thick glasses,

"La, la, ba—"

until he stood right before him.

"Fuck!"

Charlie flicked his eyes from the Asian dude to a group farther off in the parking lot. Bullshit hippie music drifted through the air.

"Now you listen *here*, little Asian boy," said Charlie. "I don't want no trouble now. I'm just buyin' my fuckin' Marlboros and—"

The Asian boy raised his fist high.

"SMOKE-TOWN-BOYS, RALLY-UUUUUUP!"

1970s

CHAPTER VII

WE USED TO SMOKE TOGETHER

"And I appreciate you tellin' me that, man.

About your brother.

That's what real friends, mejores amigos, are fuckin' for."

"IT'S YOUNG CHARLIE!"

"Get him!"

"Fuck-fuck-fuck!" Charlie sprinted past the Asian boy toward his dad's black Camaro.

"You runnin' from us, Charlie?"

Footsteps thundered behind him.

He fumbled with his keys.

"C'mon, motherfucker!" said Charlie. *"C'mon, c'mon, c'mon!"*

Couldn't even find the right fucking one.

"Fuckin' *c'mon,* now!"

The key made a metallic *click* as it slid into place.

"Yes! *Adiós,* motherf—"

"Where ya goin', Young Charlie?"

Charlie's face exploded with pain as it slammed into the car door. A thick, muscular arm coiled around his neck.

"Too slow," said Mouse. "Too slow..."

Tiny yellow sparks danced before Charlie's eyes.

Blood trickled from his nose.

Before him stood the Smoketown Boys.

***

"C'mon, *amigos!*" said Charlie. "Just lemme me alone, now! Ain't about no bullshit today!"

"Just wanna talk to ya..." Mouse tightened his arm around Charlie's neck.

"Yeah..." said Larry, rolling his sleeves up. "And maybe fuck ya up a little, too..."

Leslie and Lacey strolled over, lips between their teeth.

"Now c'mon, y'all!" said Charlie. "I didn't start no shit since then! Glick? Where's Glick?"

Tommy stepped forward from behind his Boys.

"C'mon, Tommy!" said Charlie. "Just lemme alone, man! Ain't about no bullshit, now!"

"I dunno, Young..." said Tommy.

("i hope that bitch brushed her teeth!")

"What was that shit you said..."

(*"i hope that bitch brushed her t—"*)

"...about my fuckin' girlfriend..."

(*"i hope that bitch—"*)

"...brushin' her fuckin' teeth?"

Tommy clenched his hands into fists.

"Oh, c'mon, *amigo!*" said Charlie. "I was just talkin' shit! You know how—*UUGGGH!*"

In a blur of motion, Tommy slammed his fist into Charlie's stomach.

His Boys cheered.

Charlie keeled over, coughing.

"...fuckin' *cabrón*..."

Blood pounded in Tommy's ears.

"Have *you* brushed your teeth today, Young Charlie?"

'*Cause you're gonna fuckin' need to...*

"...fuckin' *hijo de tu puta madre*..." said Charlie. "...told ya I didn't want no bullsh—*UUGGGH!*"

Another blur of motion—Tommy's fist crashed into Charlie's stomach.

His Boys cheered louder.

"*Hit 'em in his teeth, Tommy!*"

"*Knock his fuckin' teeth out!*"

Charlie gasped for air.

"...st-op..."

Mouse snickered. "You goin' for his teeth next?"

Tommy nodded.

Mouse released his headlock and grabbed Charlie's face, directing it toward Tommy.

"There ya go, Young. Just look at Tommy, now. Look right at him..."

"*Knock 'em out, Tommy!*"

"*Knock his fuckin' teeth out!*"

The evening sun glinted off Charlie's tear-streaked face. As he clutched his stomach, wheezing for air, blood and spit dangled from his chin.

"...I'm...sorry..."

"What?" asked Tommy. "What'd you say, Young?"

"Sorry..." He coughed, spraying blood. "...I said that..."

(*"i hope that bitch brushed her teeth!"*)

Tommy's pulse pounded in his ears, heat crawling up his neck.

No.

"Sorry" didn't fucking cut it.

He drew his fist back, zeroing in on Charlie's two front teeth.

One good punch.

One good punch to knock those fuckers out.

"You're gonna brush the blood off *your* fuckin' teeth, Char—"

"We used to smoke together!" said Charlie.

Tommy's eyes widened.

("you can come to my place anytime...")

("we'll fuckin' chill and smoke, like true amigos, *man...")*

"We used to smoke together, man!"

("hey, what kinda cigarettes you like?")

("i like fuckin' marlboro's...")

("ya know, the red-and-white label kind...")

Slowly, Tommy lowered his fist.

("ya know I can speak, fuckin', español?")

("that's spanish, for fuckin' spanish, man...")

They *did* used to smoke together.

("maybe you can learn español, *too...")*

("then we can talk in code and shit...")

("ain't nobody'll know what we're sayin'...")

They used to smoke together, and chill together.

And that *meant* something.

"What're you doin'?" asked Mouse. "Fuck his shit up!"

"Fuck his shit up, Tommy!"

"Knock his fuckin' teeth out!"

"No..." said Tommy. "Roll out."

"What?" asked Mouse and Larry.

"Roll out," said Tommy. "Gonna talk with Young. One-on-one."

"But Tommy—"

"I said, *roll-the-fuck-out!"*

*

The disco ball rotated with a dreamlike quality, casting brief reflections of light upon the Crow County Prom attendees.

"Would you like to sign the Prom Promise?"

"Huh?" asked Tommy.

The question came from a chick at a nearby booth in the corner of the dance floor. Some nerdy girl with glasses whose name Tommy never cared to remember.

"Prom Promise?" asked Jack, his arm around his date.

"What's that bullshit?" asked Larry, holding hands with his.

"Is it like," asked Lacey, "where each girl promises to dance with like, five different guys?"

"I get to dance with all y'all, then!" Leslie rubbed against Tommy's shoulder like a cat, and he almost wrapped his arm around her, but didn't.

"Nah," said Tommy. "Read the sign. Just some bullshit."

"Sign the PROM PROMISE!" *read the banner on the booth.*

"And PROMISE, that on PROM NIGHT you:

1. Won't do drugs!
2. Won't drink alcohol!
3. Won't have pre-marital sex!

And then PROMISE that you'll just have a good ol' time!"

"That's hilarious!" Jack laughed and slapped his knee.

Larry cackled. "Who even came up with this shit?"

"Just the idea behind it," said Jack, "is hilarious!"

"Prom Promise, huh?" Mouse stepped forward. "I'll sign that shit, give it up." He snatched the pen from the four-eyed chick.

"Dude," said Jack, "are you for real?"

"Here ya go..." said Mouse while signing. "I...fuckin'...promise..."

"Mouse," said Larry, "are you really signin' that bullsh—"

"I promise to get high!" said Mouse.

He threw the pen to the floor, spreading his arms wide.

"I promise to get fucked up! On drugs and shit!"

Everyone laughed.

"I promise to bust a nut!" said Mouse. "Deep inside of Lacey!"

The laughter grew to a roar.

"Oh, c'mon, Mouse," said Lacey, blushing. "Don't be sayin' all that..."

"Fuuuuuuck..." said Leslie.

The lights dimmed and the air pulsed with a soft, romantic melody, coaxing everyone back to the dance floor.

"C'mon, Tommy!" said Lacey. "Dance with me!"

As his Boys and their dates sauntered away, still cackling about Mouse's "Prom Promise" joke, Tommy glanced back at the four-eyed chick standing awkwardly in the booth. Despite the dimmed lights, her face, now beet-red, remained visible.

"Here's your pen," said Tommy, returning the pen Mouse had thrown on the floor. "Sorry about my Boys. They like to joke and shit."

The four-eyed chick just stood there, like a statue.

"You havin' a good time tonight?" he asked.

No response.

"Cool," said Tommy. "I'll see ya around..."

Whatever...

"Jesus," he said, returning to Leslie. "Who the hell comes to prom to do that bullshit?"

"Who gives a fuuuuuuuck," said Leslie. "Let's dance! I'm your fuckin' date, Tommy! Dance with me!"

Tommy scanned the dance floor.

Where was she?

Samantha?

And that piece of shit Bill Cunningham?

"Let's get some punch first..."

***

Tommy ladled punch from the glass bowl into his cup. Someone had already spiked it, and getting fucked up on its cheap, vodka-infused fruitiness remained the only good thing about the bullshit night so far.

(where are they, tommy?)

(where's samantha and bill...)

For the fifth time in a row, he scanned the dance floor for the two people responsible for ruinin' his fuckin' night.

(maybe they snuck off somewhere...)

No, they didn't.

Just couldn't see their faces in the dark.

That's all.

(you sure about that, tommy?)

"*Fuuuuuck, Tommy...*" *said Leslie.* "*You gotta dance with me. Samantha's dancin' with—*"

"*Shut the fuck up, already!*" *said Tommy.* "*I told you, don't even mention her fuckin' name.*"

Leslie turned away.

Soft music pulsed in the background, the rhythm slow and steady as the dancers moved together, lost in the moment. Everyone seemed to be having the time of their lives.

Everyone except him.

He sighed and turned to Leslie, still faced away.

Shouldn't have talked to her like that.

Wasn't her fault Samantha-fuckin'-Henson was a queen-fuckin'-bitch who just had to go to prom with Bill-fuckin'-Cunningham, who he never fuckin' liked.

"*Hey,*" *said Tommy.* "*Sorry I snapped at ya. Drink some of this. Get you fucked up a little.*"

Leslie sipped the punch, still refusing to meet his gaze. A tear rolled down her cheek.

Oh shit...

Is she cryin'?

Is she cryin' at prom?

"*Hey,*" *said Tommy.* "*You look good tonight. I mean, damn good.*"

It was true—most guys in school would've killed to go to prom with Leslie. Her dress showed off her body in a way that made dudes melt. But he didn't feel...attracted to her. He tried. He tried hard as hell to work up the desire to fuck her. And he did admire things about her—her tits, her legs, her ass. Admired the hell out of 'em. But even fucking her, no strings attached, like all his Boys already had, like she wanted him to, turned him off.

She wasn't smart, cool, or funny like Samantha.

She wasn't her.

She wasn't Samantha.

And knowing that Samantha—his Samantha—rested in the arms of Bill-fucking-Cunningham made him want her even fucking more.

(where are they, tommy?)

(what are they doing?)

Leslie wiped tears away. "So why won't you even dance with me?"

"Not in the mood yet," *said Tommy.* "Ya know, with all the bullshit—"

"Just beat that Bill dude's ass, then!" *said Leslie.* "Or stop mopin' around and dance with me!"

She shot him a glare that could stop an army.

"Actin' like a bitch don't suit you, Tommy."

Her high heels click-clacked as she stormed to the bathroom.

"Leslie!"

Damn.

Tommy stood alone by the punchbowl, feeling foolish.

Small and foolish.

First time he'd ever heard Leslie talk like that.

Didn't even know she could *talk like that.*

Out of instinct he reached for his cap—nope, no Mikey to give advice this time.

He turned back to the dance floor. Everyone seemed focused on dancing as closely as possible with their dates, basically fuckin' with their clothes on, while he just stood there.

Like a loser.

Like a bitch.

He clenched his hands into fists.

Maybe Leslie was right—

—maybe he should *beat the fuck outta that shithead's face tonight. Right in front of Samantha, right on the fucking dance floor so she'd see Bill's teeth fucking fly, and then he'd look into her eyes and say—*

"Glick," *said a voice beside him.*

Charlie Young poured clear liquid from a flask into the punch bowl.

"Young Charlie," *said Tommy.* "I was gonna spike the punch, but I guess ya beat me to it."

"Sí, sí..." *said Charlie.* "But you can always spike it up again."

He ladled punch into his cup and stepped beside Tommy, eyes on the dance floor.

"You havin' a good time tonight?"

"Yeah..." *said Tommy.* "I mean, it's alright. Whatever."

Charlie took a sip from his cup.

"Sí, sí...*Prom is kinda bullshit, ain't it?*"

"Yep," said Tommy. "*Kinda is...*"

He glanced around.

If Young was nearby, maybe Bill was, too?

With Saman—

"Hey," said Charlie, "*speakin' of bullshit, heard you was talkin' some?*"

"Huh?"

"*Some bullshit, man?*" asked Charlie. "*Heard you was talkin' some? Sayin' you was gonna beat Bill's ass tonight? Right here on the dance floor?*"

Tommy squeezed his cup.

"I mean," said Charlie, "*correct me if I'm wrong, now. If I misheard that shit, then, fuckin', olvídalo, man. Just olvídalo that shit.*"

Tommy swallowed his punch, then turned to face Charlie.

Didn't know what olvídalo *meant.*

Nor did he give a fuck.

"Nah," said Tommy. "*You didn't mishear shit. That's what I said, and what I might fuckin' do. Before the night's over.*"

"Is that fuckin' so?" *Charlie took a long sip from his cup.*

"It is," said Tommy. "*But that's between me and Bill. Ain't got no problem with you, Young. We used to smoke together. We're cool.*"

Charlie nodded. "Nah, see, that's where you're wrong, ese. 'Cause if you fuck with Bill, then you fuck with me."

"Is that so?" asked Tommy. "*You know my Boys'll back me up if you get involved, right? So I'd fuckin' stay—*"

"Did you make a Prom Promise, Glick?" asked Charlie.

Tommy locked eyes with him.

"Nah, I ain't about that bullshit," said Tommy. "*Did you?*"

Something cold and terrifying darkened Charlie's face.

"Nah, but I'm about to, right the fuck now."

The music cut off.

An eerie silence enveloped the dance floor.

Everyone glanced around, confused.

"I promise I got a knife in my right pocket," said Charlie.

"And if you fuck with Bill,

I'll cut your goddamn nose off."

*

Tommy and Charlie leaned against Charlie's dad's black Camaro. The setting sun's rays shifted from orange to crimson. After Charlie had finally stopped coughing and clutching his stomach, Tommy spoke.

"Need some tissues? For your nose?"

Charlie wiped his nose, flinging blood onto the pavement.

"Don't need no fuckin' tissues, man..."

He snorted and spat.

"How's your stomach?" asked Tommy.

Charlie glared. "How you think, *hombre?*"

Tommy nodded. Gettin' punched in the stomach twice could make a guy pissy.

"You hit pretty hard," said Charlie. "I'll give ya fuckin' that..."

Tommy nodded again, satisfied with himself.

Glad you realize that, Young...

I do hit hard.

Hard and fast.

"For what it's worth," said Tommy, "I only meant to *egg* your house. The bricks through the windows and shit, that was all the Possibles. Didn't tell'em to do that."

He shook his head.

"They're hard to rein in sometimes..."

Charlie spat another blood-loogie on the pavement.

"The fuck are 'the Possibles'?"

"That's what we call the guys who might join us," said Tommy. "If we let'em."

"The Possibles, huh..." Charlie seemed on the verge of making a smartass comment, but stopped.

Good...

Best not run your mouth, Young...

Or I will knock those fuckin' teeth out.

"Actually," said Charlie, "the eggs pissed me off more than the windows."

"Really?"

"*Sí,*" said Charlie. "I mean, gettin' the windows fixed cost a shit-ton of money, man, but I got a dude to fix'em up real quick. Those eggs, though..."

He shook his head and scowled.

"...started smellin' real bad, *ese*. I'm talkin' *los-huevos*-fuckin'-*horrendos*..."

Tommy fought back a grin. "Hot summer sun'll do that, won't it?"

"It sure fuckin' will," said Charlie. "And scrubbin'em off was such a pain in the ass. And then ants and bugs started crawlin' all over the house, tryin' to eat them *horrendos* fuckin' eggs..."

He spat.

"Fuckin' nightmare..."

"Could've used your hose," said Tommy.

"Huh?"

"Your water hose," said Tommy. "Could've used it to power-spray the eggs off the sides of your house. Didn't need to actually scrub'em off."

Charlie narrowed his eyes.

"Ya know," he said, "I didn't even think of that..."

Tommy shrugged. He reckoned Mouse's elephant-dung sized poop on Young's living room carpet posed the *real* nightmare, not the eggs, but it seemed better not to mention it.

"I know how you are," said Tommy, "about keepin' shit neat and tidy. I just had to get under your skin, after y'all talked all that bullshit at Dairy Queen."

He paused, considering how much to reveal.

"Honestly, I would've preferred to have egged Bill's house," he said. "But ya know, his fuckin' dad and all..."

"*Sí, sí,*" said Charlie. "Not a bright idea, to egg the fuckin' sheriff's house..."

A strikingly hot mom loaded groceries into a nearby van while her kids practiced dance moves. She leaned forward, exposing a full view of her cleavage.

Charlie whistled. "That's a *mamacita madre* if I ever saw one..."

The hot mom cast a knowing glance in their direction, as if to ask, *"Y'all boys like that?"*

"She is hot..." said Tommy. "So you still speakin' that Spanish shit real good, huh?"

"*Sí,*" said Charlie. "*Tú también deberías.*"

Tommy didn't know what that meant, nor did he give a shit enough to ask. He needed to drill down, find out what Young was planning. Even without Graham, they had to be planning something. *They had to.*

"How much fixin' the windows cost ya?" asked Tommy.

"A hundred bucks per fuckin' window."

Tommy whistled. "Damn..."

"Y'all done broke my piggy bank," said Charlie. "And you know I live alone now, right? My dad's in jail again. Mom's doin' whatever. So it's not like my parents can pay for that shit."

"Sorry to hear that..." said Tommy. "Didn't know your dad was in jail, man."

He really wasn't sorry about it, not one fucking bit, but if he wanted any truth from Young he had to play it that way.

"Smoke Monkey with me?" He pulled out a tin of hand-rolled Monkey cigs.

Charlie reached to take one, then hesitated.

"Go ahead," said Tommy. "Help you chill out..."

"Nope." Charlie pulled his hand back. "Think I'll just smoke my Marlboros..."

"Right on, man," said Tommy. "Right on..."

They lit their respective cigs and took their first puffs.

"Still like that red-and-white label kind, huh?" asked Tommy.

"Only kind that's worth smokin'," said Charlie. "Ain't about no cartoon camels."

"I gotcha, I gotcha..."

Young was likely the only person in the world who actually gave a shit how cigarette packs looked. But, if Tommy really thought about it, a cartoon camel did seem kinda ridiculous.

"I'll tell ya what, Young," said Tommy. "I feel bad about the windows. So how about this: we start buyin' coke from you."

Charlie's eyes widened.

"You for real, *ese?*"

Tommy nodded. "Two hundred dollars' worth a week. For a couple weeks to start off. See how shit goes."

"You ain't fuckin' with me, are ya?" asked Charlie. "'Cause I'm tired of the bullshit, man, I don't want no more—"

"I ain't fuckin' with ya, Young," said Tommy. "Just gotta clear it with the rest of the Boys. We don't spend squad money without a vote. But I'll make it pass."

Charlie looked at him with suspicion.

"That *would* help a lot, man. If y'all actually fuckin' did that..."

"We will," said Tommy. "And if we can sell it all, which, *if* your shit is good—"

"It is," said Charlie.

"—then we could start doin' business together. On the regular. And then you can make a shit-ton of money. Way more than those windows cost."

Charlie took a puff of his cigarette, eyeing him cautiously.

"That's pretty decent of ya, Tommy. If ya actually mean that."

"I do," said Tommy. "But I wanna ask you some questions, first."

Charlie nodded.

"Adelante."

Tommy took a good, long look at Charlie, studying him the way he'd studied Graham, searching for any trace of a lie; any *hint* Charlie might be hiding something.

"Back at prom," said Tommy, "you remember what you said to me?"

Charlie met his gaze.

"I sure fuckin' do."

Tommy drew deeply from his cig.

"Did you really have a knife on ya?"

Charlie didn't blink.

"I sure fuckin' did."

Tommy remained still, letting the smoke drift from his mouth.

"Uh-huh," he said. "And were you really gonna cut my nose off?"

"Naaah," said Charlie, never breaking eye-contact. "Was probably just gonna stab ya or somethin.'"

Tommy laughed.

Charlie stared for a moment, looking confused, then laughed a little, too.

"You talk shit good, man," said Tommy, his laughter fading. "Almost believed ya there. For a second."

He took a long drag, turning away as he exhaled smoke.

"You're a good actor, man..."

He turned back to Charlie and stared.

"You actin' now?"

Charlie stared back, unblinking.

"Whatcha mean, *ese?*"

"The Young Charlie I knew," said Tommy, "would've went *berserk* if someone fucked up his house like we did. Would've fought twenty lions in a cage, man. Barehanded. For even less."

Charlie stroked his circle beard, eyes twinkling.

"Want me to be honest with ya, *ese?*" asked Charlie. "I mean, *real* fuckin' honest?"

"Adelante," said Tommy, unsure of what the word really meant. He'd never taken Spanish and barely remembered what Charlie had taught him. *Adelante* sounded good, though.

"We'd planned to, that fuckin' night," said Charlie. "Was gonna bring down the mother of all ass-beatins' on y'all. Like a holy-fuckin'-reckonin'. But Graham started actin' like an asshole, sayin' he wanted more coke after already snortin' half my shit, and then he wouldn't roll with us if I didn't let him fuckin' key up beforehand."

Tommy stared straight into Charlie's eyes.

"Is that so?"

"Sí," said Charlie. "I mean, that's the *main* reason. 'Cause we didn't have Graham-cracker."

Tommy blew smoke in the air.

Nope.

Too simple.

Had to be more.

"That the only reason?" asked Tommy.

Tell me the truth, Young...

Or, by God, I will knock all your fuckin' teeth out...

Right here in this goddamn Walmart parking lot.

Charlie fixed Tommy with a pale stare. "I mean, I was fuckin' pissed at y'all, *ese*. But Bill held me back, said only me, him and Kenny didn't stand a chance, since y'all had the numbers and shit. So we decided to bide our time, come up with some badass plan to get revenge. I'm talkin' epic revenge, man, straight-up *brutality*, just like Black—"

For a moment, something flashed in Charlie's eyes,

("ya desayunaste?")

something cold and terrifying,

("desayunaste, glick?")
something Tommy had glimpsed at prom,
("desayunaste?")
but only for a moment.
("DESA-FUCKIN'-YUNASTE?")
"And?" asked Tommy. "When's that 'epic-fuckin'-revenge' gonna happen, huh?"

Charlie shook his head, as if recalling something unpleasant.

"Then me and Bill got into it..." said Charlie. "...and Kenny took *his* side."

Tommy squeezed his Monkey cig between his fingers.

Truth.

Finally.

Fucking—

—truth.

"So you and Bill ain't a little Posse no more?" asked Tommy.

"I don't even hang with that fucker anymore."

"Oh?" asked Tommy, his gaze never leaving Charlie's face. "What happened?"

"Man," said Charlie, "that *hombre's* got some weird fuckin' things about him..."

"Like what?"

"You ain't gonna believe this shit," said Charlie, "but he actually believes that—"

He paused.

Tommy raised an eyebrow. "Believes what?"

Charlie stared at the sunset, lost in thought.

"Believes *what*, Young?"

"...that his fuckin' *dreams* tell him stuff. Like the future and shit. Or what he should do."

Tommy nearly dropped his cig.

"The fuck?"

"That's what *I* said, man," said Charlie. "And he was wantin' us to, like, *follow his dreams* and some bullshit..."

Tommy brought his cig to his lips.

"Follow his dreams, huh..."

Sounded like some Charles Manson shit. Probably snorted too much coke, fucked his brain up.

("find it, tommy...")

("the temple...")

He grimaced, forcing those thoughts aside.

"So Bill's not only a bitch-ass cowboy," said Tommy, "but a fuckin' psychopath, too?"

"*Sí,*" said Charlie. "A fuckin' psychopathic cowboy. And on top of that, I got the feelin' he just wanted my coke, too. Fair-weather *amigo,* ya know what I mean? Snortin' my coke for free, not even helpin' sell it or chip in for it. Not really. Just spoutin' bullshit about his dreams..."

Tommy fought back a grin.

Well, well, well...

Looks like Bill's little cocaine Posse fell apart real fuckin' quick...

Thanks to his psycho-dreams-bullshit...

"Fair-weather friends..." said Tommy. "I don't need none of those, either. Me and you, we're the same that way."

He took a hit of Monkey, held it, then exhaled toward the sunset.

"I gotta ask ya, Young," said Tommy. "Who ya gettin' your coke from?"

Charlie fell silent, blowing smoke out the side of his mouth.

"Can't tell ya that, *ese.*"

Tommy nodded. He could respect that—a guy who knew to keep his mouth shut. Besides, at least now he'd confirmed the supplier was likely *not* Sheriff-fuckin'-Cunningham.

"But you still have the ability to supply us?" asked Tommy. "On a regular basis?"

"I sure fuckin' do," said Charlie.

"And you can guarantee that?"

"I sure fuckin' can."

"Alright." Tommy flicked his cig to the pavement. "I'll talk it over with my Boys and give you a call. Your number still the same?"

"*Sí,*" said Charlie. He stared at the sunset as if still processing something.

Tommy extended his hand. "We got a deal, then."

Charlie turned from the sunset, did a double-take, then shook Tommy's hand firmly.

"Sorry about punchin' you in the stomach and shit," said Tommy. "Should've talked to you first."

Charlie's face darkened for a second, then cleared.

"Gracias," he said. "Appreciate that."

"I'll see ya around, Young."

Tommy released Charlie's hand and turned to walk away, but something stopped him. Something about the setting sun and memories of how much fun he used to have with Charlie—*Young Charlie.*

What'd he used to say?

"Don't call me Ol' Charlie, 'cause I'm Young—Young Charlie."

He'd say shit like that while they smoked weed and laughed and tried to speak *español.* Young hadn't changed much at all—still about his red-and-white labeled Marlboros and speakin' that Spanish shit real good and chasin' *mamacitas* and crackin' stupid jokes. Still had that same down-to-earth quality his Boys had, the same quality he wanted *all* his Boys to have. Talkin' with him just now, really *talking* with him, it almost felt the same again, even years later. They almost felt like—

—*friends* again.

Tommy turned around.

"Hey Young," he said. "I just wanna let ya know—I always wanted you to be one of *us,* man."

Charlie's cigarette, poised for a last puff, froze mid-air.

"I always wanted you to be one of the Originals," said Tommy. "But then you started hangin' with that Bill-fuckin'-Cunningham, and I *never* liked that dude, from the very fuckin' beginning."

Charlie grimaced, eyes tinged with regret.

"That was my mistake, *amigo,"* he said. "Maybe I should've—"

Tommy held up his hand.

"If this coke deal goes good," said Tommy, "if we can do some solid business together, learn to trust each other again, then you could still be... *one of us."*

Charlie's mouth dropped. He looked astonished—like he'd been told he won the lottery.

"If you want to," said Tommy. "Open invitation."

"Gracias, man. *Muchas gracias,"* he said. "That means a lot to me."

He puffed his cigarette, his hand trembling now.

"Hey *amigo,* if we can learn to trust each other again, and if your Boys'll be cool with me, and—"

"*They will,*" said Tommy. "It was Bill who started all that shit, not you. You were just backin' him up. I get that. Gotta back up your bros, right? But we both know it's *always* been Bill-fuckin'-Cunningham. *He's* the fuckin' problem. If it wasn't for him, none of this shit would've ever happened."

Charlie nodded, seeming at a loss for words.

Tommy started to turn away.

"Hey, hey Tommy!" said Charlie. "I just...I just wanna apologize, man. For all the shit I said back at Dairy Queen. For everything."

He flicked his cigarette to the ground.

"*No lo siento, cabrón. Para nada.*"

A warm smile spread across Tommy's face—a *genuine* smile—the kind he and Young used to share all the time, back when they used to smoke together. Didn't know what that Spanish shit meant, but it sure sounded good.

"Just a bump in the road, *amigo,*" said Tommy.

He gave Charlie one last look before strolling to his car, bathed in the rays of the setting sun.

***

Charlie watched Glick drive away.

He snorted, spat blood on the pavement and crushed his cigarette beneath his cowboy boot.

His lips curled into a sneer.

AUTHOR'S NOTE: CODA

Still here? Good.

If you're walking away with more questions than answers, that's by design. This book doesn't end because the story's over—it ends because the ground has started to shift. This is only the beginning.

Book Two—now available for preorder—ushers in the war.

Prepare yourself for *The Battle of the Smokehouse*.

- ATS

ABOUT THE AUTHOR

Ashley is the author of the award-winning Kentucky Blood series, a gritty, uncompromising Southern Gothic saga that explores complex characters and raw emotion. Raised in the rural enclaves of western Kentucky, he survived for 11 years in Tokyo's cutthroat corporate world and now splits his time between countries. He often roots for the bad guys in stories and hopes his books inspire you to do the same.